Perfect on Paper

Perfect on Paper

The (mis)adventures of Waverly Bryson

MARIA MURNANE

PUBLISHED BY   PRODUCED BY

  MELCHER
                       MEDIA

Printed in the United States of America

10 11 12 13 14 15 16 / 10 9 8 7 6 5 4 3 2 1

Published by AmazonEncore
P.O. Box 400818
Las Vegas, NV 89140

Produced by Melcher Media, Inc.
124 West 13th Street
New York, NY 10011
www.melcher.com

Library of Congress Cataloging-in-Publication Data
2009913663

ISBN-13: 978-0-98255-504-0
ISBN-10: 0-9825550-4-0

This novel was originally published, in a slightly different form, by Booksurge in 2009.
Cover design and interior illustrations by Alison Forner
Interior design by Jessi Rymill
Author photo by Chris Conroy Photography

SUSTAINABLE
FORESTRY
INITIATIVE

Melcher Media strives to use environmentally responsible suppliers and materials
whenever possible in the production of its books. For this book, that includes the use of
SFI-certified interior paper stock.

＊ ＊ ＊

This book is dedicated to any woman who has ever been on a really bad date or realized halfway through the workday that her skirt is on backward.

And to Mom and Dad . . . for absolutely everything.

＊ ＊ ＊

PROLOGUE

"I still can't believe this is happening." I leaned toward my reflection in the standing full-length mirror in my living room and knocked a piece of fuzz off my long white dress. Then I turned toward my friends McKenna and Andie, who were sitting on the sofa across the room. "I'm already so nervous. I don't know how I'm going to make it down the aisle in front of all those people," I said.

McKenna stood up and poured herself a glass of red wine. "Well, you'd better start believing it, because in two weeks about three hundred very well-dressed people are going to be expecting one fantastic party."

I ran my hands over the long silk skirt, then rested them gently on my waist. My breath felt thin and cool as I exhaled. "I can't believe I'm really getting married."

Andie sighed. "I can't believe the freak show is really closing."

I pointed a finger at her and tried not to laugh. "Hey now, Miss Barnett, you know how much I hate it when you use that description, however accurate it may be."

She pushed her short blonde hair behind her ears. "Yeah, yeah, but it's like the end of an era, you know?"

McKenna nodded. "I know. It's sort of hard to believe, isn't it?"

"Thanks a lot, Mackie," I said, pushing her shoulder. They were totally right though. My dating life at times *had* been borderline ridiculous, and while I certainly wasn't going to miss living it, I was definitely going to miss laughing about it. How could one person have so many romantic disasters? I'd clearly been making up for McKenna, who had been with her boyfriend for forever and a half. Andie was single and had her share of stories, but I was by far the queen.

"Remember that investment banker guy who asked the waiter to separate the alcohol and food on the bill so he could expense your date using his work per diem?" Andie said.

I nodded. "That would be the first date."

McKenna looked at me. "Didn't that guy also live with his parents?"

I nodded again. "That would be yes."

"Excellent," McKenna said, sipping her wine. "I loved cheap investment banker guy."

Knowing what was coming, I put a hand in the air. "Please tell me we're not having this conversation today, okay, ladies? Have you ever noticed that we have this conversation, like, all the time?"

"But it's so entertaining," McKenna said, putting her arm around me. "I love rehashing Waverly moments."

"Me too," Andie said as she grabbed my still-extended hand and squeezed. "There's just so much material there. Remember that date when you forgot to put a camisole on under your sweater and then took the sweater off at the restaurant?"

I laughed and shook my head. "Lovely memory there, oh so lovely," I said.

McKenna turned toward Andie. "Remember that time her calf totally cramped up when she was hooking up with that guy Tyler on the couch?" she said.

"That was the BEST," Andie said, chuckling. "I told everyone I know about that one." Then she looked at me. "Without using your name, of course."

I cringed and walked over to said couch, which at the moment was covered by a mound of bridal magazines that collectively weighed more than the couch itself. "Hey, I think it's bad luck to talk about this stuff while in a wedding dress," I said, sifting through the pile. "I'm pretty sure I read that in a magazine somewhere."

Ignoring me completely, Andie turned back to McKenna. "Remember that guy who showed up for their second date in a pair of sweatpants?" she said.

McKenna nearly spat out her wine. "Sweatpants guy! He was a classic. Or what about that time she was getting the calluses on her feet scrubbed off at the mani-pedi place down on Chestnut Street and the guy she was going out with that night walked by with three of his friends?"

"Ah, yes, the huge hottie Nate Miller," I said, wincing. "That was the day of our first date." It was the day of our last date, too. Shocking.

Andie was tearing up now. "I think my favorite Waverly moment might have been when that guy she met at an Oktoberfest party got her contact information but never asked her out, then put her on a mass e-mail to his 'closest friends' asking to borrow fifteen hundred dollars for an LSAT class."

McKenna nodded and laughed. "Oh my God, I'd forgotten about LSAT guy. So excellent. I think *my* favorite Waverly moment was that time she put on too much self-tanner for that guy Mike's company holiday party, then tried to act like she was naturally that tan in the middle of December."

"Oh God, please don't mention that ever again," I said, closing my eyes and briefly reliving the unfortunate Oompa-Loompa imitation.

"Oh, we will, my dear," Andie said. "We definitely will."

As they regaled themselves with some of my legendary dating mishaps, I turned away to look back at the mirror, then became lost in my own thoughts. It was late on a Saturday afternoon in November, a little over a year since I'd met Aaron at a black-tie fundraiser for the San Francisco hospital where McKenna's boyfriend had just started his residency. Aaron was a partner at a major law firm downtown, following in the footsteps of his parents, who were both big-time corporate attorneys.

When I first met him I didn't think much of it because, well, why would I? He was rich, smart, good-looking, and several years older than I was. He owned a two-story Victorian up on Nob Hill and a brand new cabin in Lake Tahoe. I didn't even have a parking spot. He'd grown up in the affluent hills of Tiburon, just north of San Francisco, and his parents were regular fixtures at the opera. I'd grown up in a middle-class neighborhood near Sacramento, but my dad was currently living in what I called the Valley Pines "garden community," although most people would call it the Valley Pines "trailer park."

Aaron was one of San Francisco's most eligible bachelors. I was, well, I was standing next to him at the buffet table.

We knocked elbows while reaching for the jumbo shrimp, or—better said—in a Waverly moment, I knocked into him while reaching for the jumbo shrimp and spilled cocktail sauce all over his arm. I apologized, and before I knew it we were talking. My proclivity for senseless chatter went into hyperdrive like it tends to do when I get nervous, but he was funny, and he was nice, and I really enjoyed talking to him. To be honest, I kept waiting for the *It was nice to meet you* as he headed back to the supermodel with a Ph.D. who I assumed was waiting for him. But he wasn't there with a date. He was there talking to me.

When he asked me for my phone number, I nearly choked.

Our first date was a casual drink at a tiny wine bar in North Beach. Our second was a walk along the ocean followed by a late lunch at the Cliff House. Our third was a romantic dinner at Aqua, and after that there was no looking back. Within two weeks we were a real couple.

Seven months later, at the top of Coit Tower, he asked me to marry him. It seemed a bit fast, but it was all so exciting and romantic, I jumped into his arms and said yes. I couldn't believe it. Aaron Vaughn III wanted *me*, Waverly Bryson I, and he was going to sign legal documents to prove it. After twenty-eight years of *What if I never find that perfect person?* I had finally found him.

"Hellooo ... Waverly?"

McKenna's voice snapped me out of my daydream.

I looked at her and blinked. "I'm sorry, did you say something?"

She handed me a glass of wine. "I said, how are things going with your dad now that the wedding is so close?"

I sighed. "I don't know. It's better, I guess, but I still, well, I still think he thinks Aaron's out of my league. And are you really handing me a glass of red wine right now?"

"Oops, my bad." She laughed and turned back toward the kitchen. "I'll get you some white."

Andie picked up my wedding invitation sitting on the coffee table. "Man, getting hitched at the Ritz-Carlton in Half Moon Bay. You know, once you're officially part of the illustrious Vaughn family, you're going to have to get used to having to rough it like that." The Ritz was just a thirty-minute drive from my San Francisco apartment but about thirty light-years away from my bank account.

McKenna handed me a glass of stain-free wine and pulled the ponytail holder out of her hair. "I'm sure she'll manage. So, do you think I should wear my hair up or down for the wedding?"

"You'll induce a rash of neck sprains either way, Miss *Hi I'm Six Feet Tall with Naturally Blonde Hair*," I said. "And besides, no one is supposed to be looking at you anyway, right?"

McKenna nodded. "This is true."

"Are they allowed to look at the five-two bridesmaid with unnaturally blonde hair?" Andie said, pointing to her highlighted locks. "I could use a good hookup."

I laughed. "If it leads to a good hookup, then okay, it's all good. So should we go over the rules?"

Andie nodded. "Rule number one for being Waverly Bryson's bridesmaid is: Don't get sappy and make her cry off her makeup before the pictures."

I nodded with her. "Exactly. And the second rule is?"

McKenna pointed at Andie. "Don't bring up any Waverly moments at the wedding."

"Right," I said, laughing. I had a big mouth, but Andie's was at times truly unbelievable. "And rule number three?"

Andie took a sip of her wine. "Don't hit on the father of the groom?"

"Andie!" I said. Case in point.

"Okay, I'm kidding. But you've got to admit that Aaron's dad is pretty pretty. Now *that* would be a sweet wedding hookup," she said.

I looked over at McKenna. "Mackie, can you help me out here? Sometimes I swear you two are like an angel and a devil sitting on my shoulders."

"Ooh, I like that," Andie said, nodding and rubbing her hands together.

"Be nice now," McKenna said to her.

"So what's the third rule again?" Andie said. "I'm blanking here."

"I am too," McKenna said.

"You two are killing me," I said. "Rule number three, my dear friends, is DO NOT let me hold a bottle of any kind. Wine glasses and champagne flutes only, okay?"

"Ah, that's right," McKenna said, looking back at Andie. "Remember how mortified Whitney was when she saw all those photos of herself drinking out of a bottle in a four-thousand-dollar wedding dress?"

"I'd be mortified too if it looked like my wedding had been sponsored by Bud Light," Andie said.

I turned back to my reflection in the mirror and bit my lip. "Does this dress scream *I didn't go to private school?*"

McKenna put her arm around me and squeezed. "Wave, it doesn't matter what Aaron's last name is. That man is in love with you because you're incredibly loveable, and you two are going to have a great life together."

I sighed. "I wish my dad agreed with you."

The ring of the doorbell made us all turn our heads.

McKenna walked over and pressed the intercom. "Who is it?" she said.

A deep voice filled the room. "It's Aaron. Can I talk to Waverly?"

Aaron? Now? I jumped behind the mirror.

McKenna looked at me. "Were you expecting him?" she said.

I shook my head. "I told him I was doing wedding stuff all afternoon and then having dinner with you two. Can you ask him what he wants?"

"Do you mind if I ask what this is about? The bride is, um, rehearsing at the moment," McKenna said.

Aaron's voice echoed through the apartment. "I just need to talk to her, okay? It's important." He didn't sound amused.

McKenna looked at me again and raised her eyebrows. I motioned for her to buzz him into the building.

I lived on the first floor, so Aaron walked through the door about ten seconds later.

"This is highly unusual, Aaron, highly unusual," Andie said, crossing her arms in front of her chest.

He walked right by her and didn't say anything, which *was* highly unusual. His footsteps seemed too heavy for my delicate hardwood floors, as if they knew bad news was coming. Andie looked at me and made a *What the hell?* expression.

McKenna gathered their stuff in a hurry and shoved Andie out the door. "Call us later?" she whispered.

I nodded as she quietly closed the door behind them, and then I looked at Aaron. "Hi, honey, what's up?" I was still poking my head out from behind the mirror. "You know this is bad luck, right?"

He sat down on the couch and looked up at me. When I saw his red and swollen eyes, I forgot all about superstition and hurried out from behind the mirror.

"Hey, is everything okay? Did something happen?" I sat down next to him and put my hand on his cheek.

He nodded slowly. "I didn't really sleep last night."

My mind began to race. "Is it your dad?" Aaron's father had a heart condition. "Is he all right?"

He continued to nod. "He's fine."

I took his hands in mine. They were cold and clammy. His hazel eyes seemed focused on something that wasn't in the room with us.

"Aaron, what's going on? Are you all right?"

The nod of his head slowly turned into a shake.

"Aaron, honey, talk to me."

His eyes finally cleared, and he looked straight at me. But he didn't say anything.

"Honey?" I said.

Still nothing.

"Aaron?" I squeezed his hands.

"I ... I ..." It was barely a whisper.

I waited several seconds for him to speak again.

"I ... I don't think I can marry you," he finally said.

Time froze. I did too. My insides turned to ice, and it hurt to breathe.

He was silent for a few seconds. Then he took a deep breath.

"I'm sorry," he said. "I think we rushed into this, and I know I was the one who pushed for it, but ... I think it was a mistake."

I let go of his hands. The room began to spin, and I started to shake. I reached for the wall to hold myself up, even though I was already sitting down.

"A mistake? Wh- ... why do you think it was a mistake?"

My question hung in the air. One small word, awaiting what a thousand more couldn't make me understand.

After what seemed like forever, he finally looked at me. "I just don't think we're right for each other."

I held his gaze. We both knew I needed, deserved, a better answer than that.

He looked away and put his hands on his knees.

And I waited.

And waited.

Finally, he turned and looked me right in the eye. "I'm not in love with you, Waverly."

The tears that had welled up in the back of my eyes started to push their way out. Little beads of pain that made my head throb.

"Oh ... oh ..." My mouth was open, but the words I wanted to say stayed somewhere deep inside me. In their place came tears, which quietly streamed down my cheeks.

"I'm so sorry. I never should have let it get to this point. ..."

One by one my tears turned into sobs.

His voice was nearly a whisper. "It's just that it seemed so perfect in the beginning ... and I got caught up in it ..."

His voice trailed off, and we sat there for a long time.

Him not saying anything, me sobbing.

Side by side, for the last time.

When he finally stood up to leave, it was dark everywhere. He walked slowly to the door, the cloud of guilt surrounding him nearly visible.

He turned back to look at me.

"I never meant to hurt you, Waverly," he whispered.

And then he quietly closed the door on what I had thought was my happily ever after.

Ever felt like
spending the rest
of your life in bed?

Honey, get that sleep.
Eventually you'll wake up,
and just think how nice
your skin will look when
you do.

Three Months Later
· · ·
CHAPTER ONE

SATURDAY

2:07 p.m. "Hey, it's Andie. I just ate a king-size Snickers. Call me back. Bye."

Delete.

3:12 p.m. "Hey, it's McKenna. Are you still in bed? Call me."

Delete.

5:40 p.m. "Hey, it's Andie. Where are you? McKenna and I are grabbing pizza later if you want to come. Call me."

Delete.

7:13 p.m. "Hey, it's McKenna. I'm with Andie at Dino's. We have a cold pitcher and a hot pizza waiting for you. Come meet us, okay?"

Delete.

8:32 p.m. "Are you alive? It's Andie. We're heading to the Blue Light for drinks. Call us."

Delete.

10:35 p.m. "C'mon, Waverly, we miss you. Come have drinks with us, please? There are lots of cute guys here."

Delete.

11:15 p.m. "Hello?? Where are you? Waverly, you can't spend the rest of your life in hiding."

Delete.

11:47 p.m. "C'mon, babe, get out of those pajamas and join the living again."

Delete.

Delete. Delete. Delete.

Can't face the dating scene after a breakup?

Honey, hit the bar, and hit it hard. Beer goggles are the lonely girl's Cupid.

Three Months Later
. . .
CHAPTER TWO

Beer goggles are the lonely girl's Cupid.

Or at least that had been Andie's advice since Aaron had dumped me. Not that I'd actually acted on it yet. But there I was, finally out of social hibernation and on my first real date since the breakup.

Okay, it was a setup, but it still counted, right?

I looked across the table at him and his familiar brown eyes. He was a nice guy . . . but . . .

No, an entire case of Corona couldn't help me with this one.

I looked around the festive Mexican restaurant and searched for something, anything, to fill the silence. The place was packed, everyone immersed in loud, lively conversation and clearly having more fun than I was. Words and laughter bounced off the walls. It was like the entire place was having a ball watching me flounder through my first attempt at dating again.

I held up my beer and took a sip. "So, Rick, how long have you lived in San Francisco?"

"About two years," he said. "You?"

"Since I finished college, so I guess that's about eight years," I said.

"Wow, a long time."

"Yeah, a long time."

More awkward silence. Why couldn't I think of anything to say? Pre-Aaron I couldn't shut up. Now I sounded so lame and boring. Was I really that lame and boring?

I looked back at Rick and wondered why I wasn't attracted to him. He was cute, and he met my height requirement, which was shrinking with each Friday night I spent watching TV. But those eyes . . . and that chin . . . there was just something familiar about him that wasn't doing it for me. What was it?

"So you work in sports PR?" he finally said. "That must be fun. Are you big into sports?"

I shook my head. "Not really. I'm not very athletic, actually. Jogging in a straight line for thirty minutes is about all I can handle. If I'm feeling adventurous, I jog for thirty-five minutes, maybe even thirty-six."

"But no real sports?" he said.

"Um, does beginner's yoga count as a sport if you go once a month?" I laughed weakly and took a huge sip of my beer.

"What about watching sports? Football? Baseball?" He was obviously grasping for straws. We both were.

I shook my head again and tried to laugh. "Not really my thing," I said.

He wasn't laughing back. "So why did you get into the field?"

I picked at the paint on my beer bottle. "Um, my dad used to play professional baseball, so I sort of grew up around sports."

He finally seemed interested. "Really? For what team?"

"Oh, uh, he played AAA for the San Jose Giants."

"No way. What position did he play?"

"Pitcher."

Rick was clearly more impressed by this new information than he was by me. "That's so cool. Did he ever get called up to the big leagues?"

I bit my lip. "That was the plan, but he had to retire early, right when he was about to get his big break, unfortunately."

"Injury?"

"Something like that," I said. "It's a long story."

The look in his eyes changed to one I'd seen many times before. He wanted to know more but was too polite to ask.

He took a sip of his beer. "Does he still work in sports?"

"Not quite," I said, shaking my head.

"Oh. Well, it's cool that you do. It sounds pretty glamorous."

I picked some more paint off my beer bottle and gave my standard response to that comment. "Yeah, it's a great job," I said. If he had only seen me two days earlier, picking out the green M&M's from the bowl in our conference room because the tennis player endorsing our client's sports bras "doesn't do the green ones."

More silence. Have you ever noticed how loud silence can be? What's up with that?

"So, um, do you like being a lawyer?" I said.

"It has its moments," he said, not elaborating.

"Oh, cool." I looked down at the table. For some reason I assumed all lawyers in San Francisco knew Aaron and thus all knew that he had dumped me. Does the American Bar Association keep records on dating history?

More silence.

As if she sensed our pain, the waitress mercifully appeared and served us two more Coronas and a sampler plate of buffalo wings, nachos, and quesadillas. I, of course, immediately went for the beer. Why didn't Coronas come in the forty-ounce size? They could label them the *Bad Date Edition*.

I reached for a quesadilla. "So you're sure we haven't met?"

He nodded. "I'm sure. I would have remembered a name like Waverly, you know, because of the cracker from way back when."

I nodded too. "Yeah, I still haven't forgiven my parents for that one. Thank God they don't make those anymore. So you're really sure we haven't met?"

"I'm sure," he said.

I narrowed my eyes. "One hundred percent sure or only ninety-nine percent sure?"

He smiled but didn't look all that amused. "I'm sure." Then he leaned over and picked up another buffalo wing. "Mmm . . . buffalo wings are my absolute favorite food. I love them even more than pizza."

"No way," I blurted. "That's exactly what Aaron always says."

He looked up at me. "Who is Aaron?"

Crap. Why was I such an idiot?

I looked down at my hands. "Oh, uh, he's uh, my ex, uh, my ex-fiancé."

He looked surprised. "You were engaged?"

"Um, uh, yeah."

"When?"

"Um, a few months ago."

"Oh? What happened?"

I felt my cheeks go hot. I swallowed and pushed my long dark hair behind my ears. "Um, well, to be honest . . . we sort of rushed into it, and I really wasn't ready to get married, and I realized that he wasn't the right guy for me." I could feel myself sweating, and I knew the tears weren't far behind. I took a sip of water, but what I really needed was a stapler for my big fat mouth. Big fat stupid lying mouth.

"Oh," he said.

"Yeah," I said.

Silence.

I put my glass of water down and looked across the table at him. We had hit rock bottom.

Or so I thought.

Suddenly I knew why he looked so familiar. How hadn't I seen it right away?

Rick was right. I hadn't met him before, but holy Appalachia, he was a dead ringer . . . for . . . my . . . father. Minus a few decades and a pot belly.

Cough.

I stood up. "Hey, I'm going to use the ladies' room. I'll be right back, okay?"

"Uh, sure, are you okay?" he said. He looked a little worried.

"I'm fine, thanks." I steadied myself on the chair and smoothed my hand over my hair. On the way to the restroom I pulled my phone out of my purse and called McKenna.

She answered on the second ring. "Hey, aren't you supposed to be on your big date?"

"Uh, yeah, but I'm hiding in the bathroom," I said.

She laughed. "That bad?"

I looked at my reflection in the mirror, then covered my eyes with my free hand. "Oh my God, Mackie, I'm just not ready for this. I'm a disaster. And get this, he looks exactly like my dad."

"No way, really?"

"SO really. And I also broke our pact and brought up Aaron and nearly started crying, although I swear it was by accident. Seriously, I have to get out of here. What do I do?"

"Why don't you just tell him?"

"What am I am supposed to say? *Um, it's been nice meeting you, but this is my first date since I basically got left at the altar, and I can't deal with it, so I need to get the hell out of here. Oh, and by the way, you look exactly like my dad, which is weirding me out even more. So thanks for the sampler platter and the drinks. See ya.*"

The girl washing her hands next to me smiled sympathetically and mouthed the words "Good luck" on her way out.

I leaned my hip against the sink. "You should have heard me out there, Mackie. I was the conversational equivalent of a fish flailing around on the deck of a boat. How can I get out of here?"

"Hmm, maybe you could say you have an early meeting?"

"It's only eight o'clock!"

"Headache?"

"Are you kidding me?"

"You need to feed your cat?"

"Okay, you're not helping here."

She laughed. "It looks like you may just have to stick this one out."

"That's it? *Stick it out?* That's your advice?" I said.

"I'm sorry, Wave, I can't think of anything good. Unless you want to pull the food poisoning thing again?"

I raised my eyebrows. That had been my go-to move back in the day. "Ooh, good call. That could work."

"Hey, at least you tried, right?" she said.

"Yeah, I guess so. Thanks, Mackie."

I shut the phone and splashed some cold water on my face. Then I slapped my cheeks a couple times and put on my best *I just barfed* face. Damn that sushi I had for lunch. . . .

I walked back out to the table just as Rick was standing up.

He grabbed his coat and held out his hand. "I'm sorry, Waverly, but I have an early meeting in the morning, so I'm going to have to call it a night. But it was really nice meeting you."

"Uh, okay," I said softly, shaking his hand. What else could I say?

He put on his coat. "So, I'll see you around?"

"Um, yeah, sure." I couldn't believe it. He was really up and leaving? Actually, I could believe it. I sucked.

He handed me a fifty-dollar bill. "This should cover the check. Have a great night." He smiled, then turned and walked away.

I slowly sat down and stared at the huge tray of food in front of me. "Bye. I hope you feel better," I said to the quesadillas. I tried not to look around in case anyone was watching me, the girl who just got out-ditched. Rick was probably already on his cell phone outside, telling one of his buddies that he'd been set up with a basket case.

I picked up my beer and looked down at the outfit I'd chosen so carefully. Dark jeans, cute red top, black flats. Was the outfit at least more attractive than my conversational skills? I pulled my hair into a ponytail and looked down at my chest. Apparently I needed to invest in some remedial dating classes. And maybe a push-up bra.

They say you learn something "valuable" from every experience?

Honey, "they" have obviously never "experienced" a Brazilian bikini wax or a weekend visit to IKEA.

One Year After the Breakup

...

CHAPTER THREE

"Shane Kennedy, the NBA star?" McKenna said.

I nodded and blew hot air into my fists. "Yep, that's him."

"Hunter's going to love that one," she said. It killed her boyfriend that I didn't really like sports but got paid to work with professional athletes, even though most of them treated me like, well, paid help.

It was early on a cold morning in November, and McKenna and I were on one of our semiregular walks before work. We'd been doing them for years, and our route was always the same. We met in front of Peet's Coffee on the corner of Fillmore and Sacramento in Pacific Heights, then walked down the steep slope of Fillmore to the Marina Green yacht harbor, over to the Palace of Fine Arts, and back up the steep steps of Lyon Street. It took about an hour, and getting up early was brutal (we'd long given up trying to get Andie to join us), but it was well worth it. As we walked we talked about everything under the sun, which had been very cost-effective (i.e., free) therapy for me since the breakup.

"Well, if this guy's like most of the professional athletes we deal with, I can only hope he's not a total nightmare," I said. The next day I was off to Atlanta for the Super Show, the largest trade show in the sporting goods industry. Shane Kennedy was flying in to launch a new basketball shoe, and the whole world wanted to interview him.

"Hunter's going to be so jealous. He's still talking about that time he got to treat Barry Zito in the ER," she said.

"Who?" I said.

"Exactly," she said. "So how are you doing today?"

"I'm fine."

"No, I mean, how are you *doing?*"

I looked at the sky. "What are you talking about?"

She pushed my arm. "I know why you turned off your phone yesterday, and don't pretend you didn't get my message."

"Yesterday? What was yesterday?" I said, looking at the ground.

"You are such a bad liar."

"What?" I said, looking at the sky.

"C'mon, Wave."

"Okay, okay. It sucks." The day before had been the one-year anniversary of what would have been my wedding. I'd spent it at the movies and then on the couch, alone.

"Have you talked to him lately?" she said.

I shook my head. "The last time I saw him was months ago, when I picked up the rest of my stuff from his house."

"He wasn't that cute, you know," she said.

"*Now* who's the bad liar?" I said, smiling.

She laughed. "Okay, you're right. He was extremely cute. But it doesn't matter. Your year of mourning is over, right?"

I looked at her. "Year of mourning? What am I, a black-clad widow in Italy?" Although I *was* wearing a black fleece and sweatpants and was seriously wishing I had on my black gloves.

"Just trying to help," she said.

I glanced at my watch. "I know you are, and I love you for it. Hey, let's step it up, okay? I've got a ton of work to do before I leave tomorrow."

We sped through the rest of our walk, and by eight fifteen I was in the lobby of K.A. Marketing. The two hundred employees who staffed our San Francisco office took up all four floors of a bright white building with high ceilings, dark hardwood floors, brick walls, and funky exposed piping. We had moved in two years earlier and renovated the whole place, so while the architecture was actually really modern, the design was sort of a retro warehouse theme.

I stopped by the coffee cart in the lobby to pick up a carton of chocolate milk and a chocolate chip bagel. My department, which managed publicity for the sports and entertainment division, had a staff meeting every Monday morning, and they were less painful when I had a sizeable amount of chocolate in front of me. And ever since Mandy Edwards had transferred from our Chicago office a few weeks earlier, *painful* was the unfortunate standard.

I walked upstairs and weaved my way through the cubicles to my office. People were slowly trickling in, everyone chatting about their weekends. I put my milk and bagel down on my desk, hung my coat on the back of my door, and walked over to the window to look at the view. Sometimes I think I secretly liked that view more than I liked my job.

"Hi, Waverly, how was your weekend?"

I turned around to see Kent Tanner standing in my doorway. "Oh, hey, Kent. It was good, thanks, nothing too exciting. Yours?"

He shrugged. "The usual. Once you have kids, your weekends are pretty much a blur of cartoons, toys all over the house, barf, and dirty diapers."

I smiled. "Mr. Tanner, somehow you always know when I need a nice dose of reality to start my day. Now, are you ready for your first Super Show? It's a lot different than the technology trade shows. Think you can handle the chaos?" Kent had joined our department a couple months earlier.

"Are you kidding? Compared to pitching enterprise software, this will be a vacation."

"Cool. Let me just check to see if there's anything important I need to know before the staff meeting." I sat down at my desk and logged into my e-mail account. "Ahhh, there's a message from Mandy Edwards to the entire department. Sent on Sunday afternoon, of course."

"Of course," he said.

I shook my head slowly. "What is wrong with her? Doesn't she see how transparent the constant 'from home' e-mailing is?" A lot of people at our company had BlackBerrys, but our company culture was hardly one of sending work e-mail around the clock, especially on Sunday afternoons.

"She's new. She'll learn."

"Learn what? That being a suck-up doesn't work in this department?"

He put his hand on my shoulder. "Want to tell me how you really feel?"

I looked back at my computer screen. I was sure Mandy would reiterate whatever her weekend epiphany was at the meeting. "Bye-bye, you suck-up."

Delete.

Kent laughed and walked out of my office. "C'mon, the meeting's about to start."

"Just a second, I'm right behind you." I had just noticed an e-mail from Andie that said to call her as soon as I got to the office. It was written IN ALL CAPS, very un-Andie.

I shut my office door and dialed her work number.

"Andie Barnett," she said.

"Hey, it's me. What's up?"

"Are you sitting down?" she said.

"Yes." I wasn't.

"Seriously, are you sitting down?" she said.

"How do you always know?" I sat down and slouched in my chair.

"Okay, I'm sitting down now. What's the big news?" I said.

"Well . . . don't shoot the messenger, but . . ."

"But what?" I said.

"Waverly, I hate to tell you this, but Aaron is getting married."

I sat up straight.

"WHAT? To who?"

"To some girl named Stacy Long. It's in today's *Nob Hill Gazette.* I wanted to tell you before you heard it from someone else."

Aaron was getting married? Already? In the year since we'd broken up, I'd been on exactly three dates, all setups who never called me again.

Before I could speak, Kent knocked on my door and poked his head in.

"C'mon, Waverly, everyone's waiting for you."

I nodded at him and took a deep breath. "I gotta go, Andie. I'll call you later." I put the phone down and closed my eyes. It took all my willpower not to lock the door and google Stacy Long right there. I tried to put my work face back on as I stood up to go to the meeting, but I didn't think anyone was going to buy it.

. . .

Jess Richards, the VP in charge of our department, walked into the conference room holding a cup of coffee and a manila folder.

"Good morning, people. Let's have a quick run around the room to see what's on everyone's plate for the week. Waverly, you and Kent leave for the Super Show tomorrow, right?" he said.

I tried to smile. "Yes, sir. Atlanta here we come."

"So I hear JAG is flying in Shane Kennedy?" JAG was short for Jammin' Athletic Gear, my biggest account.

I nodded. "Yep."

"And I assume the press is lining up to talk to him?" Shane Kennedy was the reigning MVP of the NBA and had just signed a $150 million contract with the New York Knicks. I couldn't even begin to think about how much money that was per month. Per week. Per game. Per trash-talking incident. Per out-of-wedlock child.

I took a sip of my chocolate milk and nodded again. "It should be quite a week. We already have more than thirty interviews set up for him, plus dozens of others on the waiting list. Davey's really pleased." David Mason was the director of marketing at JAG, i.e., the guy who paid our invoices.

Kent rubbed his hands together. "This is going to be fun."

"I hope so," I said. "Because Waverly Bryson doesn't know if she can sit through three days of interviews with a guy who talks about himself in the third person."

Jess laughed. "Well, he can sure sink a three, no doubt about that. Nice work lining up all those interviews."

"Thanks, Jess. It's been a real team effort," I said.

"I imagine it's pretty easy getting interviews for a celebrity like that?" Mandy Edwards said.

I looked at her.

"Easy?" I said.

"I mean, did you have to do much to get the press interested?"

"What's your point, Mandy?" The press was definitely interested, but that didn't mean we hadn't worked hard to put together a great schedule.

She smiled. "No point. Since I'm new to this department, I'm just trying to learn how things work around here. In foods, the teams I managed never had celebrities to rely on, so we had to be really creative to get the press to pay any attention to our products."

I glanced at Kent, who slyly rolled his eyes. Then I looked back at her.

"We'll let you know how it went when we're back in the office next week, okay, Mandy?" I knew I was being a bit short, maybe even a bit rude, but I just couldn't deal with her, especially not then.

"Okay, thanks, Waverly. That would be great." She smiled again. Ugh.

. . .

When I got home that night I went straight to my mailbox. I hadn't checked it in a few days, so of course it was packed with a bunch of crap that wasn't even for me. I still received a ridiculous amount of junk mail for my old roommate, Whitney, whose bedroom I'd turned into an office after she'd moved out to get married. I had no idea how to stop the deluge, and it drove me crazy. Once I even wrote *deceased* on the envelope of a credit card application addressed to her and put it in the mailbox on the corner. It didn't help.

I sat down on the couch and flipped through the monster stack of mail. Junk, bill, junk, Pottery Barn catalog, bill, Pottery Barn catalog, bill, more junk. Finally, there it was, the *Nob Hill Gazette*. I just had to see it for myself.

I took a deep breath and slowly turned the pages one by one.

And then I saw it, on page eleven, right above the horoscopes:

Aaron Christopher Vaughn III and Stacy Elizabeth Long, both partners at Vaughn, Miller and Hyde, will marry at Grace Cathedral at 7 p.m. on New Year's Eve. The ceremony will be followed by a black-tie reception at the Fairmont Hotel. . . .

Suddenly feeling like I'd been kicked in the stomach, I leaned back into my couch and looked up at the ceiling. I couldn't believe it. Aaron was getting married. Married. Hitched. *Casado.* And he hadn't even called to tell me. I knew a year was a long time, but part of me still felt like it had all happened yesterday.

And while part of me had gotten over the pain, a bigger part of me hadn't.

Slowly I put the newspaper down on the couch. Then I put my head down on top of it and cried.

. . .

Our flight to Atlanta the next morning left way too early for my taste, but luckily it wasn't that crowded, so Kent and I each had our own row to stretch out in. It was my dream to have a client who would fly me in business class, but for now the only way I was sitting in business class was if I enrolled in one at the local community college.

Shortly after we took off, I leaned my head against the window. Within minutes I fell into a deep sleep, only to be awakened moments later by a flight attendant with very big hair asking me if I wanted something to drink. I looked up at her, half asleep. "You had to wake me up to ask that? Couldn't you just leave some water or something here on my tray?" I said. It's not like they were actually going to serve me *food*.

"But I need to know exactly what you want, sweetheart. We have a wide assortment of beverages on board."

"Okay, uh, I'll have coffee, please," I said. I will never understand people.

After that I couldn't fall back asleep, so I pulled out my laptop and booted it up. I ordered another cup of coffee and took a quick look at the row behind me. Kent was sound asleep.

As I saw the screen flicker to life, my thoughts turned to Aaron and the new life he'd created. He'd obviously had no trouble jumping back into the dating pool, whereas I could barely keep my head above water. Flirting? Dating? Playing hard to get? I truly sucked at it all. One day I'd even started jotting notes on my life as a born-again single woman, because it all seemed so ridiculous.

At first it was just a free-flowing hodge podge, but somehow it had morphed into something more: an idea for a line of greeting cards. Aaron's pet name for me had always been "Honey," and I would often leave him sticky notes on his pillow, windshield, bathroom mirror, etc. So in a feeble attempt at irony, I called the cards Honey Notes. I hadn't told anyone about them yet out of fear of being ridiculed.

WAVERLY'S HONEY NOTE IDEAS—NOT TO SHOW TO ANYONE OUT OF FEAR OF BEING RIDICULED

Front: So, he dumped you?
Inside: Honey, he was ugly anyway.

Front: Why is it so hard not to think about a boy when he's the one thing you're trying not to think about?
Inside: Honey, for some questions there just aren't answers. But there's always chocolate.

Front: Can't take another blind date?
Inside: Honey, if you take a few tequila shots before them, they're a lot less painful.

Front: Know that overwhelming feeling of inertia that kicks in when you're thinking about getting up and going to the gym?

Inside: Honey, where the hell is that inertia when you're thinking about getting up and going to the refrigerator?

Front: Is it okay to have really long hair in your 30s?

Inside: Honey, HELL YES!

(I wasn't 30 just yet, but I was getting way too close.) I typed in the following idea:

Front: So, the ex is getting married, and you're still on the market?

Inside: Honey, think of yourself as a prime piece of real estate—your value is only going up.

I scrolled through the rest of the list and bit my lip. It sometimes hurt to write them, but I thought the cards were funny. Would anyone else, though? I had clearly lost all perspective.

I closed my eyes to rest, and before I knew it the plane began its descent.

. . .

Pink, pink, pink. Not sure who had designed my room, but it was the hotel industry's equivalent of a chick flick. I set my suitcase down and looked around. A vase of pink flowers on the desk. Light pink-and-white sheets. Pink roses in the wallpaper and carpet. Pink soap in the bathroom. There was so much pink that I suddenly felt myself craving cotton candy. But I really couldn't complain, because the room was truly gorgeous. JAG was taking care of us.

I walked over to the window and opened the drapes. I gazed down at the beautiful swimming pool twelve stories below and wished it were summertime. How I longed to lounge by the artificial waterfalls with a good book and a margarita! The only times I ever stayed at fancy hotels were when I was working or when I'd been with Aaron, and when I was working I never had much time to enjoy them. And as for the times with Aaron, well, enough said.

I walked back across the room and opened up the closet.

Ahhh, there it was.

The Robe.

Fluffy, white, usually priced around $150.

I loved lounging around in The Robe.

I looked across the room. On top of the TV was a basket full of fruit, nuts, and candies topped off with, surprise, a pink bow. I opened the card from Penelope French, the firecracker of a woman in charge of JAG's trade show logistics.

Hi Waverly!

Some energy snacks to get you through a crazy week. Good luck!

Penelope French and JAG

Wow. In total there would be about fifty people representing JAG at the show, and in addition to handling all our travel and accommodations, plus the thousands of details involved in getting the booth together, Penelope had taken the time to send out goodie baskets with personalized cards.

I opened up a bag of cashews, kicked off my shoes, and tried to convince myself it was going to be a fun week.

Afraid to show your vulnerable side?

Honey, that's better than showing your cellulite side.

CHAPTER FOUR

The next morning, I received a wake-up call at 6:45, which was hell enough, but given that my West Coast body thought it was 3:45 a.m., I seriously thought I was going to die. Thank God I'd preset the fancy coffee maker the night before, because the smell of caffeine was the only thing that got me out of bed.

I flipped on the lights and turned on the TV as I stumbled toward the pot. A hot shower and two very strong cups of coffee later, I was ready to face the day. As I got dressed, I listened to Matt Lauer and Meredith Vieira discuss their favorite sites for online holiday shopping. Then I recognized the voice of Scott Ryan, a field reporter I'd become friends with over the years. His report was on an 80-year-old man in Dallas who owned a hundred cats.

"A feature on a man with a hundred cats? You paid how much to go to journalism school, Scotty?" I said to the TV.

I arrived at the conference center a few minutes after eight and made my way through the massive complex back to the JAG booth. I couldn't see Kent or Davey, but nearly the entire JAG sales department was already there. The show didn't open until nine o'clock, but we were all expecting a rush and wanted to be prepared. The first day of every trade show is always the craziest.

The Super Show had thousands of exhibitors every year, and it seemed like each company was set on outdoing the next with a fancy booth and "extras" to attract attention. Those extras ranged from girls in tiny bikinis handing out protein shakes to tiny gymnasts performing on balance beams to promote leotards. JAG was no exception. Our booth was enormous. We had several private meeting rooms, but the icing was a huge display room in the front area that resembled a sporting goods store, plus half of a regulation-size basketball court with a ball and a real referee for impromptu guest and/or employee pickup games.

I said hello to everyone and beelined to the coffee counter at the back of the booth, where I immediately noticed that the entire catering staff was wearing the exact same outfit I was.

Nice.

"Uh, I'll have a chocolate chip bagel and a mocha, please," I said to the girl behind the counter as I looked at her white button-down shirt and black pants.

She handed me my bagel and yelled. "Mocha coming right up!!"

Whoa—down, girl. She was way too perky for 8 a.m.

"Good morning, Waverly."

I turned around to face Gabrielle Simone, the icy new VP of sales at JAG. She was dressed in an expensive navy blue pantsuit and pearls, her short black hair slicked perfectly behind her ears.

She quickly looked me up and down, then over at my outfit twin behind the counter.

Crap.

"Um, hi, Gabrielle, how are you?" I said.

She ran her long skinny fingers over her pearls. "I'm fine, thank you, just eager to get started. If we're going to hit the aggressive sales targets I've set for this quarter, we're all going to have to push ourselves pretty hard this week."

I nodded as the girl handed me my mocha. "Um, yes, it's going to be a lot of work."

Gabrielle fingered her pearls again. "Well, I expect that you'll do your job well. David Mason mentioned what we're paying your agency each month, and it is quite a bit higher than I would expect for the amount of press coverage you seem to be generating."

There's no good way to respond to a comment like that.

I cleared my throat. "Um, well, we're working hard. We're excited about all the interviews we have lined up this week for Shane Kennedy."

She nodded. "Good, glad to hear it. We don't want to be wasting our money now, do we?"

Again, no good way to respond.

I smiled. "Of course not."

"I'm glad we agree. Now if you'll excuse me, I have a meeting with the CEO." She turned on her heel and walked away.

When she was gone I looked down at my mocha. It was shaking.

I made a mental note for a Honey Note:

Front: Scared to death by your clients?
Inside: Honey, it's better than being scared to death by your unemployment officer.

I walked into the back room marked for press interviews and sat down at the conference table. I took a sip of my mocha and heard a knock on the open door. I looked up. Shane Kennedy was standing in the doorway.

"Hi there, I'm Shane Kennedy," he said. Like I didn't know.

I tried to smile and look casual as I stood up. "It's nice to meet you, Shane. I'm Waverly Bryson." I was a little stunned at how huge he was in person. He offered his hand, which was about three times the size of mine. He had light brown eyes and a flawless complexion the color of, well, the mocha I was drinking.

Just then Davey Mason and Kent walked in behind him.

"Top of the morning, Waverly," Davey said, looking up and down at my outfit. "And can you please fetch me a double tall latte and a scone?"

"Don't start," I said, pointing at him.

He laughed. "I see you've met our guest of honor?"

I nodded. "Yep, we go way back to about one minute ago. Hey, how was the King?" Davey and Penelope French had flown in from JAG's San Francisco headquarters a couple days earlier to oversee the setting up of the booth, and Davey had popped over to Graceland for a visit. Yes, Graceland.

He sat down next to me. "It jailhouse rocked, Bryson. Did you get your goodie basket at the hotel?"

"Yes, what a great idea," I said. "I already inhaled a bag of cashews. I doubt anything will be left of that basket by the time I check out on Saturday."

He scratched the back of his head and nodded. "At first I vetoed the idea, but I changed my mind when Penelope pointed out that the same bag of cashews in the minibar would cost my marketing budget five dollars. At Costco they're only a buck."

I punched him lightly in the shoulder. "You're a ruthless businessman, Mr. Mason. But then again, that's probably why you own and I rent."

Davey looked around the table. "So, is everyone ready? The media's already lining up outside like a bunch of dorks in costume at a *Star Wars* premiere, so it's going to be a busy day," he said.

I turned to face Shane. "I guess this media crush won't be anything new for you. Do you mind press interviews?"

He leaned back in his chair and put his gigantic hands on his humongous knees. "Not really. It can be a little draining, but I'm willing to suck it up for a couple days to get the word out on the new shoe."

"Cool, that will make our job a lot easier," I said. "As Davey has probably told you, Kent and I will take turns managing your interviews, and Davey will be here to answer questions regarding the design or marketing of the shoes. We'll try to limit each interview to fifteen minutes to keep them from getting too boring. Here's a copy of today's schedule, and we'll give you a heads-up on any late additions. I hope it's not too much."

"It'll be a layup," Davey said, pretending to shoot a basket.

"Got it," Shane said. "Thanks."

He was thanking us? Was he for real? So polite! So grounded! So unusual for a professional athlete! No multiple gold chains, and he even appeared to be tattoo-free.

. . .

At 9 a.m. sharp, the show doors opened, and the chaos began. It was like the running of the bulls as the huge arena filled up almost immediately. Kent and I watched it all as we stood at the front of the JAG booth and waited for our first press appointment to show up.

"Hey, I'm going to run to the ladies' room for a minute. I'll be right back," I said.

"Don't get lost," he said.

I headed to the back of the pavilion and put my hand on my hair as I walked to gauge the static. Walking on trade show carpets was like a high school physics experiment.

On the way back from the restroom I grabbed a couple fun-size Milky Ways from the freebie bowl at the booth of a small exercise equipment company. I unwrapped one and popped it in my mouth, which I immediately regretted because I proceeded to start choking. I coughed and pounded on my chest a couple times until the half-chewed Milky Way flew out and into my hand. I stopped and glanced around for a napkin or a trash can but didn't see one anywhere, so I tossed the Milky Way back in my mouth and started chewing on it again. I knew that was pretty gross, but hey, candy is candy, right?

I started back toward the JAG booth and hoped Gabrielle Simone wouldn't see me on the way. My eyes were totally watering, and I was sure my face was red and puffy. Just then my cell phone rang. I looked at it and groaned when I saw the name on the caller ID. Now was not the time to deal with a call from my dad, the perennial early bird. Usually I had my phone off when he called at the crack of dawn back home. I sent him to voicemail and put the phone in my purse.

When I looked up, I saw a cute guy walking right at me.

A very cute guy.

"Are you okay?" he said. He was about six foot four with short, messy dark brown hair, tanned skin, and bright blue eyes. And he was smiling. Maybe even chuckling a bit.

I looked up at him, but the candy in my mouth made it hard to speak normally—not that speaking normally to such a good-looking stranger would be easy for me under any circumstances. "Um, yeah, I'm fine," I mumbled. Had he really just witnessed me putting a chewed-up, coughed-up Milky Way into my mouth?

I was so embarrassed that I didn't even stop. I just kept walking right on past him without even looking back. I turned the corner and headed back to the front of the JAG booth, where Kent was still standing.

"Are you okay?" he said. "Your face is all red and puffy."

Great.

"I'll live," I said.

"This show is so cool," he said. "I just saw Mia Hamm and Nomar Garciaparra, and I think I saw Wayne Gretzky, too, but I couldn't be sure because he had a hat on."

Over Kent's shoulder I saw a familiar face in the crowd. "Hey, there's Scotty Ryan."

"Who?" Kent said.

"Scotty, or Scott, Ryan. He's a features correspondent for the *Today* show who used to work out of San Francisco. I actually saw him on TV this morning. C'mon, I'll introduce you." I raised my arm. "Hey, Scotty, over here!"

Scotty turned his head, then said something to his camera crew and trotted over. "Why, Miss Waverly Bryson, what a pleasure to see your lovely face, although it's looking a bit red and puffy at the moment. Are you okay?" He gave me a quick hug.

"I'm fine, or I will be after a date with my makeup case," I said. "Scotty, this is my coworker Kent Tanner from K.A. Marketing."

"Hi there, it's nice to meet you," Scotty said. They shook hands, and then Kent took off for the restroom himself.

"I didn't know you were going to be here, Scotty. Your name wasn't on the registered press list," I said.

"It was a last-minute decision. We're doing a story about all those protein bars on the market. They're all the rage, you know." He winked, his eyes more green than ever.

I touched his arm. "Hey, while you're here, do you want to interview Shane Kennedy about his new line of basketball shoes?"

"Sorry, darling, I can't," he said, shaking his head.

"Are you sure? It would really make us look good to score an interview with *Today*."

"You know, for you I'd do anything, and believe me, I wish I could, because Shane Kennedy is one attractive man, but I'm flying out in a couple hours to cover a movie premiere in L.A. Then tomorrow morning I'm back to the home base in Dallas."

"A movie premiere? Man, you have the best life," I said. "By the way, I saw your feature this morning on that guy with the cats. Nice piece of investigative reporting, my friend. What would your journalism professors at Northwestern say?"

He grinned. "I know, I'm a sellout. But sweetheart, if you knew what they paid me for that fluff, you'd understand."

"Believe me, my credit card bills and I are very jealous," I said. "So you're really out of here today? I wish we could at least have dinner or something. And JAG is throwing a big party on Friday night."

"Yep, I'm on a noon flight to L.A., so unfortunately I'm going to miss all the fun. Hey, I've really gotta run now and film this story. Keep in touch, okay?"

"Okay. Bye, Scotty."

. . .

Nearly ten hours later, we were all back in the press interview room, fully exhausted and fully complaining about it. In addition to the media, our booth had been jammed with buyers, industry bigwigs, and employees of other exhibiting companies, all of them with one form or another of business with JAG, and most of them hoping to steal a glimpse of Shane Kennedy in the flesh. We had run around all day trying to attend to everyone, and it had been absolutely crazy.

Kent loosened his tie and leaned back in his chair. "I feel like I was just run over by a train. Did any of you even get a chance to walk around the show floor and check out the other booths?"

"Are you kidding me?" Davey laughed. "I barely had time to use the restroom."

I pressed my face flat on the conference table. "I need a margarita. And a massage. And did I mention a margarita?"

"I haven't even seen the trade show bunnies yet," Davey said. "What a rip-off."

Shane looked at him. "Trade show bunnies?"

"You know, the lovely ladies hired to attract visitors to the various booths," Davey said.

"Also known as trade show bimbos, in some circles," I said, my face still flat on the table.

Davey laughed. "In your circles, you mean."

I raised my head and pointed at him. "Hey now! Someone needs to take a stand against the shameless exploitation of women, right?"

"Oh please, like you didn't want to be a Dallas Cowboys cheerleader when you were a kid?" Kent said.

I laughed. "Okay, busted."

"So who's up for a huge dinner on JAG to celebrate a job well done?" Davey said. "I'm starving."

I raised my arm. "Count me in."

"Me too," Kent said.

Shane nodded. "Sounds good to me."

A half-hour later we were seated at a large booth at the back of Morton's Steakhouse. When he'd seen who we were with, the maître d' had been kind enough to put us in a back corner where Shane wouldn't be super-noticeable, not that a six-foot-eight man isn't super-noticeable everywhere. Then we ate and ate and ate until we couldn't eat anymore.

I tapped my fork against my wine glass. "All right, gentlemen, I would like to make an announcement."

"This should be good," Davey said.

"For the record, I'm going to work out every day for a week straight when I get home. Understood?" I said.

They all nodded.

I smiled. "Excellent, I'm glad we're clear on that. Now may I please see the dessert menu?"

The waiter brought out a dessert cart with every possible sweet you could want: pastries, cakes, sundaes, pies, and cookies. And I wanted everything. Everything! But I controlled myself and decided on the cheesecake . . . and a chocolate cookie.

I swallowed a bite of cheesecake and turned to Shane. "So, Mr. Kennedy, how are you able to take a few days off to be here with us? Isn't the NBA in full swing?"

He pushed his sleeves about thirty-six inches up to his elbows. "Actually, we play the Hawks here in Atlanta on Saturday, so we had today off, and tomorrow and Friday I'll practice with the team in the afternoon."

"Thank God for that," Kent said.

I nodded. "No kidding. Who would care about those stupid basketball shoes without you?"

"Good point," Davey said, pointing his fork at me. "But keep that to yourself."

"Hey, Shane, is Kristina doing any work at the show?" I said.

Kent looked at me. "Who?"

"His wife, Kristina Santana. You know, the Olympic figure skater?" I said.

"You're married to Kristina Santana? Really? I didn't know that," Kent said to Shane.

I rolled my eyes. "Hello? How can you not know that? Don't you watch *Entertainment Tonight*?"

"Is that on ESPN?" Kent said.

"Guys are worthless," I said. Kristina Santana was as famous for her beauty and brains as for her jumping ability. After winning a silver medal at the Olympics, she'd gone on to become a pediatrician. She was also the new spokesperson for Whisper perfume, so her face was everywhere.

"She's amazing. You two are going to have bionic children—very smart, attractive bionic children," I said to Shane.

He smiled. "She's actually coming into town on Friday to watch my game on Saturday night, so maybe I can introduce you."

I clapped my hands together. "I would love that! Are you going to bring her to the big JAG party on Friday night?"

"I don't know if we'll be able to make the party, but we'll try," he said.

"Don't forget to introduce us, too," Kent said. "Man, married to Kristina Santana. Go figure."

I punched him in the shoulder. "*Go figure?* Who says that?"

"Chill, Bryson," he said, rubbing his shoulder. "So, how long have you and Kristina been married?"

Shane picked up a forkful of tiramisu. "Almost five years. Are any of you married?"

"Four years, two kids," Kent said.

"Living in sin, five years, no kids," Davey said.

They all looked at me.

"Can you pass the sugar, please?" I said.

Davey shook his head. "Waverly is what you call a heartbreaker," he said to Shane. "Stomps all over them."

"That's not true," I said.

"She even broke off an engagement last year," Davey said.

Kent looked at me. "You were engaged? I didn't know that. What happened?" he said.

I swallowed and looked above him at the wall. "Um, it, uh, it just didn't work out," I said.

"She crushed the dude," Davey said. "Called it off two weeks before the big day. Poor guy never had a chance."

I poured some sugar in my coffee and sighed. "Can we please change the subject? I'm sure Shane doesn't want to hear about this."

"You know, Waverly, you've got to lower your standards," Davey said. "The way I see it, dating is like being in the jungle. Now, a relationship is a vine, and when things don't work out,

you're basically hanging from a vine that ain't swinging anymore.
Now, you may *want* to jump to another vine, a healthier vine, a
more supportive vine, or maybe a more exciting vine, but if none
of the other vines are good enough for you, or if you just don't
have enough energy to make the jump, you're going to spend
the rest of your life clinging to the lifeless bottom of a dead vine
just so you don't fall into the abyss below." He accompanied this
speech with sweeping apelike arm gestures and a variety of ani-
mal sounds.

There it was, my dysfunctional love life, acted out in a crowded
restaurant by a 34-year-old monkey.

"Well done, man. Well done." Kent stood up and clapped.

Davey bowed his head. "I'll leave a tip jar outside my room."

"Thank you for that, Davey, now will you please stop talking?"
I said.

Shane looked at me. "Why do you call this guy Davey anyway?"

I pointed at Davey. "Just look at that cute little boy face. How
can you not call him Davey? And I'm sort of a nickname person."

Davey rolled his eyes. "Thanks, Bryson. *Cute little boy face* is just
what a grown man wants to hear. Anyhow, Shane, I really think
Waverly should put herself out there more, because in my professional opinion—"

I looked up from my coffee cup. "In your *professional* opinion?"

He nodded. "Yes, in my professional opinion, Miss Bryson here
is a classic ringleader of what I like to call the Circle of Hatred,
which for centuries has defeated even the bravest of single men."

Shane and Kent both put their forks down.

"You've got to be kidding me," I said. "The Circle of Hatred?
What is that?"

"It's the ring of negative energy emitted by packs of pretty
women in bars. Do you know how terrifying it is for a mere mortal
to attempt to cross that force field? Just trying to strike up a conversation can cause years of emotional damage."

"The Circle of Hatred?" Shane said.

Davey nodded. "Totally toxic."

"Oh, Davey, you've outdone yourself this time." I buried my face in my hands.

"Bravo," Kent said.

Shane was smiling, but he clearly thought we were insane.

· · ·

After dinner, Shane headed back to his hotel, and Davey and Kent went off to a party thrown by Nelson Tennis. I briefly toyed with the idea of going with them, but when it was time to pull the trigger, I just couldn't rally.

I shook my head. "Sorry, boys, but my pink sheets and free pay-per-view sound much more appealing than a crowded room at this moment."

"C'mon, Bryson," Davey said, putting on his coat. "Don't be anti-social."

"You sure?" Kent said, standing up. "The man of your dreams might be there. . . ."

I yawned. "Then tell him I'm sorry we couldn't meet, *again*. If I want to stay awake at the booth tomorrow, I need to get in about fifteen hours of sleep tonight. Aren't you guys tired at all?"

Davey shook his head. "Nope, gotta enjoy this hall pass."

"Me neither," Kent said. "I'm fired up for a free night out."

They took off, and I headed to the ladies' room. A hall pass? That's what they called it? I washed my hands and shook my head. While Davey and Kent both welcomed a night out without their significant others, I felt a wave of loneliness hit me that I hadn't felt in months.

A free night *out*? I wished I had someone to curl up on the couch with every night, someone who wanted to hear about my day and rub my tired feet. I looked down and tried to remember if anyone had ever rubbed my feet. Aaron definitely hadn't been a foot rubber.

Sigh. Why was I still lying about how our engagement had ended?

I pulled my ponytail holder out and shook my head, running my fingers through my hair and stretching my neck from side to side.

Good Lord, only one day at the booth and already I felt like I was 130 years old. I thought about all the interviews I'd sat through, all the people I'd talked to, all the follow-up work I'd have to do when I got back to San Francisco. Ugh. I ran my hands through my hair again and looked at my reflection. The Atlanta air was always kind to my hair, and despite the convention arena air-conditioning, it felt healthy and strong and . . . WHAT?

I leaned close to the mirror and grabbed at a strand of hair on the right side of my head.

It was grey.

WHAT?

I yanked it out and held it up in the light. It was grey and thick, and did I mention it was grey and thick? It was like someone had woven a strand of dental floss into my scalp.

Sweet Jesus.

I tossed the hair into the trash can and looked at myself in the mirror. This couldn't be happening, could it? I mean, what the hell? I had to get out of there. I pulled my hair back into a low ponytail and quickly walked out into the empty hallway.

My cell phone rang, but I tossed it back in my purse when I saw my dad's name on the caller ID. Then I leaned up against the wall and closed my eyes. A grey hair? Was I over the hill already?

"Hey, are you okay?" a male voice said.

I opened my eyes and saw Shane standing outside the men's room.

"I just found a grey hair!" I blurted out, then immediately covered my mouth with both hands.

"Oh God, please tell me I didn't just say that," I whispered.

He smiled and shook his head. "Sorry, too late."

"I thought you left," I said.

He pointed to the men's room. "Pit stop."

"Oh my God, I'm so embarrassed, Shane. Please don't tell Kent and Davey, okay? They'll crucify me."

"For a grey hair?" he said.

"For anything related to getting one step closer to spinsterhood."

He nodded. "Those guys definitely like to tease you, but it's all in good fun, isn't it?"

"Yeah, but, well, sometimes, well, sometimes they go a little too far. And this week is already sucking enough."

"It is?" He sounded surprised.

"Oh, it has nothing to do with you and the show. It's just that, well . . ."

I looked up at him. There was something in his eyes that told me I could trust him. Or maybe it was the two glasses of wine I had drunk at dinner telling me I could. But regardless, I was suddenly overwhelmed with the urge to confide in someone who wasn't a part of my life in San Francisco. Right there, near the restrooms, at Morton's Steakhouse.

"Can I be honest with you, Shane?"

"Sure."

"Well, I, I didn't call off my wedding at the last minute. My fiancé did . . . and I just found out he's getting married to someone else." As soon as the words were out of my mouth I regretted them. "Oh God, I'm sorry. I don't know why I just told you that."

"You don't have to apologize," he said.

"But I'm being totally unprofessional. I'm sorry."

"Really, it's okay," he said.

I could feel the tears lining up to make their entrance. "I just can't bring myself to tell people the truth about what really happened. I know that's stupid, but I was so humiliated by the whole thing. And I doubt Kent and Davey would understand anyway."

"Hey, you might be surprised. Everyone's been on the losing end of a breakup at some point."

I frowned. "But being left practically at the altar takes it to a whole new level, you know?"

He stayed silent, sensing that I wasn't done yet.

"And now he's getting married and I'm still all alone and now I'm going grey and it's like time is flying by and I'm missing the boat and I don't know what I'm doing wrong . . ." The tears made their debut. "Oh God, I'm rambling. I'm so sorry, Shane, I'm being totally ridiculous." I wiped my eyes with the back of my hand. "I can't believe I'm crying and saying all this."

He shook his head. "No sweat, Waverly. Seriously, it's okay. Things will work out."

"You think so?" I said.

He nodded. "Hey, I want you to try something, okay?"

"You want me to *try something?*" I narrowed my eyes. "That sounds a bit shady."

He smiled. "I promise, it's totally legal. My sports psychologist makes me do it when the pressure starts to get to me."

"When the pressure of being rich and famous gets to you? Are you crazy?" I said.

He laughed. "It's just a mental exercise. Now close your eyes and tell me what you see."

I closed my eyes and immediately felt like I was going to topple over. Nice equilibrium. I reached over and put my hand on the wall. Then I stared into the back of my eyelids. I saw, well, nothing.

"Uh, Shane? I'm not seeing anything."

"Just keep your eyes closed. Now I want you to think about something that makes you feel happy, okay?"

"Okay." I tried, but I still saw nothing.

"Is this a trick?" I said.

"Nope, just keep concentrating."

I tried again. After a few moments a vision of a car-size Snickers suddenly popped into my head. My own snicker followed it.

"Good, now what do you see?" Shane said.

"I see a huge candy bar."

"Good, that's perfect. Now keep thinking about that image."

I kept thinking. Mmm.

"Okay, now open your eyes," Shane said.

I opened them and looked at him. "Well?"

"Do you know what you just saw?" he said.

"Uh, didn't I just tell you that?"

He smiled. "Work with me here, Waverly. What I mean is, do

you know the meaning of what you just saw?"

"Uh, that I'm a pig?"

"Nope. Well, maybe. I mean, I just met you. But that's not the point."

"Okay, well what then?"

"It means that you just smiled, *to yourself*."

"So?"

"And now don't you feel better?"

I thought about it. He was right. "Yeah, I do feel a little better."

"And why do you feel better?"

"Because I'm a pig?"

He smiled. "No, you feel better because you saw something in your own mind that is special to you, something that no one else in the world could see."

"So?"

"So that should show you that you can't always rely on the outside world to make you happy, Waverly. Most of the time it's really up to you."

I opened my mouth but couldn't think of anything to say.

"Think about it, Waverly," he said. "Your life isn't a basketball game. No one is keeping score but you, so don't worry so much about what everyone else is doing and what everyone else thinks."

This was coming from an NBA player? Talk about shattering stereotypes. Was he going to start ballet dancing next?

"Uh, I don't know what to say, Shane, I'm really impressed."

"Surprised you, didn't I?"

I nodded slowly. "More than you know. Thank you, I really need to get a grip."

"If you think I'm tough, wait 'til you meet my wife," he said.

I put my hand on his arm. "Hey, uh, while I really appreciate it and all, can we pretend this little encounter never happened?"

He shook his head. "Nope."

"Why not?"

"Because outside of practicing with my team, having dinner with you guys, and talking to my wife on the phone, this is pretty much the first conversation I've had all week that wasn't about me. Do you know how boring it is to have to talk about yourself all the time?"

I crossed my arms. "Hmm, I guess I never thought about that. So you're saying that my freak-out over dying old and alone with a head full of grey hair is a welcome change for you?"

He laughed. "Yeah, I guess it is."

"Well, I'm glad I could comfort you, Mr. Kennedy. And if you refuse to forget this conversation, can you at least promise me that we'll keep it between you and me?"

"Yes, we'll keep it between you and me," he said.

"You promise?" I held out my hand. "We have a deal?"

He shook it and smiled. "Deal."

When I got back to my room I booted up my computer and typed in a few more ideas for Honey Notes.

Front: Found that dreaded first grey hair?
Inside: Honey, think of the alternative. Can you say George Costanza?

Front: Do your married friends tell you that you're too picky?
Inside: Honey, they settled. Either that or they're not really your friends.

Front: Feeling down because you're still single?
Inside: Honey, keep your spirits up. Then down a few of them and go find yourself a hot guy to smooch.

Front: So your life isn't turning out how you thought it would?
Inside: Honey, no one is keeping score but you, so just go with it.

That night I dreamt that I divorced Davey to marry Shane and got into a fistfight with Kristina at our drive-through Vegas wedding. Aaron was the minister. He was dressed in an Elvis suit and dangling from a vine.

At least I woke up laughing.

Ever wish you could turn back the clock for just one night?

Honey, you and anyone who wore shoulder pads to the prom.

CHAPTER FIVE

At seven o'clock Friday evening, Penelope French and I were among the last of the JAG staff left at the booth. The show had officially ended at six o'clock, and most everyone, including Kent and Davey, had bolted shortly thereafter to hit happy hour.

I kicked off my shoes and sat cross-legged on the floor. "Thank God it's over. I'm absolutely exhausted."

"Tell me about it, sugar." She patted her fire-red bouffant hair, which never seemed to move, and cracked her knuckles. "I've been working like a dog for the past six months getting this thing together, and I'm no spring chicken anymore. Once I'm back in San Francisco, I'm heading straight for the nicest spa I can find and having every sort of body and beauty treatment imaginable, all on JAG."

"That sounds heavenly," I said.

She nodded. "Oh, it will be. And if any of those tightwads in accounting complain about the bill, they can take this show and stuff it up their cheap asses."

I laughed, and just then Gabrielle Simone emerged from one of the private meeting rooms.

"Hi, Gabrielle," I said, quickly standing up and putting my shoes on.

"Hello, Waverly," she said with a slow nod. "I trust you had a good show?"

"Excellent show," I said with a little too much enthusiasm. "A bunch of great press interviews."

"Glad to hear it." She looked down at Penelope. "And I assume you weren't serious about charging JAG for your personal spa time?"

Penelope looked at the floor. "Yeah, I was just kidding."

"Good. Well, I'll see you two back in San Francisco. Have a nice flight home." She turned and walked away.

"Meow." Penelope clawed the air when she was gone.

"That woman scares me," I whispered.

"I bet she kicks puppies for fun," Penelope said, standing up and stretching her tiny arms over her head. "So what do you say, señorita? Should we grab a bite to eat and a glass of wine before heading over to the party? It's been a long week, and it's going to be a long night. And I, for one, plan to get good and tanked."

I held my arm out to let her pass. "Show me the way."

. . .

An hour and a half later, Penelope and I were inside the Zellerbach Center, the huge venue JAG had rented. The party didn't officially start until nine o'clock, so the hall was still pretty empty except for the planning staff and the numerous caterers, bartenders, and security guards milling around.

The room looked stylishly festive. Large black and white helium balloons covered the entire ceiling, and there was a full bar in every corner, each flanked by waist-high black vases bursting with white roses. Half of the room was filled with tall, round tables of various diameters, each adorned with a black-and-white checkered tablecloth and surrounded by black barstools. A long, narrow buffet table full of appetizers and desserts lined one wall. Atop it sat large ice sculptures that spelled out *JAG*.

On the other side of the room was a dance floor, above which hung a giant disco ball. The band was tuning up on a stage that ran along the middle part of the far wall.

"This is going to be such a great party," I said. "I heard JAG hired Big Bangs to play."

Penelope nodded. "Yep, the events department finally realized that '80s cover music is the way to go, or at least the way to go for parties where the majority of the crowd is over the age of 22."

"Excellent decision," I said. I absolutely loved '80s music. Madonna, the B-52s, Duran Duran, Prince. I could dance all night, just as long as they didn't play any Bryan Adams. *Barf.*

We walked over to the nearest bar, which was staffed by an attractive guy in a tuxedo. He was really cute: tall with dark hair and dark eyes, no wedding ring. His name tag said "Chad."

I leaned down to whisper in Penelope's ear. "Well, if there's no one interesting to talk to at the party, I can always hang out by the bar with this guy."

"You ain't kidding," she whispered back, nodding.

Chad turned to face us and spread his hands out on the bar.

"What can I get you, ladies?"

Penelope batted her mascara-caked eyelashes. "Sugar, with that smile you can get whatever you darn well please. But I'll have a gin and tonic." She was always dating younger men and had no problem flirting with guys half her age or younger.

"Sure thing. And you?" He looked at me and smiled.

"Um, what do you recommend, Chad?" I said.

"How about a rookie?" he said.

"What's in a rookie?" I tried to sound cute. But how does one sound cute?

"Vodka, orange juice, pineapple juice, and Red Bull. It's pretty popular these days."

My ears perked up. "Red Bull? As in caffeine?"

He nodded. "Yep."

"Sounds good to me. Pass one over."

"Coming right up, ma'am," he said with another smile.

Pause.

Ma'am? Why didn't he just yell out *Nice grey hair there, Grandma!* to the whole room?

Chad turned his back to fix our drinks, and I leaned over to Penelope.

"Okay, he just called me ma'am. Next drink we hit a different bar, okay?"

She patted me on the arm. "No problem, dollface. It happens to the best of us."

We thanked Chad for the drinks and turned around. It was nearly nine o'clock, and we could see a big crowd forming outside.

"Check out that line," I said. "This place is about to be flooded."

Just then I heard the ring of my cell phone. I looked at the caller ID and bit my lip. It was my dad . . . again.

I touched Penelope on the shoulder. "Hey, I have to take this call, okay? I'll catch up with you later." I walked toward the nearest powder room and flipped open my phone. "Hi, Dad."

"Hi, baby, are you okay? I've left you all sorts of messages."

I hated it when he called me "baby." I pushed open the door and plopped down on a plush purple couch. "I'm fine, Dad. I'm in Atlanta for work this week, so I've been really busy."

"Atlanta? What's in Atlanta?"

"Just a trade show."

"The Super Show?"

"Yes, Dad."

"That's nice. Are all the big guns there?"

"Yep."

He didn't say anything else, so I knew what was coming.

"So what's up, Dad?"

The warmth left his voice. "Do I have to have a reason for calling my only child?"

I took a deep breath. "No, Dad, it's just that I'm sort of in the middle of something. How are you?"

"I'm good, doing all right. That job I had lined up at the factory didn't work out, but it wasn't my fault."

Of course it wasn't. "I'm sorry to hear that," I said.

"Those bastards in management had it in for me from the start. I never had a chance."

"Uh huh."

"But I'm looking into some new opportunities."

"You are?"

"Yep, been kicking around the idea of getting into magazine marketing."

"Magazine marketing?"

"It's a great opportunity," he said. "They'll train me right at the call center."

"Call center? Do you mean telemarketing?"

"It's marketing, Waverly. That's what they're calling it these days. Hey, maybe one day I'll be working right alongside you at K.A. Marketing."

"Yeah, maybe."

"So hey, listen, kiddo, I've got to pay for this training course, so if you could send me a little something to help with expenses while I'm not drawing a paycheck, not that I need your help, but if you wanted to I would appreciate it."

I made a fist with my free hand. "They're making you pay for the training course? That sounds pretty shady, Dad."

"Hey, Waverly, this is a great opportunity for a guy like me. Not everyone got the chance to go to college, you know."

I sighed. Always the college card. "I don't know, Dad. The last time I sent you money you promised it would be the last time."

"So I've had a bit of bad luck since then. It's not my fault, you know. More than anyone, you should know that, Waverly."

I stood up and put my hand on my forehead. "Fine, I'll wire you some money when I get home."

The warmth immediately returned to his voice. "Thanks, kiddo, I appreciate it. So are you seeing anyone these days?"

"No, not at the moment."

"That boy Aaron still in the picture at all?"

"Not really."

"You shouldn't be so picky, you know, letting him go like that. Boys like that don't grow on trees, you know." The *for girls like you* was left unsaid.

"I know, Dad. Listen, I've really got to go now, okay?"

"Sure, baby, you have a nice evening now."

I hung up and closed my eyes, trying to tell myself that it didn't matter.

When I finally opened them, I looked around and was struck by the difference in beauty between the powder room and the conversation I'd just had. The room was practically regal. The restroom part had marble floors, but the lounge area was covered with thick, expensive gold carpeting and boasted several plush velvet couches and love seats in various shades of dark purple, green, and yellow. The walls were lined with a number of fancy mirrors, each with its own table and a purple velvet stool.

I sat down on one and faced the gold-trimmed mirror. Then I put my drink on the table and opened my purse. To erase, or at least to camouflage the effects of three days at the booth, topped off by that lovely chat with my father, I brushed my hair, applied a bit of black mascara to my eyelashes, and swept a pale-pink blusher over my cheeks. I decided to paint my lips a dark red. Chad the bartender may have called me ma'am, but, whatever, I wasn't a total fossil yet.

Ready to have some fun, I walked back to the main hall and immediately noticed how much the party had filled up since Penelope and I had arrived. There were already several hundred people inside, and I wondered if I would ever find her again. The band had started playing, but the dance floor was still empty as the guests swarmed the bars and buffet tables.

I decided another drink was in order and glanced around to get a look at the non-Chad bartenders. I headed straight for the only one staffed by three females. I wasn't taking any more chances of being mistaken for someone's mom. I waited in line for a few minutes and listened to the band play Duran Duran's "Hungry Like the Wolf." When I reached the front of the line, a petite blonde bartender greeted me with a big smile and a southern accent. "What can I get you, miss?"

"A rookie, please," I said with a big smile of my own. Thank God for under-eye concealer.

Fresh drink in hand, I turned around to scan the crowd for familiar faces. Nothing. The room was getting really crowded, and I wondered where all the people from JAG were. I didn't see anyone I recognized, except for a handful of celebrity athletes. I had already spotted two players from the Red Sox, a couple of wide receivers from the Steelers, and an unbelievably short Olympic gymnast who didn't look old enough to drive, much less drink.

I wandered around the party for a few more minutes and still didn't recognize a soul. I looked at my watch and noticed that my drink was almost empty. Then I realized that I'd skipped lunch, hadn't eaten much at dinner, and was suddenly feeling a bit tipsy, so I headed over to the buffet table. I scoped out the offerings and filled up a tiny party plate with cheese and crackers.

I munched on a cracker and stood on my tiptoes to look around for a familiar face. Still nothing. Suddenly I felt uncomfortable, as if all the people in the room were looking at me. My face began to feel a little flushed. My burst of confidence vanished, to be replaced by a feeling that the whole room was wondering who the loser in the red lipstick was.

"Hey there, can I tell you that you look really hot in those jeans?"

I looked to my right, and then I looked down, and then I met the glance of a middle-aged man who looked like he had eaten every meal for the past twenty-five years at McDonald's. He was about five foot five and balding, with what remained of his thinning hair brushed into a tragic comb-over. He wore a white button-down shirt with a collar so tight that the folds of his neck hung over the side, and it looked like he was wearing a tire around his waist under his shirt. I tried not to look too closely at what was below his waist, but I believe his shirt was tucked into a pair of black Levi's. To top it off, he was wearing a pair of snakeskin cowboy boots.

Oh, and he was sweating.

I'm pretty sure you can imagine what I was thinking in this situation.

"Uh, thank you, I guess," I said. I wondered how I could escape.

Where was everybody from JAG?

"I'm Chuck Jenkins. What's your name, pretty lady?" He was chomping on a greasy buffalo wing covered in ranch dressing.

"Um, I'm Waverly. Waverly Bryson."

"Did you say Waverly? Waverly, as in the cracker?"

I sighed. "Yes, as in the cracker." My name could either be a fun conversation starter or a major annoyance depending on who was on the other end of the conversation.

"Well I'll be damned. Waverly." He licked the ranch dressing off his fingers, then wiped his hand on his black jeans and extended it to me for a handshake.

Was he kidding? I smiled politely and made a gesture that my hands were both occupied. *Sweet Jesus, please just go away.* I was sort of drunk, but not drunk enough to deal with this asshole.

He ate another buffalo wing and looked me up and down. "Ya know, you are one gorgeous woman, Waverly. With that lean body, I bet you're a volleyball player. Am I right? Beach volleyball? What company are you representing? Is it a bikini manufacturer?"

"I work for Jammin' Athletic Gear," I said with another sigh. "I'm a publicist."

"A what? For what?"

I glanced over his shoulder. "A publicist, for Jammin' Athletic Gear. I manage media relations for the sporting goods company throwing this party."

"Ya mean y'all handle press conferences and things like that?"

"Yes, exactly," I said. His southern drawl was really getting on my nerves. I looked around the room for someone to rescue me. No one.

I looked back at him and tried not to think about his male muffin top. "Um, what do you do, Chuck?"

"My company sells hot dogs to the concession stands at the convention center." He had his greasy fingers back in his mouth.

Hot dogs? More than one inappropriate comment came to mind.

"Oh, so you're not in town just for the show?" I said.

He shook his head. "No, no, sweetheart. I work with all the shows that come through here. But I dig the Super Show because of all the hot broads like yourself who come along with the package. Are you married?"

Was this fat little man serious? To hell with being polite. I had to get out of there. I put my plate down on a table and decided to make a run for it.

"Uh, well, it was nice talking to you, Chuck, but I need to meet up with some friends. Have a nice night."

I turned to leave, but he grabbed my arm with his greasy, chubby hand. "Hey now, sweetheart, don't leave just yet! We were just getting started. Ya know, there are all sorts of ways to enjoy a Waverly cracker. Maybe we could have a little snack in your hotel room?"

Did he really just say that? I yanked my arm away and began walking toward the dance floor. "I'm sorry, Chuck, but I really have to go now."

"Save me a dance!" he called after me.

Ugh. I kept going and didn't look back.

I escaped to a corner on the other side of the room and looked at my watch again. Where were Kent and Davey? Where was Penelope? I finished the last bit of my drink and put it down on one of the small round tables. My attempt at securing nourishment at the buffet had been thwarted by Chuck, and now I was more buzzed than ever.

I could still feel the clammy touch of his hand on my arm and wondered if there was any disinfectant on that tray of products in the lounge. So gross! Just my luck that of all the guys at the party, it was Chuck in his black Levi's who had come up to talk to me. Did I look like a Chuck type of girl? Was my dad right about me?

Just as I was beginning to rethink the whole red lipstick thing, someone tapped me on the shoulder.

"Waverly, is that you?"

I swung around and found myself face-to-face with the third button of a perfectly pressed white cotton shirt. Then I looked up about two feet and saw Shane Kennedy looking down at me.

I smiled wide. "Hey, Shane! I'm so glad to see you. Apparently I don't know anyone here." I hoped I wasn't yelling, because after a few drinks I had a tendency to talk way louder than necessary.

"Well, that makes three of us." He nodded to the person standing next to him, and my eyes followed.

No way.

It was the cute guy I'd seen the first morning of the Super Show, right after the unfortunate Milky Way incident.

"Waverly, this is Jake McIntyre," Shane said. "He was my roommate in college and is the head physical therapist and trainer for the Hawks here in Atlanta." Then he looked at Jake. "Waverly managed all the press interviews for JAG at the show."

"Hi, uh, um, it's nice to meet you, Jake." I held out my hand, hoping it wasn't too sweaty.

"It's nice to meet you, too." He shook my hand and smiled, and I could feel my cheeks getting red. Did he recognize me? I wasn't sure I wanted to know.

"Um, uh, so you two were roommates in college?" I played with my earring and wondered if I had any breath mints in my purse.

"All four years," Shane said. "Longest years of my life. Hey, are Kent and Dave here?"

I shrugged. "I have no idea. I've been standing around by myself for the last hour wondering where they are. Have you ever noticed how lame it can make you feel wandering around a party by yourself?"

I hoped they couldn't tell I was so buzzed, especially since I'd just told them that I didn't know anyone there. What kind of loser gets tanked by herself at a party?

Jake laughed. "Shane's never at a party by himself. He's too famous."

I looked up at Shane. "Too many admirers, Mr. Kennedy?"

"Just slightly," Jake said. "Press, fans, general hangers-on. It's crazy. I have to make an appointment weeks in advance just to beat this clown at Madden Football."

Shane coughed. "Like you ever win."

"Hangers-on?" I said to Shane. "What does your wife think about the hangers-on who are of the female disposition?"

He laughed. "They don't want to mess with Kristina, let's just say that."

"Hey, is she coming?" I said.

Shane shook his head. "She got stuck at the hospital."

"Oh no, really? Darn it. I was really looking forward to meeting her."

He put his arm around Jake. "Well, my man Jake here isn't nearly as hot as my wife, but he's not all that bad, is he?"

I must have turned even redder, because Shane laughed, and Jake hit him on the side of the head. "You're a jackass, Shane," he said. Then he looked at me and smiled. "Ignore him, Waverly."

I looked at Jake but didn't speak. I felt like a female deer caught in the headlights of a speeding car being driven by a very hot male deer. Or would that be a buck? Whatever the word, he was hot and I was not cool.

He and Shane were obviously waiting for me to say something in response, but I couldn't think of anything witty.

Or anything at all.

Anything.

Anything!

"Uh, um, that's okay," I finally said quietly. McKenna and Andie would kill me for being so pathetic.

I made a mental note for a Honey Note:

Front: Ever get tongue-tied talking to a cute boy?
Inside: Honey, if his tongue wasn't involved, you're a loser.

I finally broke my gaze from Jake and turned back to Shane. "So, um, hey, Shane . . . didn't you say you had a game here tomorrow? Then I guess you guys sort of play against each other?"

He nodded. "Yep, tomorrow night. Dave and Kent are coming, so you should come, too. I'll leave you a ticket at will call. Hey, I just spotted a couple of my buddies who play for the Yankees. I'm going to go say hi. I'll see you kids later."

He walked away before I could tell him my flight home was the next morning, and as he disappeared into the crowd, he turned and winked at me. Or at least I thought he winked at me.

My vision was getting a little too blurry to be sure.

"Would you like a drink, Waverly?" Jake said.

I looked at him and blinked. I knew the last thing I needed was another drink. But for some reason I couldn't get my mouth to listen to my brain, and I heard myself say, "Sure, I'll have a rookie," as we walked over to the bar and got in line.

"So I almost didn't recognize you without that candy bar in your mouth," Jake said as he handed me a fresh drink, which I proceeded to drop on the ground.

"Are you okay?" He walked back to the bar and grabbed a handful of napkins, which I used to sop up the drink that had splashed all over my jeans. Then he ordered me another drink, which I needed like a hole in the head.

I stood back up and bit my lip. "Um, you remember that?"

"I thought I might have to give you the Heimlich," he said, laughing.

I coughed and looked everywhere in the room but at his blue eyes.

"Uh, yeah, that wasn't exactly my proudest moment. Can we maybe talk about something else?"

He smiled and handed me the new drink. "Okay, but you've got to admit that it was pretty funny."

"Okay, busted," I said, finally looking back at him. "Have you ever noticed how hard it is to chew a Milky Way and walk at the same time?"

He laughed and took a sip of his beer. "So you do media relations, huh? Shane said you guys worked him pretty hard this week."

I couldn't stop staring at his eyes. Calling them blue didn't do them justice. They were more . . . well, BLUE.

"Waverly?"

I snapped out of my trance.

"I'm sorry, what did you say?"

"I said that Shane said you worked him really hard this week."

I nodded. "Yeah, we did, but he was great about it. It was impressive. So, uh, what were you doing at the show?"

"I do a little product consulting for BA Rocks and for Adina Energy, you know, for nutritional stuff, so I wanted to check out the new products on the market."

"Ooh, Adina Energy," I said. "I bet you just loved those dancing Adina Energy girls at their booth. I hear they're very nutritious."

He laughed. "No comment."

"I bet," I said, smiling.

There was a bit of an awkward silence just then. It was the first *good* awkward silence I'd had in a very long time.

"So, where do you live?" he said.

I took a sip of my drink. "San Francisco. Have you ever been?"

He nodded. "Yeah, but never for more than a night or two, because it's always been for a trip with the team. I'd like to spend more time there though. What a beautiful city."

"Yeah, it's pretty spectacular. Just please promise me that you will never, *ever* call it Frisco or San Fran, okay?"

He laughed. "I'll try to remember that."

"Seriously, Jake, remember it. Fingernails. Chalkboard. Me. Outta here." I pointed to myself and then to the exit.

He laughed again. "Okay, I promise. But it's true, I've always thought it'd be fun to live in San Francisco. I love the beach."

I swallowed and shook my head. "Actually, that's a myth."

"A myth?"

I nodded. "A myth."

"There's no beach in San Francisco?"

"Okay, I'm slightly exaggerating. What I mean is that the weather in San Francisco isn't what you'd expect, given that it's California and all."

"What's it like?"

"It's cold there, Jake, C-O-L-D."

"Really?"

"Really. It can be nice during the day, but it's usually foggy, and it's always freezing at night. And you can practically play ice hockey on the ocean."

"Wow, I had no idea."

I nodded. "You're not alone. I've noticed that every year I meet transplants from all over the country who have moved to San Francisco expecting to hit the beach before they even unpack. And they're always bummed out when they come down with frostbite. It's sort of sad, actually, like we've let them down." I frowned and wiped a fake tear from my cheek.

"It's really that cold? It always looks so nice in the movies."

I shook my head. "That's because those movies are conveniently filmed on rare sunny days, never on the days when the fog is so thick you can't see the Golden Gate Bridge."

"Wow, I never knew that."

I put my hand on my hip. "I mean we've got October, which is gorgeous, I'll give you that. And then there's the occasional balmy day here and there, but those days always seem to happen on a Tuesday—never on a weekend when you could actually do something about it, ya know?"

He smiled. "Nope, I didn't know."

"Oh yes. I'm still waiting to go to a barbecue without having to bring a warm coat."

"A warm coat to a barbecue?"

I nodded. "I've noticed that nearly every girl I know has a perfect sleeveless barbecue outfit hanging in her closet that she never gets to wear because it's always too cold."

"Perfect barbecue outfit, huh?"

"Perfect *sleeveless* barbecue outfit. Big difference."

He laughed. "So San Francisco's really that bad?"

I shook my head. "No! It's not bad at all. It's cold, but it's the best. On a clear day with the sailboats dotting the bay? Are you kidding me? It's absolutely spectacular. You couldn't pay me to live anywhere else. Besides, if you drive ten miles in any direction outside of the city, it's usually pretty hot, at least in the summer, which will do nicely if you need to defrost." I smiled and sipped my drink.

He scratched his right eyebrow. Did he think I was crazy? That had been quite an outburst, even for me.

"I still think San Francisco would beat Atlanta," he said.

"What's so bad about Atlanta?" I gazed up at him and tilted my head. God, he was pretty.

"Atlanta's not that bad, but it's not where I would have chosen for myself. I grew up in Florida and love the water, so I really miss living on the coast. That's one of the things that I don't like about working in the NBA. You don't have much say in where you live."

"I guess I never thought about it that way. From the outside it all seems so glamorous and fun," I said. Hmm. Just like *my* job did.

"Did you grow up in San Francisco?" he said.

"Sort of, near enough," I said, dreading the inevitable next question.

"Where does your family live now?" he said.

I looked at the floor. "Um, it's just my dad—he lives near Sacramento. My mom died when I was little."

"Oh, wow, I'm sorry to hear that."

"Thanks," I said quietly.

"That must have been really hard on both of you."

I nodded, my eyes still looking at the floor. What a buzzkill.

"How did she die?" he said.

I looked up, surprised that he had asked what most people never ever did. At this point in the conversation most people just tried to change the subject.

"Breast cancer," I said softly, taking a sip of my drink.

"How old were you?"

"Just a baby."

"Oh, man, so you never got to know her at all?"

I shook my head. "Nope."

"Growing up without a mom must have been difficult."

"Um . . ." I tried to read those blue eyes, which seemed to be telling me that he wasn't just being polite, that he really wanted to know.

I took another sip of my drink and nodded. "Yeah, my dad did what he could, but he just, well, he just wasn't a mom, you know?"

He nodded. "Moms are pretty amazing."

It was the perfect chance to shift the spotlight and ask him about *his* mom, who I was sure was an angel given the way he'd said that, but the idiot in me kept me talking about mine.

"Yeah, well . . . it was really hard because my dad had just started pitching in the minor leagues when they had me, and apparently he had a really promising future ahead of him, but then my mom got sick, and he had to give everything up. . . ."

He nodded again but didn't say anything, sensing that I had more to say, just like Shane had done at Morton's. Polite, sensitive, respectful. Wow.

I took a deep breath. "And after he quit baseball, he wasn't able to get it together with a real career or anything . . . you know . . . so things were hard . . . you know, financially . . . and he and I . . . well . . . we just . . . well, we're just so different . . . so it was hard that way too . . . actually, it's still pretty hard . . . and . . . and, well, I help him out sometimes, but he's still struggling a bit with managing his money." My voice trailed off again, and I looked back down at the floor. Why was I telling him all this?

"I'm sorry," he said.

I took a sip of my drink, my gaze still down. "I'm not sure why I'm telling you all this. I'm not really used to talking about it."

"You feel guilty, don't you," he said. It wasn't a question.

I looked back up at him and tried to laugh. "Am I that obvious, Mr. McIntyre?"

"Well, you're clearly doing well for yourself now, and if he's still having a hard time, it's only natural to feel a little guilty about that."

I shrugged. "I guess. My dad sure knows how to make me feel guilty about it."

"I'm sure you're more important to your dad than a career in baseball would have been, Waverly."

I shook my head. "You're really sweet, but I don't think so."

"You honestly think that baseball is more important to your dad than his own daughter?"

I nodded. "Sometimes."

"Are you serious?"

I smiled weakly. "Okay, I'm only half serious, but I've noticed that I'm not always sure which half. And now that I've officially rained all over this parade, I'm changing the subject back to you. Where do *your* parents live?"

He put his hands up. "Okay, I'll back off with the amateur psychoanalysis. My parents are still in Miami, in the same house where I grew up. I have an older brother who lives a few miles away from them and an older sister who lives in Boston with her husband and kids."

"That's nice," I said, wondering how I could change the subject even further away from family and families. I glanced over at two security guards by the fire exit and then looked back at Jake. "Hey, have you ever noticed how almost all cops have mustaches?" I said.

He smiled. "What?"

"Security guards, too. What's that all about?"

He shook his head. "I never really thought about it."

I shrugged. "It's just something I've noticed. It's quite fascinating when you start to pay attention. I wonder what the percentage is compared to the general population."

"You spend a lot of time noticing things, don't you?" he said.

I shrugged again. "A little. Oh, crap."

"What?"

"I'm sorry. I just remembered that I forgot to set my DVR to record *American Idol* this week."

He laughed. "*American Idol?* Seriously?"

"Oh, yes," I said, nodding. "It's my favorite show."

"Your favorite show? For real?"

"Yep. I even went to the concert last year."

He smiled. "I'll pretend I didn't hear that."

Had I really just told him that I went to the *American Idol* concert on the heels of talking about my mother's cancer and my screwed-up childhood? Was I insane? I was so flustered that I honestly had no idea what I was saying anymore. And the alcohol wasn't helping. My head was all foggy, and I'd already forgotten half of what I had said just five minutes earlier. Sweaty Chuck was a distant memory.

I pushed my hair behind my ear and told myself to get it together.

"So, um, you said not being able to choose where you live is one of the few things you don't like about working in the NBA. What are the other things?" I said.

"If I tell you, you'll laugh."

"Try me."

He cleared his throat. "Well, sometimes it's hard to—"

"Jake McIntyre! I thought you might be here. How are you, darling?"

We both turned around as a supertall, stick-thin brunette with matching stick-straight hair and bangs nearly jumped into Jake's lap, or what would have been his lap if he had been sitting down.

Jake blushed, and my wobbling self-confidence took a nose dive.

"Hi, Carolyn, how are you?" he said.

"I'm just wonderful, darling. Busy with the new Prada line, but doing great. We're off to New York on Monday to start the winter season."

She looked at me with a frosty smile. "Hi, I'm Carolyn Weller."

"Waverly Bryson," I said quietly, suddenly feeling like a sixth grader in a high school locker room. How could something that skinny have such huge breasts?

She turned her attention back to Jake and put her arm around his waist. She whispered something into his ear, and he laughed. I took that as my cue to make a gracious exit. I softly said *Nice meeting you both*, but neither of them seemed to hear me, so I backed away and headed through the crowd to the bar.

Then I ordered another drink and decided that getting trashed wasn't such a bad idea after all.

· · ·

"Forty-eight, forty-nine, fifty. Fifty. Fifty. Fifty." I was sitting on a bar stool at a high round table in the corner of the room, counting out loud the white roses in the vase to my right. "Fifty roses. That's five dozen roses. No, that's six dozen roses. Hell, I have no idea how many dozen roses that is."

I gazed down at my half-empty glass. How many drinks had I had? How long had I been sitting there? It's never a good sign when you lose track.

I looked over at the huge, blurry crowd. What had I been thinking? Jake wasn't interested in me. Why would he be? He was just being polite. My dad was right. Aaron was right. I was right. I was damaged goods, destined to sit on the back of the shelf until my expiration date.

I stood up and steadied myself, which took way too much effort. I picked up my drink and decided to go find Davey and Kent. They had to be in the crowd somewhere. I swung around and smacked right into a young couple standing by my table, spilling what was left of my drink all over the floor.

"Oh my gosh, I'm so sorry," I slurred.

"No worries," the fresh-faced guy said. "Are you okay?"

I smoothed my hands on my jeans. "Yeah, I'm fine. Sorry." Fine? I was nearly seeing double.

"You look familiar." The young blonde standing next to him cocked her head to one side. "Do you live in San Francisco?"

"Um, yeah," I said.

She held out her hand. "I'm Kristi Benton. This is my boyfriend, John Callahan. We work at Reebok's advertising agency. What's your name?"

"Amanda Woodward. I work at D&D Advertising," I said, shaking her hand.

"Hi, Amanda, it's nice to meet you."

I shook my head. "Actually, I was just kidding."

Blank stares.

"You know, D&D Advertising, miniskirts, *Melrose Place*?" I said.

More blank stares.

Okay, I'm way old. "Uh, I'm Waverly Bryson. I work at K.A. Marketing."

Kristi smiled. "That's it. I knew I'd seen you before. My older sister's roommate works there. Mandy Edwards."

"Oh, yes, Mandy works in my department." Definitely slurring.

"We met Mandy for lunch at her office a few weeks ago. She says she loves working there."

I nodded. "It's a good company." If Mandy only knew that no one else loved her working there.

"Well, it's good to meet you, Waverly. I'll tell Mandy I saw you."

"Great," I said. *Crap.* "It was nice talking to you."

I turned to escape and bumped smack into someone else. Good God. I needed to drink a gallon of water and put myself to bed.

"Hey, there you are. I thought you left."

I looked up and saw Jake standing there.

I casually reached for a barstool to keep my balance. "Um, nope, not yet. How's it going?"

"Are you okay?" he said.

"Yeah, I'm fine. Why? Did something happen?"

He shook his head. "You just disappeared. Where did you go?"

"Did I? Oh, sorry. I had to use the restroom. And you, uh, well, you seemed busy."

"Busy? I seemed busy?" He smiled, and I could feel my heart beating faster.

I played with my earring. "Well, I mean, with your friend and all, you know, it looked like you had things to talk about, and I didn't want to intrude. . . ."

He said nothing for a moment, just looked at me.

Then he spoke.

"Waverly, do you want to dance?"

Did I want to dance? Was he kidding? I wanted to spring to the stage and pay the band ten grand to play a slow song.

"Uh, sure."

"After you." We turned toward the dance floor. As we began to walk, he put his hand on the small of my back to guide me, and the heat I felt when he touched me could have burned a hole right through me. We maneuvered our way to the dance floor, where I spotted Kent and Davey dancing with two girls I didn't recognize. They waved us over.

"There you are! We've been looking everywhere for you!" Davey pulled me through the crowd and introduced me to his and Kent's dancing partners, two sales reps from Nike. I could barely hear him above the sound of Madonna's "Vogue" blasting from the stage.

"This is Jake!" I belted over the music. "Jake, this is Davey and Kent!"

"Hi, Jake!" Davey yelled.

"It's nice to meet you!" Kent shouted.

"Nice to meet you, too!" Jake said in a near scream.

"Should I go find a bullhorn?" I slurred at a normal decibel. But I don't think anyone heard me.

The tiny hole that had opened on the dance floor quickly closed, and Jake and I got swallowed up in the crowd. And then, as if the gods had listened to my prayers, "Vogue" ended, and the band started playing what may be the best slow-dance song ever, "Who's Crying Now?" by Journey.

Jake looked down at me. "Should we keep on dancing?"

I shrugged. "Whatever."

"Whatever? That's your answer?"

I smiled. "Yeah, whatever."

"Waverly, you are something else." I looked up, and he laughed and put his arms around me. I rested my head on his chest, and suddenly we were dancing.

I felt my entire body heat up, and a tingling sensation ran from my head all the way to my fingers and toes.

"Waverly?" he whispered, looking down at me.

I closed my eyes and sighed. "Hmm?" I felt like I was floating.

"Can I ask you something?"

I was about to look up and answer him, but once I closed my eyes, the harsh reality of major overintoxication kicked in with a vengeance. And suddenly I felt really dizzy. Horribly, horribly dizzy.

I had to get out of there. I had to get to a bathroom. Fast.

I broke away from him and covered my hand with my mouth

as I started walking away. "I have to go now."

He grabbed my hand. "Are you okay? Where are you going?"

I didn't know what else to say. I was suddenly so terribly drunk that I couldn't really see or think straight, but I knew I had to get away from him, away from everyone. I pulled my hand away and pushed my way through the blurry crowd.

When I got off the dance floor, I kept moving and headed toward the lounge, nearly knocking over Mandy Edwards's friends on the way. I ignored them and knocked open the doors to the restroom. I hurried through the plush carpeted area and ran to the last stall.

Then I threw up. Over and over and over.

. . .

When I woke up on Saturday morning, I could have sworn that I had an entire bag of jumbo-size cotton balls stuffed in my mouth. My whole body ached, and I felt like a very large nutcracker was squeezing my head. I rolled over and looked at the clock on the nightstand.

It was 7:14. What time had I gone to bed? How had I gotten back to the hotel?

I sat up and held my pounding head in my hands. Then I looked down at the bedspread. The bed was still made, and I was on top of the covers. I glanced over and saw my coat, purse, and sweater on a chair. In addition to my clothes and shoes, I was still wearing my earrings, necklace, and watch.

"Well, at least I didn't lose anything other than my dignity and my dinner," I said to no one. But I didn't feel like laughing.

I kicked off my shoes, then crawled across the bed and reached over to the top of the dresser for the manila file folder that held my itinerary. I opened it up and pulled out my flight info. My flight back to San Francisco was at ten o'clock, which meant I needed to leave for the airport by eight thirty. At least I hadn't slept through my flight.

Very, very slowly, I stood up and walked to the minibar. I opened a four-dollar bottle of water and drank the entire thing without stopping. Then I pulled off my clothes, threw them in a pile on the floor, and walked into the bathroom. I turned on the shower as hot as I could stand it and gently stepped inside. The steam was so thick that I couldn't see anything, which was just as I wanted it.

I leaned my head against the glass door and sighed. I was pretty foggy on the details, but the main events of the previous evening were painfully clear. Getting plastered and throwing up? What was I, a cast member of the *Real World*? And at a client event, no less. In the image-driven world of PR, that's the professional equivalent of, hmm, maybe being a driving instructor and running over your student's grandparents?

The last thing I could remember clearly was being on the dance floor and suddenly feeling too dizzy to stand up. I vaguely remembered getting sick in the bathroom, and that was it. I didn't even know how I had gotten home. Had Jake seen me like that? Had anyone else seen me like that?

If it were possible to die from shame, that morning would have been the end of me. I looked down at the big freckle on the top of my left foot. If they found me dead in the shower, the coroner would declare humiliation as the cause of death, and McKenna would have to fly in to identify my naked body. That stupid freckle I'd always hated would finally serve for something.

Before it had been speculation, but now it was official.

I was the biggest loser ever.

. . .

At 8 a.m., the elevator doors opened to the lobby, although my stomach felt like I was still moving. I shakily walked out wearing a pair of dark sunglasses and black clothes to reflect my state of hangover-induced near-death. I checked out and left my suitcase with the concierge, then headed over to the breakfast buffet to get some coffee and eggs. One of the only things I learned in college that I still remember is that a plate of salty scrambled eggs with cheese is the world's best cure for a hangover.

I sat down at a booth and ordered a cup of coffee, then took off my sunglasses and looked around. The lobby and restaurant were relatively empty, and I was praying that I could make it out of there without having to speak to anyone.

I put my head in my hands and groaned. I don't think I'd ever been so hungover, or at least not since before I'd met Aaron, who wasn't much of a drinker. I loved a tasty cocktail as much as the next person, but puking in a public restroom? Please. And for the first time since Aaron, I'd met a guy I was actually interested in, and I'd managed to screw it up before we'd even had one dance. Nice.

I boarded my plane an hour later, and neither my pounding head nor the three cups of coffee I'd drunk could keep me from crashing out. I fell into a deep sleep and dreamt that the captain came back to the main cabin to speak to me. He said he'd met me the night before at a bar. His name was Chuck, and he offered me a complimentary rookie if I would come up to the cockpit and sit on his lap.

When I woke up, we were landing at San Francisco International Airport. I had been asleep for nearly five hours. We waited for what seemed like an eternity to be let off the plane, and of course everyone insisted on jumping out of their seats the second the plane came to a stop, even though it was obvious that we weren't going anywhere. I had the aisle seat, and the guy next to me and his wife stood all hunched over me for, like, five minutes. I will never understand people.

By the time I got back to my apartment, it was nearly two o'clock, and despite my marathon cross-country siesta, I was still exhausted. I dropped my suitcase on the floor of the bedroom, kicked off my shoes, and buried myself under the covers, where I decided to stay until the year 2037.

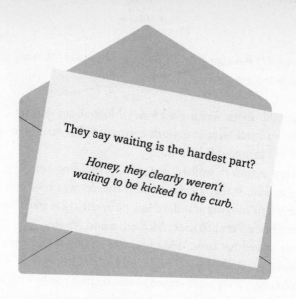

They say waiting is the hardest part?

Honey, they clearly weren't waiting to be kicked to the curb.

CHAPTER SIX

When I opened my eyes Sunday morning, I didn't know where I was. For about six seconds, I was blissfully unaware. And then I remembered everything. I put my head under the pillow and groaned.

At least my hangover was gone.

I shuffled into the kitchen wearing my robe and slippers to make some coffee. I leaned one hip against the counter and watched the water slowly drip into the pot, wondering if it would ever finish. Have you ever noticed how coffee pots seem to know when you're standing there watching them? It's like they're friends with the regular pots.

While I waited for the coffee, I grabbed a piece of paper from the shopping list magnet on my fridge and sat down at the kitchen table.

Front: Ever drink too much at a party and make a fool of yourself?
Inside: Honey, that's okay. At least you weren't home alone watching Touched by an Angel *reruns.*

Front: Feel like you never do the right thing?
Inside: Honey, look at it this way—if you always did the right thing,

you'd probably have no friends, because who wants to hang out with someone that boring?

I thought about writing a Honey Note about getting fired for acting like a total idiot at a work event, but that struck so close to home that I just couldn't do it.

At two o'clock I walked out of my building into the bright November sun. It was a cold day, but the sky was blue and clear. I pulled my hair into my standard low ponytail as I walked down the street to Dino's Pizza to meet McKenna and Andie.

Andie waved me over. "Hey, woman, sit down and have a beer and some pizza." She blew a huge bubble and popped it. "I'll pour you a cold one." They were seated at our regular booth with a frosty pitcher of Bud Light and a large pepperoni pizza between them.

I shook my head as I sat down and reached for a glass of water. "Believe me, a beer is the last thing I need right now."

"Big party week? Did you stalk any figure skaters?" McKenna said. At the Super Show the previous year, I'd taken a picture of Michelle Kwan at the food court with my phone and texted it to her and Andie. They had yet to let me live it down.

"Not this year," I said, my sour mood raining all over their good one.

Andie took her gum out of her mouth and stuck it on the side of her plate. "So I'm guessing Aaron hasn't called you yet?"

I shook my head. "Nope."

"Are you serious? I can't believe that," McKenna said. "Do you think he ever will?"

"Who knows?" I said. "If he hasn't already, I'm guessing he's not going to."

"Has the news sunk in yet?" McKenna said.

I bit my lip and tried to smile. "It's still sinking, along with my self-esteem."

She leaned over and squeezed my shoulder. "Hang in there, Wave, you'll get through this."

"So, did you have fun in Atlanta?" Andie said.

I leaned back in the booth. "Fun? No, I really couldn't say that. Well, I almost had fun, but it didn't work out."

"Because of Aaron?" McKenna said.

"Not really."

"Not really? What kind of half-ass answer is that?" Andie dipped her pizza in ranch dressing. "Details, please."

"Well, I sort of met a very cute boy at a party, but then nothing happened."

"A cute boy?" Andie said.

"What do you mean 'sort of'?" McKenna said.

"What do you mean 'nothing happened'?" Andie said.

"What party?"

"Did he ask for your phone number?"

"Why didn't it work out?"

"What was his name?"

"How old?"

"Was he hot?"

"Single?"

"Married?"

"Divorced?"

"Straight?"

I put my hands up in front of my face. "Hold on! Hold on . . . let me speak! Talking to you two is like being strapped to the wall in front of a tennis ball machine."

"Well?" they said in unison.

I took a sip of my water and slowly put it down on the table. "Okay, ladies, since you asked so nicely, I will tell you."

And I did.

When I'd finished divulging the details, I took a bite of pizza and looked at them.

"Well?" I said.

"Hot damn," Andie said.

"You really threw up?" McKenna said.

I nodded. "Yep, and I can't even remember how I got back to my hotel. For all I know, the CEO of JAG carried me there."

"Ouch," Andie said.

"Well at least you were attracted to someone new, right? That's huge," McKenna said.

I frowned. "I guess so, but I'm not sure how much consolation that'll be if I get fired."

"I highly doubt that'll happen. You think this guy Jake will try to contact you?" McKenna said.

I put my finger on my chin. "Hmm . . . given that I literally sprinted away from him to go barf up my dinner, I'm guessing . . . no."

"Ouch," Andie said again. It was the first time I'd ever seen her relatively speechless. But then she quickly recovered. "Well, I have a story that might cheer you up," she said.

I tried to smile. "I doubt even one of your stories could cheer me up today, but go ahead."

She put her hands on the table. "Okay, here goes. My sister's friend Lena called me last week and said she wanted to set me up with this banker friend of hers named Jeff. She said he was tall, successful, and kinda cute, so I figured, why not?"

I nodded. "Sounds reasonable."

"I thought so too," she said. "So he and I talked one time briefly on the phone, and it went fine, so he asked me to sushi. And I made the mistake of looking forward to it."

"You looked forward to a blind date?" McKenna said.

Andie rolled her eyes. "I know, I know—you'd think I'd learn. Anyhow, when he picked me up, right off the bat I was a little disappointed, because I wouldn't exactly classify him as good-looking. But he wasn't totally butt, so I was determined to give him a chance. We walked a few blocks down the street to this sushi place on Fillmore, and the hostess said there was a wait for a table, but if we wanted to, we could eat at the bar."

"Wait, back up." I said. "He didn't make a reservation anywhere?"

"Nope."

"Strike one," McKenna said.

Andie took a sip of her beer and shook her head. "No reservation, and then he said he didn't want to wait for a table. So the hostess walked us over to the bar, which was way too brightly lit and definitely the sort of place you'd sit for lunch alone, not on a first date for dinner. But oh well. We sat down on these low swivel stools, which are really uncomfortable for trying to talk to someone next to you. And Jeff had long legs, so he didn't really fit that well. So he swiveled toward me and basically straddled my stool."

"Wow," I said. "That's quite a visual."

She pointed at me. "Bingo. And not a good one. Then the waiter came by and gave us each a hot towel to clean our hands, and Jeff used it to totally scrub his face and neck! And when he finished, he looked at me and said, 'Aaaaah.'"

"He said, 'Aaaaah'?" I said.

"He said, 'Aaaaah,'" she said.

"Ick," I said.

"Exactly," she said. "And it gets better. So then we ordered, and we started chit-chatting a little, and my neck was killing me from having to look over at him from my stool. But even more painful was the conversation itself. Throughout the whole meal he kept name-dropping and talking about how much money he has and how successful he is and blah blah blah blah blah. It was way boring. Plus, he didn't ask me *anything* about myself. By the end of the meal I pretty much hated him."

I took a sip of my water. "Go on."

"When we finished dinner, we walked out of the restaurant, and as we passed the hostess, we noticed she had a tattoo on the small of her back that was barely visible between her top and her skirt."

"And?" I said.

"And then Jeff put his hand on the small of *my* back."

"He did *not* put his hand on the small of your back," McKenna said.

She nodded. "Oh, yes he did. And he then said, 'Do you have a tattoo like that for me to see later?'"

"Oh God, please tell me he didn't say that." I covered my mouth with my hand.

"Oh, yes he did," Andie said. "So I politely moved away from him and lied that I was tattoo-free. I wanted to run screaming down the street, but it was still super early, and I just didn't know how to gracefully get out of the date. He wanted to hang out some more but had nothing planned, so I figured the best thing to do was to take him to Solstice, you know that cute tapas bar on California and Divisadero? A friend of mine was cocktailing there, and I knew a handful of her friends would be there, so I wouldn't have to be alone with him anymore."

"Good call," I said.

"So Solstice was literally five blocks away, but he said he wanted to drive, and I knew it was probably because he wanted to show off his car. So we got to his car, and of course it was a fancy Porsche. Oh, and he also bragged that he had paid twenty dollars to the attendant at the gas station to park there illegally. So we got into the six-figure car to drive five stupid blocks, and I was counting the minutes until I could go home."

"I would be too," I said. "What happened next?"

"Well, my thoughts of escaping the date were interrupted by a putrid stench."

"A putrid stench?" McKenna said.

"He farted," Andie said.

McKenna lost it and put her face down on the table.

"No way!" Now I was totally laughing too.

"Way. It was totally silent, but so obvious and so heinous, and he didn't say anything about it. We just sat there in awkward stinky silence, and I was wondering if it would be rude to roll down the window."

"A silent but violent? That's unbelievable!" I said.

"Oh, believe it. And parking is a total bitch in that area, as you know, so I breathed through my mouth as we circled and circled for a spot. He thought he saw one on the other side of the street, but I could tell it was a handicapped spot and told him not to bother, but he didn't believe me and made a crazy illegal U-turn to get it. And of course when we pulled up, he saw it was indeed a handicapped space. And you know what he said?"

I picked up a piece of pizza. "I'm not sure I want to know."

"He said, 'Goddamned handicapped people. They have too many parking spots in this city.'"

"No way," I said. McKenna was still facedown, laughing.

"Way. So finally, after fifteen minutes of circling, we got lucky and found an open spot right across the street from Solstice. And get this: when we got out and started to cross the street, he reached his hand back to grab mine."

"He tried to hold your hand after he ripped one in the car like that?" I said.

She nodded. "Yep. And I would have rather put my hand into a bowl of hot vomit, so I just pretended not to notice. Then we went into the bar, and about five of my friends were sitting down at a table, so we sat down next to them. And believe me, I made a point of sitting on the opposite side of the table from him."

"I would have too," I said.

"So then he went to the bar with this girl Bev I know and bought us all a round, which was nice enough, but I had no intention of ever being close enough to him where I might risk any sort of actual contact. After about fifteen minutes, he got up to go to the restroom, and my friends asked me the scoop on him. I told them that it was a blind date from hell and quickly listed the highlights."

"What did they say?" McKenna said, coming up for air.

"Bev said that he had farted AGAIN when they were standing next to each other at the bar."

"Oh God, tell me you got the hell out of there before he came back," I said.

She shook her head. "I know I can be mean, but I just couldn't be *that* mean, even though I was totally grossed out. Plus I was afraid of dating karma coming back to bite me in the ass. So after he got back from the restroom, I waited about fifteen more minutes and then told him I had an early swim session in the morning and had to go to bed. I said I was training for a triathlon."

"A triathlon? Classic," I said. Andie hated all forms of exercise and never got up before eleven o'clock on the weekends.

She laughed. "I know. The chances of my training for a triathlon are about as good as the chances of the Olsen twins' spearheading a reunion show of *Full House*."

I took another sip of water. "Did he drive you home?"

"Yep, and I don't think the car had come to a full stop when I jumped out. I didn't even give him a chance to speak. I just thanked him for dinner and bolted."

"Do you think he'll call you again?" McKenna said.

"Oh God, I hope not. And do you know what the kicker is?"

"There's more?" I said.

She nodded. "Yep, get this: I told my sister the story today, and she said that Lena had tried to set her up with Jeff a few years ago, but that he didn't call for a year and a half after Lena gave him my sister's phone number!"

"A year and a half?" I said. "Are you serious?"

"Yep, a year and a half. So when he finally called my sister to ask her out, she was like, *Uh, I'm engaged, you moron*."

"Oh, man, what a loser. Did you tell Lena?" McKenna said.

Andie put her gum back in her mouth. "Not yet. But believe me, she's gonna hear about it."

"Good God, that *is* quite a story," I said.

"It might even crack my top ten for the year," she said.

"So after hearing that, do you feel better?" McKenna said to me.

I smiled. "You know, I actually do. It's sad to admit, but hearing other people's horror stories always cheers me up. It's like for a brief moment my life doesn't suck as much as I thought it did."

Andie laughed. "That's why reality TV shows are so popular."

After lunch, the three of us wandered about our neighborhood and window-shopped. McKenna and Andie both lived around the corner from me in Pacific Heights, which was filled with picturesque Victorian houses and quiet, tree-lined streets. I loved it because it had everything I could ever want within two blocks: great restaurants, three coffee houses, a bank, a supermarket, a bagel shop, a combo coffee house/laundromat, a bunch of cute boutiques whose clothes I could never afford but liked to look at, a video store, Dino's Pizza, and the Kilkenny, our favorite neighborhood pub. Plus the people who lived there were friendly and always picked up after their dogs. So despite the creepy movie of the same name from the late '80s, I felt really safe there. And I had rent control, so I wasn't going anywhere. Thank God I hadn't given up my apartment before the "wedding," although I'd realized afterward that Aaron had never officially asked me to move in with him.

"Hey, there's Brad Cantor." McKenna pointed across the street to a tall, lanky jogger.

"A Brad Cantor sighting? How unusual," I said. Brad had gone to college with us, and he was nice enough, but for some reason we saw him all the time. *All* the time.

Andie put her hand on my arm. "Oh, I forgot to tell you guys. I had a sighting the other day before work."

"Did he invite you to one of his theme parties?" I said. Brad Cantor was the master over-Eviter.

She shook her head. "He didn't see me. He was on the other side of the street from the Jamba Juice by my office. I ducked in there to hide and crouched behind a tall potted plant."

I laughed. "Aren't there, like, eight hundred thousand people who live in San Francisco?"

"So they say," McKenna said.

"So doesn't the frequency of our sightings defy some law of probability?" I said.

"Probably," Andie said.

I counted on my fingers. "Parties, street fairs, coffee shops, bars, restaurants, bus stops, on and on and on. How come we don't run into anyone else that often? Why Brad?"

"You've got me," McKenna said.

"At least you're not running into Aaron all the time," Andie said.

"Very good point," I said. "Remember that time we were at Pasta Pomodoro on Union Street?"

Andie bit her lip. "Oh God, how could I forget?"

"That one was by far my favorite," I said.

A couple years earlier, Andie had literally been crying in her pasta one night over a recent breakup, and Brad walked by. He saw us through the window, waved, came in, and walked right up to our table to say hello. He asked us what we were talking about, and we told him we were having a very serious GIRL talk about very serious boy problems. And, no kidding, he said with a smile, "Can I join you?" And then he sat down and ordered a glass of wine.

Andie shook her head. "I still can't believe he asked if he could sit down with us."

"I know. Hello? *Could I be more everywhere?* is what he should have asked," I said.

When Andie and McKenna waved goodbye an hour later, I yelled after them, "I'll let you know if I get canned tomorrow."

"Shut up!" they yelled back.

. . .

Monday morning I sat down at my desk and opened my e-mail account. I wasn't sure exactly what I was expecting, but there was nothing from Davey. I looked at my watch. It was 8:25. Davey rarely got into the JAG office before nine o'clock.

I decided to beat him to it.

To: David Mason
cc: Kent Tanner
From: Waverly Bryson
Subject: Super Show wrap-up

Good morning, Davey. I hope you had a nice flight home from Atlanta. Looks like the show was a huge success. We'll get working on the report this morning and will send it over to you by the end of the day.

Regards,
Waverly

All I could do for the time being was pray that Davey, or anyone else for that matter, didn't know what had happened at the party.

A half-hour later, I walked into the conference room and sat down. Kent wasn't there yet. Everyone was chatting about their respective weekends. I smiled and nodded and pretended to be listening to the various conversations going on around me, but my head was floating somewhere above them. I couldn't believe how nervous I was.

At nine o'clock sharp, Jess walked in, followed by Kent and our admin Nicole, who was carrying a big pink box of donuts. Everyone immediately jumped up to grab one. Bear claw in hand, Kent came over and sat down next to me.

"Hi, Waverly. Traffic was a bitch this morning. How's it going?"

I fidgeted in my seat. "I'm good, thanks. You?" If he knew anything, he wasn't letting on.

"As good as can be for a Monday, especially after such a long week. Hey, did you have a good flight home?"

"Yeah, uneventful. I slept most of the way. How was golf on Saturday?"

"Awesome. JAG hooked me and Dave up with a tee time at Augusta. It was unbelievable. I couldn't make a putt to save my life, but I didn't care. I mean, it was Augusta!"

"What does it cost to play there?" I said.

"Four hundred."

"You're kidding. Four hundred dollars? As in forty thousand pennies?"

He nodded. "Yep. Four hundred smacks. Why do you think I never play golf?"

"I guess I never really thought about whether or not you play golf."

"Not anymore I don't. Check out the parking lot of any of the nicer courses in San Francisco. Some of the cars cost more than my house did. Once we had the first kid, I pretty much hung up my clubs, unless, of course, a client's paying."

"Damn," I said.

"No kidding."

Just then, Jess stood up and shushed the group to get the meeting started. Kent and I stopped talking and turned our attention toward the front of the room.

I was off the hook. For now.

. . .

When I got back to my office, I sat down at my desk and looked at my e-mails. There was nothing from Davey. Where was he? There was, however, a message from Cynthia Hopyard, a senior VP in our New York office, asking me to call her. A few months earlier, she'd gotten engaged to Dale Payton, one of the top sports agents in the country, and moved to New York to live with him.

I adjusted my ponytail and sat back in my chair. Then I checked to make sure my door was closed and quickly dialed McKenna's number at work.

"McKenna Taylor," she said.

"Hey, it's me."

"Hey. Well?"

"Well, it looks like no one here knows about my Friday night adventure. Can you believe it?"

"Are you serious? No one saw you?"

"Well, if anyone did, no one's letting on. Wait, wait, e-mail from Davey just popped into my in-box. Hold on a sec while I open it."

I clicked on the message and held my breath.

To: Waverly Bryson
From: David Mason
Subject: Re: Super Show wrap-up

Hi Waverly. Glad to see you made it back safely. We looked everywhere for you at the Jammin' party but lost you in the crowd. Good times. I look forward to seeing the report.

Cheers,
Dave

"Well?" she said.

I leaned back in my chair and exhaled. "It looks like the fisherman is throwing me back."

"Waverly Bryson, you are one lucky girl."

"Okay, I would hesitate before using the word *lucky* to describe the big picture here, but for the small picture I may have to agree with you," I said.

I heard something beep in her office. "I'm sorry, Wave, but my ten o'clock just arrived, so I gotta run. Talk later?"

"Okay, bye."

I stood up and walked to the window. I pushed my forehead against the glass and looked at the view. My breath fogged up a little patch of glass, and I drew a little happy face with my finger.

Thank God.

Just then there was a knock on my door. I walked over to open it.

"Hey, Waverly, you got a minute? I'd like to talk to you about something."

My stomach dropped.

"Sure, Jess, what's up?"

"Could you drop by my office in a few minutes?"

"Um, okay."

"Thanks."

I shut the door and leaned my back against it. This didn't look good.

Five minutes later I walked over to Jess's office and knocked lightly on the open door.

"Hi, Waverly, have a seat." He got up and shut the door behind me.

I set my coffee cup on his desk and folded my hands on my lap. I tried to sound casual. "So, what's up?" I said.

He looked me straight in the eye. "Well, I'm not going to sugarcoat this."

I bit my lip.

"It's come to my attention that you were severely intoxicated at JAG's party on Friday night. Severely intoxicated."

All the blood in my body suddenly rushed to my cheeks. I seriously thought they might explode.

I looked at the floor and didn't say anything.

"Is that true?" he said.

I nodded slowly.

He sighed. "I was hoping you wouldn't say that. Okay, I don't need to know the gory details, but I've got to tell you that I'm pretty disappointed in you, Waverly."

I kept looking down at my hands. "I'm sorry, Jess."

We sat there in agonizing silence for a few moments, and then he finally spoke. "Waverly, I know that trade show parties can get a little crazy, but you're an account director, and I expect you to behave more professionally than that. I *need* you to behave more professionally than that, or it may damage the relationship K.A. Marketing has with JAG. Do you understand?"

I looked up at him and nodded. "I understand."

"I would hate for this incident to jeopardize your career here. But this is a large company, and gossip spreads fast. So you've got to realize that people expect you to behave in a certain way, okay?"

"Okay," I said softly.

"All right then. I trust it won't happen again?"

I shook my head. "It won't, Jess. I promise."

"Good."

More awkward silence.

"Um, Jess?"

"Yes?"

"Who told you?"

"That's not important."

"Was it Davey?"

"No. And that's the last question I'm answering about it."

"Okay."

I looked down at my hands again.

"Jess?"

"Yes?"

"I'm sorry."

I stood up and slowly walked out of his office, squeezing my coffee cup so hard I thought it might break. I turned and looked back at him. "I really am sorry."

He nodded, but he didn't say anything.

I walked to the kitchen to get some water. My legs were shaking so much I had to put my hands on the counter to steady myself. I had the sinking feeling that Jess had planned to fire me but had changed his mind when he saw my face. How could I have screwed things up so much?

"Hey, Waverly, I heard you had a great time at the Super Show."

I turned around and saw Mandy Edwards in the doorway.

"What?" I said.

"Sounds like that party on Friday night was a rager. Sorry I missed it." She smiled and walked away.

Not quite making the impression you'd like?

Honey, the only impression you should worry about is the one you make on the couch. If it's too deep, you need to get off it more.

CHAPTER SEVEN

Somehow I made it through the rest of the week, although I don't really remember actually doing anything. I avoided everyone and spent the days holed up in my office, wondering if anyone would notice if I never came out. When the weekend finally arrived, I planned to spend it holed up in my apartment, wondering if anyone would notice if I never came out.

"C'mon, Waverly, let's go out for happy hour," McKenna said early Friday afternoon. "Maybe it'll make you feel better."

"I'd rather visit my dad," I said. "Does that tell you anything?"

"Fine, fine. But I'm calling you again tomorrow."

"Good luck with that," I said.

When Saturday afternoon rolled around, I decided to get off my butt and go for a run. I doubt there are many places more beautiful to run than San Francisco on a crisp winter day, so I hoped it would cheer me up. As I headed down the hill toward the Golden Gate Bridge, I looked out at the spectacular view below. The water was sprinkled with sailboats, and I could see a number of touch-football and pickup soccer games going on at the Marina Green. Back in college I always wore headphones when I ran, but once I moved to San Francisco I had stopped using them. The scenery was entertainment enough, so for years I'd been enjoying my runs with only the gentle rhythm of my breathing to accompany me. I often ran through the Presidio, part of the Golden Gate Recreation Area, and there was something about the feel and sound of leaves crackling under my feet that invigorated me. This particular Saturday was a typical December day, cold yet not freezing, and once I warmed up, the cool air on my face was refreshing.

I weaved through the Presidio and made my way toward the Golden Gate Bridge. When I reached the path leading up to the entrance, I looked at my watch. I had already been running for my standard max of thirty-five minutes, but I wasn't tired yet, so I decided to keep going and started the trek across. I couldn't go very fast though, because it was really crowded. The pedestrian walkway on the bridge was always packed with tourists, the majority of them dressed in the ubiquitous FISHERMAN'S WHARF or PROPERTY OF ALCATRAZ fleeces they'd had to buy because they hadn't realized how cold it was going to be. Sometimes the fog was so thick you couldn't even see the bridge, much less Alcatraz, but those cheesy fleeces were hard to miss.

When I got to the other side, I looked at my watch again. I'd been running for nearly fifty minutes, and now I was definitely tired, and I still had to get back. Oops. Nice distance management. But I didn't mind. It was such a gorgeous day, and I wasn't in a hurry, so I decided to walk leisurely back to the San Francisco side of the bridge and up the hill to my apartment. The sun was slowly melting my bad mood away.

On the way back, I watched all the groups of guys playing football and soccer on the grassy Marina Green. Some of them looked pretty cute, and I wished I could stop to watch and casually strike up a conversation when a loose ball flew my way, just like happens in the movies.

But this wasn't the movies, so my feet kept moving. They carried me to the Coffee Roastery three blocks away on Chestnut Street, and I was glad I had tucked a five-dollar bill into my pocket. It was a cold day, and a hot chocolate and a warm banana nut muffin were calling my name.

Unfortunately, the snacks weren't the only ones calling my name.

"Hey, Waverly, how's it going?"

I turned around, and there was Brad Cantor.

"Oh, hi, Brad, how are you?" Everywhere, that's how he was.

"I'm good, good. What a gorgeous day!" He stood too close to me, as usual, and I found myself stepping backward.

"Yep," I said, looking over his shoulder for help.

He stepped a little closer. "I'm just grabbing an afternoon snack. I love the chocolate cake here."

I smiled and took another step back, then looked at the cashier. "Can you change that to go please?" I whispered.

"So, are you coming to my holiday party next weekend?" Brad said.

I bit my lip. "Uh, a party next weekend? I don't think I know about it."

"Oh, well I sent you the Evite, but I can tell from the master list that you haven't opened it yet."

Oops, busted. I had, of course, received the Evite but had immediately deleted it. "Oh, it must be lost in my in-box. I'll have to dig through it and look."

"It's next Saturday. The theme is elves and reindeer. I'll send you a reminder e-mail as soon as I get back to my apartment."

Elves and reindeer? "Okay, see ya." I took a sip of my hot chocolate and started walking toward the door.

"Wait up. I'll walk with you. Which way are you going?"

It was a classic Brad Cantor question. No matter how I answered, I was screwed.

I gambled and told the truth. "Um, up the hill to Pacific Heights."

"Cool, me too. Hang on a sec. I'll get my cake to go."

Ugh.

When I was finally alone in my apartment a half-hour later, I sat down on the couch and cursed myself for not just telling Brad that I really wanted to enjoy my walk home, alone. Instead I had spent the last thirty minutes listening to him ramble on about his strategy for winning an online Doom tournament he was signed up to play in that night.

I grabbed a notebook off the coffee table and jotted down an idea for a Honey Note.

Front: Is it worse to be fake or bitchy?
Inside: Honey, just face it. If you're asking, you're probably both.

Still in my sweats later that afternoon, I drove down to the Marina Safeway, which had the reputation of being more of a pickup joint than a supermarket. People even said that girls put on makeup just to shop there. *Ick.* I normally stayed away from that whole scene, but the Mollie Stone's by my apartment was closed for renovation. And the only non-condiment in my fridge was a fat block of cheese, so I was desperate.

Once I was ready to head to the checkout line, I rounded an aisle and smashed right into another shopper. I hit his cart so hard that a box of super jumbo tampons went flying right out of mine.

"Oh God, I'm so sorry." I bent down to pick up the box. Of course it would be the tampons. Did I mention they were super jumbo?

"Hi, Waverly."

I froze at the sound of his voice. No no no no no why why why why why?

I stood up and adjusted my dirty ponytail. "Uh, hi, Aaron, how's it going?"

"Good, it's going good. How are you?"

"I'm fine, thanks," I said. I was painfully far from fine. And it was painfully obvious that he wasn't alone.

He looked to his right and then back at me. "Um, Waverly, this is my fiancée, Stacy Long. Stacy, this is Waverly Bryson."

I looked at the brunette next to him. Supermodel, of course.

"Uh, hi, it's nice to meet you, Stacy." I glanced from her trendy pants and boots down to my dusty running shoes. Who wears trendy boots to go grocery shopping? And could my sweatpants be any baggier?

She smiled. "It's nice to meet you, too."

"Um, congratulations," I said. "I saw the announcement in the paper."

"Thanks," Aaron said. "I was going to call you to tell you, but we've just been so busy."

He'd been too *busy*? That's why he didn't call?

My mind raced for something witty to say, but I couldn't think of anything, and the three of us just stood there in silence.

Awkward, soul-killing silence.

Then I looked at my cart and almost laughed out loud. It was packed with frozen dinners and canned vegetables. Nothing screams *I haven't had sex in a year!* better than a shopping cart full of single-serving frozen dinners.

I looked over Aaron's head, wondering how I could escape such torture. Where was Brad Cantor when I needed him? I tried to repeat Shane's mental exercise and think of something funny to keep me from bursting into tears, but the only funny thing I could think of was that box of tampons flying out of my cart. I mean COME ON!

I took a deep breath. To hell with being polite, I was getting out of there. "Well, uh, I gotta go," I said. "It was good seeing you, Aaron. Nice to meet you, Stacy."

"It was good to see you, Waverly," Aaron said. "Take care."

Take care? From the man I nearly married? I pushed my cart past them and swore I would starve to death before ever going back to the Marina Safeway.

I walked to my car and put the groceries away, then realized that I'd forgotten to buy sugar, the ONE thing I couldn't live without. I cursed myself and headed back toward the entrance. I was about fifty feet away when I saw Aaron and Stacy leave the store with their cart, heading right for me.

I don't know what came over me, but without even thinking, I jumped to my left and ducked behind a car. I crouched down and hid there, praying that they hadn't seen me. And praying that if they had, I could think of a believable explanation for why I was squatting behind a car.

I tried to keep quiet and control my breathing, which suddenly seemed way louder than it should be. I sat down on the ground and curled my knees up to my chest. I couldn't believe what I was doing. Was I really nearly 30 years old?

About fifteen seconds later, I could hear the sound of a cart and footsteps passing by. I lifted my head up and watched until they got in their car and drove away, then slowly stood up. I wiped the dirt off my butt and looked around. A woman getting out of her car gave me a strange look, but otherwise I was in the clear.

Did I mention that I'm never going back to the Marina Safeway?

When I got home, I jotted down an idea for a Honey Note.

Front: Ever run into an ex looking like crap?
Inside: Honey, next time you need to run OVER him. Then have a margarita.

. . .

After a hot shower, I reread the Honey Note and decided that a margarita was exactly what I needed. Enough wallowing.

I called McKenna and got her voicemail.

"Hey, it's me. I need a margarita, and I need it yesterday," I said after the beep.

Then I called Andie.

"Hey, it's me. I need a margarita, and I need it yesterday," I said.

"Sweet. I'll pick you up in one hour," she said.

Having two best friends comes in very handy sometimes.

Two hours later, Andie and I were on our second margarita at Left at Albuquerque on Union Street. We were sitting at a high round table in the bar area, mowing through our second bowl of chips and salsa like champs.

"The tampons really flew out of your cart?" she said.

I nodded. "Like a pigeon in front of a moving car."

"And she was pretty?" she said.

I nodded. "Very pretty."

"And he looked good?"

I nodded. "Very good."

"But did he look happy?"

I nodded. "Very happy."

"And you looked gross?"

I put my elbows on the table and covered my face with my hands. "Very gross."

"Damn," she said.

"My life is a bowl of crap," I said, motioning to the waitress. "Can we get another round of margaritas and some more chips and salsa over here please?"

Two margaritas later, we were well on our way to Sloshistan.

"Ya know," I slurred to Andie and raised my glass. "Who needs men? Here's to girlfriends."

"Here's to girlfriends," she slurred back, raising her glass. We clinked our drinks together and polished them off.

"I'm going to call Mackie and tell her how much I love her," I said, pulling my phone out of my purse.

Just then, a tall guy in a light blue button-down shirt and khaki pants walked up to us. (I would bet my life savings that at any given time at least 40 percent of guys in the Marina district are wearing this exact same outfit, give or take a fleece vest.)

"I hate to interrupt," he said, "but my friends and I couldn't help but overhear what you just said about not needing men. Can we buy you a round of drinks to try to change your minds?"

Andie and I looked at him and then over at his friends. Three tall, cute boys. Then we looked at each other and smiled. Why not?

. . .

The next morning I woke up at eleven with a hangover and a craving for scrambled eggs with cheese. I dragged myself out of bed and walked a half block to Noah's Bagels. I smiled at the cashier. "Large coffee and a poppyseed egg mitt with cheese, please." An egg mitt was a scrambled egg on a toasted bagel. YUM.

"Coming right up." He handed me my change, and as I waited for my order, I looked at the other people in line and nodded. Yep, they pretty much all fit the profile. On weekend mornings, Noah's had two shifts of customers. Before ten o'clock, it was filled with early birds eager to take on the day: spandex-clad bikers fresh from a fifty-mile ride in the Marin Headlands; yuppie couples dressed in match-ing khaki pants and white sweaters, baby stroller in tow, on their way to the farmer's market; the overly enthusiastic Team in Training pack after a ten-mile run. And after that, the sloths rolled in: sleepy, dressed in baseball hats and sweats, and looking for a hangover cure. It never failed. When I was with Aaron, I'd usually been part of the early shift, but on my own I was more likely to be pulling up the rear. I looked down at my sweatpants and put my hand on the baseball hat I was wearing and chuckled. Today was no exception.

When I got back to my apartment, I kicked off my shoes, sat down on the couch, and unwrapped my egg mitt. Then I opened the newspaper and immediately flipped to the comics. I'd noticed that the best way to read the newspaper is to start with the comics, because everything else is so depressing.

After breakfast, I called McKenna. She picked up on the first ring.

"Hey," she said

"Hey," I said.

"Sorry I missed you guys last night. How was the big night out?" she said.

"I'd give it a seven and a half, although I'd give my hangover a solid eight. We missed you though. How was dinner?"

"Delayed. I waited for Hunter for nearly two hours at the hospital."

Just then I noticed a business card lying on the coffee table. I picked it up and turned it over. "Darren Anderson? Who the hell is that?" I said.

"What?" McKenna said.

I put my hand on my forehead. "Oh Jesus, Darren. I totally forgot."

"Wave, what are you talking about?"

"Oh, sorry. I just found this business card from a guy I met last night."

"And?"

"Well, I'm not sure who it is."

"What?"

"I mean we met two Darrens, one early on and one really late, and I'm pretty sure I kissed the late one."

"Excellent. What does he look like?"

"Which one?"

"Hello? The one you macked?"

"Uh, I sort of don't remember. Brown hair maybe?"

"You don't remember?"

"Nope. Many margaritas were consumed."

"Excellent. And the other Darren?"

"He was very cute."

"But you don't know which one's card you have?"

"Nope. I thought I'd exchanged cards with both of them, but there's just one sitting here."

"Excellent. Now that's the Waverly I know and love. Okay, I'm on my way out the door to run some errands, so I'll catch you later."

"Okay, bye."

I put Darren's card down and leaned back on the couch, where I spent the next half-hour leafing through the newspaper. Then I did a nose dive into my bed and slept for the rest of the day.

. . .

Andie called me at work Tuesday morning.

"We're going to the Warriors game tomorrow night," she said.

"The Warriors? As in basketball?" I said. "But we hate basketball."

"Should you say that out loud while you're at work?" she said. "I mean, isn't that, like, your job?"

"But we hate basketball," I whispered.

"Well, the Warriors play the Hawks tomorrow, so we're going. Maybe seeing that trainer guy Jake again will help take your mind off running into Aaron."

"Take my mind off who?" I said.

"Waverly . . ."

"Hey, do you think it's going to rain tomorrow?" I said.

"Waverly," she said. "Enough of the act. I know you're hurting right now."

"Okay, okay," I said. "It's just easier to change the subject."

"I'm on the Warriors' Web site right now," she said. "No arguing."

I bit my lip. Maybe seeing Jake again *would* help. Those blue eyes . . . God, he was so cute.

"All right, let's do it."

A few minutes later we had tickets to the game. They were semi-nosebleeds, but we were going.

. . .

The next afternoon I was getting ready to leave work early so I could go home before the game. I knew my chances of seeing Jake there were smaller than the chances of Barry Bonds coming back to San Francisco to take the press on a tour of his chemistry lab, but I was still looking forward to going.

I was walking out the door of my office when my phone rang. I set my coat down and walked back to my desk.

"Waverly Bryson," I said.

"Hi, Waverly. It's Darren."

I froze.

"Uh, from the other night?" he said. "How are you?"

All I could do was run with it. I sat down in my chair and faked a smile in my voice.

"Hi, Darren. I'm good. How are you?"

"I'm good too, thanks."

Awkward silence.

He cleared his throat. "Well, it was really nice meeting you, and I, um, was wondering if you'd like to have dinner with me on Friday."

Hmm.

Was it too late to ask him an identifying question? Like, perhaps, *Did we swap spit?"*

I took a deep breath.

What the hell. Why not?

"Okay, sure, that sounds nice," I said.

"Great, great. There's a new restaurant in Russian Hill that I've been wanting to try. Have you been to Lola's?"

"No, not yet, but I've heard it's good," I said. At least mystery Darren was up on the hip new places to eat.

"Yeah, me too. How about I make a reservation there?"

"Okay, sure, that sounds fine."

We made plans to meet up on Friday night at the Kilkenny for a drink before dinner. Then we said goodbye and hung up.

I stood up, put on my coat, and turned off the lights. Oh well, at least I wouldn't be sitting home alone on Friday night.

· · ·

At six thirty that evening, I walked out of my apartment wearing a pair of charcoal grey flare trousers with a sleeveless black sweater, a thick pink silk scarf as a headband, and a jean jacket. The outfit wasn't entirely weather-appropriate, but what cute outfit was weather-appropriate anyway?

As I headed for my car, I suddenly remembered that I hadn't moved it that morning. Damn it. When I approached the old green Saab, I immediately saw the parking ticket under the windshield wiper. I don't think I'd ever gone a full month without getting a ticket for not moving my car during street cleaning. It was just too complicated to keep track of which days those trucks were going to come by and on which side of the street and at which hours.

I pulled the ticket off the windshield and tossed it between the seats. Then I turned the key in the ignition and drove over to pick up Andie. Hers was my favorite building on the block—a dark red brick with bright white shutters that always looked recently painted. I pulled up in front and called her from my cell phone.

"Hey," she said.

"Hey, I'm outside."

"I'll be right down."

Two minutes later, she came outside and jumped in the car.

"Hey, hot stuff, how's it going?" she said.

"Good. Hey, have you ever noticed that no one in San Francisco actually rings anyone's doorbell anymore?" I said.

"Huh?"

"We always call outside from the cell phone. Why?"

She shrugged. "I don't know. I guess it's just easier to stay in a warm car than double-park."

"But doesn't it seem weird that no one finds this rude?"

"I guess I never really thought about it."

"Oh well, whatever. Anyhow, I like your outfit." She was wearing a long brown corduroy skirt, knee-length brown boots, and a bright yellow denim jacket over a yellow Tweety-Bird baby T-shirt. "I don't know how you pull it off, but you can wear the craziest stuff and make it look fashionable."

She looked down at her outfit. "This thing? Totally old."

"Well, it's super cute. I can't wear yellow. Makes me look too pasty."

"I guess that's one benefit of being a blonde, even if I have to pay a hundred and fifty dollars a month for it."

I laughed. "I think McKenna's the only blonde I know who doesn't pay her hairdresser for the privilege of having more fun."

"That bitch," she said, taking off her jacket. Then she picked up the parking ticket and looked at it. "Street cleaning, huh?"

"Of course."

"Ya know, it's really not that complicated to figure out when you have to move your car," she said.

"I know, I know. But I just can't be bothered to pay attention. And besides, sometimes it's easier to pay forty bucks than give up a good parking spot."

"Good point. I've got some friends in North Beach who pay almost as much in parking tickets each month as they do in rent," she said.

"That's what they get for living in North Beach. Have you ever noticed that it's easier to go to China than it is to find a parking spot anywhere near Chinatown?"

She nodded. "*That*, my friend, I've noticed."

. . .

It turned out that our seats to the game weren't semi-nosebleeds at all. They were full-on nosebleeds, and I was pissed.

I took my coat off as we walked up and up and up toward our "midlevel" seats in outer space. "All right, I'm writing a letter to the VP of marketing," I said.

Andie looked at me. "The VP of marketing? Why not customer service?"

I shook my head. "Nope, gotta go with marketing. I've noticed that it's the marketing people who actually care about the image of their company. Plus, they're the ones who have the most power to give you free stuff to keep you happy. Maybe I can score us some courtside seats to a future Warriors game."

She patted me on the shoulder. "Let me know how that works out."

We finally reached what was nearly the very last row and put our coats down. "We should have brought a sherpa," I said. "All right, I'm heading back down to earth for peanuts and a beer. You want something?"

She gave me an *Are you crazy?* look. "You're going back down already?"

I shrugged. "What can I say? I'm hungry."

I clomped back down the steps, and fifteen minutes later I was loaded up with a cardboard tray of snacks for us, fighting my way through the crowded circular hallway of Oracle Arena to start the steep hike back up the stands. When I entered the main dome, I looked down toward the court. The players from both teams had emerged from the locker rooms and were doing warm-up drills to a hip-hop song I was clearly not cool enough to recognize. I scanned the court until my eyes stopped, and I froze.

Jake was standing on the sideline, talking with a player.

He was even better looking than I remembered.

"Hi, Jake," I whispered.

I was only about ten rows up from the floor level, so I thought I'd wait there for a little while just in case he happened to look up.

As the crowd pushed past me, I kept my eyes on him and tried not to spill any of the food on my tray.

After nearly five minutes, he still hadn't looked up, so I decided to throw in the towel and head back up to my seat. Maybe I would try again at halftime. I turned around to face the stairs and looked up to make sure I was in the right aisle. I took my first step, then turned my head back toward the court once more. In that exact moment, Jake glanced up, and our eyes locked for just a second.

He smiled, and my heart stopped beating.

I wanted to smile back, but my stupid body was still moving up the stairs, and before I could do anything at all, I bumped smack into a group of little kids, lost my balance, and fell down. No kidding. I literally fell on the ground, and two beers, a mustard-covered pretzel, a bag of salted peanuts, and a carton of garlic fries came raining down on top of me.

Holy crap.

"Are you okay?" The father of one of the little kids jumped out of his seat to help me up.

I picked about twenty-five garlic fries from my chest. "Uh, yes, I'm fine. Thanks."

The man helped me stand, and on the way up I grabbed a couple of napkins from the dropped tray to help clean the mess off my pants and sweater. "Look, no broken bones," I said, trying to laugh.

"My son and his friends need to be more careful. I'm really sorry about that."

I shook my head and patted a napkin on my right shoulder to sop up the beer. "Oh no, no, it was my fault. I wasn't watching where I was going. Really, I'm fine. I think I'm just going to head to the restroom for a few minutes to clean up."

"Are you sure you're all right? My wife can go with you if you like." He turned toward where he had been sitting. "Pumpkin, can you help this young lady to the restroom?"

A short, stocky woman with a blond beehive in a blue-and-yellow Warriors sweatshirt leapt to my side and took me by the elbow. "You okay, sugar? Can I help you get cleaned up?"

"No, really, I'm fine." I tried to smile. "Thanks so much, but I'll be okay, really." I didn't want to make a scene, and I just wanted to get the hell out of there.

"Okay, sweetheart, but you be careful. If you need anything, we'll be right here."

"Thanks, you're very kind." I touched her lightly on the shoulder and turned back toward the circular hallway surrounding the arena. I looked down to see if Jake was still there, but the court was empty, save for an army of silicone-enhanced cheerleaders.

I walked back toward the concession area, and the bright arena lights dimmed. I heard the booming voice of the announcer introducing the players from both teams. The game was about to start, so fortunately the restroom was empty. I stood in front of the mirror and pulled a handful of paper towels from the dispenser. I held them under the running water and took a good look at myself in the mirror. I had beer, peanut dust, and garlic salt all over me, plus a ton of mustard, some of which was even in my hair. Mustard highlights. Nice.

By the time I made it back up to Andie with a fresh tray of snacks, I had spent more than fifty dollars, and the game had already started.

"What happened to you? I was getting ready to put out an APB," she said.

I put the tray of food down and pointed to my sweater and pants. "Slight accident."

"Ouch, looks like you really bit it. What happened?" She took a bite of a garlic fry.

"Hand me a cold beer first," I said. Then I told her the story.

When I was done, she took a sip of her beer. "Ya know, you're really clumsy, have you ever noticed *that?*"

I punched her in the shoulder. "Ya think?"

"Do you want to try to head down there after the game to talk to him?" she said.

I looked down at the basketball court, then at the small meal mashed into my chest and hair. "God, he's so cute, but seriously, would *you* want to talk to me like this?"

She laughed. "Maybe we should come up with another plan."

"I suck," I said.

She laughed again. "You said it, not me."

Ever had to work with
a total nightmare?

Honey, just wait until the
company holiday party. We'll see
who's all alone in the corner.

CHAPTER EIGHT

The following morning I was sitting at my computer writing a launch plan for a line of JAG hockey sticks. About halfway through I hit a wall, so I stood up to stretch. I put my arms over my head and closed my eyes. Then I put my hands on my hips and decided that a snack was in order, and I headed toward the lobby.

"Hey, Waverly, how's the launch plan going?" Mandy Edwards was walking down the hall right at me.

"Fine, Mandy. Everything's going according to schedule."

"Glad to hear it. Clients can be so demanding, don't you think?"

I looked at her. "What do you mean?"

She smiled. "Just that even when you think they're happy, sometimes they're not. At least that's been my experience. Gotta stay one step ahead of them, ya know? That's what I was just telling Jess at lunch yesterday."

I told myself not to bite.

But then I immediately caved.

"You went to lunch with Jess?" I said.

"Yes, yesterday."

"Why?"

"Just to chat."

I raised my eyebrows. "And?"

"I told him I'm happy to help out with the JAG account if you guys need it. You never know when a fresh perspective might come in handy."

"Uh, okay, thanks, Mandy. But I think we're doing fine."

"Well, I'm here if you need me. I'm always looking for ways to be a team player."

Team player. Yet another Mandy-style euphemism for *suck-up.*

"Okay, thanks, Mandy. See ya later," I said.

"No problem. Bye, Waverly."

She walked away, and I pretended to shoot her in the back.

When I sat back down at my desk, I checked my e-mail and recent meeting notes to see if there was anything important I needed to deal with on any of my accounts. Stupid tattletale Mandy.

I looked at my computer screen. At the top of my in-box was a message from an old coworker I hadn't seen in, like, five years. The subject line was "Traveling man update." As I clicked on it, I realized that it was a mass e-mail. Great . . . I was on another vacation spam e-mail list. I just couldn't understand why people sent around long, rambling e-mails about their travels to apparently everyone they'd met in their entire life. And don't even get me STARTED on inane status updates on Facebook.

Delete.

I sat up and forced myself to concentrate on the plan I'd been writing. But before I started writing again, I pulled out a notebook from my drawer and jotted down an idea for a Honey Note.

Front: What is the deal with people who send e-mail blasts to the whole world?

Inside: Honey, I'm still trying to figure out why people hang things from their rearview mirrors.

Several hours later, I finally put the finishing touches on the launch plan. I looked at my watch; it was nearly four thirty.

Where had the day gone? I realized I hadn't eaten lunch and was suddenly starving.

My midmorning snack wasn't cutting it anymore. I sent the plan to Jess and Davey for their review, then saw an e-mail from Cynthia Hopyard in our New York office asking me to call her because she wanted to talk about something.

She wanted to talk to me about something? Uh oh. Then I remembered her e-mail from the week before, in which she'd asked me to call her. I must have accidentally deleted it, because I'd completely forgotten about it since then.

This did not look good.

I ran downstairs to grab a sandwich, then shut my office door and dialed her number on speakerphone. I munched on my sandwich and punched a straw into the tiny chocolate milk carton.

"Cynthia Hopyard," she said.

"Hi, Cynthia, it's Waverly. Sorry for the speakerphone action, but I'm eating a sandwich. I promise to get off as soon as I'm done."

"No worries," she said. "I remember that you're not a big fan of the speakerphone."

"Ugh, I loathe it. I'm convinced it's a power move most people use just to make you think they're really busy when they're probably just sitting there doing nothing, ya know?"

She laughed. "Waverly, I must say that I miss your observations. How are you?"

I twisted my right earring and waited for the clunk of the other shoe. "I'm good, I'm good, and hey, I'm really sorry that I didn't call you last week. How are you? How's the wedding planning going?" I looked down at my watch. It was nearly 8 p.m. in New York. "And by the way, what are you doing in the office so late?"

"Oooh, don't remind me how late it is. This wedding is taking over my life. I spent half the afternoon on the phone with the caterer and the florist and the photographer, so now I'm stuck here with the cleaning crew, finishing up some real work."

"When's the big day anyway?" I said.

"January 30. The invitations go out tomorrow. And just to let you know, you're invited. I hope you can make it. That's why I wanted you to call me."

That was the other shoe? Damn Mandy for making me so paranoid.

"Really? That's so nice of you, Cynthia. I'd love to come. Where's it going to be?"

"Here in Manhattan. My parents aren't too thrilled about that, but since Dale and I are both so busy with work, it was easier to plan this way. My family will just have to make the trek from Seattle."

"Do you have a big family?"

"You wouldn't believe how big. My parents are both remarried to people who have grown children of their own, and I have five full brothers and sisters who are all married with kids, so counting everyone, we're talking at least fifty people in my sort-of immediate family."

"Sweet Jesus, that's like a pack of hamsters. How many of them are coming?"

She laughed. "That's the magic question. I keep telling everyone that they need to make up their minds now, because if too many of them wait until the last minute to tell me they're coming, we may not have enough wedding cake."

"Well, I'd love to come." I pulled my calendar up on the computer screen and clicked ahead to January 30 to mark the date. "Hey, wait a minute. Is that Super Bowl weekend?" Guys always said that having a wedding on Super Bowl weekend was a big no-no, and that no groom ever really wanted that date, regardless of what he told his fiancée.

"Actually, it is, but we did that on purpose because of our jobs. Since so many of the people we're inviting work in sports, we thought it'd be fun to throw a big Super Bowl party for everyone the day after the wedding."

"Cool. That sounds like a great idea. I love Super Bowl parties," I said.

"Me too. And this one will be full of fun people, I promise you that. Anyhow, Waverly, I know how expensive a weekend in New

York can be, so I'll schedule some meetings for you at our office that week. That way the travel and hotel will be on the company."

"Really? You'd do that?" I made a rough mental calculation of how much money that would save me. Roughly, it was a boatload.

Sweet!

"Sure thing. Hey, it's my wedding day, and I want you there, and technically you work for me. So I'm sure we can find some legitimate business reason for you to be here. And if I can't pull some strings, what's the point of being a senior VP, right?"

I took another sip of my chocolate milk. "That sounds fantastic, Cynthia. Thank you so much, really."

"No problem. You'll be getting your invitation in the mail soon. Okay, hon, I've gotta run or I'll miss dinner with Dale. Take care."

"Bye."

I hung up the phone and smiled.

Free trip to New York? Score!

. . .

That night I took my first and last spinning class at the Crunch gym near my house. My date with mystery Darren was the next night, so I thought I should at least try to get in shape for it. I sweated through the entire hour while wondering how it was humanly possible for my male instructor's butt to be smaller than the bike seat. Seriously, it was like a hard little peach. I was fascinated.

After the class, I sat down for ten minutes and waited for my legs to stop shaking. At one point I thought I might never walk again. When they finally calmed down, I showered and took a long steam sauna, then blew my hair dry and bundled up for the four-block walk back to my apartment. On the way home, I noticed a number of houses already had strings of bright holiday lights hung up outside and Christmas trees on display in their windows.

I was planning to buy my tree that weekend. I had a big box of decorations in storage in the basement of my building, and it now included a bunch of fancy ornaments I had bought for 75 percent off right after Christmas the year before. For years I'd been promising myself that I would stock up on cute ornaments for crazy cheap during the post-Christmas sales, but invariably I just couldn't be bothered. Finally, however, the year before, I had bothered to be bothered, and I owed it to McKenna, who had dragged me out of my apartment and to the sales despite my gloomy mental state at the time. She was 100 percent no-nonsense and always got me to do things I was too lazy to do on my own. She also didn't mess around when it came to getting rid of old crap, which included many of the outfits previously filling my closet.

Before I went to bed, I added an idea for a Honey Note to my list.

Front: How do you know when it's time to clean out your closet?
Inside: Honey, if you've seen anything you own on a rerun of Friends, *get your butt down to Goodwill ASAP.*

I fell asleep dreaming of Joey, Chandler, and the perfect Christmas tree ... until my alarm went off at the ungodly hour of 6:15 a.m. What the ...? What was going on? Then I remembered that I'd made a date with McKenna to go walking.

Fifteen minutes later, I limped out of my building bundled up in a black fleece over a long-sleeved T-shirt and grey sweatpants. I spotted McKenna in front of Peet's, her blonde hair loose under the light blue ski hat she always wore on cold mornings.

"Hey, woman, happy Friday," I said. "Can I just tell you how much my poor legs hurt right now?"

"You tried the spinning class?" she said.

I nodded. "I'm never going back there. What is up with all these muscles I never even knew I had? They're all pissed off and screaming at me for waking them from a twenty-nine-year-long nap."

She laughed and pulled on a pair of black knit gloves. "Let's get moving. I'm freezing."

"Hey, so how's Hunter doing?" I said, as we headed down the hill. "I haven't seen much of him lately."

She smiled. "He's good, just really busy at the hospital. He thinks he may have a shot at chief resident, so he's been working like a dog."

"Chief resident? Really? Good for him."

"Yeah, it's great, but I'm actually a bit worried about him, Wave. He's so stressed out that he's not sleeping, or barely sleeping. And with the crazy schedules those residents have, they really need to sleep when they actually have time to do it."

I crossed my arms over my chest to keep warm. "When will they make the decision?"

"Next Friday. He's been through several rounds of interviews with the hospital management, and now all he can do is wait."

"Waiting can be stressful," I said.

"I think the real pressure is coming from his dad," she said. "He's really hard on him. If Hunter doesn't follow in his footsteps, he'll feel like he's a failure in his dad's eyes."

I looked over at her. "Hunter's dad will think Hunter's a failure if he's not named chief resident because *he* was once a chief resident?" I said.

She nodded.

"But Hunter is a SURGEON for God's sake. Who cares if he's the boss?"

"I know," she said.

"Well if his dad's such a jerk, why does Hunter even care what he thinks?"

She looked at me. "You know, I could ask you the same question."

I stopped walking.

"Well?" she said. "Couldn't I?"

"You're right," I said. "I guess no matter what, you want your parents to be proud of you."

She put her arm around me and squeezed. "Exactly."

We started walking again. "Speaking of parents, it's my dad's birthday tomorrow," I said. "Gotta suck it up and go visit."

"You want some company for moral support?"

I shook my head. "Thanks, but I prefer just to get in and get out, you know?"

"Okay, call me if you change your mind. I'll probably be at Hunter's in the morning."

"That boy is quite a catch, you know," I said.

She smiled. "Believe me, I know." And then, as if she could read my mind, she reached over and touched my arm. "Don't worry, Wave, they're out there."

I thought about my imminent date with mystery Darren and laughed to myself. *I just wish I could remember them.*

Then I changed the subject like I always did when the subject was my dad. "So speaking of being proud, you'll be proud to hear that I have a date tonight."

She perked up and looked over at me with bright eyes. "Really? Excellent! Who with?"

"Uh, well, that's sort of a difficult question."

"What do you mean?"

"Well, I'm not exactly sure who the date is with." God, it sounded even more pathetic when I said it out loud.

She looked confused. "Is it a blind date?"

"Not exactly," I said, scratching my head.

"Internet dating?"

"Nope."

"Well then, what the hell?"

I winced. "Um, remember when I told you about those two guys named Darren I met at Lefty's last weekend, the night Andie and I drank a poolful of margaritas?"

She nodded.

"Well, apparently I have a date with one of them, but I'm not sure which one," I said.

"Seriously?"

"Seriously."

"You have no idea?"

"I have no idea."

"But how can you not know?" she said.

I held out my hand. "I'm sorry, have we met? I'm Waverly Bryson."

She shook her head and laughed. "Excellent. I can't wait to find out which one it is."

"You and me both," I said. "I honestly don't know. His phone call caught me off guard, and I couldn't think of a fast enough way to find out who it was before he asked me out."

"Didn't you kiss one of them?" she said.

I nodded. "Yep."

"But you were interested in the other one, right?"

I nodded again. "Yep. I only talked to the cute one for a few minutes, and it was in a group setting, but he was definitely a cutie. And as for the other one, since I kissed him, he can't be all that bad, right?"

"Hmm, I don't know about that. Remember what you were like before you met Aaron? Get a few drinks in you, and you were pretty much willing to kiss anyone."

I laughed. "Remember how I used to say that I suffered from AIKS?"

"That's right, your Alcohol-Induced Kissing Syndrome! I loved that one. Man, those were the days."

"I'm so out of dating shape," I said. "Screw that horrible spinning class. It's my dating muscles I need to start exercising again."

"Well, I hope it's the cute Darren. And whichever one it is, he must like you lots, because he asked you out for a Friday. That's a huge step for a guy," she said. One of the unwritten rules of dating in San Francisco was that early dates usually took place during the week or on Sundays. Apparently no one wanted to give up a weekend night unless it was serious. To me that was totally ridiculous, especially given how many weekend nights I'd sat at home in the last year, wishing I had a date.

"We'll see, Mackie. We'll see," I said.

"You'd better call me tomorrow morning with a full update."

I gave her a salute. "Will do. And by the way, tell Hunter that he's a stud, regardless of what his dad thinks."

"So are you," she said. "Don't forget that."

· · ·

At seven thirty that evening, I stood in front of my closet with my hands on my hips, still in my robe and slippers. I was supposed to meet Darren at eight and had no idea what to wear. First date.

Friday night. Drinks and dinner. Fifty percent chance of it being Right Darren, 50 percent chance of it being Wrong Darren. So I wanted to look good, but not too good. I flipped through the hangers as if I was in Bloomingdale's, looking for something to try on, rejecting item after item. I had pretty much settled on dark jeans and high-heeled black boots, but I needed something on top.

When I had nearly reached the back of my closet, I noticed a blouse I had totally forgotten about. I had bought it on sale at a boutique in Sausalito a year or so before but for some reason had never worn it. It was a light cotton material, a dark red with blue and green swirls on it, and sleeveless. The neck was a soft, deep V-shape that fell nicely against my collarbones.

I pulled the blouse off the hanger and tried it on with my jeans. Then I pulled on a wide black suede belt with a dull silver buckle and opted for black sling-backs instead of boots, a better match for a sleeveless blouse. I looked in the mirror and turned sideways to check out the view. It was a bold move to wear a sorta-sexy top on a first date, but since I assumed this would probably also be the last date, what did I care? It would be a good test run for my dating fitness plan.

At 8:05 I walked into the Kilkenny and spotted the owner, Jack O'Reilly, behind the bar. When he saw me approaching, he put down the glass he was cleaning and smiled. "Waverly, love! Where have you been?" He pointed to an empty bar stool. "Have a seat."

I sat down in front of him. "Hi, Jack. I know I've been a terrible customer, and I promise to come in more often after New Year's. McKenna said your annual holiday party is next weekend?"

"Yes, love, a week from tonight. I hope you can make it." After 115 years in San Francisco, Jack had an Irish accent that was still so thick, at times I had to concentrate to understand him. When he said things like *He's an ass*, it sounded more like *His on arse*.

"I wouldn't miss it, Jack. I promise."

He tapped his palms on the bar and smiled. "Brilliant. Now what can I get you?"

"Actually, I'm waiting for someone, so maybe I'll just—"

"Actually, she's waiting for me, so since I'm here, how about a couple of beers?" I was interrupted by a touch on my shoulder.

I took a deep breath and turned around.

Crap.

It was Darren Anderson, the Darren I had kissed. And apparently I'd been wearing serious margarita goggles at the time, because he was not cute.

"Hi, Darren, how are you? Have a seat." I motioned to the bar stool next to me and looked at Jack, who was busy sizing Wrong Darren up. He hadn't seen me with anyone but Aaron in ages, so I could see the curiosity on his face.

Darren sat down and smiled. "You look great, Waverly. I love that blouse."

Sigh. It was going to be a long night.

. . .

Three hours later, I walked into my apartment, leaned against the door, and shook my head. Thank God it was over. Wrong Darren had turned out to be a nice enough guy, and despite his non-cuteness, I had really wanted to give him a chance. But unfortunately, he had nearly bored me to death. At the Kilkenny, he had talked so much about his job that I had almost fallen asleep in my beer. He had gone on and on about tax credits and tax shelters and tax loopholes without noticing that I neither understood what he was talking about nor cared, AT ALL. How could anyone find corporate tax law that exciting? And then at dinner, he had launched into a monologue about the house he was buying, filled with mortgage and real estate jargon that was a foreign language to me, the perennial renter. By the time dinner was over, he had barely asked me anything about myself, but I didn't care anymore and had to get away from him.

I changed into my pajamas and walked into the kitchen to open the freezer. It was empty. Then I walked into my office, sat down at the computer, and pulled up my list of Honey Note ideas. I added a few more.

Front: Regret giving your phone number out after a few too many drinks?

Inside: Honey, stop whining and be thankful that someone besides the New York Times *subscription office is calling you.*

Front: Have a crush on a guy you'll probably never see again?
Inside: Honey, that's okay. At least this way he'll never crush YOU.

Front: What's worse than a really bad first date?
Inside: Honey, realizing you're out of ice cream when you get home.

Maybe if K.A. Marketing ever fired me I could get some work writing ads for high-calorie dessert products?

Not everyone can have a cookie-cutter family, right?

Honey, I'd cut your losses and settle for the cookies.

CHAPTER NINE

Saturday morning I got up early and read the paper over two big bowls of Lucky Charms. When I was finally ready to face the day, and my father, I pulled on a pair of jeans and sneakers, with a navy blue Cal Berkeley sweatshirt, then grabbed the car keys and headed outside. I pulled my hair back into a low ponytail and tried to remember where I was parked. Where the hell was the car? I was forever forgetting where I had put it. Once I was convinced that it had been stolen and was about to call the police, until, of course, I remembered that it was parked right around the corner.

I stood still for about thirty seconds, closed my eyes, and concentrated. Then it came to me. I headed two blocks south to the corner of Steiner and Pine and spotted my green Saab. I jumped inside, threw my purse onto the backseat, and headed for Sacramento.

I flipped through the stations until I found a U2 song. Have you ever noticed that if you give it about four minutes, you can always find a U2 song on the radio? It's really quite amazing.

Halfway through "Beautiful Day," my cell phone rang. I dug it out of my purse and glanced down at the caller ID: Davey. I flipped the phone open and put the hands-free earpiece in my ear.

"Hey, Davey, what's up?"

"Waverly, you got me all shook up." It was practically a yell.

"What?"

"C'mon, Bryson, don't be cruel. Please, let me be your teddy bear."

"Davey, are you listening to your Elvis greatest hits CD again?"

"It's now or never, you know."

"All right, Mr. Mason, what can I do for you today?"

"Okay, okay. Now I promise not to take too much of your precious Saturday," he said. "I just wanted to see if you could send your last few status reports to my personal account. There's something wrong with our server, and I can't access my JAG e-mail from home."

I swallowed hard. "You're reviewing our status reports on a weekend? Why?"

"Nothing major. I'm just putting together a PR presentation for our sales team, and I need to have it ready Monday morning."

"For the sales team?"

"Yep. Gabrielle Simone requested it Friday afternoon, but I didn't get to it."

"Sales wants a PR presentation?"

"What?" he said. "You're cutting out."

"What?" I said. "You're cutting out."

"What?"

"What?"

"Can you hear me now?"

"What?"

"Caller, are you there? Waverly from San Francisco, you're on the air."

I laughed. "I hear you now. Tell me this, Davey. Why does the cell phone coverage in Silicon Valley, which is supposed to be the technology capital of the *entire world*, SUCK SO MUCH?"

"I'm not sure. But assuming your call to the complaint line doesn't get dropped while you're on hold for two hours, I'm sure some friendly customer service guy in India will tell you there's nothing he can do about it."

"All right, I'll send you the reports tonight when I get home. But I'm billing you extra for this, Mr. Mason."

"Miss Bryson, I would expect nothing less."

"Bye, Davey."

. . .

Two hours later I pulled into the Valley Pines complex and wound my way around the dusty streets to my dad's double-wide in the back. I thought about the first (and only) time I'd brought Aaron there. He'd been so sweet about it, but he was clearly uncomfortable, and the image of his nine-hundred-dollar coat hanging next to my dad's orange hunting jacket will be forever burned in my memory.

The dust floated up around my car as I pulled into the gravel driveway. When it settled, I kept my hands on the steering wheel and looked out the window at the flower pots lining the walkway up to my dad's trailer. Bright violas and pansies, healthy and full of life. As I did every time I saw them, I wondered how my dad could be so nurturing to his plants yet raise a daughter who wondered if he even liked her that much.

Finally I got out of the car and walked up to the screen door. I knocked lightly, holding his birthday present behind my back. It was a new game of Scrabble. My dad loved Scrabble, and when he was in a good mood I loved playing it with him. Playing Scrabble and Boggle were staples of my childhood memories and probably had more to do with my high SAT verbal scores than some of the English classes I took in high school, where many of my classmates had never given college a second thought. Sometimes I wondered if my dad would've been happier if I hadn't either. *Not everyone is college material,* he'd said when I'd told him I wanted to go.

I knocked again. No answer. I waited, then knocked again.

Then I noticed that his truck wasn't in the driveway.

I looked at my watch. It was 2:05. I'd told him I'd be there at two to take him out to lunch for his birthday.

I pulled out my phone and called his landline. I could hear the *ring ring ring* inside. No answer, no answering machine. And he didn't have a cell phone, so that was the end of that.

I sat in my car for nearly thirty minutes, then finally got out and propped his present behind the screen door. As I was walking back to my car, his neighbor came out of her trailer and sat down on the rocking chair on her porch.

"Why, Waverly, how are you doing, dear? Come on over and say hello." Mrs. Williams had lived next door to my dad since the day he'd moved in, which had been practically the same day I'd left our tiny house for college. It had been more than twelve years, yet somehow she always looked exactly the same: plump, rosy-cheeked, and smiling, like everyone's favorite grandmother.

I smiled. "Hi, Mrs. Williams. I'm good, how are you?"

"I'm fine, dear. Looking for your daddy?"

I nodded. "It's his birthday. We were supposed to have lunch. Do you know where he is?"

"I saw him a couple hours ago gettin' in his truck. He said he was heading to Thunder Valley to blow off some steam—didn't say about what though." She laughed. "I didn't know it was his birthday. Maybe he's just angry at getting older. I know I am."

"Thunder Valley?" I said. "What's that?"

"A casino, dear, over at the Indian reservation."

"He's at a casino?"

"I think so, love. Do you want to come inside for some coffee? Maybe he'll be back soon."

I shook my head and looked at my watch. "It's really sweet of you to offer, but I think I'll just get going."

She crossed her short arms on top of her massive chest. "It's a shame you can't stay. We don't see enough of you around here."

"Oh," I said, kicking some gravel. "I've been really busy."

"Your daddy loves it when you come by, you know."

I looked up at her. "He does?"

"Sure does. He's always talking about you and your big job in San Francisco."

"He is?"

She nodded. "You come back again soon, okay, dear?"

"Okay, I will. I promise. Bye, Mrs. Williams."

"Bye, love."

I looked back at my dad's pristine potted flowers, then drove back to San Francisco.

...

I got back to my apartment around five o'clock and lugged the Christmas tree I'd bought on the way home into the living room. Every year, I told myself I should go to one of the many gorgeous tree farms along the hills of the Peninsula and cut one down myself for the experience of it all, but on my *You know you're a real grown-up when* list, cutting down your own Christmas tree was on a par with buying a house. So as usual, I'd just stopped at Target.

I headed downstairs and dug around in my basement storage closet until I found my tree stand and all my new and old decorations. I hauled everything back upstairs and plopped it all on the couch. Then I went into my office to e-mail Davey our reports and picked up my landline to call McKenna. The stutter dial tone alerted me to a new voicemail.

"Hey, baby, it's your old man. I'm sorry I missed you today, but I had a hot lead on a horse. You know how it goes, gotta strike when the iron's hot, right? Anyhow, thanks for the Scrabble set. You'll have to come back soon and teach me some of those big city words you love so much. Bye, kiddo."

Ugh. At least he didn't ask me for money this time.

I deleted the message and called McKenna.

"Hey," she said.

"Hey, I'm back."

"How'd it go?"

"It didn't."

"You didn't go?"

"Oh, I went," I said.

"What?"

"I went, but it didn't go."

"Okay, you lost me."

"He wasn't there," I said.

"What?"

"He wasn't there. I drove two hours, then waited for a half-hour, and then his neighbor told me he'd gone to a casino."

"You're kidding."

"You think I'd kid about something like that?"

"No, of course not. I'm sorry, Wave."

"Hey, what can you do, right? So are you ready to come over?"

"Yep. Did you get the chocolate mint bells?"

"Of course. The holiday playlist is all queued up, too," I said.

"Cool. I'll go pick up Andie. We'll be over in a bit."

I hung up the phone and looked at the empty tree in my living room. For as long as I'd lived in San Francisco, McKenna and Andie had helped me decorate my tree and apartment for Christmas. We'd eat chocolate mint bells, listen to holiday music, and, cheesy as it sounds, get in the spirit. It was strange now that I thought about it, but even the one Christmas I'd been with Aaron, they had been my decorating committee. I don't even think he joined us that night.

A half-hour later I took their drenched raincoats and umbrellas.

"When did it start raining? Thank God I already brought the tree in," I said.

They walked through my living room and sat down at the kitchen table. Andie shook her wet head and ran her fingers through her short hair. "This is ridiculous. I walked three blocks *with* an umbrella, and look at me."

"It's so nice and cozy in here. Do you have anything hot to drink?" McKenna said as Frank Sinatra sang "Have Yourself a Merry Little Christmas" in the background.

I hung their things up on the coat rack and walked into the kitchen. "It must be raining puppy cats out there. And if you can believe it, I do have something to drink. Coffee, tea, or hot chocolate?"

"No real drinks?" Andie said.

"Oops," I said. "Of course. Would you like some red wine?"

Andie nodded. "That's my girl."

"I'll have tea, please, with lemon if you have it," McKenna said. "And did you just say that it must be raining puppy cats out there?"

I nodded.

"And what exactly is a puppy cat?"

"It's a small cat, you know, like a puppy." I held my hands in front of me about six inches apart.

"Do you mean a kitten?"

"Yes, exactly," I said, nodding. "I've just noticed that I like the word *puppy cat* better than *kitten*. Sounds more descriptive."

McKenna rolled her eyes. "I don't even know how to respond to that."

We started pulling the decorations out of the boxes on my couch and got to work. I grabbed a pair of scissors and cut the tags off my new ornaments. I held up a large silver ball. "Okay, let's talk about how proud of myself I am for getting these decorations. This will be my prettiest tree ever!"

McKenna stood on a chair to hang a string of lights above the built-in bookshelves and looked down at me. "Hey, you haven't told us about the date last night. Which Darren was it?"

"Oh, yes, do tell," Andie said, unwrapping a chocolate mint bell.

I made a face. "Ugh, so not worth a conversation. Wrong Darren, wrong personality, wrong time to agree to a Friday night date. Wrong, wrong, wrong."

"So I guess we won't be meeting him anytime soon?" McKenna said.

I pulled a wine-colored ball out of the box and hung it on the tree. "I think the chances of that happening are about as good as the chances of finding Aaron on my doorstep tomorrow morning with a rose in his mouth and my dad standing next to him offering his blessings."

"Has Aaron called you yet?" Andie said.

I shook my head. "Nope. And now that I ran into him, I don't think he ever will."

"So . . . what, you're just going to never talk to him again?" McKenna said.

I put my hands on my hips and frowned. "I guess not. I have no idea."

"And what about cute Mr. Trainer Guy?" Andie took a sip of her wine. "Are you ever going to talk to him again?"

I raised my eyebrows. "Jake? I wish, but I just don't know how I would."

"You never know what might happen," McKenna said.

I sighed. "He's so cute. When he smiled at me at that basketball game, or at least when I think he smiled at me, I felt all melty inside."

"*Melty?* Is that even a word?" McKenna said.

"I have no idea," I said.

"So you're never going to talk to either one of them again?" Andie said.

"I have no idea," I said.

"Well who *are* you going to talk to?" Andie said.

I frowned. "I don't know. I have no idea."

"What *do* you know, Miss Puppy Cat?" McKenna said.

I unwrapped a chocolate mint bell and tossed it in my mouth. "Apparently, I know nothing."

Looking forward to a fresh
start in the New Year?

Honey, I'm with you, but I can't
seem to leave my behind behind.

CHAPTER TEN

The Friday before Christmas I ran into Kent in the office kitchen.
He grabbed my arm, nearly knocking the Snickers I had in my
hand to the floor.

"I have some good gossip, Waverly, fantastic gossip." He looked
down the hall to make sure no one could hear him.

"Oooh, I love gossip. What is it? What?" I filled my mug with
coffee and sat down at the round table in the middle of the kitchen.
"Well? Don't leave me hanging."

He walked over and shut the kitchen door, then sat down next
to me. "I heard a rumor that Paige Beckerman is going to make a big
announcement after the holidays." Paige Beckerman was the CEO
of K.A. Marketing. She was based in our New York office.

"And?"

"If everything works out, she's going to announce that we landed
a major account."

"A major account?"

He nodded. "A *very* major account, and we won't even have to
pitch it."

"No pitch? Why not?" Winning big accounts in the world of

public relations and marketing without a pitch was extremely unusual. Clients were notorious for making agencies jump through hoops of fire before finally making a decision, and the whole painful process was often stretched out for months and months.

He lowered his voice. "Word is, the head of marketing at Adina Energy called Beckerman himself and told her he wants K.A. Marketing to handle all their publicity and events. Apparently, word on the street is that we're the hot agency for product launches, and they want us."

I sat back and tried to absorb what I had just heard. Adina Energy? No way. Adina Energy was one of the biggest brands in sports and was quickly becoming one of the biggest brands in anything. It was seemingly everywhere, the Brad Cantor of brands.

"You're kidding." I took a bite of my Snickers.

"Nope. Not kidding. It should all happen by the end of January. And guess what else?"

"What?"

"There's a very good chance we'll be handling the campaign out of this office."

I dropped my Snickers on the table.

"Really?" I said.

"Yep. That would mean us, Waverly. This could make our careers. After this we'll be able to write our own ticket in sports PR, especially you, as the account lead."

When I got back to my office, I took a deep breath and thought about the news I'd just heard, the news that, as Kent had said, could literally make my career. I tapped a pencil on my desk. Would I be running the account? I was the most qualified person, right? But then why hadn't Jess told me about it yet? Was he being coy because of the Super Show fiasco? Or was it just a rumor? Hmm . . . the scoop on what could be the biggest account of my life would have to wait until after the holidays.

But I had a very good feeling about it.

. . .

Several hours later, I was at the Kilkenny holiday party with

McKenna, sitting at the bar with a plateful of appetizers and two beers in front of us. The place was packed, and it was hard to hear each other over the music and the chatter of the crowd.

"What time did Hunter say he'd be here?" I said.

"A little after nine o'clock."

"I still can't believe he's going to be chief resident. I'm so impressed."

She smiled. "I know, I'm really proud of him. And so relieved too. And I'm so proud of *you* for getting that big account! We've got to celebrate."

I put my beer down on the bar. "Hey, now, let's not count our chickens. We don't even have the account yet."

"But if you do, you're pretty sure it's going to be yours to run, right?"

I nodded. "It should be, but nothing's been confirmed yet."

"But it looks good, right?"

I smiled and thought about the great work we'd done for JAG over the years, especially the recent launch of the Shane Kennedy shoes. I'd put in a lot of solid hours on that account and was proud of the results. "Yeah, I think so."

"That's awesome. And you said that trainer guy Jake does work for Adina Energy, right? So would you see him?"

"Now *that* I don't know. He said he does some consulting for them, but I don't know how PR would play into it. But maybe I could work out some sort of boondoggle to run into him, totally by accident, of course."

"Gotta love the boondoggle," she said, then touched the fabric of my blouse. "I love that top. I remember when you bought it, but I've never seen you wear it before. What took you so long?"

I looked down at the top. "I'm not sure. I wore it for the first time on that horrible Wrong Darren date, so I put it on again tonight in hopes of avoiding any negative wardrobe-association issues."

"Well, it looks great on you. Hey, here comes the chief resident."

Hunter made his way through the crowd and gave McKenna a soft kiss when he reached us. "Hey, you," he said quietly to her in his boyfriend voice, his standard greeting that always made me jealous but happy for her at the same time. Then he turned to me and gave me a bear hug. "Hi, Waverly, it's great to see you."

"Happy birthday, Mr. *Re . . . si . . . dent*," I sang in my best Marilyn Monroe voice. "Congratulations, you genius. I'm seriously impressed."

"Why, thank you," he said with a big grin. "Now, what can I get you ladies to drink?"

Four hours of celebratory drinking and dancing later, McKenna, Hunter, and I were sitting in Pizza Orgasmica on Fillmore, a popular late-night pizza spot filled with drunken holiday revelers, us included.

"So are you coming to my New Year's Eve party?" Hunter said to me.

I extended my hand. "I'm sorry, have we met? I'm Waverly Bryson."

"Waverly's boycotting New Year's Eve," McKenna said.

"Boycotting New Year's? Why?" Hunter said.

"What?" I said.

"Why are you boycotting New Year's Eve?"

"I'm sorry, did you say something?" I said.

"Waverly . . .," McKenna said.

I put down my slice of pizza. "Okay, I'll tell you why. I may have forgotten how to be single, but one thing I do remember is that you DO NOT want to be single on New Year's Eve."

"Waverly, you're being way too dramatic," McKenna said.

"Am I? Tell me this: when else is there so much pressure to be fabulous and to find that perfect dress and the perfect guy to kiss at midnight? It's like prom night all over again, without the big hair."

"I've seen your prom photos," she said. "Ouch."

"Shut up," I said, pointing at her. "You're right, but shut up anyway."

"C'mon, Waverly, it'll be fun," Hunter said. "Maybe you'll get a good kiss out of it."

"And maybe you'll actually remember the kiss this time," McKenna said.

"Touché," I said with a laugh, then looked down and realized I had a big blob of tomato sauce and cheese on my blouse. "Oh, frick." I grabbed a napkin and dabbed at the spot.

"Hi, Waverly. Hi, McKenna. Happy holidays!"

We all looked up and saw Brad Cantor standing next to our table, by himself. He was always by himself, no matter what time of day or night it was, and apparently no matter where he was.

"You've got to be kidding me," I said under my breath.

"What?" Brad said.

"Hi, Brad, um, I was just cursing myself for dropping pizza on myself." I pointed to the mess on my top.

"Ahhh, you can barely see it. And that's a great top on you, Waverly. Mind if I join you guys?" Before I could say anything, he sat down next to me and smiled. McKenna buried her face in Hunter's shoulder and tried not to laugh.

Two strikes and you're out. The blouse was going straight into my Goodwill pile.

. . .

On the afternoon of New Year's Eve, I started to freak out. Aaron was getting married in a few hours, and I didn't even know who I was going to kiss at midnight.

McKenna was helping Hunter get ready for his party, so I called Andie.

"I'm starting to freak out," I said.

"Deep breaths, deep breaths," she said. "If you can get through tonight, a brand new year is waiting for you tomorrow morning, right?"

I nodded. "You're right, I just need to get through tonight. I can do that. Got any advice on how to do that?"

"You know what my go-to advice for this type of situation is," she said.

"The beer goggles thing?"

"Yep, you know it's true. They *are* the lonely girl's Cupid. We'll find you someone to smooch to help ease the pain. You'll be fine."

"You think so?" I said.

"Well, realistically you will probably have a meltdown at some point, probably close to midnight, but that's totally understandable. So just do what you can, and we'll deal with it."

I had to laugh. "A meltdown?"

"Hey, babe, you knew before you called me that I would tell it to you straight, so no complaining, okay? McKenna's the soda fountain to go to if you want soft-serve."

"True, true," I said. Andie was anything but soft-serve.

"Okay, hon, I gotta run and get myself waxed. See ya at the party," she said.

I put the phone down and chuckled. Andie could probably make me laugh as I was being pushed over the edge of a live volcano.

To clear my head I decided to go for a run to the Golden Gate Bridge. The cold, crisp air chilled my cheeks and forehead as I jogged down the hill toward the water. The streets were practically empty, so I assumed everyone was probably inside resting up for the big night.

There were a few sailboats sprinkled over the bay, and as I gazed out at them I remembered a sailing trip Aaron and I had taken when we'd just started dating. He and I had held hands during the entire trip and had even sneaked below a few times to kiss. And tonight he was declaring his lifelong love for someone else. *Yuck.*

While I'd tried my best not to think about his wedding, the reality of it was hitting me now. He still hadn't called me, even after I'd run into him, which I guess just proved that we weren't a part of each other's lives anymore—that we would never be again.

I wished I could just stop thinking about it. Why did I still care so much? Why did it still hurt so much? I found myself fighting back tears, running faster and faster along the lush grass of the Marina Green, then along Crissy Field toward the hill leading to the pedestrian entrance of the bridge. I wiped my forehead with my sleeve, breathing harder and harder.

It hurt. A lot. But I knew it had to do with more than just Aaron. It also had to do with the fact that I obviously hadn't really known him. I mean, how could I not have seen that he wasn't in love with me? Shouldn't that be pretty obvious? Had I been so eager to prove to myself (or to my dad?) that I was marriage material that I'd buried my head in the sand about what marriage really was? And more than that, why hadn't Aaron been in love with me? Wasn't I loveable?

At least a little bit?

I raised my left hand to wipe the tears from my eyes as I ran up the dirt hill toward the bridge. Once I reached the top, I looked ahead toward the pedestrian entrance and picked up the pace until I was nearly in a full sprint. But I didn't feel tired. I didn't feel anything. I just wanted to keep running. I wanted to leave everything behind and keep running and running and never stop.

Suddenly I realized that I was headed straight toward a huge tree branch that had fallen in the center of the path. And I was running so fast that I couldn't stop and didn't have time to go around it. I tried to jump, but my foot got caught, and before I knew what was happening, I was tumbling head first onto the dirt.

I wasn't sure what I felt about anything anymore. But when I fell over that branch, I did feel something for real.

I felt my ankle break.

. . .

New Year's Eve in a San Francisco emergency room, even in a fancy Pacific Heights emergency room, is a freak show. There are no other words to explain it appropriately. It was barely six o'clock when I got there, and the waiting room was already packed with weirdos. It was hard to tell who was on drugs and who was truly in pain. I could only imagine what it would be like as the night wore on.

After my fall, I had crawled to the side of the path and had sat there for about ten minutes. My ankle hurt so much that I couldn't imagine trying to make it to the ranger's cabin at the bridge entrance. So I'd just sat there in a state of semi-shock and waited for someone to appear. The next joggers to come by were a friendly married couple, and they'd helped me back to the main road where their car was parked. They drove me to the emergency room and let me use their phone to call McKenna, who was now on her way to pick me up.

I looked at the X-ray technician. "Is it broken?"

She helped me off the cold table and into a wheelchair. "Sorry, only the doctor is allowed to tell you that."

"Oh."

She winked. "But you're young, you'll heal fast."

Uh, thanks for the tip, Miss Confidentiality.

Thirty minutes later, I had a cast up to my knee, a set of crutches under my arms, and an appointment with a specialist for the following week. I was also still in my sweaty, dusty running clothes. Only two hours earlier I had been thinking about what to wear to Hunter's party. Frick.

I crutched back into the crowded lobby, where McKenna and Hunter were waiting. McKenna ran over and put her arms around me.

"Oh, sweetheart, you poor thing. Are you okay? How did it happen? Does it hurt? How long will you have that thing on your leg? And how in the world are you going to shower?"

I looked at her and tried to smile. "I tripped over a branch on the jogging trail. I wasn't paying attention to where I was running, and boom, I went down like a portfolio of Enron stock."

"What sort of pain medication did they give you?" Hunter said.

"I have no idea." I pulled out the prescription from my pocket and handed it to him. "They also gave me something in the casting room, and it's making me feel really woozy."

He looked at the prescription. "Vicodin. Good, it'll help you sleep tonight. We'll fill this on the way home, but first I'm going to ask the doctor what they gave you in there, just so I know. I'll be right back."

He left me and McKenna by the door and walked over to the triage desk. McKenna watched him with a dreamy look in her eyes, then put her arm around me. "All right, we need to get you home and comfortable. Let's think about what you're going to need. How long do you have to stay off your leg?"

I leaned forward and rested on my crutches. "The doctor said I have to spend a week on the couch with my leg propped up. If it swells up too much, it'll put pressure on the cast and start to throb."

"Ouch. That sounds terrible. When Hunter gets back he'll pull the car around, and then we'll take you home and get you settled." She put her hand on my back and wiped off some of the dust still coating my fleece. "We also need to get you cleaned up. I'll help you shower."

"Can I watch?" An old man in a pink tutu with waist-length pink hair looked up at us from his seat and grinned. No teeth.

Nice.

. . .

"All right, you've got *InStyle, People, US Weekly, Entertainment Weekly, Glamour,* and *Cosmopolitan,* plus your standard chick-flick classics: *When Harry Met Sally, Clueless, Sixteen Candles, Notting Hill, Legally Blonde, Love, Actually,* and *27 Dresses.*" McKenna propped my leg up on a pillow and handed me the remote.

"Uh oh, we forgot to get *Top Gun,*" I said.

"*Top Gun* is a chick flick?"

I held both my hands up in the air. "Hello? Volleyball scene?"

"Oh, yes, of course. I'll bring you that one tomorrow. You're sure you don't want me to stay with you tonight?"

"No, no, go to Hunter's party. This is his big night, and I don't want you or Andie to miss it just to babysit me."

"You sure?"

I picked up *People* magazine and shooed her away. "Yes. Now get out of here. I need to catch up on my celebrity gossip anyway."

"All right, all right. I'm going. I'll come by to check on you first thing in the morning."

I smiled. "Thanks, Mackie."

So that's how New Year's Eve, the night my once-perfect fiancé married someone else, went for me. No fancy party, no perfect dress, no perfect kiss. Just me, my DVD player, and my Vicodin. And I didn't even have any ice cream in the freezer.

The next year had to be better.

Wondering when you're finally going to know what you want out of life?

Honey, I'm still wondering what I'm going to have for lunch.

CHAPTER ELEVEN

My first day back at work after the holidays was, well, a pain in the ass. I know that sounds really crude, but maneuvering around on crutches totally sucks. Just getting myself showered, dressed, properly caffeinated, and out of the apartment before 8 a.m. had me ready to flop back into bed.

When I crutched out of my apartment building, the crisp January morning air smacked me in the face like a *Jerry Springer* guest. I wished I'd worn my hair down, because my ears immediately felt like they might chip off at any moment. I had about a third of my hair pulled back into a loose twist clasped with a thick silver clip, the rest hanging straight down my back. Several strands of my hair fell loosely to my chin, and I hoped it looked like it was supposed to be a bit messy on purpose, because the truth was that I was disheveled and exhausted. I hadn't been dressed and off the couch in nearly a week, and the last thing I could be bothered to worry about was my hair.

I wore a backpack full of stuff that would normally be in my purse, and as I crutched along, I was suddenly hit with the familiar sensation of being back in high school, when a backpack was as much a staple as the unfortunate scrunchie. For a moment I was on the way to my locker before first period chemistry. I started humming "Tearin' Up My Heart" by 'N Sync, but then I quickly realized that anyone currently in high school was probably in diapers when that band was popular. That made me feel about 90 years old and snapped me out of my morning daydream. Ouch.

I continued to crutch down the street and could practically see the grass growing on the way. The path from Fillmore down to California was on a slight but definite slope, and I was totally scared of taking a wrong step and biting it. After what seemed like forever, I finally made it to the bus stop and crutched to the back of the line for the number 1, also known as the Chinatown Express, for its voyage through what the casual observer might mistake for a village outside of Beijing. I knew I should take a cab to work, but I felt so ridiculous for the way I'd broken my ankle that I was determined to overcompensate by being strong and independent.

So I sucked it up and took public transportation.

"Here, take mine." A fresh-faced boy wearing a suit that was way too big for him jumped up and motioned for me to take his seat on the bus.

"Uh, thank you." I couldn't believe how young he looked. Was he some sort of high school intern? I sat down and hoped no one would bump into my leg. Then I looked out the window at the dark sky, which looked much darker than it had when I had left my apartment. I prayed that it wouldn't rain.

My prayers weren't answered.

Within two minutes it started to pour, and I wondered how in the world I was going to manage getting off the bus once we reached downtown. And then I wondered how in the world I was going to manage being downtown once I got off the bus. I decided that the ride home that evening would definitely be in the back of a cab. Score: *Toughing It Out, 0; Wimping Out, 1.*

"Let me help you. I'm getting off, too." The prepubescent in the suit took my arm when we reached my stop, and he even insisted on walking me to my office and holding his umbrella over my head.

"You're so sweet to do this. Seriously, thanks so much," I said.

He smiled. "It's no problem." I don't think his voice had even changed yet. I gave him my card and told him to call me if he ever needed a fake ID.

When I finally hobbled into my office, I used a crutch to shut the door and sat down at my desk. I looked at the window and saw that it was still pouring outside. I'd been at work for approximately three minutes, and I was completely exhausted.

Holy crap.

. . .

"So how's it feeling?" Andie said.

"So much better," I said. "I've pretty much got the crutch thing down, and I gave up the GI Jane attitude weeks ago and now take cabs to work. And at least I can drive if I need to." It was Sunday afternoon a few weeks later, and Andie, McKenna, and I were having lunch up in Marin, about fifteen minutes north of San Francisco across the Golden Gate Bridge.

"You're taking cabs to work?" McKenna said.

I nodded. "It's costing me a small fortune, but it makes my life so much easier. And Jess said I could work at home anytime it's raining or if I'm too tired to come into the office, which I've been doing about twice a week."

"You can stay home anytime you're too tired to come into the office? I wish I could swing that deal," Andie said.

"So when do you get the cast off?" McKenna said.

"Tuesday. If everything checks out at my doctor's appointment, they'll switch me to a walking cast."

"Cool."

"I can't wait to be able to walk again. Cynthia's wedding is a week from Saturday, and I really don't want to go on crutches. Sitting at the singles table again is going to be hard enough."

"Like a walking cast is going to look any better with a cocktail dress? I don't think so," Andie said.

"Thank you for reminding me," I said.

"So, any word on that big account yet?" McKenna said.

"Adina Energy? Not yet. But the rumors are flying that the announcement will be made next week, when I'm in the New York office," I said.

"So it's still looking good?"

I smiled. "Yep, very good. This could be a huge step forward in my career."

Andie patted my head. "Glad to hear it. You certainly deserve some good fortune."

"Thanks, honey," I said.

"Hey, speaking of honey, have you done anything with those greeting cards yet?" McKenna said. After breaking my ankle, I'd finally decided to bite the bullet and let her and Andie read my Honey Notes. To my delight, they both thought the idea was fantastic.

"Still coming up with ideas nearly every day. Want to hear one I wrote after some kid helped me on the bus and made me feel like a total grandma?"

"Shoot," Andie said.

"Okay, the front of the card says: *Ever wish you were a teenager again?*"

They both nodded.

"And when you open it, it says: *Honey, apparently you've never suffered from an unfortunate outbreak of adult acne.*"

Andie laughed. "Classic. Remember that summer when you had that acne on your back?"

"Uh, you mean my bacne? Don't remind me," I said, making a face.

She put her hand on my shoulder and squeezed. "Oh, I'll keep reminding you, my dear. That's one thing you can count on."

Two hours later we were on the way home, winding through the cobblestone streets of Mill Valley, perhaps the cutest town in Northern California. It was full of quaint restaurants, coffee shops, art galleries, and boutiques. And the weather was always perfect. The three of us had spent countless weekend afternoons in the main plaza, drinking coffee and people-watching and fantasizing about actually being able to afford a house there.

"Hey, did you guys hear that Hillary Weston is pregnant?" McKenna said.

"Again?" I said. "Is that three?"

McKenna nodded. Hillary had been the first one of our college friends to get married. We were only 23 at the time. It was like one minute she was opening beer bottles in the door jamb of our dorm room, and the next she was picking out china patterns. It had scared me to death.

"I'm never having kids," Andie said. "People who have kids are way too annoying. I don't want to be that annoying."

I laughed and turned to McKenna. "What about you? Do you still want to have kids?"

She nodded and smiled. "Someday, yeah."

"And you definitely don't?" I said to Andie.

Andie shook her head. "No way."

"What about you, Wave? Still not sure?" McKenna said.

I nodded. I wondered how they could be so sure about what they wanted when I was the one who'd nearly gotten married—and I still didn't know.

"All those girls from college are all so grown up now," I said. "But look at me, still heating frozen dinners in the microwave."

Andie laughed. "I love your cooking allergy. It's like my commitment allergy. You know, the other day my mom told me that she feels like a failure because apparently she didn't teach me how to land a man."

"Land a man?" McKenna said. "Are you kidding me?"

Andie shook her head. "No joke. Her exact words were *land a man.*"

"Wow," I said. "What did you tell her?"

"I asked her if she wanted another martini with her breakfast."

I looked out the window. "Is that so scary that I nearly got married without knowing if I even want kids?" I said.

"Life is scary," McKenna said.

I looked at her. "That sounded like avoiding the question to me."

She laughed. "So you said your ankle's feeling better?"

Andie laughed too.

I tightened my grip on the steering wheel. "No wonder Aaron didn't want to spend the rest of his life with me. Seriously, you guys, look at me. I need at least nine hours of sleep. I can't cook. I make fun of people who drive minivans. I have thirty-five pairs of black shoes. How am I cut out for breast-feeding and bake sales and PTA meetings?"

"I have forty-five pairs of black shoes," Andie said.

"I'm a mess," I said.

"Oh, be quiet," McKenna said. "You're not a mess, you're just getting to know yourself better. That's a good thing."

"But what if all I'm learning is that I'll never be ready to grow up?" I said. "It seems like everyone I know has grown up and knows what they want out of life, and I'm still eating cereal for dinner."

"You're plenty grown up," McKenna said. "Look what you've done with your life after a pretty rocky childhood. Getting an academic scholarship to college isn't easy, Waverly. You need to give yourself a little credit."

I sighed. "Yeah, but I can't blame everything on my dad, you know. If I hadn't come along, he might have had a real shot at a baseball career. But look at him now, bitter and wondering what could have been, stuck with a daughter who throws like a girl."

McKenna squeezed my arm. "It was his choice to become a father, Wave. And it's not your fault that your mom got sick. You need to stop feeling guilty about being born."

Her words made me think of what Jake had said when I met him. Did I really feel guilty about being born?

"What did Aaron think about that?" Andie said.

"About my dad?" I said.

"About your mom, your dad, everything."

I shook my head. "We didn't talk about it that much. I didn't want him to feel sorry for me."

McKenna took a deep breath. "Seriously, Wave, you've got to start trusting people to believe in you."

I looked down and bit my lip. "I trust you guys," I said softly.

"We don't count," Andie said. "We didn't almost marry you."

I looked at both of them. "You two are always so logical about everything. Why am I the one who is always freaking out?"

"There's one in every group," Andie said. "Keeps things interesting."

I leaned forward and turned on the radio to find a U2 song. "Okay, that's enough out of you two." I paid the toll at the Golden Gate Bridge and drove back into the city. We wound our way through the streets of the perfectly manicured Marina district, past the grassy parkway of the Marina Green field and the adjacent yacht harbor. The area was still full of joggers, kite flyers, and volleyball players trying to make the most of the weekend before the sun set and Monday reared its ugly head again.

After I dropped off my friends, I parked my car and walked up to my building. Once inside, I put on my pajamas and slippers and pulled my hair back into a low ponytail. Then I made a peanut butter and jelly sandwich and walked into my office. When Whitney had moved out, I didn't have much to put in there at first, but eventually I'd bought a nice oak desk, a chair, and a bookcase. To add a bit of personality to the room, I'd recently sprung for a heavy mustard-colored wooden chest, a thick rust-colored area rug, and a series of framed black-and-white pictures of random people posing for some random photographer from the 1940s. Mainly I used the office for paying bills, surfing the Internet, and writing the occasional letter, birthday card, or thank-you note. And now that I worked at home once in a while, the five-second commute was pretty sweet.

I booted up my computer and added a few more Honey Notes to my growing list.

Front: Afraid that your childhood will haunt you forever?
Inside: Honey, it will. Now get over it.

Front: Dreading sitting at the singles table?
Inside: Honey, as far as anyone knows, your boyfriend is performing

heart surgery and thus unfortunately could not attend. Or, if there are hot guys there, you are totally available. Work it as you see fit.

Front: Wondering if the whole white picket fence thing is for you?

Inside: Honey, not everyone has to be June Cleaver. Now go get yourself a facial.

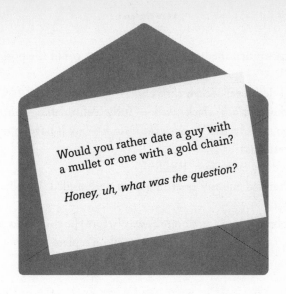

Would you rather date a guy with a mullet or one with a gold chain?

Honey, uh, what was the question?

CHAPTER TWELVE

A week later, I was on a plane bound for New York. The official reason for my trip was to attend some meetings at our Manhattan office, but of course I was really there for Cynthia's wedding. And I was crutch-free! My cast had been replaced by a walking cast, which to the untrained eye looked exactly the same, but it was much lighter. The biggest difference was that my new cast came with a little bootlike contraption around my foot that allowed me to walk. The doctor had told me how important it was to try to walk normally to avoid overcompensation injuries, but for the time being I couldn't do it. No matter how hard I tried, I walked with a noticeable limp, and the people at the office had taken to calling me the Hunchback of K. A. Marketing. Just what a girl loves to hear.

I flew out of San Francisco early that Tuesday afternoon. Everything seemed like business as usual at the airport, but when I got to the front of the check-in line, a miracle happened.

"Uh oh," the agent said. "It looks like coach is overbooked."

She typed five hundred words a minute into her keyboard and stared at her computer screen.

"What does that mean?" I said.

She continued the breakneck pace. What could she possibly be typing?

"Well, let's see"—*click click click*—"you have a full-fare economy ticket"—*clack clack clack*—"fully refundable"—*click click click*—"so it looks like"—*clack clack clack*—"we'll have to upgrade you to first class."

I raised my eyebrows. "Really?"

She handed me my boarding pass and smiled. "Really. Enjoy your flight."

I grabbed the pass and bolted away before she could take it back. Actually, I was moving more like a snail on a plate of honey, but it worked.

• • •

Thirty minutes later, I leaned back in my spacious leather seat and looked at the empty one next to me. "Are you expecting anyone to sit here?" I said to the flight attendant.

"Not today, Ms. Bryson. It's all yours."

Aaah. This was definitely my lucky day. Chatting with someone across the aisle is fine, but seriously, who wants to sit smack next to a random for a cross-country flight? My friend Whitney had met her husband on a plane, and he had even proposed during a flight by hiding the ring in the snack pack. But usually it was some lady who shared way too much information about her gout.

The extra leg room was perfect for my ankle, and once we were airborne, the flight attendants brought me a special ottoman to prop it up. They also brought me a Diet Coke and a bowl of mixed nuts. As I picked through the nuts and ate the cashews first (a habit I will probably take to my grave), I looked over the menu of gourmet lunch selections, thrilled that I would actually be fed on a plane without having to pay for it. Then I opened the in-flight magazine to see what free movies I could watch on my private screen. I looked at my watch. The scheduled flight time was about five hours, and already I didn't want to land.

I looked back at the curtain dividing first class and business class on the huge plane, and I thought of the curtain dividing business class and coach even farther back. I'd only been upgraded a few times in my life, but each time I was invariably seized by an irrational sense of superiority over the passengers in coach. It was like an evil part of me that only reared its ugly head at thirty-five thousand feet. It was horrible, and I knew it, but I couldn't help it. When I was in coach, I didn't have a problem with anyone, but put me in business or first class, and immediately I was a closet snob with an attitude. I hoped no one noticed.

I must have drifted off to sleep as I was contemplating this *Lord of the Flies* side of my personality, because I was suddenly being awakened by a flight attendant.

"Excuse me, Ms. Bryson?"

"Huh? What?" I sat up and shook my head. I knew it. They were booting me back to coach.

"It's nothing major, just a little motion sickness up in row three. Would you mind if we moved a passenger next to you to give the woman who is ill a little space?"

"Huh? Oh, sure, of course." I picked up my purse from the empty seat next to me.

"Thanks, Ms. Bryson."

"No problem." Hey, at least I was still in first class. I started flipping through the channels on my personal movie screen, and a few moments later I felt my new seatmate sit down next to me.

"Excuse me, do you have the time?" she said.

I looked down at my watch. "California time or New York time?"

"Oops, good question. Um, New York time."

I moved my watch ahead three hours. "It's just about five thirty. I think we'll land around ten o'clock."

"Thanks. And I'm so sorry to take this seat. I know it's always nice to have the extra space."

"No problem. I was upgraded anyway, so who am I to complain?"

I looked over at her with a smile and froze.

I was looking at Kristina Santana, Shane Kennedy's wife.

"Oh, Jesus," I blurted. Nice composure.

"Are you okay?" she said.

I pushed my hair behind my ear. "Um, yeah, fine. I just didn't realize who you were. I'm a big fan, um, I mean of your skating career. I saw you in the Olympics." God, so lame.

She smiled and flashed the whitest teeth I had ever seen. "Thanks. What's your name?"

"Waverly, Waverly Bryson."

"Waverly? Like the—"

I smiled and cut her off. "Yes, just like the cracker from way back when."

She laughed. "You must get that a lot. It's nice to meet you." She reached over to shake my hand.

"Actually, I did some work with your husband a few months ago," I said. "I work for JAG."

She narrowed her eyes. "Did he behave himself?"

I nodded. "He was great. In fact, he was a real sweetheart. In my line of work I have to deal with some prima donnas, and he definitely broke the mold. He even fetched me coffee a couple of times."

She laughed again. "That's not surprising. I wouldn't have married Shane if he had an attitude. Hell, I probably wouldn't even have dated him." She took a sip of her sparkling water. "I've met my share of cocky athletes too, and believe me, I got tired of that years ago."

"I'll drink to that." I picked up my Diet Coke. "I once had to arrange a press tour for a baseball player who was representing a line of catcher's gloves. God, he was a piece of work, totally full of himself and crazy rude to everyone around him when the cameras weren't running. Anyhow, he was so conceited that he nearly walked out of an on-field interview on the *Today* show when he found out the reporter had never heard of him."

"Really?"

I nodded. "And get this. After the interview, when the player was gone, the reporter laughed and said he of course knew who the guy was but wanted to mess with him."

"That's brilliant," she said.

I smiled. "I know, isn't it? I told him I'd wished I'd thought of that one myself. After that press tour, I never had to talk to that horrible ballplayer again, but the reporter and I are still good friends." Good ol' Scotty Ryan.

Kristina and I ended up talking nearly the entire flight, starting with how I had hurt my ankle, and then moving on to work, family, and, of course, Olympic medals (hers, of course). She and Shane had met six years before at a charity event in Chicago, where they had both grown up. She was juggling medical school and competitive skating at the time, and he was a young NBA star. Apparently, it was love at first sight, and within a few months they were engaged. Talk about the perfect couple.

She took a bite of her chocolate truffle cake. "So what about you? How's the romance in San Francisco?"

I looked at her and raised my eyebrows. "Hmm, where should I start? Would you rather hear about how my ex-fiancé just got married or how I haven't had sex in about eleven years?"

She nearly choked on her dessert. "Oh my God, you're hilarious."

"Okay, I'm exaggerating," I said. "But let's just say I'm in a bit of a dry spell at the moment."

"Ahhh, I hate dry spells. Don't worry though, it sounds like you're due," she said, digging through her purse. She pulled out a lipstick, reapplied it, and tossed the purse between us. "Breaking a dry spell was always my favorite part about being single."

I laughed and leaned back in my seat. "I sure hope you're right, because breaking open a carton of ice cream for dinner is currently *my* favorite part about being single, and my jeans are not exactly thrilled with me for it."

A few hours later, we were outside baggage claim in New York. I picked up my suitcase and handed her my business card. "This has my work and cell numbers, so please get in touch if you're ever in San Francisco, okay? And please tell Shane I said hi. It was so nice to meet you."

"Will do. It was great to meet you, too. Bye, Waverly."

"Bye."

I hobbled into a cab to head for the brightly lit streets of mid-town Manhattan. A few miles later, as we entered the city, I looked up and saw Kristina's face smiling down at me from a billboard for Whisper perfume.

. . .

At 11 p.m. I checked into my hotel, then went upstairs to my room and opened my suitcase. I pulled out the wrinkleables and hung them up in my closet. If at all possible, I wanted to avoid having to bust out the iron. I hate ironing. Hate it hate it hate it. I make a point of almost exclusively buying clothes that were perfectly wearable if fluffed up in the dryer, so the sight of me with an iron is about as common as the sight of Sean Penn at a Republican convention. But there are no clothes dryers in hotel rooms, and sometimes the cutest clothes have to be ironed, so then I cave. But I still hate it hate it hate it.

I put on my pajamas, then pulled my hair into a ponytail and ordered a ham and cheese sandwich and a green salad from room service. As best I could with my cast, I sat crossed-legged on the bed and turned on the TV.

"Room service." A knock on the door alerted me to the arrival of my late-night dinner. Like Pavlov's dog, immediately I was starving. I carefully got up off the bed and limped over to the door. The bellman wheeled in the tray. "Can I get you anything else?" he said.

"How about a boyfriend and a new ankle?"

"I'm sorry?"

"Kidding, kidding." I handed him a few dollars for a tip and shut the door. Then I looked down at the bill I had just signed: $28.50 for a ham and cheese sandwich, a green salad, and a bottle of water. Thank God for expense accounts.

An hour later I was about to turn off the TV and go to sleep when I decided to check my e-mail and work a little bit on my greeting cards. I booted up my laptop and, after deleting approximately seven thousand pictures of Whitney's sleeping baby, typed the following ideas to add to my master list:

MORE HONEY NOTE IDEAS

Front: Why do people have to e-mail you dozens of pictures of their newborns? Why won't one or two do?

Inside: Honey, just wait until they put those ridiculous "My child was student of the month" bumper stickers on their cars, oops—I mean, on their minivans.

Front: In a bit of a dry spell lately?

Inside: Honey, just think of how much money you're saving on fancy lingerie and waxing treatments.

I took a sip of water and read over what I had typed. It definitely came across as a little bitter.

Hmm. Was I really that bitter?

I clicked on the document and added one more:

Front: Feeling a little bitter lately?

Inside: Honey, that's okay. Just take a deep breath, smile, and imagine a car-size Snickers.

• • •

Late the next morning, Paige Beckerman announced the Adina Energy win to the entire company via videoconference. She said we'd signed a seven-figure, one-year contract for product launches and that the account would be handled out of the San Francisco office.

I smiled and looked around at the people sitting next to me in the crowded New York conference room, wondering if anyone would realize that I was the one who would be managing the account, that I was the one who would be running the show.

Then Paige Beckerman said the team would be led by Mandy Edwards.

• • •

"So, um, do you know what products Adina Energy has coming out this year?" I was sitting in Cynthia's office an hour later, updating her on the JAG account while trying not to cry, and hoping she wouldn't notice.

She shuffled through some papers on her desk. "Not a clue. But I've been so distracted with the wedding plans that even if I knew, I probably would have forgotten."

"Yeah, I guess you've got more important things to worry about. So, um, do you know why they chose Mandy Edwards to run the account? I mean, because, well, she's still pretty new to the sports division." Was I the only one who had thought I was the best choice for the job? Was I the only one who thought I'd been screwed?

She kept looking through the papers. "Jess said she's expressed quite an interest in taking on more work. And she's done a great job with her other accounts, so it looks like this is her chance to get more involved in the sports side of the agency."

"Oh." I looked at the floor and bit my lip. That weasel. Expressing an interest in taking my job was more like it. But then again, why hadn't I lobbied for more work, too? Should I have? I truly sucked at office politics.

I cleared my throat. "So, um, is everything all set for the wedding?"

"Knock on wood, but I think so. As long as Dale doesn't stand me up, we're all good."

"Oh, please. It's going to be perfect."

She stood up and put her coat on. "I sure hope you're right. Okay, Waverly, I'm sorry to be so rushed, but I've gotta get going. I'll see you on Saturday?"

"Okay." I looked at my hands in my lap.

She stopped and looked at me. "Hon, is everything okay?"

"Yep."

"Are you sure? You seem a little down."

I forced a smile and nodded. "Yep." I wasn't about to make this week about me.

. . .

Saturday morning I woke up early, wrapped a plastic bag over my cast, and took a long, hot shower. When I got out and could finally see through the steam filling up the bathroom, I wrapped myself up in The Robe and walked over to the bedroom window facing the street. Cynthia had chosen the luxurious Waldorf-Astoria as the location for her wedding, and I was at the smaller yet lovely Hôtel Plaza Athénée. It was just a few blocks away from Central Park, which was blanketed with a thick layer of snow, and its windows framed a spectacular portrait of a pristine Manhattan winter. The boutique hotel reminded me a bit of Buenos Aires and the European-style architecture so typical of the Argentine capital. I had spent a few weeks in Buenos Aires right after college and had fallen in love with everything about it, especially the gorgeous men there. My South American AIKS (Alcohol-Induced Kissing Syndrome) had kicked in big time.

After I dried my hair, I headed downstairs. The wedding wasn't until five thirty, so I had as much time as I wanted to enjoy and explore, although I wasn't planning on walking around all that much because of my hunchback limp. But I wanted to check out the neighborhood. I love Manhattan—its vibe and appearance can change so much from block to block that every few minutes it's like entering a brand new city. The sheer magnitude and boundless energy of it never cease to amaze me. I consider myself a city person and always say I will live in San Francisco unless I am delivered in a body bag to the suburbs, but New York is on a completely different level. Every time I go there I feel like a freckle-faced country bumpkin with a show pig under her arm, all alone in the big city for the very first time.

An hour later, I was reading the newspaper at a café when my cell phone rang. It startled me so much I nearly dropped my coffee in my lap. I dug the phone out of my purse and didn't recognize the number.

"Hello?"

"Waverly?" It was a familiar female voice, but I couldn't place it.

"Yes?"

"Hey there, it's Kristina from the airplane the other day. How are you?"

Kristina? What? No way.

"Oh, hi, Kristina. I'm good, thanks. Just hanging out at a café near my hotel. How are you?" I said.

"All good on this end, just hoping it doesn't snow anymore. Anyhow, I know this is a long shot, but by any chance did you pick up my appointment book by accident? I can't find it anywhere and think it may have fallen out of my purse on the plane. Maybe it ended up in yours?"

I frowned. "An appointment book? What does it look like?"

"It's very small and dark green. Leather binding."

I cradled the phone between my ear and my shoulder. "Okay, let me dig through my purse. Just a second . . . what do I have here . . . wallet . . . lipstick . . . brush . . . chapstick . . . sunglasses . . . another lipstick . . . pen . . . pen . . . pen . . . checkbook . . . God, I have a lot of crap in here . . . wait! Yes, here it is. One green appointment book. Wow, I'm sorry, I have no idea how it got in there. I didn't mean to pull a Winona on you."

"Oh, please don't apologize. I'm so relieved to have found it. I can't seem to get myself out of the dark ages and buy a BlackBerry, so without that book, I'm lost."

"Well, consider yourself found. How can I get it to you?"

She paused. "Hmm, I have today off, so is it okay with you if I come pick it up right now? I need to get out and do some shopping anyway. Hey, want to come along? I know it's last-minute, but are you free?"

"Are you kidding? I'd love to! I don't know anyone in New York except for my friend the bride, and she's obviously busy today. And the wedding isn't until later, so I really don't have any plans except for finishing this third cup of coffee."

"Are you a caffeine addict too?"

"On occasion. You too?"

"Oh yes, I got hooked in medical school. Shane knows not to talk to me in the morning before I've had my latte. He says hi, by the way. I told him how we met. So how about I pick you up at your hotel in forty-five minutes? Sound good?"

"Kristina, you are my kind of woman. That sounds perfect,

although if we're going shopping, I should warn you that my 'get up and go' sort of got up and went when I broke my ankle."

"No worries, I'll take care of you. See you in a flash."

I looked down at my outfit. I had a date with Kristina Santana? Did I look okay? I was wearing jeans and a cream flared-cuff cashmere turtleneck sweater with a green-and-blue flower embroidered over the left part of the chest. Would it do? Sadly, it was the most excited I'd been about a date in a long time, so I didn't want to blow it by showing up in a JV outfit.

. . .

Later that afternoon, Kristina and I sat in the comfy lounge chairs in the lobby of my hotel, drinking green tea and admiring the fruits of our shopping spree. She'd picked me up in a cab and taken me to several hip stores in SoHo with great deals that were in my price range. I'd bought so many things that we'd picked up a cheap duffel bag for me to store my loot on the flight home.

"Kristina, you are amazing." I looked at the pile of shopping bags surrounding us and shook my head. "I thought I was a bargain shopper, but you take the cake. I'm going to have to start calling you Bargain Betty."

She sipped her tea. "Yeah, I know. I love shopping, but I just can't bring myself to buy things that are obviously overpriced, ya know?"

"I'm the same way, but I shop for bargains because they're all I can afford. Now you, on the other hand . . ."

She put her hand up. "I know, I know. But my family was pretty poor when I was a kid, and I still remember what it felt like to worry about money. And now that I *have* money, I prefer to give it to those who really need it, and that group doesn't tend to include fancy boutique owners."

"Hey, I'm not knocking it. If you had taken me where the rich and famous of Manhattan shop, I wouldn't have been able to afford a pair of socks."

She held up her cup. "I'll drink to that."

"And I'll drink to my new wedding outfit." I had brought three dresses with me to New York, but Andie was right: did any dress look good with a cast? Uh, that would be a no. So Kristina had helped me pick out something much better: a sleek black pair of semi-flared crepe pants with a slim cream-colored satin band outlining two large pockets in the back. A matching spaghetti-strap top had the same satin band running under the bust and a two-inch slit up each side of the waist. It was simple, elegant, and pretty. And it did a great job of hiding my cast.

"You really want to help me with my hair and makeup?" I said.

"Sure, I'm happy to do it. When I'm not working and Shane's on the road, I tend to get bored, so this will help fill up my Saturday afternoon."

"You really don't have some movie premiere or awards show to attend? Or maybe some lives to save?"

She waved a hand at me. "Girl, your idea of what my life is like is so off base it's not even funny."

"So it's not all glamour and glitz?"

"Not even close. I may fly first class, but I do my own laundry, remember?"

I laughed. "It's been so fun hanging out with you. I just wish you could be my date to the wedding. I'm not exactly bouncing off the walls with excitement about sitting at the singles table."

"It won't be that bad. Maybe there'll be some good-looking men there."

"And maybe not."

"C'mon, don't be such a pessimist."

"I know, I know. I'm just not excited about putting that scarlet S back on my chest."

"Waverly, you're just being dramatic."

I crossed my arms and sighed. "Maybe I am, but that's the power of the singles table."

"You're being ridiculous. So you didn't get married, big deal. Do you even want to be married?"

I looked at her and bit my lip. "Well, I, it's just that everyone else . . ."

"You shouldn't be worrying about everyone. You should be worrying about you."

"But—"

"But nothing."

"But—"

She grabbed my wrist. "Waverly, I know I haven't known you that long, but I want you to listen to me."

I looked at her, my mouth open.

"Nothing bothers me more than a woman who looks for validation in the eyes of others, okay?"

I closed my mouth.

"If you want to get married, that's great. I think marriage is wonderful. But if for one second you actually believe that I would think *more highly of you* just because you were married, then you've really underestimated me."

"Well, I—"

"I'm not through. I like you, Waverly. I really do. But I can't deal with women who care too much about what other people think of them. I really can't."

"You can't?"

"Nope. And once someone gets on my bad side, that's it."

I smiled. "*That's it?*"

"Yep, so don't blow it." She smiled back.

I laughed. "Are you threatening me?"

She shrugged. "I prefer the term 'tough love,' but if you want to see it that way, then yes."

"Man, Shane was right when he said you were hard-nosed."

She smiled again. "Girl, you have no idea."

We lugged our shopping bags up to my room, hung my outfit for the wedding in the closet, then plopped everything else in a corner. I plugged in my hair straightener and showed Kristina the makeup I had with me.

She looked through my stuff. "I'm thinking that you should wear your hair down and straight, with smoky eye shadow and plum-colored lipstick."

"Sounds good to me," I said. "After that speech downstairs, I'm not about to get in your way."

She laughed. "Watch it."

I turned on the TV set and clicked through the channels until I settled on MTV, which was, shockingly, actually playing a video, a Madonna video marathon, in fact. "Ooh, I love Madonna," I said as I walked back to the bathroom. "Her music reminds me of getting ready for high school dances. So what was the deal with dances anyway? Did you notice how halfway through high school they suddenly weren't cool anymore? Or was that just my high school?" I leaned my hip against the sink as she finished selecting my makeup.

She applied a light layer of foundation to my face with a cotton ball. "Hey, you're right. That happened at my school, too. Suddenly no one went anymore. I have no idea why."

"And did you ever notice that getting ready for the dance was usually more fun than the dance itself?"

She stepped back and smiled at me. "Waverly, where do you come up with all these observations?"

I shrugged. "I'm a single woman with no pets. I have a lot of free time."

"Waverly . . ."

"Okay, okay, no more complaining about being single. Hey, can I ask you a question?"

"Sure." She leaned toward me and swiped a concealer stick underneath my eye.

"Um, well, I was just wondering, do you know Shane's college roommate, Jake McIntyre?"

She dusted a large brush over my cheekbones, then had me close my eyes and applied eyeliner and shadow. "Jake? Sure I know him. He was in our wedding party. Why?"

"Oh, well, Shane introduced me to him at a big party JAG threw at the end of that trade show back in November. I thought he was really cute."

"He's a sweetheart," she said, then turned my head to the left and applied more blush. She held my chin in one hand and examined my face. "Okay, I'm done with your makeup, but now I want to tweeze your eyebrows a bit, just to give them a little more shape. You mind?"

She dug through her purse and pulled out a pair of tweezers, a tiny brush, and a pair of eyebrow scissors.

"Not at all, please, go right ahead." I closed my eyes. "My blonde friends like my eyebrows because they're dark and thick, but to me they're a nightmare."

"Just leave them to me. I've always thought that if I hadn't become a doctor, I would've opened up my own beauty salon. I love this stuff. Now don't move."

I held my breath. She finished my right eyebrow, then leaned back and squinted. "Perfect. Now hold still while I do the other."

I closed my eyes again and listened to Madonna sing "Like a Virgin" in the background. I let myself get lost in the song and pictured her prancing around Venice in her wedding dress. Man, I was like a virgin for all intents and purposes. How long had it been? Ugh. I was a born-again virgin.

The sound of Kristina's voice snapped me out of my reverie.

"Okay, I'm done with the eyebrows. Now let me just straighten your hair, and we'll be done." She picked up my straightener in one hand and a chunk of my hair in the other.

"Kristina?"

"Yeah?"

"Well, um, I was just wondering what you know about Jake. I mean, does he have a girlfriend?"

She reached for another chunk of my hair and clasped the straightening iron around it. "A girlfriend? Hmm . . . I have no idea. It's been quite a while since I've seen him. But I could ask Shane about it."

"NO! I mean no, you don't have to. I was just curious, that's all. Working for the Hawks, he must have a thousand girls chasing after him."

She moved behind me to work on the back part of my hair. "He might, but I bet none of them look as good as you do right now."

She rubbed a touch of shiny gloss on her fingers and ran them through my hair. Then she put her hands on her hips again and smiled. "You have a fantastic stylist, if I do say so myself."

I turned to face the mirror, and I had to admit that I looked pretty good. My hair and makeup had been done professionally a couple times to be a bridesmaid, but the whole look had never turned out so well. And the new shape of my eyebrows really brightened up my eyes.

"Wow, Kristina, you've made me into a hottie!"

"Waverly, you were already a hottie. Now you're totally on fire." She unplugged my straightening iron and started putting my makeup back into its case.

I laughed and held my hand up to hers for a high-five. "Singles table, watch out."

. . .

The church Cynthia had chosen for her wedding was called St. Luke's. I figured it was going to be gorgeous, because I had noticed that most guys named Luke tended to be gorgeous. And I wasn't disappointed. It was high and narrow with breathtaking stained-glass windows lighting up the walls and ceiling.

I couldn't believe how many people were crammed into the pews. Seriously, there were like fifty thousand of us. I hadn't asked Cynthia how many people she had invited, but now that I thought about it, a big wedding made sense because of who the bride and groom were. Dale Payton was a big-shot sports agent, and Cynthia was a senior VP at an international marketing firm. Being successful in both professions required some serious people skills and also led to some serious financial rewards.

I slid quietly into a pew and glanced around. I leafed through the wedding program and tried to look nonchalant as I waited for the ceremony to start. The irrational side of me felt like I had a big sign on my head that said LEFT AT THE ALTAR THE LAST TIME I WAS HERE. The rational side of me told me that McKenna, Andie, and now Kristina, too, would all kick my ass if they knew what I was thinking.

The ceremony was short and sweet, thank God. Cynthia and Dale had mercifully elected to keep it that way and cut right to the *Do you? Yes, I do. And do you? Yes, I do* chase, which was just fine by me. We all stood and clapped for the newlyweds as they glided back down the aisle. (Or is it up the aisle, since the bride walks down the aisle? Who really knows?) Anyhow, they blissfully floated past us and out of the church. Once the bridesmaids and groomsmen had followed suit, the crowd streamed out of the pews and off to the hotel, where the real party awaited.

I hobbled to a cab and directed the driver to the Waldorf-Astoria, just a few blocks away. Normally I would have walked, but it was freezing outside, and I was a major turtle in my cast. When the cab dropped me off, I checked my hair and makeup in the lobby powder room and reapplied a little bit of plum-colored lipstick. Then I headed toward the main ballroom. The place was rapidly filling up with a ton of wedding guests I didn't know. I made my way to the seating chart table in the hallway and picked out my place card:

Miss Waverly Bryson
Table 53

"Table fifty-three? Who has fifty-three tables at a wedding?" I said to myself.

"Excuse me?" The attendant behind the seating chart looked up at me.

"Sorry, just talking out loud." Oops. But seriously, where would we all fit? How would the happy couple possibly have time to say hello to everyone?

I started walking into the main dining room, but the attendant pointed down the hall and smiled. "The cocktail hour is in the Astor Salon. Dinner is in an hour back here in the Grand Ballroom."

"Uh, okay, thanks." I turned on my good heel and followed the crowd. I knew a few of the people from K.A. Marketing who were supposed to be there and wondered if any of them would be seated at my table. Or maybe I'd be seated next to someone famous. I'd already spotted several athletes and media personalities in the crowd.

The Sunrise Ballroom was filled with a variety of stations featuring appetizers and drinks from around the world: sushi, tapas, spring rolls, tacos, German beers. As soon as I walked in the door, a smiling silver-haired woman in a black-and-white catering outfit approached me and looked down at my cast.

"Hi there, do you need help with anything?"

So much for my *No one will notice my cast with these pants on* plan.

I smiled. "I'm fine, thanks. But would you please tell me where I can get a glass of wine?"

She pointed to the bar on the right. "Enjoy your evening, and please find me if you need anything at all."

I headed over to the Wines from Napa Valley island and ordered a glass of Peju merlot. Then I hobbled to the sushi bar and picked out a few California rolls and a spicy salmon roll. I turned around and spotted an empty cocktail table with high bar stools to my right. I put my glass down and took a seat, then once again scanned the room. As face after face failed to register, I began to wonder if I had wandered into the wrong party.

I gave up looking and focused on the plate in front of me. Yummy. I gobbled down the California rolls and was throwing back the salmon roll when my eyes stopped in the middle of the room. Right there, standing next to the taco station, was Jake McIntyre. And I think he was looking at me.

I quickly turned my head and took a sip of wine to help the salmon roll head downstream. Jake was there? Cute Jake? Blue-eyed Jake? No way. What was he doing there? And was he alone?

I took a deep breath, then turned back to face him with a nervous smile.

But he was nowhere to be seen.

"Hey, Sunshine, I thought that was you."

I turned around and saw Scotty Ryan from the *Today* show standing there.

I stood up and hugged him. "Hey, Scotty! I didn't know you'd be here. What a nice surprise."

"I could say the same thing," he said. "How are you?"

"I'm good, thanks. You know, just the other day, I was reminiscing about how you shot down that awful baseball player by pretending not to know who he was."

He smiled. "One of my favorite interviews."

"Are you friends with Dale or with Cynthia?" I said.

"Actually, I know them completely independently of each other, so there was no way I could miss this party."

"Please, have a seat." I gestured at the empty bar stool next to me. "I'm so glad I ran into you. I don't know anyone here and was already wondering how I was going to make it through the evening alone, so you just saved me."

"Happy to help out." He took a seat and immediately noticed the cast peeking out from under my pants. "Hey, what happened to your leg?"

"It's my ankle. I wish I could say that I broke it doing something exciting, but I tripped over a branch. Painfully boring, painfully embarrassing—just plain painful."

He put his hand on my shoulder. "Well, despite the cast, you look just as lovely as ever. You're really here alone? I find that hard to believe."

I took a sip of my wine and smiled. "Well, thank you for the compliment, kind sir, but yes, I'm flying solo. You too?"

He nodded and looked around the room. "Yep."

"Actually, this is the first wedding I've been to by myself in a while," I said, suddenly feeling courageous.

"Really?"

I nodded. "Yep, and actually, the last wedding I was supposed to go to was my own."

His eyes met mine. "You were engaged? When? What happened?"

I bit my lip and took a deep breath.

I could do it. I could tell him.

"Um . . .," I said slowly.

I pictured Kristina giving high-fives to McKenna and Andie.

I could do it.

"He, uh um . . . we, um . . ."

Scotty raised an eyebrow.

"I . . . uh, I just wasn't ready to get married, so I called it off," I finally said.

Damn it. Baby steps were harder than I thought.

"Wow, I'm sorry to hear that," he said.

I picked up my glass. "Me too, but hey, what can you do? If it's not right, it's not right, right?" At least I was learning that, if nothing else.

"Love sucks," he said, then lowered his voice and leaned close to me. "Although I probably shouldn't be saying that at a wedding."

I laughed and looked around the room. "This is by far the fanciest wedding I've ever been to. I wonder when the *InStyle* celebrity weddings photographer is going to show up."

He nodded. "Tell me about it. This place is busting with current and former professional athletes."

"Yeah, my friend Hunter would sell his soul to the devil to be here right now," I said. "What a scene."

He took my free hand and gently squeezed it. "Once the party really gets going, we'll have to check out the best-looking men and then divide and conquer."

"I'll drink to that." I held my wine glass up for a toast. "Actually, there is a guy here I'm sort of interested in, but I seem to have lost him in the crowd. Want to help me find him?"

"Sure, let me at him. The four-one-one, please?"

I leaned close, still holding his hand, and lowered my voice. "Okay, but we need to be sly, because I tend to choke around this guy, and I mean that literally."

He whispered back. "Do you want to be Starsky or Hutch?"

I made a face at him. "I spotted him a few minutes ago, but then I lost him."

I described Jake to Scotty, and he leaned over and whispered in my ear, "He sounds like a major dish. Maybe we could flip a coin for him?"

"I wonder if he's here with someone," I said. "I've gotta talk to him again, Scotty. The last time I totally blew it."

"Leave it to me, precious, leave it to me. The night is young, and there's lots of fun to be had."

We spent the rest of the cocktail hour catching up and gossiping about all the famous guests. Scotty had a lot of good gossip.

"John Shasta, the Yankees pitcher? Seriously?" I said.

He nodded. "Pitches for the other team."

"But he's always doing those truck commercials."

He put his hand on my cheek. "Don't you live in San Francisco? Wake up and smell the rainbow dust, my dear."

I looked over at the burly man drinking a glass of black paint. I mean Guinness.

"But John Shasta?" I said.

Scotty reached over and grabbed my nose. "Sweetheart, you should see the love letters I get from women all over the country who have no idea I prefer men. It's all about portraying an image to a particular audience. You should know that, being the PR princess and all."

Images. What would mine have been if I'd become Mrs. Aaron Vaughn III? Would Mrs. Aaron Vaughn III have wanted the world to know about her dad's home address? What would Mrs. Aaron Vaughn III's conservative in-laws have thought about her friendship with Scotty Ryan?

I took Scotty's hand and looked down at his perfectly manicured nails. Why couldn't I keep my own nails that nice? I looked up, and the crowd behind him briefly parted. For a second I spotted Jake in the back corner of the cocktail area. He was next to the margarita bar.

I squeezed Scotty's hand. "Oh my God, there he is."

"Where?"

"Margarita bar, five o'clock. Charcoal grey suit, yellow tie."

He stood up and finished his drink. "Did you say the margarita bar? Two margaritas coming up. How do you like yours, by the way?"

"Strong. And please be subtle, Scotty."

"Beautiful, I'm always subtle. Now don't move a muscle. I'll be right back." He set his empty glass on the table and walked away.

I watched him make his way through the crowd. The room was packed, and the margarita bar was way in the back, so it was hard for me to keep track of him without craning my neck and looking totally obvious. So I gave up and turned my attention back to wondering which other famous athletes were gay.

Five minutes later, Scotty reemerged from the crowd with two margaritas. He sat down and placed the drinks on the table.

"Well?" I said.

He frowned. "He's with a brunette."

"And?"

"And unfortunately, I'm pretty sure she's his date."

I smacked my forehead with my palm. "His date? But how am I going to seduce him if he's with a date?"

He laughed. "Seduce him?"

I blushed. "Or whatever you call it these days. I've been off the market for a while. Are you sure she's his date?"

"Yeah, I'm sure. I saw hand-holding. I'm sorry, sweetheart. The nerve of him, with you here and looking so delicious."

I was crushed. "But he makes me feel melty," I said softly.

He patted me on the head. "C'mon, let's head over to dinner. And is that even a word?"

We picked up our margaritas and followed the crowd into the Grand Ballroom. And it was even bigger. "I feel like I'm at the intermission of a Broadway musical," I said.

As we walked into the dining room, I pulled my place card out of my purse. Like most little black party purses, it was way too small to carry anything I really needed, such as a wallet, or a phone, or an emergency Snickers.

"Hey, Scotty, what table are you at?"

He pulled his card out of his pocket and looked at it. "Thirty-five. What about you?"

"Fifty-three. Are you sure this isn't one of Elizabeth Taylor's wedding receptions?"

He shook his head. "Too small."

"Hey, if you can find me after dinner, save me a slow dance, okay?" I pointed to my cast. "The Macarena and Electric Slide are out of the picture with junior here."

"You bet, sweet thing." He winked and walked the other way.

. . .

Table fifty-three was definitely a singles table. Fortunately, however, it wasn't THE singles table. Hell, the wedding was so huge that for all we knew there could have been an entire singles dining room and dance floor. The room was so enormous that I couldn't even see where Cynthia and Dale were sitting, much less Jake. I focused on the wine glass in front of me instead.

From my initial superficial sizing up of my male tablemates, that glass was the only thing my lips would be touching that night. We all introduced ourselves and slid into the standard wedding small talk:

"So how do you know the bride?"

"Oh really? Then do you know (insert name here)?"

"So how do you know the groom?"

"Oh really? Then do you know (insert name here)?"

"So where are you from?"

"You are? Then do you know (insert name here)?"

"So where did you go to school?"

"You did? Then do you know (insert name here)?"

"So have you ever noticed how small talk inevitably morphs into the name game?" I said to no one in particular.

One thing that was a little awkward about our table, and the other thirty-five hundred in the room, was the flowers, which were white and beautiful and everywhere. And everywhere included the centerpiece, which was a huge globe of white petals about two feet in diameter. It was so big that it blocked my view of the people directly across the table, and theirs of me. Given that clearly no expense had been spared to make the wedding perfect, I have no idea how this rather important detail had somehow been overlooked.

Anyhow, back to the edible details. The entrées were spectacular: a choice of lobster, chicken, or sirloin, plus jasmine rice and a grilled vegetable medley lightly topped with a sweet cinnamon glaze, and the most delicious, thickest bread I had ever tasted. I ate everything on my plate. And the flowing wine was a nice social lubricant for our table of virtual strangers. Despite the visual impairment, we managed to engage the entire group in a hearty conversation that flowed from sports and books to movies and political scandals.

Then things shifted gears, and the real fun began.

Hank Fishman, a stocky, balding coworker of Dale's, stood up and raised his glass. "Ladies and gentlemen of table fifty-three, I propose a slight change of subject to spice this party up."

"What did you have in mind?" A curly-haired blonde named Dawn leaned around the centerpiece to make eye contact with him.

Hank took a sip of his wine and set it down on the table. "Well, since we've broached the general subject of dating, I suggest we delve into the more entertaining topic of dating disqualifiers. Shallow, plain, and simple."

"Disqualifiers?" I said, leaning my head a foot to the right.

"Yep, things that will exclude any possible date from consideration, and the more superficial the better."

"That sounds quite interesting." Christopher Henson, a salt-and-pepper-haired friend of Cynthia's, rubbed his hands together. "Who's first?"

"I'll take one for the team," Hank said. "And for you ladies in the group, I'm quite aware that I'm short and bald, two attributes that often top the female disqualifier list. I take no offense at that, but for the sake of originality, let's please try to come up with something new, okay?"

I raised my wine glass. "Hank, I'm in love with the self-deprecation. It's a shame we can't hook up though, because short and bald are two of my disqualifiers."

"Ahhh, you're killing me." He pretended to stab himself in the heart. "And by the way, ladies, I also have a bit of a carpet growing on my back, so let's keep back hair off the list to keep me from throwing myself off the roof tonight." He clapped his hands. "Now, let's get this game started."

We all looked at him. Or around at him.

"For me," he said. "I must admit that my top disqualifier would have to be the cheerleader. I don't care how smokin' you are. If I find out you once had pom-poms in your locker, you're out on your ass."

A small applause erupted from the group. Hank bowed his head. "And my apologies to any of you ladies who might have been cheerleaders, but it doesn't matter because you probably wouldn't hook up with a short, bald guy with a hairy back anyway." He picked up his glass and raised it to the table, then sat down.

"Who's next?" Christopher said. "Should we just go clockwise around the table?"

"Sure," Hank said, and we all looked at the blonde to his left. Her name was Lisa.

She smiled. "Then it's me, and it's easy." She lifted three fingers in the air. "Three words: personalized license plates." She sipped her wine and put it on the table.

"Ooh, excellent choice." I pointed at her and nodded.

The list grew as we continued around the table, and by the end I was dabbing my eyes with my napkin. Added to Hank's *cheerleader* and Lisa's *personalized license plates*, we had:

Matt: *Laura Ashley bedspreads or any type of waterbed*

Dawn: *Jorts (jean shorts)*

Kevin: *Former debutantes or beauty pageant contestants*

Amanda: *Any guy who weighs less than she does*

Greg: *Ivy Leaguers who unnecessarily drop their alma mater into the conversation*

Eileen: *Sandals with socks*

Me: *Tie between black Levi's and bumper stickers*

We all agreed the best disqualifier of the table belonged to Christopher, who cracked us up with *stuffed animals in the back window of the car.*

Upon further discussion, we decided that guys with pinky rings, gold chains, or mullets were automatic disqualifiers, as were girls with muffin tops or photos of their cats in their wallets. Others that were close but didn't make the A-list included guys with beer guts, unibrows, or mustaches, and girls with man hands, square and/or fake fingernails, or an annoying laugh.

Damn, we were one shallow table.

Hank motioned for a nearby waiter, who with blazing speed refilled all our wine glasses. Then Hank raised his in the air. "Table fifty-three, you are one hell of a bunch. Here's to the goddamned singles table!"

"To the goddamned singles table!" We all raised our glasses and cheered, turning several nearby heads.

"Could we perpetuate the stereotype of the drunk singles table any more?" Dawn said to me.

I laughed. Despite my best intentions to stay sober, I had failed miserably. I sucked.

"Hell, we deserve to have fun too, right?" I said. "Table fifty-three is the Island of Misfit Toys!"

"You go, girl," Hank said.

The band began to play, and before we knew it, the best man had delivered his speech, the happy couple had cut the cake, the open bar was open again (had it ever closed?), and the crowd was heading toward the dance floor. The party was going full steam ahead.

I stood up and hobbled to the nearest restroom to freshen up. It was gorgeous, with large marble sinks and more fresh flowers everywhere. I think there may have been soft classical music piped in, but it was drowned out by the sound of the swing band on the other side of the door.

I looked over at the tiny blonde in a red dress washing her hands at the sink next to me. We were the only two people in the room.

I opened my purse. "Thank God whoever designed this place had the foresight to include several women's restrooms. There's nothing more awkward at a fancy wedding than a long line of well-dressed drunk women waiting to pee."

She laughed. "Tell me about it. I love your hair, by the way. Is it naturally that straight and shiny?"

"I wish." I looked in the mirror. Man, Kristina really knew her stuff. Not a single frizz or strand out of place. My makeup was still perfect, and my smoky eyes and plum-colored lips looked sort of exotic without looking too made up.

I reapplied just a touch of lipstick and put it away, then laughed at how truly useless my tiny purse was. God forbid I might actually want it to hold something larger than a reservation.

I said goodbye to the blonde and wobbled out of the restroom, not sure what percentage of my limp was due to my cast and what percentage was due to the margaritas and the wine.

I spotted Scotty across the ballroom at what must have been table 35 and headed in his direction. When he saw me, he flagged me over by crisscrossing his arms in the air like a clueless father next to a wood-paneled station wagon in a high school parking lot.

"Waverly, over here, over here!"

I rolled my eyes. "Gee, Scotty, I never would have seen you without the full-body spasms. Thanks for going the extra mile."

"My pleasure, sweetheart. Now let me introduce you around. Waverly, this is table thirty-five. Table thirty-five, this is Waverly." He majestically swept his arm across the half-empty table, and my eyes met the gaze of three older adults who were clearly not amused by Scotty's enthusiasm.

"It's nice to meet you," I said. They nodded and immediately returned to their conversation.

Scotty turned toward a tall, slender blond man sitting next to him and smiled. "And this . . . is Tad."

"Hi, Tad, it's nice to meet you," I said.

"Likewise," he said.

We shook hands, but Tad looked right through me and directly at Scotty. I was definitely not his target audience, regardless of how shiny my hair was.

The three of us chatted a bit about how amazing the reception was, and then the band started playing a slow song.

"Hey, Mr. Ryan, how about that dance?" I said.

"Princess, but of course." He stood up and took my hand, then looked back and put his other hand on Tad's shoulder. "You'll wait for me here?"

"You bet," Tad said with a smile. I noticed that his eyelashes were longer than mine. Not fair.

Scotty and I walked hand in hand to the dance floor and blended in with the dozens of other couples savoring the jazz number. He put his arms around me, and we began to sway to the music.

I leaned my head against his shoulder. "Well?" I said.

"Well what?"

"Hello? Mr. Blondie at your table?"

"Thirty-nine, sports agent, no kids, doesn't like dogs. Jackpot!"

"Oh, man, I'm jealous, Scotty! I mean I'm happy for you and all, but you were sort of my pretend date tonight. Now who am I going to hang around with?"

He smoothed his hand over my hair. "Now, now, Waverly, don't put on the life preserver and jump ship just yet. Let's have a dance, and then you can work the room a bit, and if after that you still feel the need for some Scotty love, just let me know, okay?"

I smiled. "Okay, I will, I will. Thanks, Scotty. And tonight's about celebrating Cynthia and Dale anyway, right? I don't want to forget that."

He squeezed me tight. "That's the spirit, gorgeous, that's the spirit."

After our dance, Scotty put his arm around me and walked me halfway back to table 53 before heading off to the restroom. I had a hard time finding the table though, because I didn't recognize anyone anywhere. No Hank, no Christopher, no girl who won't date anyone who weighs less than she does. Then I finally realized that the reason I didn't recognize anyone was because table 53 was totally empty. The band had stepped it up a notch and was now playing '80s cover music, and my entire table was busting a move on the dance floor.

"That's just great," I said, putting my hands on my hips. "An awesome band playing '80s music, and I can't dance because I tripped over a freakin' tree branch!" I could barely hear my own voice over the band, so I figured that no one around me could either, and it was sort of fun to yell. "But it doesn't matter anyway, because even if I could dance, I don't have anyone to dance with, and the one guy here I want to be with is with someone else. This totally sucks!"

"Waverly, are you all right?" A familiar voice behind me made the hair on the back of my neck stand up.

"Oh, crap." I mouthed the words and made a squinty face. Then I slowly turned around, and there he was.

"Jake! Hi, how are you?" I tried to act casual.

"I'm good, thanks. I thought that was you. I didn't expect to see you here. Are you friends with Dale?"

I played with my earring. "Um, I work with Cynthia, or at least I did before she transferred to our New York office. Um, how do you know them?"

"Through work. Dale's represented several players on the Hawks over the years."

"Oh, small world," I said.

Awkward silence. I could only hope images of my vomit weren't flashing before his eyes.

"You look really nice, Waverly. I like your hair that way."

I felt the blood rush to my face and looked down at my cast. "Um, thanks."

His eyes followed mine. "Hey, what happened to your leg?"

"Oh, it's nothing really, just a broken ankle."

"How'd you break it?"

I cleared my throat and tried to smile. "Uh, have you ever noticed how hard it is to jog in a straight line when there's a huge tree branch in your path?"

"Oh, man, I'm sorry. That must have really hurt."

"It did, but I'll be fine." I wiggled my red toes peeking out of my cast. "I get this thing off in about three more weeks. Not the best accessory for a fancy wedding, but I guess it's better than bringing bad breath or an ugly date." *Bad breath or an ugly date? Did that really just come out of my mouth?*

"Um, yeah. So, how have you been?" he said.

I grabbed onto the chair next to me. "Good, good—just really busy with work and stuff. You know, the usual. We won the Adina

Energy account, you know. Didn't you say you did some work for them or something?"

He smiled. "Yes, I do. You have a good memory. So you won that account? That's great."

I didn't respond right away, but then I practically yelled at him.

"Yeah, but I'm not going to be managing it. I thought I was, but then they gave it to the one girl in my entire company I hate."

"Oh," he said. "That's too bad."

What the hell was wrong with me? First I go blabbing about my dad's money problems back at the Super Show, and now this? Why couldn't I keep my dirty laundry in the hamper around this guy?

"So, um, how are *you* doing?" I said. "Keeping busy with the team?"

He looked over my shoulder, probably at his date, I thought. "Actually, we're having a great season this year, so things are going pretty well for me. You know, when the team wins, we all win sort of thing." Then he scratched his right eyebrow. "Hey, did I see you at the game in Oakland last month when we played the Warriors?" He cocked his head to one side and smiled, and I tightened my grip on the chair.

"Um, a Warriors game? No, I don't think so."

His smile faded. "Really? I was sure I saw you there."

I turned my head to avoid his gaze and wondered if my nose would knock the drink out of his hand. "Oh, wait, yes, I did go to a Warriors game last month, got dragged there by some clients. You know how those boring work things can be."

He didn't reply, and I kept looking around to avoid making eye contact. Why was I being so standoffish?

"Oh," he finally said.

I knew it was only a matter of time before he headed back to his date, so I decided to pull the ripcord before he did.

I held out my hand and forced a big fake smile. "Well, Jake, it's been nice seeing you, but I'm sure your date is wondering where you are, so I'll let you get back to her. I hope you enjoy the reception."

"Um, yeah, it was nice seeing you, too, Waverly."

He shook my hand and held it for just a moment, then turned and walked away.

I slumped down in my chair, feeling more alone than ever.

I picked up my wine glass and looked at it. "Mr. Merlot, looks like you're the only friend I've got tonight." Then I turned around and watched Jake cross the room, sit down next to the brunette, and put his arm around the back of her chair. It was far away, but from what I could make out, she looked gorgeous and perfect.

"Crap," I whispered under my breath.

Suddenly I was struck with another Honey Note idea. I flipped over my place card and looked around for something to write with (my purse was, of course, too small to hold anything resembling a writing instrument). I spotted a pen on the empty table next to mine and reached for it.

Front: How do you know when you really like a guy?
Inside: Honey, when you can't think of one intelligent thing to say, you're in trouble.

I folded the card and slipped it into my purse, wondering if I'd be able to decipher my writing when I sobered up, and wondering if I should hit an AA meeting then, too. Then I stood up and wobbled over to the floor-to-ceiling window lining the far wall of the enormous room. I leaned in close to the glass and gazed outside at the snowy winter night. What a gorgeous view. I stepped back a few feet and noticed the reflection of the party behind me in the glass window, as if I was watching from outside. The dance floor, the bar, the guests, all mixing and mingling and having a blast. Seeing the spectator's view from the reverse made me feel like I was watching what could have been my own perfect wedding. What had Scotty been saying about images?

I turned and leaned my back against the window and listened to the band. I stood there for what seemed like hours but was probably just minutes, completely losing track of time. I closed my eyes for a few moments, then opened them and looked back at the crowd.

After a quick scan of the dance floor, I spotted my tablemates front and center. They must have done some group tequila shots in my absence, because they were on fire. Hank and Amanda were making out. Matt and Lisa were dirty dancing. Greg had his shirt off and was twirling it over his head as if he had just scored a goal in the World Cup. They were clearly the life of the party, and I desperately wished I was in the mood or physical condition to join them.

"Waverly, you doing okay?" A hand rested softly on my right shoulder.

I turned and saw Scotty standing there.

"Hi, Scotty." I smiled weakly.

"Hi, princess. How're you doing?"

"Okay, I guess."

"You sure about that?"

I blinked slowly. "Well, actually, not so great. This whole scene is making me think of my own non-wedding a bit too much."

"Do you want to talk about it?" he said.

I shook my head. "Thanks, but there's not that much to say."

"Did you see your crush?"

I nodded. "Unfortunately. We talked for a few minutes, but I ended up sounding cold and bitchy and basically scared him away. I wasn't myself at all, Scotty. What's wrong with me?"

"Sweetheart, there is absolutely nothing wrong with you. The only thing wrong here is that such a stunning woman is standing here alone in the corner when there are tons of men in this room who would kill to be with her."

"Scotty, please." I wiped a tear from my eye and tried to smile. "I appreciate the pep talk, but let's be realistic."

"Waverly, you need to wake up and smell the testosterone." He winked and put his arm around my shoulders.

I leaned my head against him. "Thanks, Scotty. You're a good friend. You're a liar, but you're a good friend."

"Miss Bryson, I am not lying. Now normally I would whisk you off onto the dance floor and dazzle you with my white man's over-bite, but given your injury, we must move to plan B. So how does a piece of wedding cake sound? I'll even order some extra chocolate sauce from the kitchen if you want. I know how much you love chocolate." He smoothed my hair with his hand and eased me gently back toward the crowd.

"Chocolate sauce? Did you say chocolate sauce? You certainly know the way to my heart, you kind man. Let me at it." I smiled and followed him back to his table.

. . .

When I rolled out of bed the next morning and opened the drapes, what I saw outside was, well, nothing. Everything was white, white, white, a blizzard unlike anything I'd ever seen. It was like the monster centerpiece from the wedding was stuck to the hotel window.

I turned on the TV and flipped through the channels until I found a local news station. Yep, a snowstorm had invaded the entire Northeast. And apparently all flights in and out of New York were grounded until further notice.

Crap. There went my plans for spending the day window-shopping before Cynthia's Super Bowl party.

I wondered how big the party was going to be and where it even was. I couldn't remember exactly what Cynthia had said about it, other than it was at a sports bar sort of near the hotel. I needed to look at the invitation in my suitcase.

Scotty definitely wasn't going. He was spending Sunday with his new buddy, Tad, who had graciously let me be the third wheel for the rest of the reception until I'd called it a night after two more pieces of wedding cake.

Well, at least I'd gotten a decent night's sleep. Good thing, because I needed to be well rested if I was going to spend the day cooped up in a hotel room, right?

I walked into the bathroom and washed my face. If the bad news was that I was snowed in, the good news was that my hair still looked fantastic. I decided not to wash it, tucking it under a shower cap as I turned on the hot water. Why not get one more day out of a great hairstyle?

After my shower, I pulled on a pair of dark brown low-rider corduroy pants that I'd bought the day before with Kristina. They had a wide cuff at the bottom, so they didn't present a challenge to my cast, whose toe opening I covered with a thick dark brown sock. On top I chose a thin cream-colored fitted angora sweater with tiny blue flowers embroidered around a scoop neck. I admired my outfit in the mirror and then laughed. One thing I hadn't bought on my shopping spree was a snowproof tent to protect me and my cast from the elements. Seriously, what was I supposed to do if I decided to leave the hotel? As the proud owner of an *It never snows in California* wardrobe, a wool coat and scarf were the best I could do.

Down in the lobby café, I curled up in a green overstuffed chair by the roaring fire and ordered a cappuccino and a chocolate croissant. I flipped through the stack of newspapers on a nearby table and pulled out the *New York Times*. I was reading a review of a new resort in Cabo San Lucas when the waiter set down my order in front of me. I looked up to thank him, and just then the elevator doors behind him opened.

Out walked Jake and the brunette.

I pulled the paper back up. "Oh, freakin' frick, you've got to be kidding me," I said right into the ink.

"Excuse me, miss?" The waiter looked confused.

"Oh, gosh, I'm sorry. I wasn't talking to you," I said.

"No problem at all, miss." He quickly disappeared, the epitome of fine hotel service.

I held up the newspaper in front of me and hoped Jake hadn't seen me. The same hotel? How many billions of hotels were there in Manhattan?

After a few minutes, I slowly lowered the newspaper to take a peek. He and the brunette were at the reception desk and appeared to be checking out. *Oh, please, let them be checking the HELL out of there.*

The waiter came back to see if I needed anything else. I glanced at the half-full cup on the table next to me, secretly thrilled that, under the circumstances, I hadn't glanced at the half-empty cup on the table next to me.

"Actually, another cappuccino would be great, thanks. And hey, do you know anything about the weather situation? I mean, are all the flights definitely grounded?" I found myself whispering even though Jake was about three miles away from me.

He nodded and smiled sympathetically. "Yes, miss, all the airports are closed. Many of our weekend guests have already made arrangements to stay another night. The reception desk can help you with that if you need assistance."

Yeah, like I wanted to go anywhere near that reception desk. "Thank you. I'll look into that after breakfast," I said.

I looked back over at Jake and didn't see any luggage. Damn it. Were they making plans to stay another night? Was I really trapped in the hotel with them?

I continued to spy like some sort of government agent from the Department of Totally Lame People. Jake turned around briefly, but I quickly pulled the newspaper up to cover my face. I didn't know if it was because of the way I'd acted the night before or the way I'd acted at the Super Show, but I just didn't want to see the third act.

After a few more minutes I peeked over the newspaper. Jake was gone.

Hmm, what to do? I couldn't hide behind the paper all day long. I looked at my watch. It was eleven, and the Super Bowl party didn't start until five thirty. I looked back down at my phone and thought about who I knew in New York besides Cynthia. Uh, that would be no one. So I decided to call Kristina.

"Hello?"

"Hey, Kristina, it's Waverly."

"Hey, you. How was the wedding?"

"Extravagant, to say the least. I think I gained five pounds on the appetizers alone. But my hair still looks great. Hey, by any chance are you free today?"

"What's up?"

"I'm snowed in and could use a playmate."

"Actually, I am. And that sounds great."

It turned out that she had the whole day off, so we decided to go to the movies to escape the snowstorm before heading over to the party. Somehow, she made it through the blizzard and picked me up in a cab, and we spent the afternoon eating popcorn, drinking Diet Coke, and watching a sappy romantic comedy that made us both cry at the end. How is it that romantic comedies are SO predictable yet still suck me in every time?

After the movie, we headed over to Blondie's Sports, an Upper West Side bar that Cynthia and Dale had rented out for the party. Despite my fear of running into Jake again, I was actually looking forward to it just so I could say hi to Cynthia, which I hadn't done at the wedding. With ten thousand guests, it's a little challenging to get any QT with the bride.

"All these people were at the wedding last night?" I said as we took off our coats. The place was packed.

"You tell me. You're the one who went," Kristina said.

"Then how come I couldn't pick any of them out of a lineup? I mean I know there were a lot of people there, but you'd think I'd recognize *someone*."

"You don't recognize anyone?"

"Not a one. Seriously, Kristina, sometimes I think the short-term memory part of my brain never fully developed, sort of like some other parts of me." I pointed to my chest.

She laughed and put her hand on my arm. "What do you want to drink? Let's try to grab a table."

The humiliation gods had mercy on me. In other words, Jake didn't go to the party. Or at least I didn't see him there, which was good enough for me. Kristina and I had a great time enjoying the food, the beer, the crowd, and the conversation. Oh, and I almost forgot the most important thing we enjoyed: the commercials!

After the game, I finally got a chance to say hello to Cynthia.

"Do you know how long I had to wait in line just to talk to you?"

I said as I gave her a hug. "You're like Reese Witherspoon at a movie premiere, and I'm some Podunk newspaper reporter trying to get an interview."

She brushed a few strands of strawberry blonde hair out of her eyes. "I know, I'm so sorry. It's been crazy with all these people here. Did you have fun at the wedding?"

"Yes, of course! It was perfect. And you were stunning. You're still glowing! Thank you so much for setting me up with everything. I had a great time."

She smiled and squeezed my hands. "I'm so glad to hear that. You know you could have brought a date, right?"

"Yes, and thanks, but really, there's no one I wanted to bring. And my table was a riot. Did you know that a paisley bedspread or an ill-timed pair of socks could kill a potential romance?"

"Huh?"

Just then Dale pulled her arm to introduce her to a friend of his, and I decided to slip away quietly. I could fill her in on all I'd learned about dating disqualifiers when she got back from her honeymoon.

Does absence make the heart grow fonder?

Honey, I know that abstinence sure does.

CHAPTER THIRTEEN

A couple weeks after the Super Bowl, my phone rang just as I was about to leave the office to get my cast off. The number on the display looked familiar, but I couldn't quite place it.

"Waverly Bryson," I said.

"Hi, Waverly."

I definitely had no trouble placing the voice, which somehow managed to kick me in the stomach through the phone line. Or at least that's how it felt when I heard it.

I quickly sat back down in my chair. "Aaron," I said softly.

"How are you?"

"I, I'm doing okay. How are you?"

"I'm good," he said.

"Good."

"I hear you broke your ankle. Are you okay?"

"Oh, yeah, I'm fine. I'm getting the cast off in about a half-hour, actually," I said. How did he know about my ankle?

"That's good to hear," he said.

"Thanks."

"Um, so listen, I was wondering if you and I could get together later for a drink? I'd like to talk to you about something," he said.

He wanted to talk to me about something?

What did he want to talk to me about? It couldn't be to apologize for not telling me about the wedding, right? Too much time had passed for that, and he'd already sort of apologized at the Marina Safeway, right?

Did he . . . did he miss me? Did he want to get back together? Had his marriage been a mistake?

This was quite unexpected.

"Waverly? Are you still there?" he said.

"Oh, yeah, sorry, I spaced out a bit. I'm still here."

"So are you free tonight?"

I was, but he didn't have to know that, right?

"Actually, I have plans tonight," I said. Plans to obsess over why he wanted to see me.

"Oh, okay, well how about tomorrow night?"

I bit my lip. *Tomorrow night. Tomorrow night.*

I just sat there, not saying anything.

"Waverly?"

I opened my mouth, but nothing came out.

"Waverly, are you still there?"

I bit my lip even harder.

"Okay, that should work," I finally said.

"Cool. Where is good for you?"

I put my hand over my eyes. "Um, how about the Kilkenny at seven thirty?"

"Great, I'll see you there. Bye, Waverly."

"Bye, Aaron."

I put down the phone and stared at it, already mentally trying on everything in my closet.

"Hey, Waverly? You got a sec?"

I looked up and saw Mandy standing in my office door.

"Um, sure, what's up?"

She smiled. "I just wanted to ask you a couple questions about how you run the JAG account. I thought it might help me get things rolling faster on Adina Energy. Do you mind?"

Did I mind? She wanted *me* to tell her how to do the job she stole from me? Was she crazy?

I stood up and pointed to my cast. "Actually, I've got to head to the doctor right now. Maybe some other time?"

She smiled even wider. "Okay, sure, some other time. Everything's already going great with my account team, but, well, you know, this is such a high-profile client that I just thought it might be nice to chat and get your perspective on things."

"Okay." I nodded and grabbed my purse. *We'll do that right after I send Brad Cantor an Evite to my Figure Skating on a Frozen Hell theme party.*

. . .

"So you really think he wants you back?" McKenna said on the phone later that night. "Even though he just got married?"

I lay down on my bed and looked up at the ceiling. "I know, I know, but maybe, don't you think? I mean, why else would he want to talk to me in person?"

"Do you *want* to get back together with him?" she said.

I closed my eyes. "I don't know."

"Do you still love him?"

I paused.

"I don't know. I mean, I did, but . . ." My voice trailed off.

"But what?"

"But I wonder if I really knew him, you know? I wonder if I even knew myself when we were together. I wonder if I even know myself now."

She laughed. "It sounds like you're finally starting to listen to me."

I sat up. "Seriously, Mackie, part of me thinks that I was just so happy that someone so perfect wanted me that I didn't really focus on what *I* wanted, you know? And that probably didn't make me all that stimulating to be around."

"Waverly, give yourself some credit. You're great to be around. And no one is perfect, not even Aaron."

"Thanks," I said. "But you know what I mean. And now I really wonder, you know? I think I was sort of a chameleon with Aaron, molding my life around what *he* wanted, not what *I* wanted."

"And what *do* you want?" she said.

I bit my lip. "I hope I know when I find it."

. . .

At seven forty the next night, I walked into the Kilkenny and held my breath. I looked around and saw Aaron sitting at the bar, waiting for me with a Newcastle in front of him. It was like I had gone back in time. Jack O'Reilly was probably checking the year on his calendar.

I walked up and tapped Aaron on the shoulder. "Hey, you," I said.

"Hey, you, too," he said, standing up and giving me a bear hug. "What can I get you to drink?"

I was surprised at how nervous I suddenly was. "Um, a Blue Moon with lemon is fine," I said.

"One Blue Moon with lemon for the lady here," Aaron said to Jack.

"Here you are, love," Jack said a few seconds later, raising his eyebrows as he set the drink in front of me.

"Don't ask," I whispered, as I picked up the glass and turned to follow Aaron.

We walked across the bar to a table in the back. "Well," I said as I took off my coat and sat down across from him. "Here we are."

"Here we are," he said. "You look great."

I smiled. "Thanks. I've been working out a ton."

"Really?"

I laughed. "Of course not. You look good, too." And damn it, he really did.

He pointed at my leg. "So, no more cast?"

"Cast-free as of yesterday," I said, raising both arms in the air.

"That's good to hear."

"Yeah it is, uh, thanks," I said, suddenly at a loss for conversation at the sight of the ring on his left hand.

"So, how are you? How's work?" he said.

I shrugged. "It's all right."

"You still hate it there, don't you?" he said.

I narrowed my eyes. "Hate it? Why do you say that?" I'd never told him I hated my job. I'd never told anyone that. Did I hate my job?

"Just a feeling I always had." He looked around the bar. "It's sort of strange, coming in here together again, don't you think?"

I nodded. "Habit, I guess. I probably should have suggested another place."

"No, it's fine. It's just a bit familiar and unfamiliar at the same time, you know?"

I knew. "Uh huh."

When was he going to get to the point?

I bit my lip and then the bullet. "So what's up? You said you wanted to talk to me about something?"

He took a sip of his beer. "Um, yeah, well I, uh, I know this is long overdue, but I just wanted to apologize for not calling you to tell you that I was getting married."

That was the big news?

I looked at the floor. "Oh, that's okay," I said.

He shook his head. "No, it's not. I should have told you. And running into you like that, and, well, seeing you again, well, it's just that, well, I have something else I need to tell you."

"You do?" I said, raising my eyes to meet his.

He nodded, then took my hands in his and squeezed them.

I closed my eyes.

Oh my God.

This was it. But how did *I* feel? What would I say? The thoughts in my head were like bumper cars.

I opened my eyes, but he didn't say anything.

I kept looking at him.

"Well?" I finally said.

He took a deep breath. "Stacy and I are having a baby."

Stacy and I are having a baby?

"What?" I let go of his hands.

He smiled. "I'm going to be a father."

"But you just got married!"

"I know, but this is something we both really want."

Something we both really want. We know and understand each other. We are perfect for each other. We also have lots and lots of sex.

"Why are you telling me this?" I said, suddenly feeling the tears that were about to make an inconvenient appearance.

"Because I didn't want you to hear it somewhere else this time."

"Oh, um . . . then . . . congratulations," I said softly, looking at the ground. I wasn't exactly happy for him, but he was obviously thrilled.

I looked back up at him. He was smiling, and the look in his eyes was something I'd never seen when he looked at me.

Ever.

The look in his eyes was . . . melty. Aaron's wife and new life made him feel . . . melty.

"Thanks," he said. "I know you might not believe it, but hearing that from you really means a lot to me."

We both stared at our drinks, him not wanting to shower me with more details, me not wanting to ask for them. He was clearly trying to do right by me. Why was he so nice? It made everything so grey. Another thing to add to my grown-up list: *You know you're a real grown-up when nothing but Oreos is black and white.*

After a long silence, he picked up his beer and took a sip. "So, um, how's your dad doing?"

I looked back at the floor. "He's okay, the same, I guess."

"He called me, you know."

I looked up at him. "What?"

"A couple weeks ago. That's how I heard about your ankle."

"He didn't ask you for money, did he?"

He shook his head. "He called me to see how you were doing."

My dad had called Aaron to ask him about me? But my dad didn't even like Aaron. My dad didn't even really like me.

I stood up and pushed my hair behind my ears. "Wait a minute.

You called me out of pity because my father thinks I'm a mess? Is that what this is about?"

He seemed startled. "No, no, I just thought you should know about the baby. That's all. It's not pity."

"Because I'm doing fine," I said. "Really, I'm fine." *Ha.*

"Waverly, I never thought that you weren't." He held my gaze when he said it. "Never."

"Really?" I said.

"Really."

"One hundred percent really or only ninety-nine percent really?" I said.

He laughed and was about to speak, but just then his phone rang.

And I knew who it was.

His hall pass was over. And so were we.

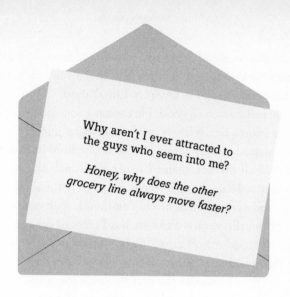

Why aren't I ever attracted to the guys who seem into me?

Honey, why does the other grocery line always move faster?

CHAPTER FOURTEEN

The very next day, fresh from a two-hour cry session on the phone with McKenna, I started working on my own baby. I finally sent sample Honey Notes to a handful of publishers, and I couldn't believe how good it felt to do it. The thought of seeing something I created all on my own come to life made me feel like, well, like a proud mother. A proud, mini-van-free, sleep-deprivation-free mother.

After I submitted them, I kept writing new cards, using our department meetings as solid doodle time and as a way to keep from listening to Mandy Edwards, who was clearly having a ball running the Adina Energy account, given her glowing status reports. She hadn't come back to me again to gloat or steal my ideas, so at least I didn't have to deal with her outside of the weekly meetings.

Fortunately (or unfortunately), the material for the cards kept on coming, doing little to change my opinion that when it came to dating, I was in a class all by myself and might not ever graduate.

One Thursday night, I met a cute boy at the Kilkenny. His name was Pierce, and at first I thought he was super sweet and totally normal. He was six foot one with light brown hair, blue eyes, and a great smile. He worked in investment banking, had gone to Princeton and then Stanford Business School, played rugby on the weekends, and had a sarcastic sense of humor. We didn't talk for very long, but when he asked for my phone number, I was more than happy to give it to him. Yahoo!

Our first date was all good. He took me to a quaint Italian restaurant in North Beach late on a Monday night, and over pasta and wine we shared stories about our jobs, our hobbies, our friends. We covered all the bases, and I made it through the entire night without any red flags flying through the air or without having to tell him about my engagement or my childhood. At first I wasn't sure if I was physically attracted to him, but I enjoyed his company, and when he dropped me off at midnight, he said goodbye with a soft kiss on the mouth that definitely piqued my interest. It had been so long since I'd had a kiss on the mouth, much less a kiss like that!

Get that press release ready, I was back in the game!

But then my team started to lose.

Fast.

The next morning I got to the office at eight thirty. I was a little sleep-deprived, but it was a good sleep deprivation—you know, the kind that doesn't bother you too much because you were up late on a date, not because you were up late watching TV by yourself.

I sat down at my desk and took a sip of coffee and a bite of my chocolate chip bagel. Then I logged onto my computer and saw an e-mail from Pierce in my in-box. The "sent" time was 5:02 a.m.

5:02 a.m.?

Then I remembered that he worked market hours, so his 5 a.m. was like another person's 8 a.m. I could only imagine how exhausted our late night must have left him. I clicked on the message to open it.

To: Waverly Bryson
From: Pierce Jansen
Subject: Lovely lady

Good morning, Waverly!

I just wanted to let you know that I had a fantastic time last night.

*I can't stop thinking about you, and I want to know when I can
see you again. It's been a long time since I've felt this much so fast.
I have a feeling this might be everything I've been waiting for and
more. I look forward to hearing from you.*

Love,
Pierce

I blinked slowly three times after reading the e-mail. Then I
read it again. Then I closed it without replying and looked ner-
vously around me, as if I had witnessed something I wasn't supposed to. *I have a feeling this might be everything I've been waiting
for and more?* After one date? Wasn't that more of a twenty-ninth
date sort of comment? Or maybe a marriage proposal sort of
comment?

I decided to postpone any response until I could discuss the situation with McKenna and Andie over lunch, which we'd scheduled
at a deli equidistant from our offices. I scrolled through my other
e-mails and saw one from a reporter at *Sports Illustrated* asking for
an interview with the president of JAG for a story she was writing
about the credibility of athletes who get paid to endorse products.
(I had always wondered the same thing; I mean, think about it!)
I picked up my phone to call Davey about it, and the stutter dial
tone alerted me to a new voicemail. I punched in my password and
listened. The message had been left at 8:25 a.m.:

"*Hi, Waverly, it's me, Pierce. I sent you an e-mail when I got to
work, but I wasn't sure if you got it, so I thought I'd call. Anyhow, I just
wanted to say hi and tell you how much fun I had last night. I really
want to see you again and was wondering if you're free tonight? It might
sound strange, but I can't stop thinking about you. Do you have any
idea how beautiful you are? Anyway, I really had a great time. Call me
please. Bye.*"

I sat back in my chair.

What the . . .?

Seriously, what the . . .? I knew I was just getting used to dating
again, but wasn't this a little bit over the top? I didn't know what to

do, so I closed the message and tried not to think about it. I had a lot of work to do that morning, so I just got on with my day.

After I called Davey, I met with Nicole and Kent in the conference room to review the status of our accounts. After that I spoke to several reporters to arrange interviews with clients, and then I worked on a launch plan for a new line of JAG tennis balls. Your basic PR grind.

Around ten thirty or so, I walked into the kitchen to get a fresh cup of coffee. To my delight, someone had left an unmistakable big pink box on the counter. I was in the mood for something sugary, so I grabbed an old-fashioned glazed donut, filled up my mug, and headed back to my office.

When I sat down at my desk, I saw a new e-mail message from Pierce in my in-box. It wasn't even lunchtime!

To: *Waverly Bryson*
From: *Pierce Jansen*
Subject: *Hello again!*

Hello Waverly!

I left you a voicemail a couple hours ago. Did you get it? I haven't heard back from you yet, so you must be having a busy day. Well, I just wanted to say hi and tell you that I had a great time last night and wanted to see if your free tonight. I hope so. Please call me.

Love,
Pierce
p.s. Looking forward to hearing from you!

Okay, this was getting ridiculous. And don't think I hadn't noticed that big fat *YOUR*. As I sat there with my mouth open, I saw that my phone had registered four missed calls, but I didn't have any voicemails. Then I noticed that all the calls were from the same number.

Could it be?

I pulled Pierce's card out of my desk drawer and compared it with the number on my caller ID log . . . bingo.

Holy restraining order. I had won the stalker lottery.

Just then the phone rang again. I looked at the number on the caller ID display.

Was he kidding me?

I looked at my watch. It was only ten forty-five. My lunch with McKenna and Andie couldn't arrive fast enough.

. . .

"You swear he seemed normal last night?" Andie said.

"And he was normal when you met him?" McKenna took a bite of her salad.

I nodded my head vigorously. "Yes! I swear! I had my crazy radar on high both times, and it didn't pick up anything. I used to be able to spot the red flags faster than this. Have I totally lost it?"

McKenna nodded and took a sip of her Sprite. "Could be, could be. You're definitely out of practice. Now let's review the situation. Did previous relationships enter into any of your conversations?"

I shook my head. "Nope. Not at all. But then again, that's one thing I always try to avoid when I first meet someone. I mean, who needs to hear about Aaron and his love child right away, right?" I said.

She took another sip of her Sprite and set it down on the table.

"Now normally I would agree with you," she said. "But in this case, a few strategically placed questions might have avoided this whole situation."

"Like what, *Are you a stalker?*" I sighed. "What a bummer. He seemed so promising. I can't believe he turned out to be that guy from *Swingers*."

"Yeah, sounds like a classic résumé boyfriend," Andie said.

I looked at her. "Huh?"

"Perfect on paper, but a total bust in person," she said.

"Ah," I said. "Exactly."

"From everything you told us, he seemed great," McKenna said.

I nodded. "He did to me, too."

"So I guess it's onto the next one?" Andie said.

I sighed. "What do I do now?"

"To avoid bad dating karma, you need to be honest with him," McKenna said. "Just be firm and let him know you're not interested."

I nodded. "Okay, I think I can do that."

Andie put her hand over mine. "But don't be a bitch about it, okay? You know you have that unintentional bitchy thing going on sometimes," she said.

I nodded. "I know, but I swear I'm working on that." I sipped my iced tea and smiled weakly.

"Pull that Band-Aid off, but with tact," McKenna said.

"Couldn't I just not e-mail him back and not return his calls? Isn't that what everyone else does?" I said.

"That's what I do," Andie said.

"You're not helping here," McKenna said to her, then looked at me. "Wave, sometimes it sucks being nice, but you are nice. Now get to it and cut that cord."

"Do I have to?"

They both nodded.

I looked at Andie. "Would you?"

She laughed. "I'm not as nice as you."

I made a face. "Ugh."

Late that afternoon, after I was sure he'd be gone for the day, I replied to Pierce's e-mail saying I was busy that night. I tried to sound uninterested, but apparently I wasn't firm enough. The next three days he e-mailed me at 4:59 a.m., 5:01 a.m., and 5:03 a.m., all asking me out for that weekend. He literally must have walked into his office and e-mailed me before even turning on the lights, either that or from his BlackBerry even *before* he got to the office. Did he have zero friends to stop him?

I deleted each e-mail without replying. He also called several times a day, but thanks to my trusty caller ID, I never picked up.

The following Monday, I walked into yet another e-mail, this one sent at 5:02 a.m. This time I finally responded to it.

To: Pierce Jansen
From: Waverly Bryson
Subject: Re: Nice weekend?

Hi Pierce,

Thanks for your calls and e-mails. I'm sorry to have taken so long to get back to you, but the truth is that I've recently been talking to my ex-boyfriend, and over the weekend we decided to get back together. I'm sorry. You're a great guy, but it's just a timing thing.

Good luck,
Waverly

I could only hope he didn't know my ex-boyfriend, because I was pretty sure we weren't getting back together.

I never heard from stalker Pierce again, but the Honey Note fodder kept on coming. A week or so later, my old roommate Whitney called. She wanted to set me up with a guy her husband, Bryan, worked with. His name was Ben, and he was an accountant at Bryan's law firm.

"An accountant?" I said, sighing into the phone. "I don't want to stereotype, but an accountant?"

"I swear, Waverly, he's a nice guy. And he's cute. And he definitely meets your height requirement."

"But is he boring?"

"No, he's not boring. Trust me. He's a nice guy, and he's our age, and he's single."

"He's not blond is he?" Ever since I'd been covered in slobber by Barry Winters at the eighth grade holiday dance, the thought of locking lips with a blond had triggered my gag reflex.

She sighed. "Seriously, Waverly, stop being so picky. When was the last time you even got some action?"

I cracked up. "Getting action" was classic Whitney. She used to say that all the time when we lived together.

"Okay, okay, have him call me," I said.

Ben called a day or so later, and we made plans to have a drink the following Tuesday after work. It seemed harmless enough, so I was going with it.

The day of the date, there was a voicemail from Ben waiting for me when I got back to my desk after lunch:

"Hi, Waverly, it's Ben Herman here. I hate to do this, but I'm going to have to cancel our drink tonight. I'm feeling a bit yucky, so I'm heading home early. I'll call you tomorrow to reschedule. I'm really sorry, but I just feel too icky to go out."

I saved the message.

Yucky and *icky?* Had he just said *yucky* and *icky?*

I replayed the message again. Yes, he had said them both.

I'm sorry, but there was no way I was going on a blind date with a grown CHILDLESS man with the words *yucky* and *icky* in his daily vocabulary.

I deleted the message and the one he left the next day, too. Whitney was pissed at me for weeks, but whatever. They were getting lower every day, but I still had some standards.

. . .

A couple weeks later, I met a guy named Eric. The scene of the crime was Mollie Stone's, the supermarket around the corner from my apartment. I went in there one Monday night after yoga for a salad. Mollie Stone's has a fantastic salad bar that is ridiculously overpriced, but I ended up making my dinner there at least three times a week. It was just too easy, too close, and too tasty.

I was trying not to crush the hard-boiled eggs with the tongs when Eric struck up a conversation. I was wearing a tattered Cal Berkeley tank top and black yoga pants, with a sweatshirt wrapped around my waist and my hair pulled up into a sweaty, messy bun. So it was obvious that I'd been involved in some sort of exercise, either that or I was just gross. Anyhow, he asked me what sport I had been doing, and we started chatting. When I finished making my salad, he asked me if he could call me some time, so I said sure and gave him my cell phone number. After stalker Pierce, I'd

decided that I couldn't deal with anymore personal calls at work. I
was all about the cell phone now.

Physically, Eric wasn't my type, but he seemed friendly and
funny, so I figured why not? His thinning hair was pretty light,
and at five foot eleven he didn't meet my height requirement, but I
had decided to get over myself and stop being so picky. What was
my problem anyway? Like I was some beauty queen? Please.

Eric called a couple days later and asked me to dinner. We made
plans to meet at Godzila Sushi (spelled with one *l*, though I have
no idea why), a popular spot on Divisadero Street about ten blocks
from my apartment. The night of the date, I left my place wearing
a pair of jeans, a white tank top, and a black shawl. I'd straight-
ened my hair and pinned a few strands to one side with a tiny clip.
As I walked toward the restaurant, I suddenly realized that it was
March 12, which meant that the next day was March 13.

I stopped in my tracks.

March 13 was the day Aaron and I had gotten engaged.

Back then we'd laughed about how our marriage was doomed
because we'd gotten engaged on Friday the thirteenth. Apparently,
we had been right.

I looked up into the starry sky and closed my eyes, then told
myself to snap out of it and kept walking toward the restaurant. *Baby
steps, baby steps.* I continued down California, and when I turned
left onto Divisadero, I saw the Godzila Sushi sign a couple blocks
away. There was a handful of people milling about outside, and I
wondered how long we'd have to wait for a table. Godzila Sushi was
always packed and annoyingly loud. And it didn't take reservations.
Did that make it a good place for a first date? I wasn't so sure, and I
wondered why Eric had picked it. On the one hand, the noise and
informality took away the pressure to be romantic, but on the other
hand, it was sort of awkward to manage small talk in a loud room.

When I walked up to the restaurant, I didn't see Eric anywhere
in the sidewalk crowd, so I poked my head inside to take a look.

"Waverly, over here!"

I turned my head to the left and saw him waving to me from the bar near the back. I made my way through the crowd and walked up to greet him. He stood up and gave me a tight bear hug, so tight that it was sort of hard to breathe. I broke away from him to smile and say hello, and when I took a step back I noticed that, I swear to God, he was wearing a yellow tank top tucked into a pair of black jorts.

"Hi, Eric." I swallowed and tried to mask the look of panic that was surely plastered all over my face. Was he kidding me?

He smiled. "I put our name down for a table. It should be just a few more minutes. By the way, you look hot."

"Oh, thanks," I said, focusing more on his outfit than his compliment.

Then I noticed that he had a large bottle of beer in front of him, the liter kind that you would normally share with someone else. I also noticed that it was nearly empty.

"Have you been here long?" I said.

"Nah, not long. About thirty minutes."

Thirty minutes? I looked at my watch. "Oh gosh, I'm sorry. I thought we'd agreed to meet at eight o'clock. Am I late?"

"No, you're not late at all. I just thought I'd come early and have a brew. Do you want something?"

"Um, okay. A light beer would be nice, thanks." Hello? Weird vibes everywhere.

He poured what was left of his huge Sapporo into his glass and ordered another. The bartender also brought out a Bud Light and a cold glass for me.

Eric poured me a beer and held his up for a toast. "Here's to the salad bar and cute girls in yoga pants." He smiled and patted my thigh.

I lifted my glass and fake smiled back. This was going to be brutal.

Just then I felt a light tap on my shoulder. "Hi, Waverly."

I looked to my right and saw Mandy Edwards standing there.

Mandy Edwards, witnessing me on a date with a guy wearing a tank top and jorts. Black jorts, no less, perhaps the only sartorial offense more tragic than regular jorts.

She was with a tall, brown-haired, very cute guy who looked

vaguely familiar. I stood up and gave them an awkward smile. "Hi, Mandy. How are you doing?" Then I turned to Eric. "Um, Eric, this is Mandy. We work together."

Mandy held out her hand. "Hi, Eric, it's nice to meet you. This is my fiancé, Darren."

Fiancé? Who would marry Mandy Edwards?

I looked at the guy next to her and momentarily stopped breathing.

Holy crap.

It was Right Darren, the cute Darren who had taken my card a few months before but had never called me while Wrong Darren had. I glanced at the huge rock on Mandy's finger. At least now I knew why he hadn't picked up the phone.

Darren shook Eric's hand and then mine. "You look familiar," he said. "Have we met?"

I took a sip of my beer and shook my head. "Uh, no, I don't think so." Then I looked back at Mandy. "When did you get engaged?"

"A few days ago, when we were wine-tasting up in Napa. We just got back today." She smiled wide.

"Wow, congratulations," I said.

"Thanks," she said. "I can't wait to start planning the wedding."

Darren kept looking at me. "Are you sure we haven't met? I could swear we have."

Before I could say anything, Mandy grabbed his elbow. "Well, we've got to get going. Nice to meet you, Eric. Bye, Waverly."

They drifted off into the crowd, and I followed her with my eyes. She was marrying cute Darren? Wow. Then I looked over at Eric, ripped from a NASCAR poster, and could only wonder what Mandy was thinking. Had she noticed his outfit? Or was I just a superficial bitch? No—who was I kidding? She had noticed. Any normal person would have noticed. But yes, I was also a superficial bitch.

I turned back to Eric. "So, uh, you were saying that you got here a bit early?"

"Yeah, man, this place rocks for people-watching. Lots of hot chicks come in here on Thursday nights."

"Uh, okay."

After that promising start, things only got better. It turned out that Eric was an exercise freak, and since we'd met on one of my rare exercise days and because I worked in sports PR, he assumed that I was one too. And fitness was ALL he wanted to talk about.

"Which gym do you go to? I belong to Gold's."

"How often do you work out? Do you like spinning?"

"What's your exercise routine? I like to mix it up a bit, ya know, keep it interesting."

"Have you ever done a triathlon? I'm doing Escape from Alcatraz in June."

And on . . .

And on . . .

And on.

We hit the iceberg as the waiter brought us a plate of California rolls.

"What equipment do you use?" he said.

Equipment? Like I ever went anywhere near the equipment.

I dipped a roll in soy sauce and wondered if his butt was smaller than mine. "Um, once I used a machine for hamstrings, but I'm not sure what it was called. And my legs totally hurt the next day, so that was the end of that."

We were sinking fast.

"I work out six days a week," he said. "It's my passion."

"Six days? Wow. That is a lot of days," I said.

"Yep, six days a week, rain or shine."

"Cool," I said.

And then we slammed against the ocean floor.

"Here, feel my muscles." He leaned toward me and flexed his bare bicep, right there in the middle of Godzila Sushi.

I winced and looked around. I'm not a religious person, but at that moment I was praying to God that no one was watching, especially Mandy. I lightly touched his upper arm with my index finger and pulled it away as if I had just touched a rattlesnake.

"Yes, uh, that's quite a muscle," I said. SOS . . . SOS . . .

When Eric walked me home later that night, he gave me another bear hug and then went in for the kiss. I dodged it and gave him the cheek.

"Can I call you?" he said.

"Uh, sure."

He called me two days later to ask me if I wanted to go for a run, but I lied and told him I had to go out of town for three weeks for work.

After an awkward silence, I lied again and told him I would get in touch when I got back. It was more dating karma out the window, but another date with him and I would have thrown myself out the window.

· · ·

A couple weeks later I met a guy I actually *liked*. And I couldn't believe it, because he liked me back! His name was Reid, and he worked at my bank. The only time I actually went inside the bank was when I needed a roll of quarters for the laundry, and that was to the teller's window, so I never noticed all those other people who worked at the desks in there. Another thing to add to my grown-up list: *You know you're a real grown-up when you have a meeting with one of those desk people inside a bank.*

I went in there one Saturday morning to get some quarters, and on my way out I noticed Reid leaning on the edge of one of the desks. He was talking to an older woman, like 90 years old older woman, and he had such a nice smile that I just sort of stopped walking and started standing there, right in the middle of the room, watching him smile at this tiny old lady.

After about ten seconds, he looked over and flat-out busted me.

"Do you need help?" he said.

"Um, no, just getting quarters for the laundry," I said, clearing my throat.

"Well, do you need some help folding?" he said with a smile.

"Ahh," said the little old lady.

For about two weeks I saw him a lot. It was so fun! He was

charming, funny, handsome, tall, and smart. He even smelled good. And he was fascinated by my job. *"You got paid to hang out with Shane Kennedy?"* he said over and over. *"Do you know how many guys I know who would pay to hang out with Shane Kennedy?"*

It was like there was nothing wrong with him.

The problem was that I wasn't the only one who thought so.

One Saturday night we went to a big charity party in the Marina, and in an unfortunate demonstration of the dateable male-female ratio in that area of San Francisco, at one point I reached for his hand, and he didn't take mine in return. I gave him a confused look, but he still didn't take my hand.

An epic Waverly moment followed.

First I looked up at him and smiled. "Hey, you, don't you want to hold my hand?" I said playfully.

He shook his head.

I smiled again and tilted my head. "Really?"

He shook his head again.

Then I sort of stopped smiling and said, "Why not?"

No response.

Then, like one of those lab mice that repeatedly shock themselves, I tried for the cheese one more time.

"Reid, will you please just tell me why you won't hold my hand?" I said.

He finally looked at me and said, "Because I'm dating three other women at this party."

"Oh," I said.

It should come as no surprise that I never heard from him again.

But I'm sure I'll run into him at the Marina Safeway someday.

. . .

So I was out there looking, but Waverly moments and Honey Notes were all I was really finding.

Front: Know what I want to know?
Inside: Honey, what are guys who wear tank tops THINKING?

Front: Is his butt smaller than yours?

Inside: Honey, run for the hills, and run fast. It's not worth the humiliation, and yours is only gonna get bigger.

Front: Want to keep yourself from going too far on the first date?

Inside: Honey, don't shave your legs. And if you need extra insurance, wear your oldest granny panties.

Front: How long should you wait before sleeping with a guy you've just started dating?

Inside: Honey, if he's hot, why are you wasting your time asking me?

Front: Been on some bad dates lately?

Inside: Honey, at least you're out and about, right? That's better than cleaning your oven, which you know you never use anyway.

Front: Found out a guy you really like is seeing other people?

Inside: Honey, let's see how he looks in about ten years. There's an inverse correlation between success as a player when they're young and success in the battle of the bulge when they're not.

Have a tendency to put your foot in your mouth?

Honey, at least that's less fattening than putting foot-long chili dogs in your mouth.

CHAPTER FIFTEEN

On occasion, May in San Francisco can do a fantastic imitation of October, and that year, April did a fantastic imitation of May's imitating October. The days were unusually warm and balmy, the daylight reaching further and further into each evening. (But don't get me wrong. It was still as freezing as a popsicle at night.)

One Wednesday morning, Scotty Ryan called me out of the blue.

I smiled into the phone. "Hey, Scotty, what a nice surprise. How are you?"

"I'm good, beautiful. Can't complain at all."

"What have you been up to since Cynthia and Dale's wedding? Are you still seeing that Tad guy?" I said.

"Actually, I am. Can you believe it? Three months and counting. I may be going soft in my old age, but I think I'm in love," he said.

I tossed my squishy stress ball in the air. "*Now* I've heard everything. So to what do I owe the pleasure of this call, Mr. Ryan?"

"Actually, I thought I might steal you for a few hours at lunchtime today."

"Today? You're in town?"

"I am indeed. I'm interviewing Bono before the U2 concert down in San Jose tonight, so since I'm here I thought I'd catch the Giants game today and hoped my favorite PR lady might want to join me. I've got two tickets to a friend of a friend's luxury box."

I sat up straight in my chair. "Wait a minute. You're interviewing Bono, and U2 is my favorite band OF ALL TIME, and you're inviting me to the *Giants* game? The Giants, who finished in last place last year, I might add?"

He laughed. "I know, I'm a horrible friend. But as usual, the producers decided on this assignment at the last minute, so I can't get any extra tickets to the concert. I'm so sorry, love. I'll make it up to you some other way, okay? I promise."

"You'd better, Scotty Ryan, you'd better."

"I will, I promise. Now what time do you want me to pick you up? The baseball game starts at one fifteen. Can you ditch work for a few hours?"

I smiled again. "Hey, if I'm spending quality time with a big-shot reporter from the *Today* show, it's not skipping work, it's professional development. Have I taught you nothing about PR?"

"Ah, of course," he said. "So does twelve thirty sound good?"

"Sounds perfect. See you then."

I hung up the phone and saw Mandy Edwards standing in my office door.

"Hey, Waverly, did you just say you're going to the Giants game with a reporter from the *Today* show?"

I nodded. Busted.

She smiled. "That's so cool. Do you think he might be interested in hearing about Adina Energy's new line of energy bars? They taste really good, you know."

"Uh, probably not. He covered that trend last year."

Her smile didn't move. "Oh, okay, just thought I'd ask. Because Adina Energy has such a high-profile brand name, we're targeting high-profile press with our campaign, you know, so I just figured the *Today* show might be interested too. So you're going to watch a baseball game in the middle of the day?"

I nodded again. "Yep, is there something else you needed? I'm really sort of busy here."

"No thanks, just stopped by to say hello. I'm really busy with this launch, you know." *Because it's so high-profile, you know.*

"So I've heard," I said.

She turned to leave. "Well, have fun at the game," she said a little too loudly as she walked away.

"Thanks, Mandy, I will," I said to the pencil in my hand, which I wanted to snap in half.

As soon as she was gone, I immediately went to ask Jess if it was okay to go to the game before Mandy got to him. Thank God he said yes. Thank God for our clients who were desperate to get their products in front of the millions of people who watch the *Today* show.

Three hours later, Scotty and I were in a half-empty luxury box at AT&T Park, watching the Giants get killed by the Padres. But we didn't really care about the game, because there was an open bar!

"So it's the real deal with this guy Tad?" I said, as he handed me a beer and a plate of the ballpark's famous garlic fries.

"It may be, my dear, he may be. But time will tell. The distance thing is forcing us to take things slowly."

"He lives in New York, right? Do you think you'll move there?" I picked up a handful of fries. "Wouldn't it be easier for your job anyway if you were in New York?"

He took a sip of his drink and nodded. "I've thought about it, and it would certainly be more exciting than Dallas, but we'll see. What about you—how's your love life these days?"

"Hey, did that guy just get a hit?" I leaned forward in my seat and pointed down at the field.

He looked over at me and laughed. "Are you avoiding my question?"

"What question?" I grabbed some more fries and stuffed them in my mouth.

"Waverly?"

I stood up and smoothed my skirt. "Hey, I'm going to run to the

restroom. Do you need another drink from the free bar? It's on me."
I pointed to the small bar by the door.

He shook his head and smiled. "Okay, okay, I won't ask anymore questions. But I will have another beer when you get back."
He handed me a ten-dollar bill. "And why don't you grab another
plate of garlic fries from the snack bar since you just inhaled most
of these."

I took the money and blew him a garlic kiss. "Okay, dearie, I'm
on it. I'll be right back." I walked out of the luxury box and headed
down the pristine corridor toward the restroom and the non-
crowded snack bar. Being a VIP at the ballpark was an entirely different experience from going as a regular spectator. In many ways
it was like the first class versus coach scenario on an airplane: free
drinks, no crowds or restroom lines, and my snob attitude that
appeared out of nowhere.

Five minutes later, I was walking back from the snack bar holding a huge tray of garlic fries. The smell was a little overwhelming,
and I could only wonder how lethal my breath must be after eating
so many of them. But man, were they yummy. I picked up three
more and stuffed them into my mouth. Thank God I was only with
Scotty, who had just kissed me on his way to the restroom and pretended to faint from the smell. I mean, could you imagine being on
a real date and scarfing down a huge pile of garlic fries and then—

I stopped in my tracks.

Standing ten feet in front of me was Jake McIntyre.

Jake McIntyre and those gorgeous blue eyes.

It'd been months since I'd run into him at Cynthia's wedding,
but seeing him still made my legs feel all wobbly. I wanted to say
hello, but for some reason I wasn't able to get those stupid legs to
listen to me. So I just kept on walking.

"Waverly?"

My stupid legs kept moving.

"Waverly?"

Finally my brain regained control of my nervous system.

I turned to face him. "Oh, hi, Jake. I, uh, I didn't see you."

He smiled and walked toward me. "What are you doing here?"

"Uh, just watching the game." I tried to swallow the fries I was still chewing as fast as I could, but the smell of them was engulfing my body.

"Who are you here with?" he said.

I smiled and immediately forgot every guy I'd been on a date with all year. "Shouldn't I be the one asking you that question since I'm the one who lives here?"

He pointed at the door to the luxury box right next to me. "Oh no, I'm sorry, I mean who are you with at this event?" On the door was a sign that said BA ROCKS VIP ROOM.

I shook my head. "I'm not here for any event. I just came this way to get some snacks."

"Oh, sorry, I just assumed because of the PR thing . . . well anyway, how are you?"

I was afraid to speak too loudly because the last thing I wanted was more garlic heading in his direction. "I'm good, good, thanks. What are you doing here?"

"Just a guest of a friend of mine who's sponsored by BA Rocks."

"Oh, cool, that sounds fun," I said. "Uh, so how are you?"

"I'm good, thanks. Well I guess not that good. We just got swept in the first round of the playoffs, so my summer vacation came a little early this year."

"Oh, I'm sorry to hear that. What do you do in the off-season anyway?" I was determined to be nice to him this time, regardless of how nervous I was. I smiled and felt the sweat beading up on my forehead. Garlic-scented sweat. Nice.

He pointed to the door again. "A couple boondoggles like this, and then I'm going to visit my parents in Florida, then spend a couple months working at basketball camps for underprivileged kids in Atlanta."

"Gotta love the boondoggle," I said. "Personally I'm a big fan. And those camps sound cool, too." God, he was pretty. Those eyes . . . *Keep it together. . . . Keep it together.*

He laughed. "Yeah, it'll be a fun summer. But first I think I'm going to spend a few weeks in South America. I've always wanted to go to Brazil and Argentina."

Alone? Was he going alone?

I was dying to ask him.

Should I ask him?

Maybe I could ask him.

What could it hurt to ask him?

Suddenly I realized that a lot of time had passed, and I still hadn't said a word.

Say something, Waverly!

"I went to Brazil and Argentina a few years ago," I blurted out. "It's a total party down there. I've never kissed so many boys in my life."

OH MY GOD.

He laughed. "What?"

My cheeks were more on fire than my breath. "Uh, have you ever noticed how much the Giants suck?" I whispered.

Just then a man in a suit walked up to Jake and put his hand on his arm. "Mr. McIntyre, there's a phone call for you inside."

Jake looked at the man and then back at me.

I raised my eyebrows. "*Mr. McIntyre?* Are you more important than I think you are?"

He smiled. "They're just being polite. Well, I guess I'd better go. It was nice to see you, Waverly."

I saluted. "You too, *Mr. McIntyre.* Bye."

He turned and walked into the suite with the man. The door closed behind them, and I just stood there.

I've never kissed so many boys in my life?

I was the stupidest person alive.

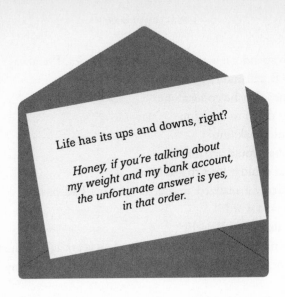

Life has its ups and downs, right?

Honey, if you're talking about my weight and my bank account, the unfortunate answer is yes, in that order.

CHAPTER SIXTEEN

A couple weeks later, I came home from work early. My throat and head were killing me, and I just wanted to lie down. I walked into the building and grabbed my mail, then unlocked the apartment door and headed straight for my bed. I flipped through the stack as I walked and saw three envelopes from publishing houses. Three very thin envelopes.

"Great," I said. I sat down on my bed and read one rejection after another. Ugh. Who knew it was harder to get into the greeting card business than it was to get into Harvard? I was trying to keep my hopes up, but the growing stack of rejection letters on my desk was hard to ignore. They all sounded more or less the same:

Dear Ms. Bryson: Thank you for your submission to (insert company name here). While we think your idea is (insert lukewarm adjective here), we don't think it is an appropriate fit for us at this time. Good luck, and thank you for thinking of (insert company name here).

Was there some sort of rejection letter template in Microsoft Word?

I lay back on my bed and shut my eyes. This truly was worse than applying to college. At least when you applied to college you knew that someone, somewhere, would let you in because they needed your money.

I kept my eyes closed, and before I knew it I was asleep. An hour later I was startled awake by the ring of my cell phone. Half asleep, I sat up, and for a second I didn't know where I was. I shook my head and tried to snap out of my groggy haze.

"Hello?"

"Hey, kiddo."

I cursed myself for not looking at the caller ID.

I lay back on the bed. "Hi, Dad."

"Did I wake you?"

"Oh no, not at all." I tried to play it off, but it was obvious that I'd been totally asleep. Why doesn't anyone ever just admit that?

"How are you doing?" he said.

"I'm okay, came home from work a little early today because I wasn't feeling well."

"Still burning the candle at both ends, huh? You never could slow yourself down."

"I guess so," I said. "So what's going on with you?"

"Well, I have some good news," he said.

Good news? From my dad?

"Really?" I said. "What is it?"

"I've got myself a new job."

"Really? That's great, Dad. Where?"

"Here," he said.

"Here?"

"No, here, not there," he said.

"What?" I said.

"Here, as in at home. I'll be working from home."

"Doing what?"

"I'll be selling vitamins," he said.

"Vitamins?"

"It's a great opportunity. If I work hard enough, I should be able to make a couple thousand a week."

"Vitamins? At home?"

"Yep, I went to a seminar and learned all I need to know. Now I just need to buy the vitamins, and I'll be able to get started."

I closed my eyes and sighed. "You have to buy the vitamins first?"

"Yes, they want to make sure you're committed to the process, so they have you buy them upfront. Then it's all profit after that."

"C'mon, Dad," I said.

"C'mon, Dad, what?"

"Dad, that's a scam. They're dumping that product on you, so all the risk is on you, not them. Don't you see that?"

"Waverly, can't you for once support me on something? This is a good investment opportunity for your old man."

I bit my lip and took a deep breath. "No."

"No?" he said.

"Dad, I can't watch you dig your own grave again. I just can't. If you want to get a job, I'm all for it. But selling vitamins out of your house doesn't sound like the best choice."

"You'll see," he said. "I'm really going to make something of this."

Here we go again, I thought. "Dad, I'm not having this conversation with you again. I love you, but I'm hanging up now."

"But—"

"Goodbye, Dad." I slowly shut my phone, put it down on the bed, and followed with my head on the pillow.

The next thing I knew my phone was ringing again. This time I looked at the caller ID display, but I didn't recognize the number.

"Hello?"

"Hello, is this Waverly Bryson?"

"Yes?" I didn't recognize the voice either.

"Hi, Waverly. My name is Becca Bentley, and I work for Smithers Publishing here in San Francisco."

Smithers *Publishing?* My heart stopped. I didn't remember sending them anything, but my heart stopped anyway.

"Hi," I said.

"We received the samples of your Honey Notes that you sent to Kara Barnett in our art department."

"Oh," I said. Kara Barnett? As in Andie's cousin? Go Andie!

"And I'm calling to see if you can come in next week to talk about them."

I tried not to fall off the bed. "Next week? Sure, I can do that."

"Great. Hold the line so my assistant can schedule an appointment. I look forward to meeting you, Waverly."

"Um, you too. Thanks for calling . . . um . . . thanks for calling." Oops, I had already forgotten her name.

Three minutes later I had a meeting on the calendar of Smithers Publishing.

I hung up the phone and sat there on my bed.

Holy crap.

. . .

That Sunday, McKenna and I went for one of our walks. We had a lot to talk about, so we decided to enjoy the sun and just do it. We met on our usual corner around two o'clock and headed down toward the water. Since we weren't pressed for time, we planned to walk all the way over the Golden Gate Bridge and back. However, we also brought a small backpack with a change of clothes in case we decided to bail out early and have a drink in the sun.

And that's exactly what we did.

Twenty minutes later, we were lounging in expensive teak lawn chairs on the deck of the ritzy St. Francis Yacht Club, right on the water of the Marina Green and facing the Golden Gate Bridge. And all for club members only. I loved that McKenna worked in investment banking.

I took a sip of my iced tea and pushed my sunglasses on top of my head. "Okay, let's get down to business and do a checklist. We've got the date, we've got your dress, we've got the place, we've got the band, we've got the caterer, we've got the maid of honor—who, by the way, is doing a kick-ass job, I must say—and we've got the guest list. Am I missing anything?"

She grabbed a nacho and chomped. "We still need to figure out the invitations, flowers, wedding cake, and dresses for you and Andie. Oops, I forgot about the rehearsal dinner. We need to find a place for that."

"No worries. We've planned tons of restaurant parties at K.A. Marketing and have contacts all over the city, so it won't be hard at all to find the perfect spot. Leave it to me. Just promise me that you won't move to the suburbs after the honeymoon, okay? Hey, what about the honeymoon anyway? Where are you going?"

She leaned back in her chair. "Hunter is in charge of that, and he won't tell me anything. He said I won't know where we're going until we're at the airport."

"Oooh, how romantic. I didn't know he had it in him. Actually, what am I saying? Anyone who spells out MARRY ME MCKENNA on a Scrabble board wins huge points in the romance category. But you hinted enough to make sure he takes you to a beach, right?"

She sipped her Diet Coke. "I did more than hint. I told him I'm only packing tropical clothes."

I leaned back in my chair and closed my eyes. "Why anyone would want to do anything but lie on a beach and drink piña coladas after the stress of planning a wedding is beyond me. Sightseeing? Museums? Honey, are you kidding me?"

"Hey, speaking of honey, are you all ready for your big meeting at Smithers?" she said.

I opened my eyes and sat back up. "It's all I can think about. Well, besides planning your wedding, of course. It's probably nothing, but still, nothing is something, right?"

"Nothing is definitely something. I'm proud of you, Bryson."

I grinned. "Thanks."

"My fingers are crossed for you," she said. "And I expect a very expensive wedding present if you strike it rich."

"I'll try to remember that. Maybe I'll even make a Honey Note for you."

"Really? What would it be?"

"Let me think." I took a sip of my drink and closed my eyes.

"I'm waiting . . ."

"Shhh. I'm concentrating."

"Still waiting . . ."

"Shhh . . . don't disturb the artist."

"I'm falling asleep here . . ."

"Shhh," I said. "I'm not good under pressure."

"I've got one for you," she said.

I opened my eyes and looked at her. "You do?"

"Yep."

"Well?"

"The front of the card says: *Happy that your best friend's getting married but afraid of losing her?*"

I swallowed. God, she knew me well.

"And when you open it, it says: *Honey, don't worry. She's not going anywhere.*"

"Really?" I said, a lump forming in my throat.

"Really." She leaned over and gave me a hug. "I need my Waverly."

. . .

Walking by myself back up Fillmore a couple hours later, I nearly strolled right in front of a car as I crossed against the light at Union Street. Oops. The honking horn snapped me out of my daydream, and I hurried across the street to safety and away from the angry glare of the driver. When I got to the sidewalk, I looked back down the hill toward the yacht club and smiled. McKenna was getting married. I was meeting with a real publishing company. It was nearly sixty-five degrees outside. Life was definitely looking up.

Speaking of looking up, I turned around and did just that, contemplating the steep trek ahead of me to Pacific Heights.

And then I saw him. Or them.

Aaron and his pregnant wife were walking down Fillmore Street, right toward me.

I froze. It was like I was in the Marina Safeway all over again. Back in my sweatpants, and totally unprepared for the encounter.

I had a choice to make.

I could say hi to them . . . face the future.

Or I could run . . . from the past.

I wanted to put on a brave face, I really did. But my legs had other ideas, and I ducked into the Coffee Roastery until they were gone.

. . .

The evening before the Smithers Publishing meeting, I went for a short run in the Presidio. My mind was bursting with questions. What would the meeting be like? What would they say? What should I wear? I was so engrossed in my thoughts that I didn't hear anything else. That quickly ended, however, when someone shouted my name from behind.

"Waverly! Waverly!"

I turned around and wished I'd been wearing my headphones when I saw Brad Cantor jogging up the hill. He was wearing a white terry-cloth headband and a green tank top that said KISS ME, I'M IRISH.

"I didn't think you were ever going to turn around," he said as he caught up with me. "I've been calling your name for a while."

"Sorry, I've got a lot on my mind," I said. I tried not to sound annoyed, but seriously, could he be more ubiquitous?

"Good stuff, I hope?" he said.

"I hope it will be," I said. "How are you?"

"I'm great. Hey, I'm glad to see your leg's all healed."

How did he know about my leg? I was pretty sure that the past few months had been Brad Cantor–free.

"My leg?"

"Didn't you have a cast or something? I saw you on Chestnut Street a few months ago with a cast up to your knee. I yelled your name, but you didn't hear me."

Ahhh, yes. I had heard him calling my name that day but had acted like I hadn't.

"Oh, yeah, I broke my ankle on New Year's Eve. But I'm okay now. Thanks."

"Party accident?"

I shook my head. "Nothing that exciting. Jogging accident, actually."

He continued to run next to me, and I wondered if he was going to follow me all the way home. "Hey, speaking of parties, I'm having one in a couple weeks. It's an all-black theme. I'm getting black lights to decorate the place, and I bought black food dye for my special punch. Watch for the Evite," he said.

"Okay, Brad, thanks. Hey, I'm going to finish my jog this way, so I'll catch you later." I dashed away on another path before he had a chance to reply. I just couldn't be bothered with Brad Cantor at that moment.

Black punch? That was one party I would definitely not be attending. Maybe I could clean out my refrigerator that night. Or shoot myself in the head.

. . .

The next morning, I woke up early and stood in front of my closet, wondering what to wear to my meeting. A suit was a must, but I normally wore jeans to work, so I didn't know how to pull it off without looking like I was sneaking out for a job interview or something equally suspicious that Mandy would certainly suspect. I hadn't mentioned the Honey Notes to anyone at work for the same reason it had taken me so long to let McKenna and Andie read them: fear of being ridiculed (plus the fact that every other publisher in the United States apparently thought they were stupid). But the last thing I wanted to do was start rumors that I was interviewing around, so I was planning to tell Kent and Jess about the cards that morning to avoid any possible misunderstandings.

I finally chose a button-down striped orange, black, and red fitted polyester blouse with a flared collar. Then I grabbed my favorite suit: a fitted black crepe jacket with matching pants that had a slightly flared leg. I thought, or at least I hoped, that the outfit would look hip and trendy, but not too funky. I decided to wear my wire-rimmed glasses with my hair pulled back into my standard low ponytail but with a deeper side part. My goal was to look smart yet not nerdy, stylish yet professional, attractive yet serious.

I looked in the mirror before heading off to work. Could I pull this off?

At twelve thirty, with Jess's approval and Kent's congratulations, I left my office and headed in the direction of Smithers Publishing, just six blocks away. I couldn't believe how nervous I was! I was literally shaking in my boots. Actually, I was shaking in my sling-back heels.

My appointment was at 1 p.m., but I highly doubted they would offer me anything to eat, so I decided to stop into Uncle Ken's Bagels for a snack. As the cashier was giving me my change, I heard the ring of my cell phone. I dug it out of my purse and looked at the caller ID: Davey. I didn't have time for a catch-up conversation right then, so I sent him to voicemail. "Bye-bye, Davey," I said and tossed the phone back into my purse.

I walked out of the store and headed in the direction of Smithers Publishing. I made it about ten feet before something hit me in the back of my head.

"What the . . .?" I put my hand up to my head in a panic. Was I bleeding? Had I been shot? I felt no pain at all. Had I been crapped on by a pigeon?

Then I looked down and saw what had hit me lying on the side-walk: a sesame bagel.

"What the . . .?" I said again.

"You are SO busted, Waverly Bryson!"

I turned around and saw Davey standing in the entrance to Uncle Ken's Bagels, holding his cell phone up in the air and cracking up.

"Oops, sorry, Davey." I walked back toward him. "I'm in a hurry and thought I'd just let you leave a message."

He put his arm around me and gave me a squeeze. "Wow, you look rather stylish this afternoon. Why are you so dressed up?"

"Just a meeting."

He narrowed his eyes. "A press meeting?"

"Not really."

"Client meeting?"

I shook my head.

"New business pitch?"

"Not exactly."

He took a step back. "Wait a minute, you're not going on an interview are you? Are you ditching me?"

I laughed. "Ditch you? Never in a million years."

"You promise?" he said.

"I promise. Now I've really gotta go, or I'm gonna be late." I turned and blew him a kiss. Then I was off.

The offices of Smithers Publishing were strikingly creative. The floors were a dark hardwood with a slight reddish hue. The high ceiling boasted an enormous skylight, and each wall was painted a different shade of green or yellow. Framed photos of book and magazine covers were staggered everywhere. Biographies, autobiographies, fiction, nonfiction, science fiction, cookbooks, home-decorating magazines. Was there anything they didn't publish? I wondered how greeting cards fit into their product mix. I hadn't been able to find anything about them on the company's Web site.

I walked up to the front desk. "Hi there, I'm Waverly Bryson. I have a one o'clock?"

The 50-something receptionist with short white hair smiled at me. "Hello, Miss Bryson. Please have a seat. They'll be out to get you shortly."

I looked at my watch. It was 12:56 p.m. I wondered if the meeting would start on time. I stood up and asked the receptionist where the restrooms were, and she pointed down the hall to the left. I looked at all the photos lining the walls as I walked, and when I reached the ladies' room, it was totally empty. The soft background music reminded me of my dentist's office.

After a quick pee, I flushed the toilet and turned the knob on the stall door. I heard a weird click, and the door didn't budge.

Uh oh.

I tried again.

Nothing.

Oh Jesus, it was broken.

Holy crap.

The biggest meeting of my life started in two minutes, and I was stuck in a bathroom stall in an empty ladies' room. Was this a joke?

I didn't know what to do. I jiggled and jostled and rattled and jiggled the latch some more, but it just wouldn't move. Then I started yanking, which yielded similar results.

After two minutes of swearing at the latch, I looked at my watch again. I had to get out of there. I tried to yank the door open one last time, but it just wasn't going anywhere.

Should I scream?

At 1:01, I decided to make a move. I closed my eyes and took a deep breath. Then I got down on my back and slithered under the door. Yes, slithered under the door. Yes, on my back. Yes, in my suit. Yes, like a snake.

Ick.

Once I made it to the other side, I stood up, washed my hands, smoothed out my suit, reapplied my lipstick, and fixed my hair. Then I took a step back and looked at myself in the mirror. Had that really just happened?

I turned and headed back out to the lobby. Thank God no one had walked in on me.

When I made it back to the reception area, I sat down, picked up a magazine, and pretended to read. Then I shook my head and chuckled. Sliding under a bathroom stall door on my back? Who does that? Sometimes I wondered if I was being secretly video-taped for some humiliation-related reality show. They could call it *Waverly's Moments*.

A couple minutes later, a Clay Aiken look-alike came out and extended his hand. "Hi there, I'm Wyatt Clyndelle, a senior editor here at Smithers. Thanks for coming in." He looked about my age, or maybe a couple of years older.

"It's nice to meet you, Wyatt. Thanks for having me." I stood up and shook his hand, trying not to squeeze it too hard and thus appear too eager, or too soft, and thus appear too wimpy. There are few things in life that bug me more than a limp handshake.

"It's our pleasure, Waverly. Please, this way." He motioned for me to follow him down the hall to a glass-walled conference room. Inside were three other people sitting at a long, oval cherry table. The carpet was a plush cream color. They probably had to shampoo it every night to keep it clean, but it certainly presented an image of success.

Wyatt opened the large glass door, and the man and two women who were sitting at the table all looked up.

"Good afternoon, everyone. I'd like to introduce you to Waverly Bryson. Waverly, this is Emily Walton, head of our fiction department, Dean Paxton, our marketing director, and I believe you spoke to Becca Bentley on the phone?"

They all stood up to shake my hand, and as I was making the rounds Wyatt offered to make me a latte.

My ears perked up. "Did you say *make?* As in you have your own espresso machine?"

Emily laughed. "We don't mess around when it comes to properly caffeinating our employees."

"Wow, I could get used to this place," I said, nodding.

Within minutes we all had various coffee drinks and pastries in front of us. We chitchatted a bit about the weather, and then Emily cleared her throat to end the small talk and officially start the meeting.

"Waverly, I'd like to thank you on behalf of all of us for coming in today," she said.

"Oh gosh, it's my pleasure," I said.

She picked up her cappuccino and took a sip. "You may be wondering why we wanted to talk to you, given that Smithers doesn't currently publish greeting cards."

So *that* was why I hadn't been able to find any information about their card division. I knew I was a bad researcher, but not that bad.

"I must admit I was sort of wondering about that," I said.

"So how did you come up with the idea for the cards anyway?" she said.

I looked at my hands and realized it was the first time anyone had asked me that question.

"Um, well . . ." I said.

I looked up at the faces sitting around the table. They were all staring at me, awaiting my reply.

Should I just come out with it?

I took a deep breath. "Well, uh, actually I started writing them after my, um, after my fiancé called off our wedding." I exhaled an entire cloud, and I was surprised at how liberating it felt to say those words out loud, even if it was to a group of virtual strangers.

"Oh," Emily said.

"Um, uh, he used to call me *honey*," I said, swallowing hard. "So it was sort of an effort to be a bit ironic, I guess."

She nodded. "Well, I'm sorry things didn't work out with you and your ex, but I can't say I'm sorry that you came up with those cards."

I smiled. "Thanks."

"The truth is that we've been thinking about starting a card division for a while, and until recently we hadn't been able to agree on a strategy. But when we saw your samples, something clicked for all of us." She gestured to the others in the room, who all nodded.

I nodded along with them, although I don't know why. Have you ever noticed that nods are like yawns?

"Waverly, we think your Honey Notes are just what we need to launch the card division of Smithers Publishing," Emily said.

I looked at her and blinked. Um, what?

"You want to create a card division around my Honey Notes?" I said.

"Yes."

"But I thought this was just an introductory meeting."

They all laughed, and Emily smiled at me. "Well, since this is our first meeting, I guess it is an introductory one, but we want you to know that we're serious about this. We think your cards are fantastic, and we don't see the need to waste time beating around the bush. There's nothing like them on the market right now, and we believe they'll really strike a chord with single women, as will your reason for creating them in the first place."

Wow. She had seriously cut right through that bush.

"If we can come to an agreement, we'd like to launch the cards this summer," she said.

This summer?

"Um, wow," I said. It was hardly a professional response, but I was in professional shock.

"There's something else, as well," she said.

"Something else?" It was a whisper.

She nodded. "When we saw the photo that you included with the cards, we decided that it might be fun to use you in the advertising campaign."

"The photo I included with the cards?" I said, looking at everyone in the room. Given that it came from Andie's photo collection, I could only hope I wasn't holding up a big fat margarita, but I highly doubted it.

Emily nodded again. "We think putting a real face behind the cards will help create a hip, fun brand identity for them, and you certainly have the right face and the right image."

"I do?" I said.

She nodded. "And meeting you in person has confirmed that you also have the right personality."

"I do?" I said again, wondering how in the world they'd managed to get that impression. What was up with my caveman answers? A hair above grunting is hardly a winning conversation style.

She smiled. "You're our Honey Notes poster girl, Waverly, what do you think?"

I felt a little light-headed and was glad that I was sitting down. I took a sip of my latte and looked around the room. Me, a poster girl for the hip? If these people had only seen me just a half-hour earlier, mopping the restroom floor with my discount suit.

"An advertising campaign?" I said.

"Yep," Dean, the marketing guy, said. "We're thinking print and billboards for advertising, plus a publicity tour to hit magazines, TV, and radio, plus the online communities and blogosphere. Maybe you can give us some advice on that side of things."

Print ads?

Billboards?

A press tour?

"Waverly, are you okay?"

I realized that I hadn't said anything for a while and that they were all staring at me.

"Can we get you anything?" Dean said.

"No, no, I'm fine." I blinked a few times and smiled. "Just fine."

Apparently I had chosen the right outfit for the meeting.

• • •

When I walked out of the Smithers Publishing offices, I felt totally numb. Assuming that I accepted what I had just been offered, my life was about to change . . . completely. Suddenly I felt like I was standing on a skateboard, and I have really crappy balance. Was I ready for this? What about my job? What was I going to tell Jess and Kent and Davey? Emily had assured me that they would accommodate my work schedule for photo shoots and interviews and such, but if I really wanted to promote my cards, I knew I'd have to devote a significant amount of time to it. To do a good job I'd probably have to take some time off and essentially be like one of my own clients.

Wait a minute.

To promote my cards I'd essentially have to be like one of my own clients.

Could I be my own client? Could I get Smithers to hire K.A. Marketing to publicize the cards?

Why not? If we could publicize tennis balls and hockey sticks, why couldn't we do greeting cards? And bringing in a new client might be just what I needed to get my career back on track.

• • •

From that point on, things started happening fast. Really, really fast. The team at Smithers didn't mess around, and before I knew it I was approving artwork, fonts, and colors for the national launch of something that had once been a Word document on my PC. And Emily Walton had agreed to hire K.A. Marketing to manage the press campaign, so suddenly I was in the position of doing PR for myself, which ironically made me my own annoying client.

"You're going to love the advertising campaign, Mackie. It's really cute," I said. We were walking down to the Marina Green one Friday morning in early June.

"Well? Tell me about it," she said.

"The slogan's going to be *Sometimes we all need a spoonful of honey*. The idea is to have me in a variety of print ads, and in each one I'm going to ask a question of an imaginary friend. Her response will always be *Honey, pick up a Honey Note to find out*. Isn't that great?"

She looked over at me and smiled. "Adorable."

I clapped my hands together. "I know. I'm so excited!"

"So how was the photo shoot?" she said.

I reached over and grabbed her arm. "Oh my God, it was hilarious. I've attended tons of client photo shoots over the years, but all I'd really ever done was hang out by the buffet and watch, ya know? It's another world on the other side of the camera."

"Lots of fussing?"

I nodded. "Exactly. With the hairstylists, makeup artists, wardrobe consultants, lighting people, directors, camera operators, ad agency people, and Smithers people, I felt like I was on a VH1 diva special."

She laughed. "Did you demand a thousand white lilies in your dressing room?"

"No, but I did request fifty gallons of Evian to wash my hair."

"Excellent. So when's the big press tour?"

"We leave Monday morning. And ask me what perk I managed to weasel into the contract Smithers signed with K.A. Marketing?"

"Something tells me you're going to tell me anyway."

I smiled. "Can you say first-class airfare?"

"Really? Well done, Bryson, well done."

I stretched my arms over my head. "*Gracias* . . . so, are we still on for the Union Street Fair tomorrow?" The first weekend in June every year, nine or ten blocks of Union Street in the Cow Hollow neighborhood were blocked off for two days and filled with arts and crafts booths, free concerts, and a boatload of drunk people.

"Of course, wouldn't miss it," she said. "Andie's coming over to pick me up at noon, then we'll come get you."

"Of all the summer street fairs in San Francisco, that one's by far my second favorite," I said.

"Your second favorite? Which one's first? North Beach?"

I punched her in the shoulder. "Hello? Fillmore Street Fair?"

"Oops. How could I forget? Is that because of the thirty-two-ounce margaritas or because it's half a block from our apartments?"

"Um, that would be both." '

"So you'd pick that one over the Union Street Fair?" she said.

I put my palms up like a scale. "Hmm, it could be a toss-up. As a single woman I'd say Union Street because there are cuter guys there, but so many of them are under 25 that it takes them out of contention."

"Andie might disagree with you on that," she said.

"This is true," I said. "To her, hooking up with younger guys is like a sport. Actually, that's probably the only sport she's actually good at."

"She *is* pretty good at it," McKenna said.

"This is true," I said again. "Anyhow, I still think it's a tie between the street fairs."

"Either way it's research for the Honey Notes, right?" she said.

I laughed. "Exactly."

. . .

The following Monday morning, Kent and I were comfortably cruising thirty-five-thousand feet above the ground and laughing at our good fortune.

I looked over at him. "Okay, Mr. Tanner, let's review the situation. No, wait, first let's have a toast with our free mimosas. Cheers!"

"Okay, but hurry up, because I have a movie to watch and a nap to take before we land. I want to take full advantage of this recliner lounger and personalized entertainment system."

"Fine, I'll hurry." I sat up straight and counted on my fingers. "Let's see. We're being paid to:

1. *Fly first class*
2. *Stay in a sweet hotel*
3. *Eat at the best restaurants in Manhattan*
4. *Bitch about being single*
5. *Promote something that could quite possibly make me rich if it works out*

. . . Not bad at all, I must say."

He coughed. "ME being the key word in that last bullet point, missy. Don't forget the little people when you give up first class for your own jet, okay?"

I smiled at him. "Okay."

"And just to clarify, you're the one who's bitching about being single, not me," he said. "I'm just along for the ride."

"Touché. But seriously, Kent, this is like a joke. Do you realize that?"

He took a sip of his mimosa and fiddled around with his private video screen. "Yes, HONEY, I do."

. . .

On our last night in New York, Kent and I met Kristina at a sports bar to watch Shane on the road in a playoff game. I had never seen Kent so nervous. We got there before she did, and he was practically shaking.

I put my hand on his arm. "Calm down, Kent Tanner. You'll be fine. Kristina is totally normal and nice, just like Shane was at the Super Show. Remember?"

"Yes, I remember, but that was Shane. Shane is a man, an M-A-N. I do not find him physically attractive. Kristina, on the other hand . . ."

"Shut up." I punched him in the shoulder. "You, my friend, are a happily married man. You have two hyperactive children who are always filthy dirty and never stop screaming and leave you zero time for yourself. Why would you want to give that up to be with a stunning supermodel Olympic-gold-medalist millionaire doctor?"

He took a sip of his beer and looked over my shoulder. "What time did she say she'd be here?"

I looked down at my watch. It was nearly nine o'clock, and the place was packed. The Knicks were playing against the Heat in Miami, but because of the West Coast TV audience, the game didn't start until nine fifteen New York time.

"Any minute now, tiger. Chill." I got up and headed to the restroom.

He held up his glass. "Don't forget to bring me back another glass of liquid courage."

Kristina arrived in a rush at 9:14, straight from the hospital and looking more beautiful than ever. She turned more than a few heads but seemed not to notice as she maneuvered her way through the tables and sat down.

"Hi, Kristina, how's it going?" I leaned over and gave her a hug. It had been more than four months since we had seen each other. "You look perfect, as usual."

"It's nice to see you, sweetie. You look great, too." Then she turned toward Kent and extended her hand. "Hi there, you must be Kent."

"Um, hi. Nice to meet you." Kent shook her hand, smiled weakly, and turned his eyes toward the big-screen TV. *Typical guy*, I thought, shaking my head and laughing to myself. Completely smitten but gives the impression of total disinterest.

"What's so funny?" Kristina took off her coat to reveal a cute fitted black tank top and jeans.

"I'll tell you later." I grabbed a handful of pretzels from the bowl in front of us. "What can we get you to drink? And let's get a menu over here. I'm starving."

After we ordered, Kristina put her hand over mine on the table. "So, how did the press tour go? Tell me tell me tell me," she said.

Kent and I looked at each other. "You or me?" I said.

"Ladies first," he said.

I cleared my throat. "Well, I don't want to sound full of myself, but the press tour was, well, a smashing success."

Kristina smiled. "Really?"

"Really," Kent said, nodding.

"Let's see, what were the phrases we heard the most? *Unique . . . hilarious . . . it's about time . . . single women need something like this . . .* what else?" I looked at Kent.

"Don't forget *striking a chord.* I sort of got sick of that one," he said.

I laughed. "Ahhh, yes, we did hear that one a lot."

Kristina squeezed my hand. "That's fantastic, Waverly. It looks like you've got something special on your hands."

"I know, can you believe it?"

"So what happens now?" she said.

"Well, in a few weeks the advertising campaign starts, and the official launch of the cards is at the end of next month, which is when the print publicity should hit. They'll do the online stuff then, too."

"Wow. So soon?"

I nodded. "Yep, it's crazy how fast this is all happening. And if the response we got this week is any indication of what's to come, soon there might be thousands of Waverly Brysons out there lining up to buy Honey Notes."

"Thousands of Waverly Brysons? God help us all," Kent said.

. . .

The Knicks beat the Heat 108 to 105, and Shane scored thirty points. The crowd went wild, and more than one drunk fan came over to congratulate Kristina. She graciously thanked each one of them and sent them all on their way without any of them even realizing that they had been sent on their way. What talent.

After the game, the three of us headed to the tiniest diner I'd ever seen for dessert. It was a serious hole in the wall, but Kristina was a big fan of their double-chocolate milk shakes, so we agreed to give it a try.

I held up my glass. "You were right, Kristina. This is the best milk shake I've ever had. Seriously, I'm in love."

"Finally. I thought it would never happen. Cheers to that." Kent took a big sip of his banana milk shake and tapped his glass against mine.

Kristina looked at him. "You thought what would never happen?"

He cocked his head toward me. "Waverly. In love."

"Why not?" She looked from Kent to me. "Why wouldn't you be in love?"

"Thanks a lot, butthead," I said to Kent. "Can we just change the subject please?"

"No really, what's the scoop? I want to know," Kristina said.

"Let's just say that Miss Bryson here is off-the-charts picky," Kent said.

Kristina raised her eyebrows.

"In other words, a guy would have to be, well, you, to grab her attention," he said to her.

"A guy would have to be me?" Kristina said.

"Well, not you, but the male equivalent of you. You know . . . attractive, smart, athletic, nice, the whole pie."

I pushed Kent's arm. "Someone sure got over his stage fright."

"Shut up, Bryson." He looked back at Kristina. "Waverly can find a flaw in every potential suitor. Just ask her."

"Is that true, Waverly?" Kristina said.

I looked at Kent. "No, it is not."

"True," he said.

"Not true," I said.

Kent took another sip of his milk shake. "You know what Dave says, Waverly. You have to run out every grounder."

I rolled my eyes. "Ugh. If I had a dollar for every time Davey brought up those stupid grounders. I am SICK of running out grounders, okay?"

"Don't worry," Kristina said, patting me on the head. "You know very well that I think you're just fine on your own."

"Thank you," I said with a smile. "I do too. I really do."

. . .

The Honey Notes were in stores at the end of July. We were,

of course, all hopeful that they would do well, but none of us was prepared for what happened.

Let's just say that what happened was good.

I don't know how or why, but the cards somehow became the craze of single women everywhere. Word seemed to spread like wildfire, and the cards flew off the shelves. It was like I'd written a bunch of new Harry Potter books, only all the characters were sexually frustrated single women, and each book was just two pages long.

I was the talk of K.A. Marketing, or better put, the butt of more than one joke. It was all in good fun though. Everyone seemed genuinely happy for my success. Except for Mandy Edwards, of course.

I ran into her one morning in the kitchen.

"Hi, Waverly. It looks like your Honey Notes are quite a hit."

I smiled. "Thanks, Mandy."

"It must be fun, working on your own account like that," she said.

I shrugged. "It's not bad. Better than working on data storage or networking systems, I suppose."

"So what does JAG think about it?"

I looked at her. "What do you mean?"

"Well, they can't be happy that you're spending so much time on another account, right? I don't think Adina Energy would be happy if I were spending so much time on another account."

"As far as I know, JAG is quite happy with our work," I said, suddenly paranoid.

"Okay, glad to hear it. I was just wondering how you manage to fit it all in without letting anything slip through the cracks." She picked up her coffee and strolled out of the kitchen.

Aargh.

Later that afternoon, I called Davey to check in and make sure everything was okay. He said it was.

A couple Sundays later, however, he left me a cryptic message on my cell phone. He wanted to "discuss something" and suggested we meet for lunch the next day at the Curbside Café, a cute little place on California and Fillmore, and one convenient block away from my apartment. I didn't feel like hiking it all the way downtown just to turn around a few hours later and hike it right back, so I worked from home that morning. Plus, I was a little freaked out and didn't want anyone at the office to see me that way.

At twelve thirty, I pushed open the restaurant door and looked around. I spotted him in a booth in the back, making a little house with the coasters.

"Hey there, Davey Mason." I took off my coat and sat down across from him.

"Hey back at you, Miss Bryson."

I put my hands on the table. "All right, let's cut to the chase. What's with all the secrecy? It's not like you to be so coy."

He looked at me and didn't say anything.

"If you're going to fire us, just get it over with, okay?" I said.

He looked surprised. "Fire you? I'm not going to fire you."

"You're not?"

"Noooo . . . why would you think that?"

"It's just that Mandy said that . . . forget it, I'm sorry, I need to get a grip. What's up then? Why did you bring me here?"

He smiled. "Because I have some news."

"You have news?"

"Yes, I have news."

"Well?"

He took a deep breath. "Okay, here goes. How does *I got married* sound?"

"What? You? Married? What?"

He grinned. "I know. Can you believe it? I can't believe it. Can you believe it? I really can't believe it."

"I can't believe it."

"Me neither. Can you believe it?"

"Married? You? Really?"

"Really."

"Well, details please?"

He waved over the waitress, and we both ordered turkey sandwiches and fries. Then he turned back to me. "I don't know what came over me, but a couple weeks ago, and I know this sounds totally cheesy, but a couple weeks ago I was watching Lindsay as she was sitting on the couch. She was just sitting there reading a magazine, and it hit me. I suddenly realized that she's the person I want to be with for the rest of my life, and she's been that person for several years now, so what the hell was I waiting for?"

"Wow. I still can't believe it."

He grinned again. "I know. Neither can I. So anyhow, after this epiphany, I went ring shopping the very next day. And then I started thinking about how I wanted to ask her, and when would be the right time. And then I chose this past Friday afternoon, because we were going to be painting the condo."

The waitress brought our drinks and set them down on the table.

I picked up my Diet Coke and took a sip. "You asked her to marry you while you were painting your condo?"

"Yep."

"I don't understand. How is that romantic?"

"Because I painted my proposal on the wall," he said, crossing his arms and smiling.

"Ooh, not bad." I nodded my head.

"Exactly." He nodded back.

"You're quite proud of yourself, aren't you?" I said, smiling.

"You bet. I take pride in being romantic in ways that you would never read about in *Cosmopolitan*."

"So wait a minute, you just proposed on Friday?"

"Yep."

"And you're already married?"

"Yep."

"Am I missing something here?"

He laughed. "We flew to Vegas for the weekend."

I nodded again. "Ahhh, that's the Davey I know and love. Did you get married by Elvis?"

"Of course." He pulled an old-school Polaroid photo out of his pocket and slid it across the table. "Would you expect anything else?"

I looked at the photo. There they were: Mr. and Mrs. Davey and Lindsay Mason, and the King.

I slid the photo back toward him and smiled. "Davey, from you I would expect nothing less."

"Maybe you'll be next," he said.

I shook my head. "Are you kidding? I can't get married now. Now that the Honey Notes are out, I have to maintain my public image as a bitter single woman."

He laughed. "So, I have more news." He thanked the waitress as she served us our sandwiches.

I took another sip of my drink. "More news? How can you top that? Wait . . . is Lindsay prego?"

"Nope."

I looked at him. "Well?"

"You ready to hear this?" he said.

"Now I'm not so sure," I said. "Is it bad news?"

He shook his head. "*I* sure don't think so."

"Well then, spill," I said.

"I'm leaving JAG."

"WHAT? You're leaving? What? Why?"

"Lindsay and I decided to quit our jobs and backpack around the world for a year. We're leaving next month."

"No way. Does JAG know?"

He picked up a fry and tossed it into his mouth. "I gave notice this morning."

"Already?"

"Already."

"Wow. When's your last day?"

"In two weeks."

"What? Only two weeks?"

He nodded. "We're putting everything in storage and renting out our place, so I've got a lot to do before we leave. Plus I have to deal with passports, visas, your standard world-traveler stuff."

"Damn," I said.

"Yep."

I leaned back in the booth and sighed. "Man, it's the end of an era, Davey." I'd worked on the JAG account for so long that sometimes I felt like Davey was my real boss, even though we didn't even work for the same company.

"I know, but I'm so excited about this, Waverly. And you guys will be fine without me."

"Who's going to take over for you?"

He hesitated.

"Davey?"

"Um, I believe it'll be Gabrielle Simone." He stuffed another fry into his mouth and looked at the ceiling.

I opened my eyes wide. "Gabrielle Simone, the ice lady? Are you kidding me?"

He nodded. "She's been pushing to get into marketing for a while, so they're going to let her manage the PR agency."

I raised an eyebrow at him.

"What?" he said, laughing.

"She's not exactly a basket of puppy cats, you know."

"Puppy cats?"

I shrugged. "Small cats, kittens, whatever, you get the point."

"Oh, she's not *that* bad. You'll be fine."

I put my elbows on the table and rested my cheeks in my palms. "So you're really leaving me?"

"Yep, my lady. I really am."

"I hate you right now, Davey Mason."

He grinned. "I'll miss you, too."

Ever feel like you don't know anything at all?

Honey, congratulations. At least you finally know that.

CHAPTER SEVENTEEN

Davey was wrong. So wrong.

Exactly two weeks later, Jess called me into his office.

"What's up, Jess?" I sat down in a chair across from his desk and put my hands on my thighs.

"Well," he said. "It's not good news."

My heart sank. "What is it?"

"Gabrielle Simone just called."

I bit my lip. "And?"

"She's not happy," he said.

"Not happy? But why? How? She hasn't even worked with us yet."

He sighed. "Apparently she thinks the Honey Notes are jeopardizing the quality of the team's work on the JAG account."

What?

"You're kidding me," I said. "How does she even know that we're working on the Honey Notes?"

"I don't know," he said.

Mandy Edwards sure knew.

I looked out the window and then back at him. "So what do we do now?"

He didn't say anything.

"Jess?"

"I'm afraid I'm going to have to pull you off the account."

"What? You can't do that to me, Jess!"

"I'm sorry, but I have to."

I dug my fingernails into my thighs. "But I've worked with JAG for nearly five years. I know that company better than most of the people who work there. And we're doing a great job for them. You *know* that."

He sighed again. "I know that, believe me, I do. But the client has spoken, and my hands are tied. I'm sorry."

I fought back the tears.

"So that's it?"

"Yes. Gabrielle was pretty clear."

"There's nothing you can do?"

"I'm sorry, but no."

"So what do I do now?"

He tapped a pen on his desk. "For now you can keep focusing on the launch of the Honey Notes. When that calms down, I'll probably put you on the Birdie Golf account."

"What about Kent and Nicole?"

"They'll stay on the JAG team."

"And the account lead?"

He looked at me.

I closed my eyes and then opened them slowly. "Don't tell me. You're giving it to Mandy, aren't you?" I said.

He nodded.

I shook my head slowly and tried to keep my composure. "Thanks a lot, Jess," I said. Then I stood up and walked out of the room.

I made it all the way to my office before I started to cry.

I looked out my window at the view I loved so much and thought about how things had gone so wrong at my job. Had Aaron been right when he said he didn't think I'd ever liked it? Had I been a chameleon at work, too? Or had things just changed?

. . .

After work I decided to walk home for the first time ever. I needed time to digest what had happened, and I just couldn't see doing that while crammed into a bus.

I headed up the steep hill of California Street and looked at the sidewalk in front of me. Booted off the JAG account. After five years. For Mandy Edwards of all people. It just wasn't fair. I'd worked really hard on that account, and regardless of what Gabrielle Simone thought, I was still working hard on it. Or at least I thought I was. Actually, maybe I really wasn't anymore.

Ugh.

Why did Davey have to leave? What was I supposed to do now? Things weren't ever going to be the same without him. And now with Mandy entrenched in my department, gloating over the Adina Energy account, and now the JAG account too . . . I didn't know if I could take it.

Yuck.

My breath quickened as I climbed up the steepest part of California Street, and I wondered why I didn't walk home more often. Who needs a gym membership when you have California Street?

When I got to Powell Street, I turned around and watched a cable car packed with tourists as it rolled past Chinatown on its way down to Ghirardelli Square. It was the middle of the summer, so of course they were all freezing, but they still looked thrilled to be in San Francisco.

As I looked down the hill, California Street led smoothly into the energy of the financial district. Behind the tall buildings I could see the Bay Bridge framing the skyline. It was the neglected stepsister of the lovely Golden Gate, but at the right angle the Bay Bridge was still a beauty in its own right.

I put my hands on my hips and sighed.

"Hey, Waverly, are you okay?"

I turned around to see Brad Cantor standing on the corner, right next to me.

I sighed again. "Oh, hi Brad. I'm just admiring the view, I guess."

"Are you okay? You look upset."

I tried to smile. "I'm fine."

"No, really, are you okay?"

"Yes, I'm fine," I said, taking a step back. As usual, he was standing way too close to me.

"Okay. If you say so."

I turned to go, but the concerned look in his eye triggered something inside of me. And instead of walking away, I started to cry.

He looked panicked. "Here, um, take this." He reached into his pocket and pulled out a handkerchief.

"Thanks." I dabbed my eyes. Was I really crying in front of Brad Cantor, the world's only person under the age of 70 to carry around a handkerchief?

"Do you want to talk about it?" he said.

I shook my head. "No, thanks, Brad—but no."

"Are you sure?"

I nodded and blew my nose.

"Okay," he said. Then he just stood there.

"It's my job," I blurted out. "I lost a big account today."

Suddenly I was back at Morton's Steakhouse in Atlanta, where I'd confessed to Shane Kennedy about my fear of dying alone. Now I was standing on a street corner with Brad Cantor, whom I'd never had a real conversation with, crying about my job.

"I'm sorry to hear that," Brad said. "Are you in sales?"

I shook my head and looked at the ground. "Public relations."

"Was it a big account?"

I nodded. "Yeah."

"Did you make a big mistake or something?"

"I don't think so," I said. "The client put someone new in charge of our agency, and I guess she wanted to go in a new direction. Either that, or she flat-out doesn't like me."

"Well then, you just can't sweat it, Waverly. Seriously, sometimes you have no control over what the client does, no matter how good you are or how hard you try."

I looked back up at him. "You think so? I've never been booted off an account before."

He laughed. "Well, then you've led a charmed life. Seriously, don't worry about it. There are many more important things in life than losing an account. And you know what they say, right? When one door closes, another one opens."

I looked up at him. When did dorky Brad Cantor get so wise?

"You really think so?" I said.

"Sure. Maybe this is your chance to do something you like even better. Life is what you make of it, Waverly, so have fun with it."

I dabbed my eyes again. "Thanks, Brad. I think I'm finally beginning to understand that." What was it about friendly gestures from guys I barely knew that made me spill my guts? Then I thought of Aaron and my dad and Davey and Kent. Was the real question why couldn't I spill my guts to the guys who *weren't* strangers?

I looked at Brad standing there in his yellow sweater vest. He really wasn't that bad of a guy, and not bad looking, either. Maybe it wouldn't kill me to be nicer to him. Maybe we could actually become friends. Maybe I could even introduce him to some of my single girlfriends . . . hmm . . . Andie already knew him, and she would eat him alive anyway. Maybe my admin Nicole? No, too young. Did I have any other single friends?

"So can you come?" he said.

I blinked and looked at him. "Huh? I'm sorry, I spaced out. Did you say something?"

"I said, Can you come to my superheroes party? It's two weeks from Saturday. I'm dressing as Spider-Man. I'm sending out the Evite tomorrow."

A superheroes party?

"Uh, I'll check my calendar," I said.

Maybe Brad Cantor and I could actually become friends.

Then again, maybe not.

. . .

Later that night I picked up the phone and took a deep breath. It was time to deal with something.

"Hello?"

"Hey, Dad, it's me."

"Waverly?"

"Do you have any other kids?" I said.

He laughed. "Now this is a surprise."

"I know, I know," I said.

"So what's up, kiddo?"

I bit my lip. "Um, do you think we could get together for dinner this week? I'd like to talk to you about something."

"Dinner? You want to have dinner with me?"

"Yes," I said.

"Well, sure." He sounded genuinely surprised.

The following night we met at an Olive Garden halfway between San Francisco and Sacramento. Normally I refused to go anywhere near an Olive Garden, but this wasn't the time for attitude. And it wasn't the place either, because I was really hungry and was all over that bottomless salad.

My dad took a bite of a bread stick. "So what's the big news?"

I looked down at my hands interlaced on my lap. "I, uh, I want to talk to you about something."

"Is this about my vitamin business again? Because I told you that I—"

"No, it's not about that," I said. I clasped my hands tighter. "It's about something else . . . something I should have told you a long time ago."

He raised his eyebrows.

"About Aaron," I said.

"Aaron?"

"Um, yes, um, about our wedding."

He picked up another breadstick.

I looked at him and bit my lip. I still couldn't believe I'd lied to my own father about something so important.

"Um, well, I . . . I wasn't the one who called off the wedding."

He put the breadstick down. "What?"

"Aaron called it off," I said.

"*Aaron* called it off?" he said.

I nodded.

"But why?"

"Because . . . because he wasn't in love with me." I looked at the wall over his head as I said it.

He cleared his throat.

"Why didn't you tell me?" he said.

I looked at him, and my voice began to tremble. "Because I thought you'd say, *I told you so.*"

"*I told you so?* Why would you think I would say that?"

"Because I . . . because I thought . . . I thought you thought he was out of my league."

He took off his glasses and cleaned them with his shirt.

"You thought that?" he said, looking at the glasses.

I shook my head. "I'm not sure . . . maybe . . . I . . . I just always felt like you thought I wasn't good enough for him."

He slowly put his glasses back on, then looked up at me.

How could you say that? I wanted him to say. *How could you think that?* I wanted him to tell me how much he loved me, that he was proud of how I'd turned out, even though it had been hard to raise me on his own. I wanted to ask him why I'd never heard him say those words, why part of me still wondered if anyone could ever love me.

But he didn't say those words. He didn't say anything.

"Dad?" I said.

"That's crazy talk," he finally said to his dessert menu. "Now are we going to order something sweet or what?"

I sighed and felt the tears welling up in my eyes.

I looked at him across the table, his eyes buried in the menu.

Then I remembered what his next-door neighbor had said that day I'd gone to see him and he wasn't home.

He's always talking about you and your big job in San Francisco.

Maybe he'd said those things *about* me, just not *to* me. Just like I'd said so many things to my friends *about* Aaron, but not *to* Aaron.

I looked at him again. Maybe he was doing the best he could. Baseball had been his talent, his future, and now he was just trying to get by with what he had. He was who he was, and maybe it was time for me to accept that for what it was.

"Dad?" I said.

"Yes, kiddo?" he said.

"I . . . I'm sorry I got in the way of your baseball career."

He narrowed his eyes. "Baby, don't you ever feel sorry about that, okay? Ever."

"But—"

"I'm serious, Waverly, I don't want to hear anymore crazy talk tonight, okay?"

I nodded. "Okay."

He looked back down at his menu. We were barely talking, but it was the deepest conversation I think we'd ever had.

I took a deep breath. "Hey, Dad?"

"Yep?"

"Have you ever noticed how hard it is to tell the people you love the most what you're really feeling?"

He chuckled. "You know, your mom used to get on my back about that all the time?"

"Really?"

"She always wanted to talk about something. That woman could talk the ears off an elephant. Me, I like to change the subject when things get too heavy."

Talk about dominant genes on both sides of my genetic equation.

"So can we have dessert now?" he said. "I know we don't agree on much, but that's one thing we've always done well together, right?"

I smiled. When it came to me and my dad, dessert was definitely the easy part.

Then I told him all about the Honey Notes, over crappy tiramisu, at the Olive Garden.

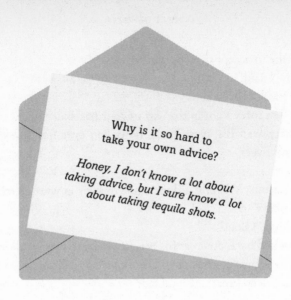

Why is it so hard to take your own advice?

Honey, I don't know a lot about taking advice, but I sure know a lot about taking tequila shots.

CHAPTER EIGHTEEN

A week later, I was sitting in the conference room waiting for the staff meeting to begin. Our admin Nicole was filling me in on her latest boyfriend crisis.

"Waverly, what's wrong with me?" she said, tears in her eyes.

"Nicole, there's absolutely nothing wrong with you. He's a total jerk for breaking up with you that way. Seriously, what a tool."

She looked up at me. "You think so?"

"Sweetheart, YES. Anyone who would break up with someone over text message is an ass. Trust me."

"You think I should call him again?"

"NO." She had cried for two days, then caved and called him. That was a week ago, and he hadn't returned her call. "You need to forget that jerk. In fact, I think I'm going to make a Honey Note about this one," I said.

"You'd do that for me?"

"Sure, why not?"

She smiled. "Really?"

That made her feel better? Hmm . . . maybe dedicating Honey Notes could be my gift to society, the blind leading the blind, one broken heart at a time.

Just then Jess walked into the room and clapped his hands. "All right, people, let's cut the chitchat. We've got work to do, work to do."

Kent slid a chocolate glazed donut across the table to Nicole, but it didn't stop and fell right off the table, then rolled along the carpet until it hit the door. Nicole picked it up, dusted it off, and took a bite.

We all looked at her.

"But it's the last chocolate glazed," she said.

Jess shook his head and laughed. "Okay, everyone, let's get this show on the road. Account updates please?"

Mandy stood up, and I sank down in my seat and stared at my shoes.

"Adina Energy is in the middle of the launch of its new high-protein energy bars, so we're pretty busy with that, but we're right on track," she said. "And everything's in order on the JAG account, too. I'm having lunch with Gabrielle Simone tomorrow, who's our new contact there since Dave Mason left." She smiled, and I wanted to pull her chair out from under her before she sat down.

"Good to hear it. Kent, what's going on with the Honey Notes?" Jess said.

Kent stood up. "Well, the account is going great. This week we have phone interviews with radio stations in Florida, New York, and Los Angeles, plus with the *Boston Globe*, the *Chicago Tribune*, and the *Philadelphia Inquirer*. We're also looking at another trip to New York to meet with more of the mainstream magazines that weren't interested the last time around but have since changed their tune. And we've lined up interviews with several popular Web sites and bloggers. The team at Smithers seems quite pleased with our work."

"Great," Jess said.

Kent rubbed his hands together. "Our only real complaint is the talent, that is, the creator of the cards, a Miss Waverly Bryson. She's a bit high maintenance and sort of a pain in the rear to work with, to be honest. Is there any way we could reduce her involvement in the account?"

"I second the motion," Nicole said. "She's a major control freak."

"Your basic nightmare client," Kent said, nodding.

I crossed my arms and made a face. "How funny you all are. Be careful people, or Smithers just may find itself a new PR firm."

Kent put his arm around me and patted my head. "Hush, little baby, don't say a word. . . ."

"Actually, I have a bit of news on the Honey Notes account that I'd like to share with the group," Jess said.

I sat up in my chair. News? What? What? I really couldn't take anymore news.

"I got a call from *People* magazine this morning," he said.

"And?" we all said in unison, leaning forward in our chairs. *People* magazine was the Holy Grail for publicists. The briefest product mention could send sales through the roof. It was almost up there with being on *Oprah*!

Jess looked right at me and smiled. "They want to include Waverly in this year's 50 Most Beautiful People issue."

A cheer went up in the room, but I couldn't hear it. I was totally numb.

"Um, what?" I said.

"No joke, Waverly," Jess said. "Apparently there was a last-minute cancellation, and someone at *People* saw your lovely face in the Honey Notes ads and thought you'd be a great replacement. Assuming that you accept the invitation, they'll be in touch this week to set up the photo shoot."

An understudy for one of *People*'s most beautiful? Talk about big cheekbones to fill.

Nicole stood up and started jumping up and down. "Oh my God! This is so exciting! Can I come to the photo shoot? Pretty please pretty please pretty please, can I come?"

Kent crossed his arms over his heart and pretended to choke up. "That's our little girl, folks, all grown up. Does anyone have a tissue?"

Mandy Edwards flashed her beauty pageant smile. "Congratulations, Waverly, that's wonderful news."

"This is truly fantastic," Jess said. "Our executive team is going to be thrilled."

I sat back in my chair in a daze. This was crazy. Me? In *People* magazine? Along with the Scarlett Johansson and Keira Knightley types? Me?

I hoped their makeup artist was good. Damned good.

Making an effort to try something new?

Honey, as long as it doesn't involve a bikini and a webcam, I'm all for it.

CHAPTER NINETEEN

I remember the three months before my ten-year high school reunion. A trip to the gym every evening after work. No chocolate. No cookies. No poppyseed muffins. A futile effort to cut back on Snickers bars. All to look my best for one superficial evening with a bunch of people I wouldn't see for another ten years, if ever again.

I can't say my crash health kick was all that successful, but at least I tried. Or at least I had the option of trying. And that was for one dinner with a couple hundred former classmates. To get in shape for the God knows how many zillions of *People* magazine readers out there, I had exactly one week. Six days, actually.

Six days.

Crap.

Oh well. I'd done a lot of thinking about the whole 50 Most Beautiful People thing, and I'd come to the conclusion that I was one of the token *not really beautiful* people on the list anyway. Have you ever noticed how they always throw a few randoms in there to create the illusion that real people are beautiful too? They're usually the noncelebrity types: an author, a politician, a chef, the occasional bungee-jumping business executive.

Add bitter single woman to the list. I could already see the angry letters rolling in:

"Dear Editors: You really blew it with this year's list. Where was Céline Dion? Where was LeAnn Rimes? You chose that greeting card writer over those beauties? I'm outraged."

"Dear Editors: Waverly who? A discontinued cracker over the lovely Taylor Swift? And where was Miley Cyrus? I'm tempted to cancel my subscription. I hope you clowns get it right next time."

"Dear Editors: Knock me over with a wet noodle. You call your-selves the voice of America but leave out Sarah Palin for that bitter Honey Notes lady? Pull your heads out of the sand and get a clue."

The letters would be signed by the Wilmas in Nebraska, the Mary Jeans in West Virginia, the Becky Sues in Oklahoma. Legions of desperate housewives who wanted Eva, not Wava.

I didn't have a chance.

. . .

The day before the photo shoot, I was sitting with McKenna on the floor of my living room. It was early Saturday afternoon, and we were flipping through issues of *Bride* and *InStyle*, look-ing for possible hairstyles for her wedding. Both our dresses were strapless, fitted, and floor-length. Hers was ivory, mine a dark bluish-silver.

"How about this one?" I held up a photo of a model with her hair pulled high into a messy-yet-somehow-classy bun.

She looked at me and nodded. "I like it. Snip it for the 'up' pile." On the floor next to us we had built one stack of photos of models and celebrities with their hair pulled up, and one stack with their hair down. McKenna was still on the fence about which way to go.

I stood up and stretched my arms over my head. "I'm tired. Want something to drink?" I headed for the kitchen.

"What do you have?"

I opened the fridge and took a look. "Um, that would be water, H_2O, and agua."

"Why am I not surprised?" she said. I couldn't see her, but I knew she was rolling her eyes.

I walked back into the living room carrying one glass of water and one glass of agua. "Hey, wanna hit Dino's for some pizza? I'm starving," I said.

"Sounds good to me." She gathered the stacks together and stuffed them into her massive wedding binder. "I've had enough of this for today."

A half-hour later, we were each working on our second slice when I saw Andie on the other side of the street.

"Hey, look, there's Andie," I said. "Wasn't she going to Tahoe this weekend?"

"That's what I thought," McKenna said.

"Lemme go catch her. Grab an extra plate, will you?" I jumped up and trotted outside to catch up to her.

A couple minutes later, Andie and I walked back inside Dino's. I pulled up a third chair and sat back down in my seat.

"So no Tahoe?" McKenna said.

Andie stuck her gum on the side of the plate in front of her and reached for a slice of pizza. "Change of plans," she said.

"I feel a story coming on," McKenna said.

"Well?" I said to Andie. "Does this involve a story?"

She nodded. "Of course it does. And if you pour me some of that beer, I'll tell you."

"Deal." I picked up the pitcher of Bud Light. "Now spill."

"Okay, but this is pretty bad, so lean in," she said. We both leaned in.

She pushed her short blonde hair behind her ears and lowered her voice. "Okay, here goes. Last night I went to a dinner party at my friend Kelly's house over in Nob Hill. It was four couples in a tiny two-bedroom, one-bathroom apartment on the third floor. She and her roommate, Brenda, invited me and our friend Jill over, and we all brought dates. I brought this cute guy Nick I met at a photography class I started taking. I just asked him on Thursday, which is why I decided not to go to Tahoe."

I leaned back and put my hands on the table. "Wait a minute. Your friend Kelly lives with a girl named Brenda?"

"Yep," Andie said.

I opened my hands wide in front of me. "Am I the only one seeing the brilliance in this?"

They both looked at me blankly.

"Brenda Walsh? Kelly Taylor? Hello? Didn't anyone here watch the original *90210*?"

McKenna handed me my beer. "Drink." Then she turned her attention back to Andie. "Go on."

"Donna . . . Martin . . . graduates . . .," I chanted softly to myself and took a sip.

"Well, as I was saying, Kelly and Brenda live in this tiny apartment, so they basically filled up the entire living room with a big table they had borrowed from a neighbor. They worked all day preparing the meal for the eight of us: grilled salmon with a caramel glaze, mashed potatoes, and steamed spinach."

"Mmm, I love salmon," I said. "Hey, Mackie, we decided on salmon as an entrée option for your wedding, right?"

"Yes." She kept her eyes on Andie. "And?"

Andie took a sip of her beer. "Well, the dinner was fantastic, and I ate everything on my plate. Everything. If I had been alone, I probably would have licked it. Then for dessert we had chocolate mousse and cappuccinos, and we started talking about which celebrities we think have had plastic surgery."

I pointed at Andie. "Oh, oh, let me guess who made the list—"

McKenna put her hand over my mouth. "Would it kill you to keep a lid on it for two seconds?"

Andie swallowed a bite of pizza. "Well, up to that point, everything was fun and perfect. And then . . ."

"And then what?" McKenna and I said at the same time.

"Shhh. You're both yelling," she said.

"And then what?" we said in a whisper.

"Everything was fun and perfect . . . and then . . . well . . . and then . . . the cappuccino kicked in."

"Oh no." McKenna put her hand over her mouth and shook her head.

Andie nodded. "Oh yes. And it kicked in like a champ. All of a sudden I really had to go. I mean I *really* had to go. So I excused myself and walked into the bathroom, which was practically on top of the dining room table, and I prayed that their conversation would drown out any inevitable, you know, noises."

I covered my mouth with a napkin. "No way."

Andie nodded. "Way. So I went into the bathroom, and everything came out okay, but . . ."

"But . . .?" McKenna said.

"But it was huge. I mean HUGE."

McKenna crossed her arms and put her head down on the table, totally cracking up.

"I mean it was so big that when I tried to flush it, it wouldn't go down. It just floated there," Andie said.

"No way," I said again.

"Way." Andie nodded and took another sip of her beer. "I tried to flush the toilet three times, but the damned floater wouldn't go down. And right on the other side of that door was my date and six other people, and I didn't want them all to hear the toilet flush, like, twelve times, ya know?"

McKenna was still facedown on the table, her shoulders totally shaking.

"So what did you do?" I was laughing so hard I barely got the question out.

Andie shrugged. "I fished it out, wrapped it up in toilet paper, and threw it out the window."

"NO WAY!" I put my hand over my mouth as I realized that everyone in the restaurant was looking at me.

"Way." Andie nodded again and took a bite of her pizza.

"What did you do then?" I said, petting McKenna's hair. She was still facedown.

"What else could I do? I went back to the party like nothing had happened."

"Wait, didn't you say their apartment was on the third floor?" I said.

"Yep."

"Well, did you see where it went?"

She shook her head and took another bite. "Didn't see, didn't want to see."

McKenna finally came up for air. Her face was totally red, and her eyes were watering. She was still laughing, and it took her a while to calm down enough to talk.

"I don't think I've ever laughed this hard, ever," she said.

Andie tossed her gum back into her mouth and shrugged. "Hey, if you can't share a story like that, what's the point of having friends, right?"

When I got home from dinner, I wrote down an idea for a Honey Note:

Front: They say laughter is the best medicine?
Inside: Honey, toss it in with girlfriends and beer, and you've found the fountain of youth.

. . .

The following Tuesday morning, I was sitting in my office looking over the schedule for a second Honey Notes press tour. A few minutes after eleven, Tracy Leiderman from *People* called. She had been my main point of contact in the coordination of the photo shoot.

The photo shoot, by the way, had been hilarious. A tall blonde woman named Liz had come by my apartment Sunday morning to pick me up. She drove me to a fancy studio in a bright loft building in the South of Market district. There she did my hair, and then a plump, medium-height redhead named Cricket did my makeup. During the makeup session, a teeny tiny dark-haired woman named Rita came in and introduced herself as the wardrobe specialist.

Between the four of us, I think we represented every possible body type and hair color. Rita dressed me in a pair of white linen pants and a white cotton tank top, and then Liz and Cricket touched up my hair and makeup.

Once I was fully primped and ready to go, the four of us got into a limo and drove to the beach out by Half Moon Bay. There we met a photographer named Jan and his four-person lighting crew, which had roped off a whole area for the photo shoot. The girls primped me again, and then Jan spent nearly four hours taking about a hundred and eighty thousand pictures of me frolicking on the beach. I felt like I was in a maxipad commercial.

The whole memory made me laugh as I picked up the phone. "Hi. Tracy, how are you?"

"I'm good, thanks. Just wanted to touch base after the photo shoot. I heard it went great."

"Yeah, I guess so," I said. "I felt a little silly prancing around on the beach like that though."

She laughed. "Don't worry. Jan and his team are the best in the business, really. I guarantee you'll love how you look when the issue comes out."

"I hope so. I must admit that this has all been a little overwhelming."

"Just enjoy it, Waverly. Besides, the fun is just getting started. I have another offer for you."

Another offer? What could top being invited to appear in *People*'s 50 Most Beautiful issue, even as a B-lister?

"Another offer?" I said.

"Well, as you know, we're big fans of your Honey Notes here at *People*, probably because a lot of us are single and can totally relate. And we have a great deal of single readers, so we thought that it might be fun to host a singles auction for charity."

I took a sip of my coffee. "A singles auction?"

"Yep. We'll auction off a dinner date with the single people on our 50 Most Beautiful list who are willing to participate, plus a number of other singles we've featured in the magazine over the last year. We'll announce the auction in the magazine and on our Web site, and then we'll have live bidding at a big party here in New York and publish the photos from the dates in the following week's issue. We think it'll be really popular with advertisers."

I took another sip of my coffee but didn't say anything. Live bidding? Photos? What if no one bid on me? Would they have to offer me at a discount? What if the photo they ran the following week had a caption under me that said *Still available?*

"It'll be fun," Tracy said. "We'll pay for all your travel and accommodations, and the whole thing will be great exposure for your Honey Notes. Plus it'll be for the American Cancer Society."

I still said nothing.

"Waverly, are you there?"

"Yeah, sorry, I'm here," I said.

"So what do you say?"

I bit my lip. "Okay, sign me up."

What was I getting myself into?

Think that your first impression of a person means everything?

Honey, the problem is that if you're wrong about it, you're an idiot.

CHAPTER TWENTY

People magazine hit the stands a couple weeks later, and overnight my life was turned upside down. I knew that a lot of people read *People*, but good God, apparently oceans of people and all their relatives read *People*.

In addition to the billion people who came out of the e-woodwork and added me as a friend on Facebook, my home phone, which was still in the good ol' fashioned phone book, rang off the hook. Old friends called to ask why I hadn't told them about it. More than a few stalker types called to ask me out. Random people on the bus and the street stared at me, and then they called me to tell me they had seen me on the bus or on the street. My dad called to say he was the talk of Valley Pines. Brad Cantor called to say congratulations and to invite me to a "make your own crepe" brunch.

I finally had to cancel the landline, which I used about as much as my oven anyway. And I used my oven, well, never. Sometimes I considered putting my nice jewelry in there just in case I ever got robbed. I mean, who would think to look *there*?

At work, the Honey Notes interview requests poured in, and I wondered if the hype would ever calm down. Magazines, newspapers, radio stations, Web sites, blogs, suddenly everyone wanted to talk about life as a single woman in San Francisco. The tech guy in our office had to reroute my direct-line calls through the receptionist to help manage the traffic (and to screen out the weirdos). It was truly insane.

Scotty Ryan called and asked if I would design a Honey Note based on him.

"A card based on you? What do you mean?" I said.

"Couldn't you make one about falling for your good-looking gay friend? That's the cliché of the day, right?"

I laughed. "Scotty, how do you manage to lift that pumpkin head of yours off your pillow every morning?"

"It's not easy, my dear. It's not easy."

Davey called me all the way from Paris to heckle.

"What are you selling in that photo, Waverly? Douches?"

"Um, that would be maxipads, Davey. Please get your feminine hygiene products straight."

"Oops, my mistake."

"How in the world did you see the magazine all the way in Paris?" I said.

"The Internet, my dear. Get out of the dark ages. But seriously, Bryson, I'm proud of you. You're really doing it."

"Doing what?"

"You know, *it*. Your own thing, following your dreams, making it happen, all that BS."

I smiled. I guess I was. "So did you hear?" I said.

"Hear what?"

"I got booted off the JAG account."

"What? Are you serious?"

"Yep."

"When?"

"The day after you left the company."

"Really? Did they tell you why? You've always done such a great job for us."

"Apparently Gabrielle Simone wasn't happy."

"Wasn't happy? Why not?"

"She doesn't seem to be a big fan."

"Of K.A. Marketing or of you?"

"Of me. I hear she just loves her new account lead."

"And she really booted you on her very first day?"

"Her very first day. She must hate me."

"Hmm, I wonder if it was because of what happened way back at the Super Show. . . ."

I sat up in my chair. "What do you mean?"

He laughed. "You know, barf barf."

"You knew about that? Why didn't you ever say anything?"

"Why would I? What's the big deal? We were all drunk at that party. Hell, it was the Super Show!"

I smiled. "I miss you, Davey Mason, do you know that? Lindsay is one lucky girl."

"Well, I miss you, too, and yes, she is. So now that you're all big and famous, promise me that you won't forget us little people who tried our best to hold you back, okay?"

"I promise."

"Cool. Au revoir, Mademoiselle Bryson."

"Bye, Davey."

. . .

Two weeks later, I got another call from Tracy at *People*.

"Hi, Tracy, how's it going?" I picked up my squishy stress ball and tossed it into the air.

"Great, thanks. How are you, Waverly?"

"I'm good—still reeling from all the attention, but good. What's up?"

"I just wanted to give you a heads-up on the singles auction. We're going to move it up a week for a number of logistical reasons that I won't bore you with. Anyhow, it will now be at the Plaza Hotel in Manhattan on October 13. So mark your calendar."

I bit my lip. "Friday the thirteenth?"

"Yep, is that a problem? Don't tell me you're superstitious?"

"Well, um, no—no, it's fine. I'll put it on my calendar."

"Great, because we'd really love to have you there. We'll get you a nice room at the Plaza for the weekend, and we'll fly you home Sunday or Monday, whichever you prefer, okay?"

I squeezed the ball. "Sure, okay, thanks, Tracy."

"Great. I'll be in touch as the date gets closer. Take care, Waverly."

"Bye, Tracy."

I hung up the phone and put the ball on my desk.

October 13. Friday the thirteenth. Ouch.

· · ·

"You're spending your thirtieth birthday at a singles auction? Are you insane?" Andie picked up a piece of cheddar cheese and sandwiched it between two crackers.

It was a rare hot Sunday afternoon, and McKenna, Andie, and I were hanging out in the shared backyard of Andie's apartment building, drinking sweetened iced tea and enjoying the sun.

"I know, I know, it's so embarrassing, but I committed before they changed the date. What am I supposed to do now?" I said.

Andie pushed her sunglasses up to rest on her head and reached for another piece of cheese. "Can't you have your assistant call and cancel? Or maybe just not show up at all? Isn't that what all you famous people do?"

"Come on, Andie, you know she can't do that," McKenna said.

Andie shrugged. "Okay, you're right. Not showing up would be a little harsh. Maybe you could just call at the last minute and say something suddenly came up?" she said.

I looked at her. "You want me to say that something suddenly came up?"

"Yeah, why not?"

"Uh, maybe because that's one of the most quoted lines OF ALL TIME? Why don't I just tell them I'm grounded because I forgot that Mom always said don't play ball in the house?"

"Hey, wasn't there a *Seinfeld* episode about this?" McKenna said.

I looked at her. "About quoting *The Brady Bunch?*"

"No, about having a first date on your birthday. There was one episode where Jerry goes on a first date with this really pretty girl, and at dinner she tells him that it's her birthday. And *she's* the one who picked the day for the date! The whole episode is about how everyone but Jerry thinks she's a loser."

I groaned. "Wonderful."

Andie tossed another piece of cheese into her mouth "What type of guy would fly all the way to New York to bid for some girl in an auction? You know whoever picks you is gonna be a psycho."

"Maybe it'll just be someone who lives in New York," McKenna said.

"Still psycho," Andie said.

I groaned. "No matter how you package it up, this is one very small notch above appearing on a reality show."

McKenna nodded. "Looks like it."

I covered my eyes with my hands. "Ugh, I'm so embarrassed for myself."

"I'm embarrassed for you, too," Andie said, grabbing another piece of cheese.

I pinched her arm. "Hey, cheese girl, how's the annual summer diet going?"

"Bite me," she said, putting the cheese down.

"Well at least it's all for charity," McKenna said.

"And at least you'll get to meet some hot single celebrities at the party," Andie said. "Maybe you'll get lucky and hook up."

I rolled my eyes.

Andie shrugged and put her sunglasses back on. "Just trying to be optimistic."

"Don't worry, Wave. We'll celebrate your birthday after the auction. You'll probably need to eat a whole cake anyway to help you get over the experience," McKenna said.

"Double chocolate?" I said.

"You got it," McKenna said.

Andie laughed. "Nothing but the best for our little maxipad model."

. . .

Kent and I scheduled the next Honey Notes press tour for the week after the singles auction. The plan was for me to fly to New York on Friday, and Kent would fly in the following Monday for the interviews. And when Tracy found out that Smithers Publishing was already paying for my plane ticket, she said that *People* would pay for me to bring a friend if I wanted. Sweet!

I called McKenna at work to give her the good news.

"Are you kidding me? I wouldn't miss it. Is Andie coming, too?" she said.

"Well, I only have two plane tickets," I said.

"Hello? I'm an investment banker, remember? I have a billion miles. Give her the ticket. I'll get my own."

"Really? Are you sure that weekend's good for you?"

"I don't care if it is or not. I'm canceling whatever's on my calendar. We can make this my bachelorette weekend, too."

"Perfect! Let's call Andie via three-way," I said, dialing her number.

"Andrea Barnett," Andie answered in her work voice, which was two octaves below her regular voice.

"Hey, Andie, it's Waverly and Mackie on three-way. Do you want to go to New York with us for—"

"I'm in," she said.

"But don't you want to know the—"

"In," she said.

I laughed and leaned back in my chair, then gave her the details.

"Besides the turning thirty part and the being auctioned off in front of a large group of people part, the weekend will be so fun," I said.

"I'm fired up," Andie said. "I plan to eat too much, drink too much, and shop too much."

"Me too," McKenna said. "I'm digging this coattails thing. So how is it being famous anyway, Wave?"

I leaned forward in my chair. "Well, I would hardly call myself famous, but these fifteen minutes have definitely been a little surreal. You know what I realized though?" I said.

"What?" they both said.

"I realized the ONE photo that apparently everyone in the world has seen of me was taken by a professional photographer with professional lighting after a professional makeup artist and a professional hairstylist worked on me for two hours."

"So? You look great in it," McKenna said.

"Yeah, but no matter how hard I try, I'm never going to look as good as I do in that picture!"

"You know, that is sad, but sorta true," Andie said.

I laughed. "I know. So sad, and so true."

"You should really be proud of yourself, Wave," McKenna said. "Those Honey Notes are fantastic. So many people have creative ideas, but turning them into something real is another story."

I smiled into the phone. "Thanks, Mackie. You know, it's so crazy, but I guess I owe all this to Aaron. Who would have thought?"

"That breakup was the best thing that ever happened to you," McKenna said.

"We should all be so lucky," Andie said.

"I'm serious," McKenna said. "You've finally stopped trying to live your life according to some ridiculous master plan. Where's the fun in that?"

"No fun for you!" Andie said in her Soup Nazi voice.

. . .

That Thursday, the three of us met at the Kilkenny after work for a beer.

"I don't believe it," I said to Andie. "Really?"

She pushed her hair behind her ears and nodded. "Yep. When the check came, he looked right at me and said, 'Shall we split it?'"

"No way," McKenna said.

"Way," Andie said, nodding again.

I sipped my beer. "And this was a first date?"

"Yep, first date."

"And he had asked you out?"

"Yep."

I tilted my head to one side. "And then he asked you to pay for half of dinner?"

She nodded again. "Yep."

"I don't get it," I said.

Andie blew a bubble. "Join the club."

"Do you think he's in the closet?" McKenna said. Every girl we knew in San Francisco had asked that question at least once. "Maybe he just goes on random dates now and then so no one will suspect?"

Andie put her finger on her lip. "You know, now that I think about it, he could be. He *was* really well-dressed. So maybe. Or maybe he's just rude."

"He's rude either way," I said. "How did you meet him?"

"At the gym," she said, nodding slowly. "Yep, I should have known better. The guys I meet at the gym always turn out to be gay."

"But you never go to the gym," I said.

She smacked her gum and smiled. "And now you know why."

"That would make a good Honey Note," I said.

"Everything's a Honey Note for you these days," McKenna said.

I smiled. "Yep, I'm done with dating to find love. Now I'm just using it as research."

"My friend Max told me an amazing dating story the other day," Andie said.

"That nice guy with the awesome apartment you call the Maxi-pad?" I said.

She nodded. "Uh huh, and get this. He took a girl out for the first time the other night, and at dinner she flat-out asked him how much money he has in his bank account."

"She did not," McKenna said.

"Oh yes, she did," Andie said.

"I will never understand people," I said. "What did he say?"

"Get this," Andie said. "Before he could even answer, the girl's BOYFRIEND showed up at the restaurant and started yelling at her."

"No way," I said.

"Way," Andie said. "He starts yelling at her for cheating on him, and get this: she pretends she doesn't know who he is!"

"You're kidding," McKenna said.

Andie shook her head. "Totally true. She acted like she'd never seen him before."

"That's awesome," I said. "What a nut job."

"Total nut job," Andie said. "And when the guy finally left, she *still* wouldn't admit she knew him. She told Max her ex-boyfriend must have put the guy up to it."

"Yeah, sure he did," McKenna said.

"I will never understand people," I said, taking a sip of my beer. "So I'm assuming she didn't get to see the famous Maxipad?"

Andie laughed. "Hardly."

"Speaking of great apartments," McKenna said, "are you ladies up for watching the Blue Angels at Davio and Alessandro's annual roof deck party this weekend?"

"Yes!" I said. "I love that party, and I love Fleet Week. The planes have been whizzing by my window all week. It's so loud, but I love it when . . ."

I stopped talking.

"You love it when what?" Andie said.

I looked over her shoulder. "Sorry. I got distracted. Check out that tall guy over there, but be casual about it. Isn't that Darren from Left at Albuquerque?"

Andie and McKenna both whipped their heads around to look.

"Ladies, that was hardly casual," I said with a sigh.

"Who?" McKenna said.

"Where?" Andie said.

"The one with the brown hair in the white button-down shirt, by the pool table," I said. "Andie, remember we met him that night we went to Lefty's after I ran into Aaron at the Marina Safeway? The night of the double Darrens?"

Andie laughed. "Ah, yes, the double Darrens. How could I forget?"

"Well, it turns out that cute Darren is engaged to that nightmare Mandy at work."

They both looked at me.

"The Mandy who practically stole your job?" Andie said.

I nodded.

"That's her fiancé?" she said.

"Yep," I said.

McKenna looked back over at Darren. "He's really cute."

I sighed. "I know. I ran into them a couple months ago when I was on this awful date. It was so embarrassing, because at Lefty's I'd given him my card hoping he would ask me out, but he never called. And then I find out he's engaged to bitch woman."

"Oops," Andie said.

"Exactly," I said. "So I pretended not to recognize him, but I don't think he bought it. Oh well, whatever. If he's marrying that nut job, he's not my type anyway."

Just then the guy standing next to us at the bar turned to face us. He shook his head and frowned. Then he looked right at me.

"Actually, Mandy's a really cool girl, not that you would know anything about being cool. I'll be sure to tell her you said hi," he said. Then he picked up the beers he'd ordered and walked across the room to where Darren was standing.

Holy crap.

I buried my face in my hands. "Oh my God oh my God oh my God, please tell me that didn't just happen. Please please someone tell me that didn't just happen."

Andie nodded. "Apparently it did."

"That was ugly," McKenna said.

My cheeks were on fire. "Good Lord, could I shove my entire leg further down my throat?"

"This town is way too small," McKenna said. "You literally never know who might be standing right next to you."

"I know," I said. "But usually it's Brad Cantor, not the friend of a girl who stole my job and hates me."

McKenna put her arm around me. "It'll be okay, Wave, maybe he won't even say anything."

"Or if she already hates you, who cares what he tells her?" Andie said.

I shook my head and felt the tears welling up in my eyes. "I can't believe I just did that. Me and my stupid big mouth."

Just then Andie's cell phone rang.

"Hello? Hey . . . okay . . . okay . . . yeah . . . got it . . . okay . . . I'm on my way . . . Bye." She hung up and threw the phone in her purse.

"Who was that?" McKenna said.

Andie smiled and stood up. "Booty call."

I wiped a tear from my eye and laughed. "Did you really just say that? What about all that talk about how hard it is to find a date?"

She blew another bubble and popped it. "Who said anything about a date? Gotta run. Bye, sweeties. Hang in there, Waverly."

McKenna stood up too. "I've gotta get going as well. Unfortunately, I have a seven a.m. conference call tomorrow. Our East Coast office has no shame."

"I'm right behind you guys." I stood up and kept my back to Darren and his buddy. "All I want to do right now is get the hell out of here."

"Sounds like tomorrow might be a good day for you to call in sick," Andie said.

I finished off my beer and put it on the bar. "No kidding. After that performance, I might as well call in dead."

• • •

The following Monday night, I met up with McKenna after work for a yoga class. On the way out of the studio, I stopped in my tracks and put my hands on my hips.

"Frick, I left my purse in my office," I said. "Just what I needed to top off this fantastic night." I was already annoyed because I'd been stuck next to one of those inappropriate yoga guys for the entire class. I wanted to punch him after all that endless grunting and groaning and moaning, and then when he started snoring in the final relaxation pose—the main reason I even *went* to yoga—I nearly lost it.

"Can't you just get it tomorrow?" she said.

"Nope, it's got my keys in it."

She patted my head. "Now you know why I've been telling you for years to give me a set of your keys."

I looked at her and held out my hand. "Have we met? I'm Waverly Bryson, not some responsible adult."

"Fine, fine. Let's go."

"It shouldn't take long. The security guard knows me. He can let us in."

Five minutes later, we were in the dark offices of K. A. Marketing, the only light coming from the soft glow of the exit signs and the kitchen, which for some reason was always lit.

"This is creepy," McKenna said. "I'm heading to the kitchen to get some water. Meet me at the elevator?"

"Sure. I'll just be a minute." I walked down the long hallway to my office and grabbed my purse. I was about to head back to the elevator when I thought I heard someone crying. I paused for a second.

Crying?

Then I noticed a single light on down the opposite hall. I walked slowly toward the noise.

"Hello? Is anyone here?" I said.

The crying stopped. I walked toward the light and poked my head into the doorway.

Mandy Edwards was sitting at her desk, wiping tears from her cheeks.

"Mandy, are you all right?" I said.

She pushed a few strands of hair away from her face and nodded. "I'm fine."

"Are you sure?"

"As fine as I can be, I guess."

I looked down at my hands and then up at her watery green eyes.

"Um, what's wrong?" I said.

She sniffled. "I don't know what to do."

"What do you mean?"

Silence.

"Mandy?"

She put her face in her hands and started crying again. "I found out that my fiancé has been cheating on me."

Her words were so unexpected that for a moment I just stood there.

"Oh God, I'm sorry, Mandy," I finally said.

She coughed, and the tears began to stream down her cheeks.

I didn't know what else to say, but it didn't seem right to leave her there, so I sat down on the chair across from her desk and let her cry.

And cry.

After about thirty seconds, I finally spoke. "Is there anything I can do? You two looked so happy when I saw you together."

She coughed again. "I love him, Waverly. God, I love him so much. I thought he was so perfect, you know?"

I nodded. Boy, did I know.

"But part of me has always known that he wasn't who I thought he was. Or who I hoped he was," she said.

Was this really Mandy Edwards sitting in front of me?

I handed her a tissue. "Well, I guess it's better to find out now than after you were married, right?"

She blew her nose. "I know, I know. And I know I have to break it off. It's just so much harder than I thought it would be. I . . . I just don't want to be single again."

I stared at her. For a second it was like looking in a mirror.

I took a deep breath. "Mandy, believe me, I know how you feel. I *really* do. But you can't be with someone who isn't right for you just so you won't be alone."

"That's easy for you to say," she said.

"What do you mean?"

"I mean, you're from around here, you went to college here. You're not alone, but I am. Besides Darren and my roommate, I don't really have any friends in San Francisco. And no matter what I do, I can't seem to make any, especially here at work."

I bit my lip.

"I know I'm not that great with people sometimes, and ever since I transferred to this department, all I've wanted to do is fit in. But no matter how hard I try, people seem to hate me," she said.

"People don't hate you, Mandy," I said softly.

"C'mon, Waverly, every time I try to talk to you, you can't run away fast enough. And I hear the things you say about me." The tears were still streaming down her face.

Me and my big humongous mouth.

"And I know what other people around here think about me. I know everyone resents me for taking over the JAG account."

I twisted my right earring. "Well, that's not exactly true."

"Please, I'm not stupid."

I couldn't think of anything to say, so I just looked down at my hands.

She blew her nose again. "When Jess offered me the account, I thought maybe I could do it. I thought maybe I could show everyone that I do belong here. But I was wrong."

I kept looking at my hands.

"I didn't want it, you know," she said.

I looked back up at her. "You didn't?"

She dabbed at her eyes with a tissue. "Waverly, I was already so over my head with Adina Energy, you don't even want to know."

"You were?"

She nodded. "And if you remember, I tried to ask you for help more than once, but I don't have to remind you what your reaction was."

"I ... I ..." I didn't know what to say. She had really been asking for *help*?

"So believe me, taking on another account was the last thing I wanted," she said.

I handed her another tissue. "But I thought—"

"Well, you thought wrong."

"Then why did you agree to take the JAG account on as well?"

She dabbed her eyes. "What was I supposed to do? Tell Jess that I couldn't handle it?"

I took a deep breath. "Wow, I honestly had no idea you felt that way. I thought you were happy running both accounts."

"Well, I'm not. I'm drowning, okay? Thank God Kent and Nicole know the JAG account so well, because without them I'd be in serious trouble."

I handed her another tissue. "Why didn't you say something?"

"What could I say? I'd already asked you for help more than once. Why do you hate me so much anyway? What did I ever do to you?"

I couldn't deny it. "Well, I guess, I guess I just don't trust you," I said.

"Why not?"

I took a deep breath and exhaled. "Well, to be honest, I don't trust you because of that whole Super Show thing."

"What Super Show thing?"

"You know, what you told Jess about me after the big party that JAG threw."

She looked at me. "What?"

"Come on, Mandy, I know it was you."

"You know it was me? What was me?"

"I saw your roommate's sister there. I know what she told you."

"My roommate's sister? What? I swear I have no idea what you're talking about."

I looked her right in the eye.

"You didn't tell Jess?"

"Tell Jess what?"

"You really didn't tell him?"

The look in her eyes was blank.

Wow. I couldn't believe how much my initial opinion of her had clouded my judgment of everything she said and did, and for so long. Talk about judging a book before you've walked a mile in its moccasins.

"Mandy, I think I owe you an apology," I said.

"For what?"

I walked behind her desk and pulled her out of her chair. "For being an idiot. C'mon, let's get you out of here."

We walked out into the hallway and nearly smashed right into McKenna.

"Uh, hi. I didn't want to intrude, but I wasn't sure where to go," she said.

"No worries," I said, and looked at Mandy. "Mackie, this is Mandy. And she needs a margarita."

As we walked toward the elevator I made a mental note for a Honey Note.

Front: Ever wonder why the new girl at work seems to hate you so much?

Inside: Honey, think back to the angst of the high school lunchroom. Then offer her a seat at your table.

Always trying to plan how your life is going to turn out?

Honey, where's the fun in that?

CHAPTER TWENTY-ONE

With three weeks to go before the auction, the planning for McKenna's wedding continued full steam ahead. We pretty much had everything in order, and when the day came to send out the invitations, we went for a walk before work for a heart-to-heart.

"So this is it, my dear. The big day," I said, as we headed down the steepest part of Fillmore toward the water. "Once those bad boys are in the mailbox, there's no going back."

"I can't believe it," she said. "I'm so nervous."

"What are you talking about?" I stretched my arms over my head. "Why are you nervous? You two are perfect for each other. And I was kidding about the *no going back* by the way."

"I know you were, and I know we are, but I'm still nervous, Wave. Seriously, so nervous."

"Really? But why?" I said.

She scratched her cheek. "I love Hunter to death, I really do. But I like doing my own thing, too, ya know? And I love spending time with my friends. I just don't want that to change once I'm married."

"I know, I know." I nodded my head. "I've realized those things about myself, too, thank God."

"I hope I'm not a horrible wife," she said.

I laughed and pushed her arm. "Mackie, please. You're great with Hunter. Believe me, I've paid attention. Besides, he doesn't want a Stepford wife, he wants you. He knows how you are, and he loves you for it. He doesn't expect you to change just because you're marrying him."

"Do you think so? Even though we've been together forever, I'm afraid things might change once we're officially married. Does that make sense?"

I put my arm around her and squeezed. "Don't worry, Mackie, you're going to be fine."

"Really?"

I laughed. "Yes, really. Ya know, I must say that I'm rather enjoying this moment."

"What moment?"

"The one moment in our ENTIRE RELATIONSHIP where I'm the one calming *you* down, not vice versa."

She laughed. "I'm glad my stress brings you joy."

"Seriously, Mackie, ask yourself this: do you want to be with Hunter?"

She nodded.

"Forever?"

She nodded again.

"Are you sure?"

She paused for a few seconds and then smiled. "Yes, I'm sure."

"Then you're going to be fine. If you're doing what you really want to do, you'll be happy. It's as easy as that."

"Ya think?"

I nodded. "Don't worry about how your life is supposed to be. Just make it how you want it to be."

Once the words were out of my mouth, I realized that I finally believed them.

Late that night, hoping he'd be gone from the office, I called Aaron. I'd noticed that attorneys tend to live at the office, so I couldn't be sure he wouldn't answer, in which case I'd either have to hang up or disguise my voice and pretend it was a wrong number (thank God his office phone system didn't have caller ID). But I lucked out and got his voicemail, so I left a message wishing him the best with the baby and his marriage and life in general. I didn't have the guts to actually talk to him, but I meant what I said and wanted him to know that I'd moved on.

I didn't mention the hiding behind a car thing though—I'd matured, but I hadn't gone insane.

I hung up and went to bed contented, finally feeling the sense of closure I'd wanted so much.

And the very next day, I did what I should have done long before.

I quit my job.

. . .

The Tuesday evening before the auction, I was walking along Union Street in the Cow Hollow neighborhood, window-shopping for a dress to wear and chatting with Andie on my cell phone.

"So after the next press tour for the Honey Notes, that's it? You're done with K.A. Marketing?" she said.

"Yep," I said. "Totally done."

"I still can't believe you quit."

"Really?"

"Yep. I didn't think you'd ever leave that place," she said.

"You didn't?"

"Nope. Besides that Mandy girl and the occasional annoying client, I thought you loved it there."

I smoothed my hand over my ponytail. "Yeah, well, it took me a while to even realize it, much less admit it, but I didn't love it, and to be honest I didn't even like it all that much anymore."

"Really?" she said.

"Yeah, I mean, it was okay, and I did like it at one point, but I always thought that I should *love* it because, well, because everyone was always saying what a great job it was, you know?"

"It did sound perfect, but I guess that was on paper," she said.

I laughed. "I could say the same thing about my relationship with Aaron. But anyhow, my heart just wasn't in it anymore. I think that's why I was so quick to judge Mandy, because she tried harder than I did. And it turned out that I was wrong about her, you know. She's actually pretty nice."

"So what happened to push you over the edge?"

"Not one thing in particular. I guess it was more a feeling that it was okay to try something new and move on, you know? That it was okay to admit that sports PR wasn't the right career for me, or at least anymore."

"What did your boss say when you told him?"

"He wasn't thrilled, but he understood. Part of me thinks he may even have been a little relieved, because it wasn't like I'd been all that busy lately. It obviously hasn't been the greatest year for me there. And now I can focus full time on the Honey Notes, which is what I've realized I really want to do anyway. I've even thought about branching the Honey brand out to other products for single women."

"Really? Like what?"

"*Honey*, I guess you'll have to wait and see," I said, laughing.

"Cool. And at least you're free of that whole annoying client thing," she said.

I smiled. "I definitely won't miss that. From now on, the only client who gets to boss Waverly Bryson around is Waverly Bryson."

"So what happens next?" she said.

"Well, after Mackie's wedding I'm going to Mexico to figure that out."

"Mexico? Nice. Who with?"

"No one, just me."

"Really?"

"Yep, I've got it all booked. Ten days at the new Playa del Sol resort in Cabo San Lucas, all by myself."

"Man, good for you, Waverly. Going on vacation by yourself takes guts."

I sat down on a bench outside the Coffee Roastery on the corner of Fillmore and Union. "Ya know, I'm actually really looking forward to it. To all of it."

"Seriously, I'm proud of you. You're so grown up," she said.

"Me? Grown up? As in a grown-up?"

"Are you kidding? Totally. Look at what you're doing with your life."

I smiled. "I guess I hadn't thought about it that way. So I guess you can be grown up and still eat cereal for dinner?"

She laughed. "Apparently so."

"Cool," I said.

"Well, I'm very impressed."

"Thanks," I said. "I mean *gracias.* I guess I should start practicing my Spanish."

Just then I spotted Brad Cantor in the crosswalk.

"Oh crap," I whispered into the phone.

"What?"

"Nothing, it's just another Brad Cantor sight—"

A vision of Mandy Edwards, alone and crying at her desk, flashed before me.

"Andie, I'll call you back."

"What? Why?"

"I'll explain later. Bye, Andie."

I shut the phone and waved my hand. "Hey, Brad, over here."

. . .

The day of the singles auction, I woke up to the sound of my phone ringing. I rolled over and looked at the clock on my nightstand. It was 5:30 a.m.

"What the . . . ?" The sun was definitely still asleep, as were all sane people in the Pacific time zone. Was it always this dark outside at five thirty in the morning? Had I ever even been awake at five thirty in the morning?

I crawled out of bed and squinted at the caller ID display on my phone. It was filled with zeroes.

"Hello?" I said.

"Happy birthday, Miss Bryson!!!"

I held the phone away from my ear. "Davey?"

"What up, chicken butt?! Are you awake?"

"I am now. Why are you calling me at five thirty in the morning?"

"It's only five thirty there? Oops, sorry about that. I can't keep these time zones straight."

"Where are you?" I said, sitting back down on the bed and rubbing my eyes.

"Bali. Lindsay and I are sipping cocktails in the hotel lounge, but I couldn't miss your thirtieth birthday."

"Wow, Davey, I'm touched. Seriously."

"Hey now, our friendship doesn't end with our jobs, right?"

"Right. And guess what? I quit mine, too."

"You quit? Because of Gabrielle?"

I shook my head. "Nope. I think it was more the fact that I liked the idea of sports PR more than I liked sports PR itself. It just took me a while to realize it."

"Wow, well, I'm sure they'll miss you," he said. "You were really good at your job."

"Thanks, and I'll miss them, too, but they can still see me, right?" I said. "Like you will when you get back?"

"True," he said. "So speaking of seeing you, are any men doing that these days?"

I crawled back under the covers. "Nothing to report, sir. And that's fine with me."

"You still breaking hearts?"

I laughed. "Never was."

"You're killing me, Bryson."

"You know, there's something I never told you about that," I said.

"About what?"

"About my wedding, and about this whole 'breaking hearts' myth that you like to perpetuate."

"Your wedding?" he said. "Are we talking about the one you called off, or have I been out of the country longer than I thought?"

"The one I called off, silly. Only I didn't."

"You lost me."

"I didn't call it off," I said.

"You didn't call it off?"

"Nope."

"So you're married?"

I laughed. "No, you butthead, *he* called it off."

"*He* called it off? Really?"

"Really," I said.

"Oh, wow. I'm sorry, Waverly."

"That's okay, I'm over it now," I said. "Finally."

"Why didn't you ever say anything?"

"Because I was a lame-o."

"Because you were a *lame-o?*"

"Well that, and a few other reasons, too. But basically because I was a lame-o who was afraid of what people would think of her."

"Bryson, I've been giving you grief about that for like two years. Who's the lame-o now?"

"I don't want to hear it, okay, Davey? I should have told you, but I didn't. End of story, okay?"

"Okay, okay. So I guess this means I can't heckle you about being single anymore?"

I laughed. "No, of course it doesn't. It just means that I'm not going to let it bother me when you do."

"Did it really bother you that much?"

"A little, but I'm done with worrying about what other people think. Now I'm just trying to focus on what *I* think."

"Wait a minute. Who are you and what have you done with Waverly? Hey, am I on the radio?"

"I'm hanging up now, Davey."

"Happy birthday, Miss Bryson."

. . .

A few hours later, McKenna, Andie, and I were cruising along in luxury seats aboard American Airlines flight 24 to New York's John F. Kennedy International Airport. We were chatting about the upcoming weekend and thoroughly enjoying a gourmet breakfast of eggs Benedict, croissants, fresh fruit, and cappuccinos.

Andie was all smiles. "I can't wait to check out some of those great boutiques in the West Village. I've been looking forever for a pair of—oh hell, it's Princeton Hopper." She pointed to a guy leaving the first-class lavatory and sitting down three rows in front of us.

I sat up straight and looked around the cabin. "Who?"

"Princeton Hopper. I met him at the Kilkenny with some work friends back in January."

"And?" McKenna said.

"And we ended up having breakfast together, if you know what I mean."

"Excellent," McKenna said with a laugh.

Andie lowered her voice. "But get this: a couple weeks ago I ran into him at the Starbucks on Montgomery Street downtown, and he didn't recognize me."

McKenna coughed. "You're joking."

Andie shook her head. "Nope. I looked right at him and got zero, zilch, nada. Not a spark of recognition! I mean, am I that forgettable?"

"Do you think he would have recognized you if you took your clothes off?" I said.

"Waverly!" McKenna hit me on the shoulder.

"I'm just asking," I said.

. . .

Six hours later we were at JFK's baggage claim. Luckily we didn't have to wait long, because the airline crew had tagged the first-class luggage and brought it out before the bags of the unwashed masses in coach. We were out of there and in the taxi line within minutes.

I looked at my watch. It was five thirty. We had two and a half hours to make it to the hotel, shower, and change for the auction. The taxi line was long, and with Friday traffic it was going to be tight.

"I'm so stupid," I said. "Why didn't I book an earlier flight? If I don't have time to take a shower, I'm going to show up at the auction with plane hair. Will you guys promise to bid on me if no one else does?"

"Don't they have a bunch of stylists to make you all beautiful?" Andie said.

I shook my head. "I wish. I guess all the real celebrities bring their own entourage for that sort of thing. We imposters get the hotel shampoo."

Traffic was nice to us, and we made it to the hotel with just enough time to get ready. The hotel shampoo turned out to be nice, too, way nicer than my normal shampoo. And our room turned out not to be a room at all. It was a suite, and it was ridiculous.

"Holy crap," I whispered as we walked in.

The living room was enormous, with a high ceiling and bright white walls. French doors opened to a large balcony with bamboo trees and pink rose bushes lining the sides. The floors were marble, the furniture a dark, rich walnut. On one side of the room was a massive home entertainment center with a stereo, a huge flat-screen TV, a DVD player, and three shelves full of movies. Facing it was a huge sectional couch that could probably sleep four people comfortably. On the other side of the room was a large desk with a PC, a fully stocked wet bar with an espresso machine, and another couch and matching love seat. An exquisite oriental rug filled the center of the room, and a large crystal chandelier hovered over it.

The bathroom in the master bedroom was the biggest I'd ever seen. In addition to two sinks and a huge shower with showerheads on both sides and steam holes along the wall, it housed a massive Jacuzzi that could easily seat six people. The bedroom itself, also huge, had two king beds, another flat-screen TV, and another desk and PC. Yet another room featured a treadmill and stair machine, both armed with headphones and hooked up to a wall-mounted TV/DVD unit.

"Wow. *People* magazine doesn't mess around," McKenna said as we walked back into the living room.

I tipped the bellboy, who bowed slightly and promptly disappeared. "Apparently not," I said.

"This place is straight out of a movie," Andie said.

A huge basket overflowing with flowers, fruit, and snacks sat on the glass coffee table by one of the couches. I walked over and picked out the card.

Waverly,

> *Welcome to New York! We hope you enjoy your stay. Anything you want from room service or any of the hotel restaurants is on the house. As a special birthday treat, the staff spa is expecting you at noon tomorrow and will take good care of you and your two friends. It's on us, so have fun!*
>
> *I look forward to seeing you at the party tonight. You've got my number, so if you need anything else, don't hesitate to call.*

Tracy Leiderman and the people at People

The spa was expecting me *and* my two friends? And how did she know it was my birthday?

"Wow. Tracy would sure give Penelope French at JAG a run for her money," I said.

"Huh?" McKenna picked through the basket and unwrapped a Twix.

"Oh, nothing, just talking to myself." I handed her the card. "Take a look at this. We're in the spa business! Now let's get a move on, or we're going to be late to the party."

. . .

At 8 p.m. sharp, the three of us stood in front of the huge mirror in the master bedroom. My dress was dark red and strapless, fitted tightly at my waist, with a line of tiny black silk roses sewn across the bust. The cut was A-line and fell two inches above the knee. Along the bottom hem was another line of tiny black silk roses. My hair was pulled straight back off my forehead and up into a high bun. I wore no jewelry except for my small diamond earrings. My black strappy heels put me at a solid five feet ten inches.

McKenna wore a simple fitted black strapless crepe dress that stopped just above her knees. Her blonde hair was pulled into a low bun, her only jewelry a thin silver bracelet. Her black strappy heels put her at a solid six feet two inches.

Andie wore a gold shimmery halter top and black pants, soft pinkish-brown lipstick, and big dangly gold earrings. She had her short blonde hair tucked behind her ears. Her black strappy heels put her at a solid five feet four inches.

"We look like Papa Bear, Mama Bear, and Baby Bear," I said.

"I think we look pretty good," McKenna said.

I nodded. "I agree, not bad at all."

"*Pretty good? Not bad?* Are you two crazy? We look HOT," Andie said.

"Hey, maybe Princeton Hopper will be there," I said. "I'd pay to see *that* reunion."

"Thanks, you beeyatch," Andie said, pretending to slap me on the cheek.

"Hey now, don't touch the makeup!" I said, laughing.

"You two are ridiculous," McKenna said.

"Sorry, Papa Bear," I said, hanging my head.

We walked to the elevator, and Andie turned to me as she pushed the down button. "Hey, Waverly, you never said how the auction is going to work. Do you have to prance around on a stage like at a beauty pageant?"

I looked for a breath mint in my purse, the same cute yet basically useless black one I'd brought to Cynthia's wedding. "Oh God, I hope not. I couldn't bring myself to ask for any details. All I know is that after the auction I'm supposed to sit at dinner with whoever bid the most on me, and I'm supposed to dance with him a bit too, you know, like a real date."

"That's supposed to be like a real date?" Andie said. "When was the last time anyone took either of you to dinner and dancing on a date?"

"Good point," I said.

"Hunter likes to dance," McKenna said with a tiny smile.

"Hunter's way too perfect," I said.

McKenna put her hand on my head as the elevator door opened.

"Yeah, but at least you'll have free health care until you get a new job. Okay, let's go. I can't wait to see this."

Andie waved her arms in the air and did a little dance. "I can't wait to see the open bar either, birthday girl. It's all good—woo-hoo!"

I pushed her into the elevator, and we were off like a prom dress.

. . .

The auction party might have been for charity, but someone certainly paid a ridiculous amount of money to put it on. It wasn't half as large as Cynthia's wedding, but the glamour was definitely on a par. And the celebrity sightings alone were worth the trip. From what Tracy Leiderman had told me, including me, there were thirteen men and women from the 50 Most Beautiful list on the auction docket, nearly all of them actors. And twelve of them were way better looking than me. There were also twenty other singles on the block who had been featured one way or another in the magazine, but I didn't know who they were, because the room was also filled with a bunch of McKennas and Andies who were there to support (or heckle) their friends.

We wandered over to the bar, ordered three glasses of wine, and checked out the crowd.

"Wow, all these guys are single?" McKenna scanned the room. She looked down at her engagement ring and then at me. "Remind me again why I'm getting married in a couple weeks?"

"Oh yeah, like your surgeon fiancé isn't a total babe. Now shut up and mingle," Andie said.

"Touché," McKenna said.

Drinks in hand, we decided to look for Tracy.

"What does she look like?" McKenna said.

"Uh, I don't know," I said.

"You don't know?" she said.

"Well, I've never met her before," I said.

"Then how are we supposed to spot her in this crowd?"

I shrugged. "I guess I never thought about that."

She laughed. "You didn't think about that?"

I held out my hand. "I'm sorry, have we met? I'm Waverly Bryson."

Just then we noticed a short, plump woman approaching the microphone on a small elevated platform at the back of the room.

The band stopped playing, and everyone turned their attention toward her.

"Welcome, ladies and gentlemen. I'm Tracy Leiderman, head of community relations at *People*."

"I guess that answers that question," I whispered to McKenna as I set my drink down on a nearby table.

"I can't say I was all that worried," she whispered back.

Tracy smiled at the crowd. "On behalf of our entire staff, I'd like to thank you for coming tonight. We know all of you have busy schedules and have gone out of your way to be here, and we very much appreciate it. Please enjoy the cocktails and appetizers. In a few minutes we'll bring the singles up on stage and open the doors to the bidders. We have thirty-three singles up for auction, but our auctioneer is very fast, so the whole thing shouldn't take more than forty-five minutes. We'll have all the singles up here together first so the audience can get a look and pick out their favorites, and then we'll go one by one with the bidding."

"Oh God, kill me now," I whispered, squeezing McKenna's and Andie's hands.

"It'll be fine," McKenna whispered back.

"I need another drink," Andie whispered.

Tracy was still talking. ". . . and when the auction is over, we'll introduce you to your dates. They'll join us all for cocktails for a half-hour or so before we move to dinner in the room next door, followed by some fun dance music. We'll have to take a few photos for the magazine, but we promise to keep it light so you can enjoy yourselves. And I promise we'll be all done by eleven."

My ears perked up. "Fun dance music? You think they'll play '80s tunes?"

"If they do, please promise me you won't try to convince them to play "YMCA" like you did at Whitney's wedding, okay?" McKenna said.

I shrugged. "Okay, okay. But I still say that crowd was on its deathbed before I took charge."

Andie took a sip of her drink and looked around the room. "I wonder how much money people are going to bid? Some of those guys are really cute."

"You're actually thinking about bidding on someone?" McKenna said.

"Hey, a girl's got needs," Andie said.

Tracy got back up on stage and motioned for the singles to join her.

I took a deep breath. "Wish me luck."

"Good luck," said McKenna.

"Don't trip," Andie said.

I walked up to the stage, where Tracy was chatting with what looked like her assistant. When she saw me approaching, she turned and held out her hand.

"Waverly Bryson! What a pleasure to finally meet you in person."

"Hi, Tracy," I said, shaking her hand.

Apparently my eyes said more than my words did, because she put her other hand on my shoulder and laughed. "Don't worry, it'll be fun. I promise."

"You promise?"

She nodded. "It may be a little painful, but it'll also be fun. And it's for a good cause, right?"

"No pain, no gain, huh?" I said.

She winked and motioned for everyone to gather around her. "Something like that."

Ten minutes later we were backstage. I could hear the noise of the crowd on the other side of the curtain and wondered how many people would be in the audience. I looked down at the huge round number seven pinned to my chest, then up at all the other singles lined up around me. Everyone was laughing and chatting, but with a nervous energy that told me I wasn't the only one who felt just a little bit foolish. I recognized a few people from the Most Beautiful list, but most of the others I'd never seen before.

"You ready, number seven?" the guy behind me said.

I laughed. "As ready as I'll ever be, number eight."

"I think I'm going to throw up," number six said.

I could hear the muffled voice of the MC announcing the auction.

Then there was a countdown. "Ten, nine, eight, seven, six, five, four, three, two, one . . ."

I bit my lip.

"Ladies and gentlemen, here are our single PEOPLE!"

The curtain went up, and for a second I thought I was looking straight into the sun. The bright lights were everywhere, and the crowd was going crazy. I heard Tracy shout *"Now!"* and our line started moving. I couldn't see anything more than three feet in front of me, so I just followed number six. We walked across the stage, and as I grinded my teeth into a painfully fake smile I wondered why I hadn't had another glass of wine.

". . . Number seven, Waverly! Number eight, Jason! Number nine, Brady! . . ."

We walked across the stage and back, all of us blindly smiling into the lights. Then we went backstage to the green room, and the waiting began. Thank God I was number seven and not number twenty-seven. I couldn't wait for number one to come back and give us the scoop so we'd know what to expect.

The problem was that number one didn't come back. And then numbers two and three copied her.

"Crap," I said, as number four got up to leave. "It's a black hole out there."

"Are you nervous, number seven?" number eight said to me. He looked so familiar, but I couldn't place him.

I nodded. "Just slightly, you?"

"Nah, I love this sort of thing."

"You love being auctioned off?" I said.

He laughed. "I love being on stage. I'm a singer."

Then I remembered where I'd seen him. "Hey, wait a minute, weren't you on *American Idol* a couple seasons ago?" I said.

He smiled.

"I love that show!" I said.

"So do I," he said. "I used to be a mechanic, and look at me now. This is way better than changing a battery."

I felt the same way about myself. This was much better than writing press releases, despite the feeling that I might throw up at any moment.

"So what do *you* do?" he said.

"Oh, uh, I have a line of funny greeting cards for single women. They're called Honey Notes."

"Cool," he said. "I dig it." He'd obviously never heard of my cards or of me, but I didn't care. It was the first time in a long time that I didn't secretly wish I had a different answer to that question.

I smiled. "Thanks, I dig it too."

The door opened, and Tracy poked her head in. "Waverly, you're up."

I stood up and smoothed my dress. "Holy crap," I said.

"Good luck, number seven," number eight said.

"Thanks, number eight," I said.

I followed Tracy out of the room and into a dark corridor toward the noise and the lights. She pointed straight ahead of us. "Okay, Waverly, when the auctioneer calls your name, just walk through that entrance to the stage, stand in the white circle, and smile."

"That's all I have to do?" I said. "Stand in the white circle and smile?"

She laughed. "Were you expecting an obstacle course or something?"

"Something like that," I said.

She put her hand on my shoulder. "We're not that mean. Don't worry, you'll do great."

"Do I have lipstick on my teeth?" I said.

She shook her head. "You look beautiful. Okay, it's nearly time."

I could hear the auction for number six in full swing, the loud voice of the auctioneer filling up the room. "THIRTY-EIGHT hundred, we have THIRTY-EIGHT hundred from the man in the back. Do I hear FOUR THOUSAND?"

"Thirty-eight hundred dollars?" I said. "That's like a mortgage payment for a really nice house!"

"Number two went for ten thousand," Tracy said.

I could feel my eyes getting really big. "Ten thousand dollars? Are you joking? Who was number two?"

"The Victoria's Secret model."

I closed my eyes and tried not to freak out.

"SOLD! . . . for thirty-eight hundred dollars!" the auctioneer said. The crowd erupted, and number six walked off the stage and past me.

"Nice job," I said.

"Thanks," she said. "Although I'm pretty sure it was a friend who bid on me."

I was fairly certain McKenna and Andie weren't about to cough up thirty-eight hundred dollars to have dinner with me.

"Okay, it's your turn, Waverly," Tracy said to me.

The voice of the auctioneer boomed. "Ladies and gentlemen, let's give it up for single number seven!"

"Good luck!" Tracy gave me a little shove, and I started walking toward the stage. *Smile and don't trip*, I thought to myself. *Smile and don't trip. Smile and don't trip.*

The noise of the crowd got louder as I approached the entrance to the stage. I paused for a moment, then took a deep breath and stepped into the lights.

The auctioneer's voice was way louder than I expected it to be, or better put, WAY LOUDER THAN I EXPECTED IT TO BE. "Number seven is WAVERLY BRYSON, featured in this year's 50 Most Beautiful People issue!!"

I saw the white circle and headed straight to it, trying to smile, and suddenly barely aware of what the announcer was saying, or screaming.

". . . comes to us from SAN FRANCISCO . . ."

I reached the circle safely and turned to face the crowd.

". . . GREETING CARDS earlier this year . . ."

I looked for a familiar face, but the lights blocked out everything. The only person I could see was a really short bald man in the front row. He looked friendly, so I smiled at him.

The announcer continued. "So let's get the bidding started. Do I hear TWO THOUSAND dollars?"

I swallowed hard. Please, please, please let someone, anyone, bid on me.

The auctioneer shouted, "TWO THOUSAND dollars from the gentleman in the corner! Do I hear twenty-two hundred?"

I shifted my weight from my left hip to my right.

"TWENTY-TWO HUNDRED, we have twenty-two hundred. Do I hear TWENTY-FIVE?"

The crowd was cheering and clapping.

The announcer yelled again. "TWENTY-FIVE HUNDRED! We have twenty-five hundred from the woman in the white hat. Do I hear TWENTY-SEVEN?"

The *woman* in the white hat? McKenna and Andie weren't wearing hats. Hmm. Well, I guess that would make for a good story, right?

"Is that three thousand I hear?" the auctioneer said. "Yes! We have a bid for THREE THOUSAND from the gentleman in the back."

The crowd went wild. Three thousand dollars? Someone had upped the bid to three thousand dollars? I squinted to see the back but still couldn't see past the bald man in the front. He was still smiling at me, but he wasn't bidding.

"THIRTY-FIVE hundred!" The auctioneer pointed his gavel to the right of the crowd. "I have THIRTY-FIVE hundred from the tall blonde woman to my right."

Tall blonde woman? Mackie perhaps? How much wine had she had?

"We have THIRTY-FIVE hundred," the auctioneer said. "Do I hear FOUR THOUSAND?"

Nothing.

I clasped my hands together in front of me and smiled. Was it over? Thirty-five hundred wasn't bad at all!

"FIVE THOUSAND!" the auctioneer suddenly yelled. "FIVE THOUSAND from the gentleman in the back!" The noise of the audience mirrored the sudden jump in the bidding and suddenly jumped a few decibels in response.

Five thousand dollars? To have dinner with me?

"FIVE THOUSAND dollars," the auctioneer said. "We have five thousand ... going once ... going twice ... SOLD! For FIVE THOUSAND dollars!"

The cheer of the crowd grew even louder, even though I still couldn't actually see anyone. I smiled into the lights and curtsied and exited stage left. I didn't know if I was more excited about having gone for five thousand dollars or having stayed on my feet.

. . .

After the auction was over, Tracy called us all backstage again. The plan was for our dates to come pick us up at the green room, and then we'd sit together at dinner. I was dying to know who had picked me. The Victoria's Secret model had been the top bid, but hey, I'd gone for half of what she had! I figured that was pretty good, given that my bra size was about half of hers, if that.

As I walked toward the green room, I heard Tracy's voice. "Hey, Waverly, can I talk to you for a minute?"

I turned around and walked up to her. "Sure, what's up?"

She pursed her lips. "Well, there was a little glitch in your auction."

Oh frick, my bidder had changed his mind. I was the girl without a bidder.

"Oh, uh, that's okay," I said. "I had a feeling that might happen."

Tracy laughed. "It's not what you think. It's just that your date had some sort of an emergency and had to leave."

Thank God! But then again, maybe that wasn't such a great thing. What happened next?

"So what happens next?" I said.

"Well, that's what I wanted to talk to you about. If you're okay with it, I'd like to ask you to have dinner with him tomorrow night. I know it's different from what you agreed to do, but if you wouldn't mind, I would really, really appreciate it."

Hmm. Saturday was supposed to be our big night out for McKenna's bachelorette weekend and for my birthday. "Will the date have to last all night? I sort of already have plans," I said.

"No, no, of course not. He'll pick you up at your hotel at seven thirty, and I promise by ten you'll be free for the night. All you have to do is have dinner with him, and we'll pay for anywhere you two want to go."

I swallowed and nodded my head. "Okay, sure. I'd be glad to do it."

"Oh, thank you so much, Waverly. I really appreciate this. You just made my life a lot less complicated."

"No problem. So who is this guy anyway?"

She looked at her clipboard and ran her finger down the page. "Feldman. Wendall P. Feldman, from Dallas, Texas."

Wendall P. Feldman? Someone named Wendall P. Feldman had paid five thousand dollars to have dinner with me?

"Can I ask you one question?" I said.

"Sure."

"Is the guy visually impaired?"

She hit me lightly on the shoulder with her clipboard. "Shush. Now get out there and enjoy the rest of your birthday with your friends."

"Hey, Tracy, how did you know it was my birthday anyway?"

She winked. "A little bird told me."

. . .

The party turned out to be a total blast. McKenna, Andie, and I made friends with the bartenders, and we lit up the dance floor, too. I hadn't danced that much since we used to go clubbing right out of college. In addition to my beloved '80s tunes, the band played hip-hop and top-40 music, so we hardly took a break.

Most of the auction winners were straight off the rack at Nerds R Us, but they were really nice people, and who could knock their enthusiasm? And the few celebrities in the group were actually pretty cool, too. At first things were a little tense, but once everyone had squirted a few tubes of social lubricant down their throats, one and all had a good time. We danced up a storm with everybody in sight, and I wished my camera had fit into my elf-size purse.

After the party ended, the three of us headed out to a small jazz club in Greenwich Village. We made our way through the crowd and sat down in the back. "Okay, ladies, what's the drink of choice?" Andie said. "Lemon drops? Kamikazes? Jägermeister?"

"Jägermeister?" I said. "That stuff is still around? Have you ever noticed that you can taste that stuff days later when you burp?"

"That's gross," McKenna said.

"Yes, yes it is," I said. "And that's why I'll be ordering a vodka tonic."

"And a lemon drop to go with it," Andie said. "You're not getting off that easy, birthday girl."

"All right, fine." I hated shots, but hell, it was my birthday. Okay, it was after midnight and thus no longer technically my birthday, but whatever.

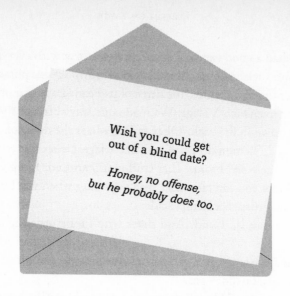

Wish you could get
out of a blind date?

*Honey, no offense,
but he probably does too.*

CHAPTER TWENTY-TWO

The next morning we didn't wake up until after eleven, and it wasn't pretty when we did. I called room service and ordered three plates of scrambled eggs with cheese, two orders of curly fries, three large bottles of lemon-lime Gatorade, a bottle of aspirin, and three Diet Cokes. Nothing was going to make our suffering go away completely, but I was pulling out all the stops to try.

When the food arrived, I tipped the bellman and rolled the huge tray into Andie and McKenna's bedroom. They were still facedown on their beds.

"Rise and shine, honey buns, time to get a move on," I said.

"I gave at the office," Andie said.

McKenna groaned and sat up with her arms crossed over her face. "Aspirin, I need aspirin."

At noon we finally made it down to the luxury spa on the second floor, all three of us wearing dark sunglasses, shorts, T-shirts, and flip-flops. I gave the receptionist my name, and she smiled and looked down at the schedule in front of her. "Welcome to the Plaza Spa, Miss Bryson. It looks like we'll be treating you and your guests to a steam sauna, a Swedish massage, and a European cleansing facial. Then we'll serve you a light lunch in our sun room, followed by a deluxe manicure and a paraffin wax pedicure. You'll finish off with a tray of chocolates and coffee, all compliments of *People* magazine, with birthday greetings from Tracy Leiderman."

Andie and I took off our sunglasses and looked at each other.

"I could get used to this life," I said.

She nodded. "Hell yes, you could."

The receptionist walked us back to the changing room, where thick robes and slippers were waiting. I looked around. Vases of fresh flowers were on nearly every flat surface.

She handed us each a steaming tea cup with tiny green flowers painted on it. "Your aestheticians will be by for you shortly. Feel free to relax in the recliner couches in the lounge area while you're waiting," she said.

I took a sip. "Okay, thank you so much." I hadn't even started my treatments, and I already felt like a princess. As she walked away, I lowered my voice and leaned toward Andie and McKenna. "It's amazing how a spa visit can make you feel so special, as if the people you're paying to saw the calluses off your feet really want to be there, ya know?"

"Totally," Andie said.

Hours later, we floated out of the spa feeling like new women. A thousand dollars worth of pampering can do wonders for a hangover. We had been rubbed and scrubbed, manicured and pedicured, oiled and spoiled, then fed and fed some more. We graciously thanked the staff and headed back upstairs.

I opened the door to our suite and walked into the master bedroom. "All right, I'm finally ready to get dressed and take on the day," I said.

"You mean ready to get dressed and take on the afternoon," McKenna said. "It's four o'clock."

I plopped down on the bed. "Four o'clock already? Good lord. Way to waste an entire day. We barely have any time left for shopping!"

Andie sat down next to me. "Are you kidding? You think spending four hours at a fancy spa, *for free*, is a waste?"

I laughed. "Yeah, I guess you're right. Look at me, already taking this princess thing for granted." I pulled my cell phone out of my backpack and was about to stick it into my shoulder bag when I saw that I had a new voicemail.

"Hi, Waverly, it's Kristina. Happy birthday! How was the party last night? I'm sorry I didn't get back to you earlier, but I've been slammed at the hospital. Shane and I are both free tonight though, so we were wondering if you'd like to get together for dinner. Give me a call when you get this message, okay? Bye."

"Darn it," I said. I'd called Kristina a few days earlier to let her know I was going to be in town.

"What's the problem?" McKenna said.

"That was Kristina. She and Shane invited us to dinner tonight, but I can't go. Why did I tell Tracy I would give up my one Saturday night in New York?"

"Because you're a good person, that's why," McKenna said.

I groaned and put my head between my knees. "You're right, you're right. But still, frick, frick, and more frick."

"Huge bummer though," McKenna said. "Hunter would totally flip if I had dinner with Shane Kennedy."

I stood up and put my hands on my hips. "Okay . . . let's get going, missy and missy, or we're going to missy out on what little remains of this beautiful day. I'll call Kristina from the road."

We headed out into the crisp October sun and decided to walk around the neighborhood a bit. In our drunken stupor the night before we'd seen some boutiques we wanted to check out.

We made it about two blocks before detouring into the very first coffee place we saw. On the way outside I called Kristina and held the phone up to my ear, then looked at the huge latte in my other hand. "Have you ever noticed that you're like a tractor beam for hungover people?" I said to the cup.

"Hey, Waverly, how's it going?" she said.

"Hi, Kristina. It's going great. How are you?"

"I'm good, just curious about this crazy singles auction you mentioned in your message the other day. Was it fun? And are you free for a birthday dinner tonight? Shane would like to see you, too."

I bit my lip. "I wish I could, but apparently the guy who bid on me couldn't stick around for the party last night, so now *I'm* stuck having dinner with him tonight. Can you do lunch or dinner tomorrow instead?" It all sounded so ridiculous.

"Hmm . . . we've got plans tomorrow," she said. "What time is your date? Maybe we could meet you for a drink before? Where are you staying?"

"He's picking me up at seven thirty, so that might work. We're staying at the Plaza. Would meeting there for a drink around six thirty work for you?"

"Let me check with Shane. Hold on a sec."

I looked at my watch. It was already nearly four thirty.

Kristina came back on the line. "Okay, that works. We'll meet you in the Oak Room bar at the Plaza at six thirty. Sound good?"

"Perfect, see you then."

I closed my phone and turned to McKenna and Andie. "Did you catch that?"

"Six thirty," McKenna said.

"At the hotel," Andie said.

I nodded. "Yep, but I guess that sort of squashes our shopping spree," I said.

"No biggie. We have all day tomorrow, and I'm too lazy to try on clothes right now anyway," Andie said.

"How about we head up to Central Park and lie in the sun for a bit before getting you ready for your big date?" McKenna said.

"That sounds absolutely perfect," I said. "Let's go."

. . .

An hour and a half later, we were back in our suite. I was in a towel with wet hair, on my knees, and rummaging through my suitcase to find something suitable to wear. I'd brought only one fancy dress with me, which I'd already worn, and everything else I had was either business casual for the following week's press interviews or super casual for lounging around and shopping. I had inexplicably forgotten to pack a cute outfit for what was supposed to be my big Saturday night out with McKenna and Andie. What was wrong with me?

Tracy had said my date would be picking me up in a limousine, so I figured the appropriate attire required a little more effort than jeans and flip-flops. Plus they were going to take our picture for the next week's issue of *People*. Oops.

"I have nothing to wear! N-A-D-A!" I yelled from the bedroom.

McKenna and Andie were sprawled out on the couch in the living room watching a DVD of *Save the Last Dance* and eating Pringles from the minibar.

"Sorry, can't help you and your shrimpy body!" McKenna yelled.

"Sorry, can't help you and your Amazon body!" Andie yelled.

We were definitely the Three Bears, which totally sucked, because they both had really cute clothes that would never fit me.

After several failed combinations, I finally walked into the living room wearing a pair of lightweight black capri pants, a red sleeveless button-down cotton shirt, and a pair of black flats with those miniature socks that make it look like you're not wearing socks. I had my hair down and wore a thick black headband.

"How about this?" I said.

Andie paused the movie and looked up at me. "You look like Skipper, Barbie's younger sister."

I frowned. "You suck."

"You asked." She laughed and turned back to the TV.

I walked back into the bedroom and stripped, throwing the pants and top into the growing pile of clothes on the floor next to my suitcase. I looked over at the clock on the nightstand. It was six fifteen, and I was still in my underwear. Crap. What was I going to wear?

Then I remembered a cute little cotton tank top I'd stuffed with my lingerie into the upper lining of my suitcase. I ran over and pulled it out. It was simple and black, with thin spaghetti straps and a built-in bra. Definitely dress-up-able. Then I headed back over to the pile of discarded clothes and began to dig. I thought I had a skirt in there somewhere that might work . . . where was it . . . c'mon, honey . . . throw me a bone here . . . bingo!

I pulled out the dark pink skirt with a thick black stripe around the hem. It was an A-frame cut and fell a couple inches above the knee. I had passed it over before because I couldn't find anything to go with it, but this black tank might do the trick. I put them both on and stood in front of the mirror. *Not bad.* Then I dug through my shoes and found a pair of black open-toed slides with two-inch heels. I slipped them on and looked in the mirror again. *Not bad at all.* All I needed now was some jewelry. I ran into the other bathroom and rummaged through McKenna's jewelry sack. She practically never wore jewelry, but she had some beautiful stuff. I found a thin silver chain with a tiny round diamond pendant. I slipped it around my neck and then put on my own diamond stud earrings. I looked at the full-length mirror. *Yes!* It was wrinkled, but it was definitely a cute outfit.

I walked back into the living room and held my arms out to the side. "Okay, Joan and Melissa, is this better?"

Andie paused the movie again and looked up.

"Well done. Good girl!" She sat up and clapped.

"You look great," McKenna said.

"Thank you, thank you very much." I curtsied, then stripped. "Hey, Mackie, I borrowed your diamond necklace. And can one of you please run an iron over these while I fix my hair and makeup? Thanks loves, you're peaches." I threw the skirt and tank top at them and ran back into the bedroom.

. . .

At six forty we headed downstairs to meet Shane and Kristina. Hunter had begged McKenna to call him and then keep her phone on so he could listen in. She had told him the wedding was off.

The bar was pretty empty, so we spotted them right away. Kristina stood up and trotted over to greet us. "Hey there, it's great to see you!" She gave me a hug. Her shiny black hair was pulled back into a low bun.

"Hi, Kristina, it's great to see you, too. These are my friends McKenna and Andie from San Francisco."

"Ahhh, the famous Mackie and Andie. It's great to finally meet you. I've heard a lot about both of you." She moved behind us and gave us each a gentle shove in the back. "Okay, ladies, let's get a move on and go meet my husband. The clock is ticking before Waverly's big date." We headed over to where Shane was sitting.

He stood up when we reached the bar. "Hi, Waverly, how's it going?" He leaned down to give me a hug.

I hugged him back on my tiptoes. "Hi, Shane. It's great to see you. Were you always this tall?"

"Yep, it must be you. Are you standing in a hole?" Then he leaned down and whispered in my ear. "So have you found anymore grey hairs?"

"Watch it, Mr. Kennedy," I whispered back. Then I playfully pushed him away and introduced him to McKenna and Andie.

"Can I get you ladies a drink?" Shane said.

I saw that he and Kristina each had a glass of white wine in front of them. I looked at my watch. It was barely six forty-five. Hmm.

"What the hell? I'll have a glass of merlot," I said.

McKenna looked at me and laughed. "Think *that* will help with your hangover?"

I held out my hand. "I'm sorry, have we met? I'm Waverly Bryson."

"Make that two glasses," Andie said.

McKenna looked at her and laughed. "You too?"

"Hair of the dog, you know," Andie said with a shrug.

"All right, make it three glasses," McKenna said.

"That's my girl," I said.

"Big night last night?" Kristina said.

The three of us nodded.

"Oh, yes," McKenna said.

"We were overserved," I said.

"It wasn't our fault," Andie said.

Shane handed us each a glass and sat down. "So what exactly is the deal with this date tonight? Is it some sort of reality show?"

I nearly choked on my wine. "Oh, God no, it's just a singles auction for charity. I was supposed to meet the guy last night right after the auction and have dinner with him then, but he bailed, so now I have to have dinner with him tonight."

"So who is he? Did they give you any scoop?" Kristina said.

"Nada. All I know is that his name is Wendall P. Feldman, and he's from Dallas," I said.

"Wendall Feldman?" Kristina said. "Seriously?"

"Seriously," I said. "And don't forget the *P.*"

"I have to pee," Andie said, standing up. "Be right back."

"What does he look like?" Kristina said.

I shook my head. "I have no idea. I couldn't see anything because of the bright lights, and Andie and McKenna couldn't see him in the crowd either. And then he left."

"Did you google him?" Shane said.

"Is he on Facebook?" Kristina said.

I lightly pounded my fist on the bar. "Darn it. I didn't even think of that. And we even have free Internet in our room upstairs, not to mention Andie's iPhone."

"We suck," McKenna said.

"Where are you going on your date?" Kristina said.

"I have no idea," I said. "I honestly know nothing."

"The guy bid five thousand dollars," McKenna said.

Kristina raised her eyebrows. "Really? Hmm . . . he must be very interested in you to spend that kind of money," she said.

McKenna laughed. "Or interested in getting his picture in *People* magazine."

"Touché," I said.

· · ·

At seven thirty-five, a short grey-haired man in a suit and chauffeur's cap walked into the bar. He approached our group with a polite smile.

"Excuse me, is one of you Waverly Bryson?" he said.

"Yes, sir, that's me," I said with a salute.

He bowed ever so slightly. "My name is Malcolm, and I'll be your chauffeur for the evening. The limo is waiting for you outside. If you'll just follow me, we'll be on our way."

I put my drink down and took a deep breath. "So we'll all meet up after my date is over?" I said to my friends.

"Yep, call me," McKenna said. She and Andie had hit it off with Kristina and Shane, so the four of them were going to dinner.

"Okay." I quickly reapplied my lipstick and stood up to smooth my skirt.

"I have to see this," McKenna said, standing up.

"Hell yes, we do," Andie said, following her.

"Me too." Kristina grabbed Shane and pulled him off his stool. Shane rolled his eyes. "Chicks."

The five of us followed the chauffeur out of the bar and into the lobby. Then I turned and pointed at them. "Okay, you can watch, but don't be all obvious and weird about it, okay? Promise?"

"Don't worry, we'll be quiet as mice. We just want to grab a peek," McKenna said.

"I hope he's not butt," Andie said.

I rolled my eyes. "Thanks, Andie. Now get out of here and keep your phone on vibrate so you don't miss my call, which I will be making the second this dinner is over. We still have a bachelorette party ahead of us."

"Bachelorette party? What?" Shane said. "Am I allowed to be here?"

"Honey, if you're lucky, we'll let you be the entertainment. Now shoo, all of you." I pushed him toward the others, then turned back to Malcolm, exhaled, and bit my lip.

"Okay, kind sir, show me the way." I tried to smile.

"After you, Miss Bryson." He gestured toward the hotel entrance.

"Here goes," I said softly.

Malcolm opened the lobby door for me, and I saw a black stretch limousine parked outside next to the curb. We walked under the hotel awning down the red carpet toward the sidewalk. I turned my head and saw my friends peering out from a window in the lobby, smiling and waving.

"Losers," I mouthed at them.

I shook my head and then turned forward to face the limousine, but I stepped funny, and my heel slipped on the carpet. I lost my balance and tried to catch myself by holding on to Malcolm's arm, but he was just out of reach, so I went down like a sack of bricks. My legs flew out from under me, and I fell flat on my back onto the carpet.

Holy crap.

"Miss Bryson, are you all right?" Malcolm and two doormen rushed over to help me up.

I struggled to my feet and smoothed out my skirt. "I'm fine, I'm fine. Totally mortified, but I'll live," I said.

I turned back to the hotel and saw the Four Stooges laughing their heads off from the lobby window. I curtsied and waved to them with a smile. I'd get them back later.

"Are you sure you're all right, Miss Bryson?" Malcolm said.

"Yes, I swear, I'm fine, thanks. Seriously, I'm okay." I had a massive raspberry on my left elbow that stung like hell, but I was too embarrassed to say anything about it. A Band-Aid would just have to wait.

"Okay, if you say so. But that was quite a tumble. Let me know if you need anything, okay?"

"I could use a big shot of tequila right about now," I said under my breath.

"Pardon?"

"Um, I said I could use a beach spot in Anguilla right about now."

"Couldn't we all, Miss Bryson. Couldn't we all." He tipped his hat and winked, then held out his arm. Malcolm was an okay dude.

I took his arm, and we started toward the limo. I prayed that Wendall P. Feldman hadn't witnessed my fall, so I could preserve the air-brushed illusion he probably expected for his five thousand dollars. Man, was he in for a surprise.

Malcolm opened the passenger door, and I leaned down and poked my head inside.

"Hi, Waverly, I'm so glad you made it. And you look gorgeous, as always."

The voice was so familiar. Could it be . . .?

I turned my head to the back of the limo and gasped.

Can Cupid strike more than once?

Honey, if everyone in France can, why can't the C-man?

CHAPTER TWENTY-THREE

I sat down inside the limousine and smoothed out my skirt. We started moving, but I felt like my stomach had been left behind on the sidewalk.

"Hi, Waverly," he said again.

I looked at him and blinked twice.

"Scotty?" Scotty Ryan . . . from . . . Dallas?

I swallowed hard. *What?*

He reached over and put his hand on my arm "Are you okay? You look a little startled."

Startled? Hellooo? Can you say *understatement?*

I could barely speak. "No, I'm fine, really. What are you . . .?" It came out as a squeak.

"It's great to see you, by the way. And are you really okay? That was quite a fall," he said.

So much for the airbrushed illusion.

"Oh, I'm okay. A little embarrassed, but I'm fine."

"Good, because I need you in top form for this date tonight. I've waited a long time for this moment, and I don't want you wimping out on me."

I touched my right earring and twisted it. "But Scotty, I don't understand."

"Don't understand what? Hey, want some champagne?" He pulled a bottle out of an ice bucket and held out a crystal flute.

I shook my head. "No, thanks."

"Are you sure? It's Dom Perignon."

On second thought, champagne suddenly seemed like a good idea. "Okay, why not?" I reached for the flute.

"Scotty?" I said softly.

"Yes, Waverly?"

"Um, aren't you, uh, you know . . .?"

"Aren't I what?"

"You know . . ."

He smiled. "Shorter than you are?"

I laughed. "No, you know . . . gay?"

His smile turned into a grin. Then he winked.

I was at a loss for words.

He lightly touched my leg. "I'll explain everything. Just wait a minute."

He touched a button to lower the black divider between us and the driver.

"Malcolm, could you please pull over for a minute at Park and Sixty-second? I need to pick something up," he said.

"Why, of course, sir."

"Thanks, my good man." He raised the divider back up.

I put my champagne flute down in one of the limo's built-in drink holders and crossed my arms. "Scotty, what's going on?"

He smiled. "Sweetheart, I just want to make sure that tonight is perfect. And there's something I need to pick up to make that happen."

"I'm really confused. Why didn't you ever say anything?" I said.

"Say anything about what?"

I whispered, "About, you know, not really being gay?"

Just then the limo came to a stop, and we heard Malcolm get out of the car. Scotty scooted forward toward the passenger door just as Malcolm was opening it.

"Just a minute, Waverly. I'll be right back." He put his champagne down and stepped outside of the limo, shutting the door behind him.

I leaned back into the deep leather folds of the seat and closed my eyes. Was I dreaming? What was going on?

Five minutes later, the door opened, and Scotty sat back down with a small velvet box in his hand.

He looked at me and smiled. "All set."

I glanced at the box. "What happens next?" I said.

"Off to a fabulous little Italian restaurant, my lovely lady. Waiting there is a romantic candlelight dinner that I hope will enchant you as much as you enchant me."

I set my champagne down again and looked him straight in the eye.

"Scotty, you still haven't answered my question."

"What question, darling?"

"We've been friends for years. Why didn't you tell me you weren't gay?"

He put his hand on my arm.

"Sweetheart, who said I wasn't gay?"

What?

"What?" I said.

"What what?"

"You're not straight?" I said.

"Nope, I'm not straight."

"So you're still gay?"

He laughed. "Yes, I'm still gay."

"Then why—"

I put my hand over my mouth. "Oh my God."

"What?" he said.

"You're here out of pity."

"What do you mean?"

"You bid on me because no one else would."

"Waverly—"

"To save my feelings from being hurt, right? I knew it. Oh my God, I'm such a los—"

He grabbed my hand. "Waverly, calm down."

I looked at him.

"I didn't bid on you because no one else did," he said.

"You didn't?"

He shook his head. "Nope."

"Are you sure?"

He laughed. "Yes, my love, I'm sure."

"Then why did you bid on me?"

He leaned back and took a sip of champagne. "Who said I bid on you?"

What?

"You didn't bid on me?"

He shook his head. "No, I did not."

"Then why are you my date tonight?"

"Who said I was your date tonight?"

What??

"Scotty, cut it out. I'm serious. What's going on?"

"Gorgeous, didn't I tell you I wanted this night to be perfect, *for you?*"

I nodded. "Yes, you did."

"And didn't I say I just needed to pick up one thing to make it perfect, *for you?*"

I nodded again and glanced at the box on the seat next to him. "Yes, you did."

"And have I ever lied to you?"

"Not that I know of."

"Well I haven't, and I'm not about to start now." He leaned over to press the divider button again. "So what do you think? Should I tell our good driver where the restaurant is so we can be on our way?"

I looked down at the velvet box, then up at the black divider as it slowly opened. Through the front windshield I could see the sign for the Plaza Hotel. We were back at the Plaza?

Then the driver turned around.

I gasped again.

The person sitting in the driver's seat wasn't Malcolm anymore.

"Hi, Waverly," he said.

"Hi, Jake," I whispered.

. . .

As I was trying to process what was happening, I heard knocking on the passenger window. Scotty opened the door, and Shane's and Kristina's smiling faces poked in.

"Hey there, Scott," Shane said.

Kristina smiled. "Hi, Waverly."

"Hi, everyone," Jake said, moving to the backseat and sitting next to me.

I looked at Jake and Scotty and then back at Shane and Kristina.

"How did . . .?" I whispered to no one in particular.

"I'll explain everything," Jake said.

"He'll explain everything." Shane pointed to Jake.

"He'll explain everything." Scotty squeezed my knee and pointed to Jake.

Then McKenna and Andie poked their heads in. "Nice ride ya got going here," Andie said.

"Mackie? Andie? What the . . .?" I said.

McKenna shook her head. "Don't ask me, you're the one with all these crazy famous friends."

"Hey now, watch your language," Kristina said.

Scotty climbed out of the limo. "All right, people, I'm outta here." Then he leaned back in and kissed me on the cheek. "Have fun at dinner, Miss Bryson. Mr. McIntyre, please take good care of her."

"I'll do my best," Jake said.

"Hey, wait a minute." I grabbed Scotty's hand and pulled him toward me.

"What, love?"

"What's in the box?" I whispered.

He pulled it out of his pocket and held it up. "This?"

I nodded.

"It's a key to Tad's apartment. He's out of town until tomorrow, but he left me a key with his doorman so I could stay at his place tonight."

"That's it?" I said.

He smiled. "That's it."

I pointed at him and laughed. "Mr. Ryan, you got me bad."

"That's why I receive marriage proposals from women across the country, my dear. Now, shoo." He kissed my hand and shut the door.

Then my real date began.

. . .

Twenty minutes later, Jake and I were seated in a quiet corner at Cacio e Pepe, a picturesque Italian restaurant in the East Village.

He poured me a glass of red wine. "So, we meet again."

"We meet again," I said, still dazed.

"Here's to *People* magazine." He lifted his glass up to mine.

I held my glass tight as I touched it against his. "So you're Wendall P. Feldman?"

He laughed. "Oh, that. Wendall Feldman was my next-door neighbor growing up."

"So he's a real person?"

He nodded. "He's a real person."

"What does the *P* stand for?"

"Poindexter."

"Wendall Poindexter Feldman? Ouch. So why the fake name anyway?"

He smiled. "I thought you might go running for the hills again if you knew it was me."

I blushed and looked down. Running for the hills? Yeah, right. If he only knew how many times I'd thought about running my fingers through his hair.

"And I thought you had a boyfriend this whole time anyway," he said.

I looked back up at him. "A boyfriend? What?"

"Yeah, actually, I thought Scott was your boyfriend. Or at least that you were dating him."

"Scotty?" I said. "Really?"

He nodded. "You two always looked rather chummy, especially at Dale's wedding, and then I saw him kiss you at that Giants' game in the spring."

The waiter set our entrees down and quietly retreated.

I pushed my pasta around with my fork and shook my head.

"Jake, Scotty was never my boyfriend."

He looked at me and smiled. "I know that *now*," he said, and I could feel my pulse start to race.

"How did you meet him?" I said.

"At a barbecue at Shane's house a few weeks ago. When he introduced me to his boyfriend, it sort of cleared things up."

"You met Scott at a barbecue at Shane's house?" I said.

He nodded, his messy brown hair nearly reaching his eyes. "His boyfriend works at the same agency as Shane's agent. Anyhow, I told him that you'd pretty much given me the Heisman every time I'd seen you since we met." He moved his hands into the position of the little guy on the Heisman Trophy, one hand behind his head and the other straight out in front of him.

I smiled and pointed at him. "I so did not give you the Heisman."

He pointed back. "You so did, but Scott set me straight, and then Kristina backed him up." He smiled and looked right at me. With those blue eyes.

"Oh," I said, thanking God I was already sitting down, because my knees were beginning to feel really weak, and I had already fallen on my face one too many times that day.

"Then Scott said he had a clever idea for how you and I could meet up again, and here we are," he said.

"So this was all Scotty's idea?"

"Yep, pretty much. He also said something about owing you."

Owing me? Oh yeah, the U2 concert he didn't take me to. Talk about making good on your word.

"But how did you work out the whole surprise thing? I mean, what if I'd seen you bid on me at the auction?" I said.

He laughed. "I have some connections."

"Connections?"

"Yep, I wasn't even at the auction. The auctioneer just knew to make the highest bidder the gentleman in the back."

"But . . . but what if . . .?"

"What if what?"

"Well, I mean, I know it sounds insane, but what if someone else had bid a lot of money on me?"

He laughed. "That's where it comes in handy to be buddies with an NBA star. Shane and Kristina said they'd take care of it if the bidding got out of my price range."

"They did?"

"Well, mostly Kristina," he said. "She said she thought we'd have a good time." Then he lowered his voice a bit and smiled. "I think she was right."

I couldn't take anymore of those sexy smiles. I took a sip of water and tried to cool myself off.

"Um, so why didn't you just do the regular auction? Were you busy last night?" I said.

He shook his head. "I wanted a real date with you . . . alone."

"Oh," I whispered, nearly falling off my chair.

"So, were Scotty and Kristina right in their prediction?" he said.

"What prediction?"

"That you'd be glad to find out that your date was with me?"

I could feel the blood rushing to my face. I looked over his shoulder and then up at the ceiling. "Um, well, yeah, but, um . . ."

He smiled. "But what?"

I couldn't believe this was really happening.

I closed my eyes and sighed.

"Waverly? Are you okay?"

I opened my eyes and shook my head to focus them. "I'm sorry. I was just . . . I was just thinking. . . ."

"Waverly?"

"Yes?"

"No more thinking, okay?"

"Okay," I whispered.

Just then the waiter appeared with a single piece of chocolate cake with a small candle on top.

I looked at the cake and then at Jake. "How did you know?"

"Hey, give a guy some credit. Now go ahead, make a wish."

I laughed. "You want me to make a wish?"

"Yep."

"Really?"

He nodded.

"Are you sure you're not related to Scotty?"

"What?" he said.

"I mean, are you sure your last name's not Ryan, too?"

"Ryan?" he said again.

I raised my eyebrows. "You know, Jake Ryan, *Sixteen Candles?*"

"Huh?"

I shrugged. "It's a girl thing." I leaned down and blew the candle out, then looked up at him and smiled.

"Happy birthday, Waverly," he said.

"Thank you, Jake McIntyre," I whispered.

He cleared his throat.

"So . . .," he said.

"So . . .," I said.

"So you still haven't answered my question."

"Um, what was it again?"

He smiled. "You're killing me."

"I'm sorry," I said. "Have you ever noticed that I tend to change the subject when I get nervous?"

He laughed. "I've noticed. Okay, I'll ask you another question. Do you remember what you asked me when we first met?"

I had no idea what he was talking about. What had I asked him? That whole night was a blur.

"Um, if you like pineapple on your pizza? If you own any Barry Manilow music? If you've ever eaten a whole chicken?"

He laughed again. "Nope."

"Can you give me a little hint?" I tapped my fingers on the table.

"You asked me what I don't like about working in the NBA. Do you remember?"

I nodded. "That's right, I did ask you that."

He scratched his eyebrow and took a deep breath, then leaned across the table and took my hands in his. His touch set off a spark that shot through my entire body, from my fingers all the way down to my toes.

"Can I answer that question now?" he said.

I nodded again. The ability to speak was gone.

"Waverly, there are a lot of beautiful women in the world, and you are certainly one of them. But appearances can be deceiving, and that night I was going to tell you how hard it is for me to meet someone who is real, someone smart and witty and independent and down-to-earth."

My eyes were slightly unfocused.

"It is?" I said softly.

He leaned closer toward me and smiled. "Yes. I wanted to meet someone who is all those things, someone who's as beautiful as she looks, but whose true beauty can't be captured in a photograph."

I swallowed hard. "You did?"

He rubbed his thumbs over my palms. "I wanted to meet someone like you."

My voice came back as a squeak. "I'm those things?"

He nodded. "I knew it from the first few moments I talked to you. You're different, Waverly. I don't know what it is, but there's just something about you."

"There is?"

"Maybe it's your sarcasm. Or your ridiculous yet adorable observations. Or that you aren't afraid to speak your mind. Or the way your eyes sparkle when you laugh."

I sat there, frozen.

"Or maybe it's none of those things." He squeezed my hands tight. "Maybe it's just that when I'm with you, all I can think about is how much I want to kiss you."

"Me?" I whispered.

He slowly leaned toward me. "Yes, you. You have something special, something very, very special, and I'm determined to figure out what it is."

"You are?"

He leaned closer and lowered his voice. "Yes."

I took a deep breath and looked at him.

"Jake?"

"Yes?" He leaned even closer.

"Can I ask you something?"

He nodded.

"Have you ever noticed that I like you a lot?" I whispered.

He put his finger on my lips and smiled. "Shhh."

I smiled and closed my eyes. I was . . . melting.

And then Wendall P. Feldman kissed me.

Does happily ever after really exist?

Honey, you only live once, so make it happen.

CHAPTER TWENTY-FOUR

The day of the wedding was unusually warm, so McKenna and I decided to go for one last walk before the big one down the aisle. We met in front of Peet's Coffee at ten. Our hair and makeup appointments weren't until two o'clock, so we were good on time. After dozens of practice runs, we'd finally decided that she would wear her hair down and straight and mine would be pulled back into a high curly bun.

Oh, and I was going to wear a tiara.

Just kidding.

As we headed down the hill, I looked out at the sailboats and then back at her. "Hey, Mackie, how many of these walks do you think we've done?"

"Oh God, a ton," she said. "I don't know, maybe a couple hundred?"

"Wow, that's a boatload of walks. You'd think you'd see some evidence of that in my calves," I said, looking down at my legs.

She laughed. "I hear you on that."

"I can't really remember what my life was like without you and these walks in it, ya know?" I said.

She put her hands on her hips. "You're not going to get all sappy on me, are you? I don't want to have puffy eyes for the wedding."

I pushed her arm. "Shut up, I'm being serious. I really want to tell you how important you are to me."

"I know, I know. I can't remember what my life was like without you either. And I don't even want to think about what it would be like without you now."

"I can pretty much assure you that you won't have to worry about that, especially if this whole 'quitting my job' thing backfires and I end up sleeping on your couch," I said.

"Oh please, you're going to do great."

"But seriously, without your friendship I think I would dry up and blow away like an old snail shell," I said.

She put her arm around me as we walked. "Lovely visual. Are you going to use that one in a Honey Note?"

"Hmm, not a bad idea."

"Ya know, I'm still waiting for some sort of royalties from all the creative inspiration this friendship of ours has given you for those cards," she said.

I extended my hand. "I'm sorry, have we met? I'm Waverly Bryson. And I don't think so."

After our walk, we stopped in front of my apartment, hugged each other a tearful goodbye, and headed home to shower. The plan was to meet back up in an hour at a cute B&B down in the Marina that we had rented out as the designated "getting ready" place for the girls. After the rehearsal dinner, both of us had spent the night there, but we wanted to shower at our own places because it was just easier.

Once inside my apartment, I walked into my room, threw my clothes into the hamper, and put on my robe and slippers. Then I picked up my phone to see if I had any messages. There was one from Jake:

"Hey, you, I just wanted to say good morning and tell you how much I'm looking forward to seeing you tonight. Enjoy the rest of the day with the girls, and I'll see you at the ceremony."

His voice still gave me goose bumps.

I saved the message and jumped in the shower.

. . .

At five o'clock, McKenna and I were standing outside the main ballroom of the St. Francis Yacht Club, classical music from the string quartet drifting out into the hall. We were peeking through the curtains to check out all the guests filling the huge room. The scent of hundreds of white roses sweetened the air.

"I can't believe this day is really here. And I can't believe how many people are sitting in those pretty white chairs," I said, staring at everyone's backs.

"What did you expect with a guest list like that?" McKenna said. "Hey, can you come here for a second and check me out? Am I busting out of this thing too much? Is it too X-rated for a wedding?" She adjusted the top of her strapless black dress and put her hands on her waist.

"You look gorgeous, but I gotta say that your rack is humongous," I said.

She laughed. "The one perk of breast-feeding."

Just then Andie walked up behind us. "You ready ladies? It's time to go." She smoothed out her black strapless bridesmaid dress.

"Yep, I'm ready," McKenna said.

I nodded. "Me too."

McKenna gently touched my cheek. "Waverly, you look beautiful. I think I'm going to cry."

"Thanks," I said softly, afraid that I was going to lose it, too.

Andie clapped her hands. "Okay people, let's get cooking. There's an open bar waiting at the reception."

The noise of the crowd inside quieted down, and my dad walked up and put his arms around us. "Ready to go, ladies?" he said. The three of us squeezed hands and nodded.

The quartet briefly stopped playing, and the doors opened. Then the music started again, and one by one my bridesmaids walked down the aisle.

Then it was my turn.

I took a deep breath and looked up at my father next to me.

"Don't trip," he said.

"Dad!"

He laughed. "Andie told me to say that."

I smiled. "I love you, Dad."

"I love you, too, kiddo."

I took another deep breath and intertwined my arm in his. I felt slightly dizzy, as if everything were in slow motion. The guests stood up, and I was vaguely aware of three hundred pairs of eyes smiling at me. Andie and McKenna, Davey and Lindsay, Kent and his wife, Beth, Hunter and new baby Justin, Kristina and groomsman Shane, Cynthia and Dale, Scotty and Tad, even Brad Cantor and Mandy Edwards (I know, I'm a sap, but they do make a cute couple).

It was really happening, and all my loved ones were there to enjoy it with me.

I took my first step down the aisle and looked straight ahead. All those eyes were focused on me, but the only ones I saw were the bright blue ones belonging to Jake, who was waiting for me at the other end of the aisle.

The End . . .?

. . .

KIDDING. Hello?? Like after all that yapping about being fine on my own and not worrying about what everyone else was doing, I was going to go sprinting down the aisle that fast? Honey, I don't think so. Give me some credit!

Here's what really happened after our walk that day:

At five o'clock, McKenna and I were standing together before the ceremony, but she was the one in the wedding dress. I did wear my hair up in a high curly bun though. We were at the Tiburon Golf Club in Marin looking out the window at the lush green hills and waterfalls surrounding the links. There were about two hundred guests seated in sparkling white chairs, all of them waiting to watch McKenna and Hunter tie the knot. The balmy weather was a perfect seventy-two degrees.

The outdoor ceremony was simple and touching. McKenna

and Hunter had written their own vows over pancakes at IHOP one Sunday morning, and they managed to combine romance with humor in a way that had all the guests laughing yet tearing up at the same time. I was way weepy.

Jake was my date. We'd been seeing each other for just a couple weeks, and a few days after the wedding I was still going on my very first vacation by myself, but we were getting along just great. Time would tell what would happen in the future, but it had been amazing so far, and I was certainly enjoying every minute. That's what it's all about, right?

Shane and Kristina came to the wedding. We'd all gone dancing after my singles auction date, and to make McKenna's bachelorette party complete, we'd even gone to a male strip club. We'd begged Shane to get up on stage to join the dancers, but he was too afraid his photo would end up all over the Internet. You know you're really famous when you can't get drunk and act like an idiot in front of total strangers anymore.

I think Hunter was more nervous about meeting Shane than about committing himself for the rest of his life to another person. And when word got out at the hospital that Shane was attending the wedding, Hunter's friends were tempted to scalp their invitations to pay off their med school loans. Men!

When it was time for dinner, I took my seat next to McKenna at the bridal party table. The white-rose centerpiece was purposely just a few inches high, so our views weren't impaired.

She took a sip of champagne and leaned over to me. "Can you believe I'm married?" she whispered.

I put my hand on her shoulder. "Congratulations, HONEY, you did it!"

"Honey, help me." She laughed and shook her head.

Just then, Hunter came up behind us and put his hands on McKenna's bare shoulders.

"What are you two ladies whispering about?"

"Just how lucky I am, sweetie." She took his hands and pulled his arms around her.

"Liar." He laughed and sat down next to her.

Dinner, as they say, was served. The salmon was delicious, and those who opted for the prime rib were equally impressed. The wine McKenna and I had chosen to accompany dinner was apparently a hit, but then again, who's going to turn down free wine?

The only real glitch in the evening was the cake. Or, more specifically, the cake cutting, because I was in the ladies' room at the time. Oops. But at least I didn't get locked in the stall. And then came the dancing. For the cocktail hour and dinner we'd hired a string quartet, but for dancing we'd picked a DJ who specialized in, of course, '80s tunes. A few songs into his first set, he put on "Bizarre Love Triangle" by New Order.

"Oh my God, this is the best dance song EVER!" I jumped up from our table and looked at Jake. "Ready to bust a move?"

He laughed. "Did you just say *Bust a move?*"

I nodded. "Oh, yes, I did."

He stood up and put his arm around me. "I'm not sure I want to see this."

McKenna and Hunter were already on the dance floor, boogying down with Andie. They spotted me and waved at me to come join them. I trotted over and zigzagged my way through the crowd. But I stepped on something slippery just before I reached them, and I suddenly felt the all-too-familiar feeling of losing my balance.

"Oh cra—," I started to yell, falling backward, bracing myself.

But the crash never came.

"Don't worry, I've got you." Jake scooped me up in his arms and gently set me back down on my feet.

I put my arms around him and looked up at his eyes.

Those beautiful blue eyes.

I smiled. "Yes, you do, Jake McIntyre. Yes, you do."

After the song was over, we starting walking back toward our table so I could have some more cake. But then the DJ began to play "Who's Crying Now?" by Journey.

I looked at Jake.

Jake looked at me.

"Well?" he said.

"Well what?" I titled my head to one side and smiled.

"If I ask you to dance to this song again, are you going to run away?"

I shook my head. "Nope."

"You promise?"

I nodded slowly and kept smiling at him. "I promise."

We turned back to the dance floor, and he put his hand on the small of my back. Once again, his touch nearly burned a hole right through me. He led me through the crowd and gently put his arms around me.

He looked down at me as we swayed to the music. "Thanks for asking me to be your date tonight, Waverly Bryson."

I smiled up at him. "Thank you for accepting, Jake McIntyre."

He smiled back and squeezed me tight.

"Hey, Jake?"

"Yeah?"

"Is *melty* a word?"

"What?"

"I was just wondering, you know, because I've noticed that—"

"Waverly?" he said.

"What?"

"Shut up and just dance with me, okay?"

I grinned. "Okay."

He squeezed me tighter, and I closed my eyes.

And this time the only dizziness I felt was the sensation of leaving the past behind and falling head over heels into the future.

. . .

The Real End

. . .

ACKNOWLEDGMENTS

THANK YOU so much to those who provided help in all shapes and sizes for this book, which began as a dreamy idea on countless morning walks with my dear friend Alison Marquiss and finally came to life with the help of my impossibly wonderful father (and highly unpaid administrative assistant), Mike Murnane. Along the way I received invaluable feedback and support from the following amazing people: Flo Murnane, Mark Murnane, Icha Murnane, Monica Morey, Luke Morey, Michele Sharkey, Brett Sharkey, Terri Sharkey, Lindsay Barnett, Lucinda Bowman, Caitlin "Kiwi" Flanagan, Mary Huck, Kat Woody, Mary Scouffas, Bridget Serchak, Tami McMillan, Christine Paul, Sean Sullivan, Jen Jasper, Doug Massa, Sarita Bhargava, Doretta Bonner, Bobby Davidorf, Sunita Rao, Billy Burkoth and Jennifer Livingstone (collectively known as "BLi"), Debbie Bolzan, Andreá Maxwell, Annie Flaig, Michele Breen, Somill Hwang, Mary Karlton, Anh Vazquez, Danny Stoian, Jenn van der Kleut, Meg Russell, Leslie Harris, Nelle Sacknoff, Max Chang, Patti O'Connell, Alex Carr, and Lori "Bosenwasser" Rosenwasser.

In your own way each of you helped turn my imagination into a life-changing reality, and for that I will always be grateful.

ABOUT THE AUTHOR

MARIA MURNANE had a successful career in public relations for nearly a decade before admitting to herself that she wasn't happy. Knowing she would be miserable if she stayed on the path she was on, she quit and went to Argentina for what was supposed to be a two-week solo trip before facing real life again. Instead, she ended up living in Buenos Aires for a year, playing semi-professional soccer for one of the most famous clubs in the world and doing what she had always dreamed about, which was to write a humorous novel based on her experiences as a single professional woman in San Francisco.

Maria was a Regents' and Chancellor's Scholar at UC Berkeley, where she graduated with high honors in English and Spanish. She also received a master's degree in integrated marketing communications from Northwestern University. She currently lives in New York and does professional business writing in addition to promoting her book.

More information is available at www.mariamurnane.com.

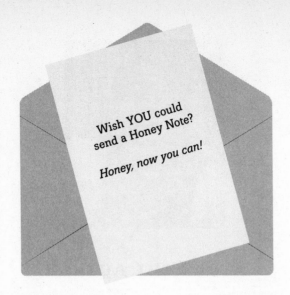

Wish YOU could
send a Honey Note?

Honey, now you can!

WWW.HONEYNOTE.COM

. . .

If you have an idea for a Honey Note, please let Maria (and Waverly) know.
They'd love to hear from you! Dating disaster stories are also welcome.